HIGH LORD of LYSTRA

Also by Robin Hardy

The Chataine's Guardian
Stone of Help

The climactic third novel in the Lystra series

HIGH LORD OF LYSTRA

A Novel by
ROBIN HARDY

Author of *The Chataine's Guardian*
and *Stone of Help*

WORD BOOKS
PUBLISHER
WACO, TEXAS

A DIVISION OF
WORD, INCORPORATED

HIGH LORD OF LYSTRA

The Scripture quoted on pp. 22–23 is Psalm 108. Scripture quote on pp. 163–164 is Psalm 116. Scripture quoted on p. 248 is Psalm 139:12. All Scripture quotations are from The New International Version of the Bible, copyrighted © 1978 by the New York International Bible Society International.

Library of Congress Cataloging-in-Publication Data

Hardy, Robin, 1955–
    High lord of Lystra.

    I. Title.
PR6058.A6754H5   1986   823'.914   86-13181
ISBN 0–8499–0574–5
ISBN 0–8499–3052–9 (pbk.)

Printed in the United States of America

5 6 7 8 9 8   BKC   9 8 7 6 5 4 3 2 1

To Ruth, whose love in Christ
spans the great chasm to comfort me;

To Glenn

How firm a foundation, ye saints of the Lord,
Is laid for your faith in his excellent Word!
What more can he say than to you he hath said,
To you who for refuge to Jesus have fled?

"Fear not, I am with thee; O be not dismayed,
For I am thy God, and will still give thee aid;
I'll strengthen thee, help thee, and cause thee to stand,
Upheld by my righteous, omnipotent hand.

"When through fiery trials thy pathway shall lie,
My grace, all-sufficient, shall be thy supply;
The flame shall not hurt thee; I only design
Thy dross to consume, and thy gold to refine.

"The soul that on Jesus hath leaned for repose
I will not, I will not desert to his foes;
That soul, though all hell should endeavor to shake,
I'll never, no, never, no, never forsake!"

John Rippon's *Selection of Hymns,* 1787

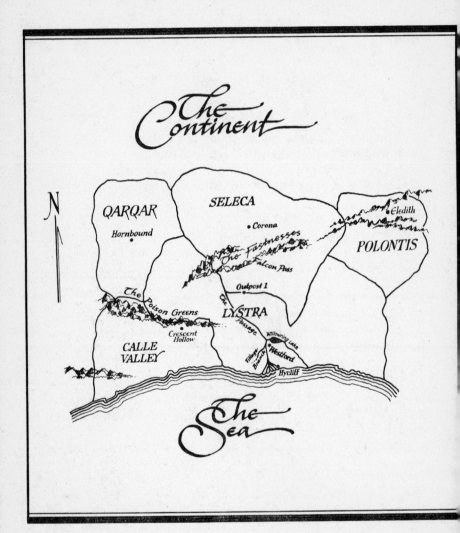

THE HISTORY
(from the *Annals of Lystra*)

. . . THE EVENTS SURROUNDING the end of the reign of Surchatain Karel of Lystra, being duly and truthfully chronicled in the aforementioned Book,* may be summarized as follows, to wit: Karel, having discerned his daughter's life to be in Peril, appointed a soldier from the standing army, a follower of the Way, to be guardian of the Chataine Deirdre, she at that time being ten years of age. The soldier, being Roman of Westford, was then twenty-two. Albeit that his coat of arms has since been shown to bear the Bend Sinister,** Roman had gained respect for his Abilities and Leadership. He performed ably in difficult circumstances as the Chataine's guardian until her eighteenth year, when she frustrated her father's intentions by choosing Roman as her Husband. In his wrath the Surchatain sentenced the soldier to die, but Roman escaped to marry Deirdre and join Commander Galapos at Outpost One.

In the face of a Dreaded Invasion by Surchatain Tremaine of Seleca, Galapos joined forces with Deirdre's uncle, Surchatain Corneus of Seir. But as the Price of that alliance, Corneus demanded that Deirdre be given to his son Jason. Roman unwillingly sent his bride to Jason in Ooster, but Corneus betrayed Galapos in Vile Treachery and aligned himself with Tremaine. At Ooster, Deirdre discovered herself to be with child by Roman.

The armies of Tremaine and Corneus surrounded the outpost to slay the defenders of Lystra, and Roman prayed in desperation to his God. It followed that, by the Power of God, the enemy were weakened

---

* Published as *The Chataine's Guardian.*
** That is, he was of illegitimate birth.

9

by a Pestilence and thereby destroyed. At Ooster, Jason learned of the battle's outcome and killed himself, having first told Deirdre that Roman and Galapos were dead. Deirdre despaired, but was supernaturally defended until Roman and Galapos, the victors, found her at Ooster. Then did she learn that Karel was dead and that Galapos, the new Surchatain, was her Natural Father.

After which followed these events,* to wit: Deirdre, soon to give birth to her first Child, unwisely allowed herself to be lured from her Husband's protection by her former nursemaid, the old woman having fallen under Power of the witch Varela. After being delivered of a son, the Chataine was kidnapped and suffered great Travail, being sold as Slave to Surchataine Sheva, who ruled Goerge from her fortress palace built on the Cliffs of Diamond's Head. There did Deirdre finally learn how to work and how to pray, being taught by a kindred slave called Old Josef.

In the mean time did Roman, unknowing what had befallen his Wife, spend three months of fruitless search in the City of Corona, now fallen into wickedness. Then did he return to Westford, broken with Dismay.

Yet at this time did Galapos the Surchatain discover his Daughter in the palace of Sheva and did forfeit his Life for her Freedom. Impelled by his Sacrifice of Love, she then freed all the Slaves of Sheva, among them being the Polonti huntsman called Nihl. It followed that Nihl returned with her to Westford to do Service under the new Surchatain, Roman; and with them came also the Palace Administrator, Troyce; and the Overseer, Sevter; and a host of former Slaves who wished to serve.

Here begins the Continuation of the Story, it being the third Summer since their return. . . .

---

* Chronicled in *Stone of Help*.

10

PART ONE

CORONA

CHAPTER 1

DEIRDRE, SURCHATAINE OF LYSTRA, opened her eyes just enough to see scattered rays of golden light leaping from behind the velvet draperies. These early June mornings were so splendid. Smiling, she stretched and her forearm brushed the bare, muscled shoulder of her husband, Roman. She shifted to watch him sleep, admiring his brown, sinewy form. In lightly smoothing the thick black hair away from his face, she uncovered the old bludgeon scar on his forehead and several grey hairs. Then she grinned. Responding to an irrepressible urge, she draped her arm over his back and bit his nearest shoulder.

He roused with a start and gathered her beneath him to kiss her in retaliation. They were locked this way when a sly little giggle was heard. Roman raised his head to see two intensely blue eyes, under a forelock of thick reddish-brown hair, peeping over the edge of the bed.

"Rascal!" Roman exclaimed, leaning over to lift the giggling two-year-old onto Deirdre's stomach. "You climbed down from your bed again! How shall we contain you, little adventurer?"

Deirdre laughed, "He is his father's son! Still, I am glad we moved him into the adjoining room. I like having him near us."

Roman lay back and smiled, watching his fair-haired wife cuddle and tickle the squealing child while the feather-filled ticking shifted gently beneath them. "Deirdre," he mused, "how did you choose the name Ariel? I do not know that I have ever heard it before."

She held the child still and confessed, "You'll think it strange."

"Tell me."

"I had a dream . . . I saw a beautiful young man riding into battle, wearing your crest. . . . Someone said, 'His name is Ariel.' I decided that would be our son's name."

Roman watched her silently, and she grew self-conscious as she bounced the child on her leg. Then he leaned over and said, "Take him to the nursemaid for a while." Which she did.

Later in the morning, Roman strode down the corridor with the slender, white-haired Counselor at his side. Basil was thumbing through a sheaf of papers. "Surchatain, the emissaries this morning are from the provinces of Qarqar, Calle Valley—and Polontis."

Surchatain Roman almost stopped in midstride at the mention of his mother's homeland. "Polontis? What is their request?"

The Counselor shuffled his papers, searching. "I am not certain. Only for an audience with you."

"They'll have that," Roman promised as he walked into the audience hall. A waiting crowd of spectators went to their knees in deference as he passed them. He nodded to Commander Nihl standing to the left of the bronze throne, then sat. He glanced at the empty air to his right and sighed. Obviously, his lectures to Deirdre on why she should sit at audience with him had not had any effect. Yet, knowing her temperament, he would not force her, for that would defeat his purpose and make her all the more impervious to learning how to rule.

To the first-time observer in the audience, Roman and Nihl might have appeared to be brothers, they were so similar in aspect. They shared the common Polonti features of straight black hair, brown skin, and large frames. Yet Nihl was pure Polonti, markedly more reserved and taut than his half-blooded kinsman. Or perhaps it was because Roman was older and never a citizen of his mother's country that he did not hold quite so rigidly to their native manners.

The Surchatain said, "I will hear first the emissary from Polontis."

A grave-faced Polonti nudged his way up from the edge of the crowd and bowed slowly to Roman. "Surchatain—it is gracious of you to hear me first, as I am the least of these here. I am Coran, who brings greetings from Bruc, ruler of Polontis. Lord Bruc wishes to establish first that he holds no ill will for the number of Polonti warriors who have left his service to join yours."

"Then why have my messengers to him never been acknowledged?" Roman asked testily.

"An unfortunate misunderstanding, Surchatain, as my lord's former Counselor gave him unwise advice concerning them," explained Coran. Roman leaned his head on his hand and looked at him. "He feared you wished to draw more men away," continued Coran, gaining speed, "and as our resources are already so depleted, a further loss would leave us indefensible."

"Against me?" Roman asked sarcastically, then turned to whisper

14

to Nihl, "Is this man really Polonti? He talks more like a Selecan statesman."

Nihl cocked his head. "Bruc sends his emissaries to the south to be educated before employing them—never to Seleca, though."

Roman turned his attention back to the messenger. "What does Bruc want?"

"To advise you of an impending crisis, Surchatain. Lord Bruc's spies have discovered evidence of an army growing in Corona—a large, savage army who have bound themselves with an oath never to rest until they have accomplished the dead Tremaine's goal of conquering the Continent. They are sure to attack you when they feel they've gained might enough," the emissary warned.

Roman shifted on the throne. "I know the situation in Corona. They have a few hundred men gathered under a crazy demagogue who thinks he is Tremaine reincarnated. I won't waste my time or my men on him. He could not take an outpost from me, much less Westford." Nihl nodded in concord with this assessment.

Coran looked down at the purple runner, thwarted in his first move. He responded humbly, "No, Surchatain, he cannot take Lystra. But he has set his eyes on Polontis as his first conquest, and we are not so secure."

"That is Bruc's problem," answered Roman, watching him.

"If we fall, he becomes that much stronger!" the messenger spilled out desperately. "Would you rather deal with him when he has a few men and delusions, or when he comes marching to you with the rest of the Continent in his hand?"

"He cannot conquer the Continent," Roman reiterated quietly.

Coran bit his lips as if choking back pride. "Perhaps not. But he could take Polontis. Help us, Surchatain. I beg you to help us."

Roman sat silently evaluating him and his request. The hall was so quiet he could hear Coran's tense breathing. "I will consider it," Roman finally said. Coran bowed in relief at having brought his case this far.

"Kam," Roman gestured, "take Lord Bruc's emissary to a guest suite and see that he is made comfortable until I have an answer for him."

"Surchatain." The stocky, black-bearded Second in Command saluted Roman and glanced at the messenger.

Coran paused in astonishment at this unusually gracious treatment of an emissary, then caught himself in time to turn and follow the Second. On his way out, he heard the Surchatain say, "Now I will hear the emissary from Qarqar."

Coran departed the hall behind Kam, who turned down a side corridor leading to the interior of the palace. Coran walked slowly to look at the paintings, tapestries, and finely wrought ornamental shields and weapons which crowded each other the length of the walls. "Your Surchatain spends much for things that entertain the eye," he observed carefully.

The Second glanced at the masterpieces of workmanship. "He bought none of them," he answered. "They came as gifts from other provinces, or from his acquisition of what was formerly Seir and Goerge."

"Ah," Coran responded. They turned down another corridor, this one lined with long, slender windows which opened out into the courtyard. Passing them, Coran glimpsed a unit of soldiers drilling on the grounds.

He slowly came to a stop as he watched them. The Second in Command, who was under the Commander and above the Captains, paused to look over the unit himself. They were practicing the art of fighting when disadvantaged by a loss of arms. Captain Colin's voice could be heard even from the corridor windows, shouting instructions. Colin was only two years older than his cousin Deirdre and son of the former Surchatain of Seir. After the death of his father, he had brought with him the wealth of his province to serve Roman.

The Polonti emissary unconsciously leaned against the window facing to see more. He caught sight of a row of weapons stalls filled to capacity, and the gear of the soldiers piled on the ground near the walkway. "Are all your men outfitted so?" he asked.

Kam straightened to a perfect vertical and said, "There is complete hauberk available to outfit each man. Offensively, they are trained with the bow, broadsword, spear, and mace, as well as hand-to-hand and on horseback, of course; then they may choose which weapons and method of fighting suit them best. After that, they are placed in service according to how their skills may best be used."

"How many men do you have, to be able to place them at their preference?" Coran demanded in disbelief.

Kam smiled. "You know I cannot tell you that. But I will tell you we have more than Tremaine did at the height of his power."

"How does he do it?" exclaimed Coran. "How does your Surchatain lure all the ablest men to his service?"

"He'll take anyone," Kam answered slowly. "He takes anyone willing and trains him to perfection. And he forgives mistakes."

Deirdre stood over a work table in the kitchen, rolling out dough, fine and thin. A simple servant's apron covered her richly embroidered dress of sapphire blue. Two young kitchen maids stood at her sides,

16

watching. "The thinner you roll it, the finer and lighter it will be," Deirdre murmured, ". . . there." She paused to wipe her hands on her apron and brush a tangled blond lock from her face. "Merry? Is the filling ready?"

"Yes, my lady, very nearly—" the hefty kitchen mistress hurried up, stirring a large crock of blackberry compote. "It must be mixed a minute longer," she mumbled apologetically.

"There is no hurry," Deirdre said firmly. "They have not even finished their meal yet, and those men would wait through the afternoon for pastry!"

"True, my lady," Merry said, pausing to let another cook add flour to the compote. This cook, a man, smiled to himself as he glanced toward the Surchataine in her apron. He had been a servant here in the palace for a long time—since before Deirdre had married. He had known her when she would rather have died than set a foot in the kitchen, and here she was, showing these girls how to make proper pastry. It amazed him. But she had been different ever since she came back from Diamond's Head. He had heard she'd been a slave there—a kitchen maid. Well, whatever did it, now she acted as if these servants were people just like herself.

The Surchataine placed a hand on his arm and said, "Brock, please see if Wesley has come back from market yet. I am dying for a taste of the new fruit wines."

"You'll have it if I have to ride to market myself, my lady," Brock replied, already on his way out.

At the table in the dining hall, Roman leaned back to empty his goblet, then set it down, inhaling deeply. Nihl, on his right, and Basil, on his left, looked up at him, silently inquiring. "I do not know what to do about Bruc's request," Roman said, casting a glance toward Nihl.

The Commander dipped a bit of bread in his plate. "You drew an accurate admission from the emissary. Polontis is in danger, but we are not."

"And what if this new tyrant does conquer Polontis?" Roman asked, looking around the table. The Second, Kam, and the Captains, Colin, Olynn, and Reuel did not offer any speculations.

Sevter, the palace overseer, might have had an opinion, but he held his tongue when he saw the administrator, Troyce, stir importantly. Troyce said, "Then he may find himself leading a lion on a rope. The mountains in that province make it hard to hold. And the Polonti are not generally a group that will submit readily to a foreign ruler, especially after so many of them were humiliated by enslavement to

Sheva." When the words were out he glanced at Nihl, who had been one of those slaves, but the Commander appeared not to take the remark personally.

Roman focused his attention on the clean-shaven, articulate administrator. "You think they would revolt."

"Without question." With a jeweled finger, Troyce casually brushed a crumb from his red velvet coat.

"Yet historically, such revolts are seldom successful at the start," Roman observed.

"This is also true," admitted Troyce.

"So they would expend resources, and lives, in attempts to shake his hold that would probably fail unless they were aided." Troyce raised his shoulders, unable to contradict this conclusion.

After a pause, Basil reasoned, "The question seems to be, Surchatain, whether you should sacrifice some of your men to contain what is essentially Polontis' problem. What shall you gain that would make the sacrifice worthwhile? Polontis?"

"No," Roman answered. "I would not annex them unwilling, and Bruc would just as soon hand over the province to this new tyrant as to me." They were silent a moment, as those who had not yet finished eating cleaned up the last bit of brewis from their plates.

Then Roman said, "I am afraid I will have to go to Corona myself."

This statement brought startled protests from those around him: "Surchatain!" "No, Roman, you must not—"

He raised his hand in a short gesture that stilled them. "Not only because of this. I have not forgotten what I saw in Corona when I was there searching for Deirdre. Now that Lystra is firmly established, I have been thinking more and more of the—the inhumanity I found there. And it has only worsened since then. The Lord has not given me this power to sit and be secure. I believe He wants to deliver Corona from the hell she has made for herself." He stopped, eyes on the far end of the table.

Before anyone could think of an argument, Deirdre appeared from the kitchen carrying a tray of pastries. "I thought you might wait for these," she laughed, setting the tray before Roman with a bow.

He turned in the great chair and encircled her waist, pressing his face against her midriff. "You are a treasure of many talents," he said softly, "and how I thank God for you."

She stroked his hair and bent to kiss his head. The others at table relaxed and settled back in their chairs, smiling. The same thought seemed to flash from mind to mind: *He won't go to Corona and leave her.*

"Sit beside me," he said, waving at a sentry to bring a chair for

18

her. She sat, selecting a pastry, and passed the tray to Nihl.

"Deirdre," Roman said quietly, taking her hand, "remember all the things I told you about what I saw in Corona?"

"The killing, and robbing, and slave trading? Oh yes!" she said, grimacing. But the pastry was really excellent so she smiled again.

"Yes, all that," continued Roman, and the others grew wary. Nihl leaned forward and Basil began to fidget. "And more trouble has sprung up. Some kind of warlord has begun gathering himself an army. Deirdre . . . it appears I must go to Corona."

She jerked her head up to gaze into his solemn brown face. "Oh no, Roman, please," she whispered. "You have such capable officers— can't you send them?" Nihl looked intently at Roman but did not dare interrupt this discussion.

Roman lowered his voice. "Please don't argue with me, Deirdre— that makes it so much harder. The Lord has laid Corona on my conscience and I must go."

"Then let me go, too," she said. "Let me go with you."

"By no means," he replied firmly.

"Roman, why not?"

"Expose you to that danger and corruption? Certainly not."

"But what do you think I endured at Diamond's Head?" she insisted gently. "I have handled danger before."

"It would be foolhardy of me to risk your life for this," he said, temper rising. "It is not your battle."

"Roman, my love, I am your wife. Your battles *are* my battles. Will the Lord not protect me as well as you? You may need me!"

"Ariel needs you," he countered.

"He needs you, also. Gusta is a faithful nursemaid and will keep him safe until we return."

"I will not risk you for this."

"Roman—"

"No!"

His sharp denial cut her so deeply that she clenched her teeth to avoid embarrassing herself with tears. But they were coming regardless, so she stiffly rose, nodded to him, and escaped from the hall.

After an awkward silence, Basil said, "It is certainly wisest to keep her here." The others murmured agreement.

Roman sat back, stroking his brow. "I suppose we must scout the situation before taking an army."

Nihl nodded. "Yes, Surchatain," agreed Basil.

"Surchatain, I request to go," volunteered Kam.

"And I," added Colin.

"Very well. Kam, and Colin, and Nihl—I wish you to accompany

19

me. Basil, you will have charge of the palace in our absence, answering to Deirdre, of course, and Troyce shall administrate, answering to you. Olynn, you will be acting Commander."

The officers looked from face to face, then Basil finally said, "Surchatain, at the risk of angering you, I must protest your going as a scout. Go if you must, but lead an army when you go."

Roman smiled tightly. "I value a man who is not afraid to speak his mind. But I have to judge for myself what should be done. And until I make that judgment, an army is unnecessary. I'll not be foolhardy, Basil, but I'll not go trusting in a large number of men to protect me when I should have used good sense instead."

No one else spoke, so Roman stood. "Kam, please see that Bruc's emissary is summoned before me tomorrow morning."

"Surchatain." He and the rest stood.

"Nihl." Roman jerked his head toward the exit. "To the mews."

The Commander joined him on a leisurely walk through the courtyard to the small building where the falcons were kept. As they went, Roman remarked, "Deirdre tells me you are reading like a scholar now."

Nihl smiled faintly. "The Surchataine's praise exceeds its object. But she has been kind and patient to teach me—I always desired to read for myself the pages of Scripture Josef wrote from memory."

Roman murmured, "They have special meaning for Deirdre, too." He lowered his head to enter the low door of the mews and paused to let his eyes adjust to the darkness, and to not overly agitate the birds within.

As he slipped on a heavy glove, he quietly whistled a bar of a song. Some flutterment overhead followed, and the tinkling of a bell, as a gerfalcon flapped down to his wrist. "Pretty girl, pretty girl," he murmured, gently putting on her hood with one hand. He untied her jesses from the perch and brought her outside.

He waited, stroking the bird, while Nihl brought out a hound from the kennels nearby. The dog, unleashed, bounded up eager for the hunt. Roman and Nihl took the animals with them to the stables, then rode southeast from the palace, toward the marshes near the river.

Under cover of trees, they left the horses and Roman unhooded the bird. Then they treaded watchfully through the marshes with the greyhound leading the way, nose to the ground.

Flushed by the hound, a flock of cranes sprang to the air ahead of them and the falcon shot up in pursuit. It targeted a lagging bird and seized it with piercing talons. When Roman whistled the call, the hawk dropped the crane disinterestedly and the hound retrieved it, bringing it directly to Nihl. The falcon, meanwhile, climbed to circle overhead.

After the first kill of the day, the hawk was calmer, so the men loosened up somewhat themselves. "It's amazing to see her hunt," Roman muttered. "I am glad Troyce thought to introduce falconry here."

Nihl agreed, "It is a good sport—far better than bows and arrows for small game. Perhaps you should include it in the games this year."

"Perhaps. But I think it more a test of the bird's skill than the man's."

"The games are scheduled to start in a few weeks," Nihl continued. "Will you delay them until we return from Corona?"

"No," replied Roman. "With or without us, they'll take place as set. It is not fair to the men who have been training to put them off."

Nihl nodded, watching the bird mount and soar. The hound ran ahead of them, nosing for small animals. Nihl added as a careful afterthought, "Troyce has brought less useful ideas from Goerge than hawking, however—such as a desire for power. I am not comfortable leaving him in any measure of control while we are gone."

Roman smiled imperceptibly. "Deirdre thinks he has done well with the household accounts."

"The Surchataine does not supervise him very closely. But the Counselor does, and he does not think Troyce so wonderful."

"Come now, Nihl—could that be due to the fact that Troyce is ambitious, and Basil feels threatened?"

"Ambitious men are dangerous."

Roman glanced at him. "Are *you* ambitious, my brother?"

"To serve you well, yes. Not to take your position."

Roman watched as the hound dislodged a scurrying hare, which the hawk pounced on and then dropped, dead. Nihl clapped his hands to hasten the hound's retrieval of the hare. "I have no justification for censuring Troyce at this point, regardless of your concern," said Roman.

Nihl's face tightened as he took the hare from the dog's jaws and dropped it with the crane in the large net bag slung over his back. "I do not speak idly about this. You know I have never lied to you or misled you."

Eyes on the hawk above, Roman hesitated. "If you have never lied to me, tell me this . . . do you love my wife, Nihl?"

Their eyes met instantly. The Commander slowly responded, "I love her, Surchatain. I could not feel otherwise. But I will never touch her."

Their eyes were drawn skyward again as screams above indicated the falcon had found more prey. Roman then answered, "I believe you, Nihl. I will give Basil authority to censure Troyce in my absence, if need be." They walked forward, Roman whistling to the bird.

When they returned to the palace they went directly to the chapel, as the bells were tolling the hour for the daily Scripture readings. The simple service was conducted by the holy man Avelon, who had won Roman's mother to Christianity.

Roman and Nihl entered the lamplit hall quietly and sat in the back. Roman looked for Deirdre in the crowded chapel, but could not find her. She must be quite upset to miss coming today.

His eye then caught the colored glass window above the wooden cross at the front. The window, which depicted a shepherd carrying a lamb, was a recent addition to admit light to the dark hall. Deirdre had seen picture windows for the first time in the cathedral at Ooster, and had convinced Roman of their desirability. Gazing at it now, he conceded it was beautiful, although part of him missed the stark simplicity of the place where he had spent so many hours in prayer.

Brother Avelon came to the dais at front and raised his hand in a benediction. "Brothers and sisters in Christ, we continue our reading in the Psalms." He paused to find his place in the heavy volume he held. His hands shook slightly with age; his thin hair fell to his shoulders in a white flow.

After a lifetime of humble service to the villagers in the name of the Lord, Avelon had finally been persuaded by Roman to serve in the palace instead. The moment of decision had come when Roman had traveled to the coast to find the once-poor villagers ensconced in fine houses, wearing purples and reds, due to their success at the fishing trade. But Brother Avelon was as poor as ever, living in wretched dependence on the haughty graces of those he had spent his life helping. The irony of it lay not just in that he had taught them to read, thus giving them the capacity to advance in business, but that in the crisis of Tremaine's invasion, it had been Avelon who had taken them to the coast and introduced them to the established fishermen!

Roman, furious at finding the holy man in such a state, had packed up Brother Avelon and brought him to the palace. And Avelon, old and tired, had acquiesced and stayed on.

Now the holy man found his place in the book and read in a voice unaffected by age:

A song. A psalm of David.

My heart is steadfast, O God;
     I will sing and make music with all my soul.

22

Awake, harp and lyre!
    I will awaken the dawn.
I will praise you, O Lord, among the nations;
    I will sing of you among the peoples.
For great is your love, higher than the heavens;
    your faithfulness reaches to the skies.
Be exalted, O God, above the heavens;
    and let your glory be over all the earth.

Save us and help us with your right hand,
    that those you love may be delivered.
God has spoken from his sanctuary:
    "In triumph I will parcel out Shechem
    and measure off the Valley of Succoth.
Gilead is mine, Manasseh is mine;
    Ephraim is my helmet,
    Judah my scepter.
Moab is my washbasin,
    upon Edom I toss my sandal;
    over Philistia I shout in triumph."

Who will bring me to the fortified city?
    Who will lead me to Edom?
Is it not you, O God, you who have rejected us
    and no longer go out with our armies?
Give us aid against the enemy,
    for the help of man is worthless.
With God we will gain the victory,
    and he will trample down our enemies.

The words sank down like a lead weight into Roman's soul: *Who will bring me to the fortified city? . . . Is it not you, O God?* and he knew his decision to go to Corona had been confirmed.

CHAPTER 2

AT DINNER, Deirdre and Roman sat together at the head of the table with the captains, the officials, and their wives sitting around it. There was an unusual heaviness at the table tonight; Deirdre's head was down the whole of the dinner. She refused the suckling pig, choosing to listlessly stir the pea pods around on her plate.

Roman sighed and glanced away, then took her hand and kissed it. "The children are dancing tonight," he said. He had chosen her favorite entertainment this evening in hopes of lifting her spirit.

"Thank you, my lord." She smiled fleetingly at him, then lowered her head again.

"Sevter, will you see if they are ready?" Roman gestured in distress to the beefy, ruddy man beside Troyce.

"Surchatain." The palace overseer left his seat. In moments he returned, leading a line of eleven children, ranging in age from ten to two. Deirdre straightened and smiled, as did all those at table, for most of these children were their very own.

The eldest, a boy, carried a small lute, and the next two, girls, held tambourines. Bringing up the rear, grinning and clutching the hand of the little girl in front of him, was Ariel.

The children bowed solemnly to Roman and Deirdre, who nodded gravely in response. Then the three instrumentalists stood aside to play, and the children began an earnest quadrille for the delight of the grownups. They stepped and twirled to the beat of the tambourines and the melody of the lute.

Ariel, however, kept missing his steps, turning to laugh and wave at his mother. The little girl who was his partner, and who felt responsible for seeing that he did it right, grew increasingly agitated until she stopped in the midst of the dance and burst into frustrated tears. The quadrille disintegrated into a confused jumble.

The adult audience quickly turned their faces and raised their cloths to conceal their laughter, and even Roman had to suppress a smile. Deirdre sprang from her chair to embrace Ariel and the little girl, consoling her, "You did well! Don't be upset—you did the best you could with him!"

The child stopped crying and hugged her neck. Standing, Deirdre patted her and added without thinking, "The men sometimes go their own way without regard for us."

24

Roman sat back abruptly; the table stilled. Then Roman stood and said, "You are dismissed." As his guests hastily rose, he determinedly held his hand out to Deirdre. Carrying Ariel on her hip, she took Roman's hand, and he led her out, up the stone stairs.

Deirdre left Ariel to Gusta's care for the night while Roman waited in the corridor, then she meekly followed him to the Surchatain's suite. They passed by the sentry into the receiving room. It held Deirdre's bill of freedom, framed and hung as a memorial to her father Galapos, who had procured that bill to free her from slavery in exchange for his own life. Seeing it always renewed in her feelings of humility and gratitude.

Wordlessly, Roman opened the door to the lush inner chamber for her to enter. It was a room trimmed in purple and gold, cluttered with treasures collected by previous rulers for over two hundred years. Inside, she turned to face him as he closed the door. She respectfully waited for him to speak first. He was angry, she was sure, or at least exasperated.

But he took her in his arms and pressed his lips to hers, his arms tightening around her. He loosed her hair from the gold band to let it fall down her back, and whispered, "Deirdre, don't defy me over this."

She opened his collar to kiss his neck. "Please, please let me go with you."

"No." He lowered her to the bed.

Unlacing her bodice, she raised her eyes seductively. "You'll need me."

"Don't torment me, Deirdre. I can't take you. I'm not allowing Kam or Colin to bring their wives."

"I am not their wives. I am your wife, and the Surchataine, and I want to go with you."

"No. That is final." He fell on top of her and she did not argue more.

As the dinner guests were leaving the banquet hall that evening, Nihl waited in the corridor, watching Troyce talk with the under-secretary. The two were standing directly under one of the many banners brightening the stone walls, carrying the coat of arms of the great houses of Lystra. The one they stood under, the largest, bore a lion and a cross, and a narrow black line from the upper right to the lower left corner. This was the coat of arms of the present Surchatain.

When Troyce ended his conversation, he departed the hall into the corridor and turned to the left, not seeing Nihl. The Commander fol-

25

lowed him up the wide stone stairway leading to the living quarters on the second floor.

Nihl stalked the administrator with catlike strides. When Troyce stopped at the door to his chambers, Nihl put a hand on his shoulder. There was no one else in the corridor.

Troyce startled. "Commander! You surprised me."

"I have something to tell you before we leave, Troyce."

"Oh?" The administrator raised an eyebrow in a manner dangerously close to condescension.

"I will have men watching you while we are gone. Do not antagonize the Counselor, and keep your distance from the Surchataine."

Troyce eyed him. "It still rankles you that you were a slave at Sheva's palace when I was a lord there, doesn't it?" Troyce carefully avoided using the epithet *drud* which had been attached to all Polonti in slavery at Diamond's Head.

"No, but I think it rankles *you* to be merely administrator here and not a lord. I think you always watch to make a step up by means of someone's bloody back."

"Nonsense!" Troyce replied, surprisingly calm at such an accusation. "I have gained my position here by doing my job well. You must admit the Treasury is bulging. If I do things that seem bold to you, why, it is only to further Lystra's interests. And as for you," his face took on an aspect of benediction, "I will pray that one day you will be free of the chains of the past, my friend."

Nihl took a moment to answer. "The past does not trouble me. But you do. I know what you are behind all your smooth talk—beneath the cover of the Surchataine's kindness. You are a snake."

"Such jealousy!" murmured Troyce, forehead furrowing in astonishment. "I had thought such rancorous threats beneath you."

"Whatever you think, just be sure to remember what I have told you, Troyce." Nihl's hard eyes bored this closing statement deep, then he turned sharply away.

At the open audience the following morning, Coran, the Polonti emissary, stood before Roman as the Surchatain said, "I have decided that we will further investigate this problem in Corona, and deal with it ourselves. You may go tell Bruc we will disarm any threat to Polontis or Lystra from there. And tell Bruc to stay apart from it unless I summon him."

Coran stood speechless at this unhoped-for success, then came to himself in time to bow. "May your wealth and power increase to match your abundant graciousness, Surchatain," he said, able only to recite an old blessing.

Roman nodded slightly, saying, "You are dismissed." The emissary bowed again and left.

Roman immediately waved Kam forward and whispered, "Tag a scout on his heels to see that he leaves Lystra without lingering." Kam nodded, but his eyes held a question. Roman answered, "We will leave tomorrow morning, after he is well away. I do not think he needs to know I am going." Kam nodded again with conviction and turned on his heel.

There were only a few other items of business that demanded the Surchatain's personal attention this morning. As the palace and city of Westford were functioning with an efficiency never before achieved, Roman had been able to delegate most of the routine official duties to Basil and his staff.

But the oft-complaining silversmith of Westford, DuCange, had asked to see him personally, so Roman motioned him up to the throne and inquired, "DuCange, what is your problem today?"

"Surchatain, I must protest the arbitrary and unjust suppression of business that your Counselor engages in," complained DuCange, bowing briefly.

"Basil? What has he done to hurt your business?" Roman asked skeptically.

"I have had a large demand for these silver toys," DuCange said, holding up a gimmal. He set it spinning to show its intriguing motion. "They are simply for amusement, but your Counselor has forbidden me to make or sell them."

Roman watched the silver rings spin, frowning. Then with a brief shake of his head, he directed a soldier, "Summon the Counselor." Basil normally attended these morning audiences, but at this moment was writing out a formal reply to Bruc for the emissary to carry.

When Basil appeared in the hall Roman asked, "Counselor, have you really enjoined DuCange from making these things?"

Basil stiffened slightly, glancing at DuCange. "Yes, Surchatain."

"Why?"

"Surchatain, I feel it is not a good use of the silver we have acquired so much of. These toys, as DuCange calls them, are used by magicians and sorcerers in their rituals, and—"

Roman swung back to DuCange. "You are not only forbidden to make them, but you are to buy back and destroy every one of those things you have sold. If after today I see even one of them around, I will banish you from Lystra."

"Surchatain—" DuCange gasped at the extremity of this stricture.

"You are dismissed," Roman instructed curtly, rising from the throne

27

to leave the hall himself. Passing Basil, he nodded briefly, and the Counselor bowed low.

As Roman strode from the audience hall, he saw something which caused him to stop and smile. Toddling toward him was Ariel, clutching a miniature bow, with a quiver of half-sized arrows slung on his back. "Lesson, Fada! Have a lesson!" he gurgled.

Roman picked him up, grunting, "Your mother must be close by. Well . . . for a moment." Ariel gave a throaty laugh of victory.

The father carried his son to the archery range. The soldiers taking practice there smiled and made room for them, but did not slacken their shooting.

Roman placed him before a target set low on the ground close to them, and helped the child put an arrow to the string. Lightly guiding him, Roman helped him draw back and release. The arrow struck the target and fell. "Good, Ariel. Now again."

As they practiced, he grew dimly aware of shrill voices from the palace, but ignored them. When someone nearby called, "He is here," though, he turned to look.

Deirdre came running out of the palace, her voluminous skirts billowing around her. When she saw Roman and Ariel, she stopped, putting a hand to her chest in relief. "Roman," she gasped, "when you bring him out here, please send word to me. I became frantic when I could not find him."

Roman straightened in surprise. "You did not send him to me?"

"No," she frowned. "I knew you were holding audience."

"But—he came to me with his bow and quiver—" he grinned suddenly and grabbed up the squealing Ariel. "Rascal! You came of your own to me!" He shook the sturdy child with pride.

Deirdre exhaled and smiled. Roman shifted Ariel to his left arm and placed his right hand at her back to walk with her to the palace. His mind turning to other things, he said thoughtfully, "Deirdre, I wish you would sit at audience with me. You need to learn to make judgments, especially when I am gone."

She lowered her head, sighing, "As you wish, my lord. But when you are gone, Basil is to make judgments. That you have already said."

"Yes, for the time being. But I want you to listen and learn, for the day when you sit alone on the throne."

Her stomach wrenched at this calm assessment of a cruel eventuality. "I do not know . . . that I can ever learn to—to make judgments— I've never had the head for sorting out problems—" she gained momentum in her difficulty, for the tears were coming and she couldn't stop them.

28

Roman faced about in dismay and held her close with his free arm. "Deirdre . . ."

Ariel patted her shoulder and cooed, "Poor ting."

"Deirdre, you *must* learn, for the day that I—"

"Don't say it again," she pleaded, putting her fingers to his lips. "I can't bear to hear it. Please don't say it again."

He hesitated, not wishing to hurt her, but convinced it must be said. "I will not always be with you, my love."

She gazed at him while the tears ran freely down her face. She and he had stopped under one of the pentices of the courtyard; workers and soldiers went about their business but kept a discreet distance. "You think you will not return from Corona," she said.

"I may not," he replied softly. "I've no idea what awaits me there, and I want you to be prepared."

"Do you know how wretched it is to sit waiting, not knowing if your beloved will ever return, and unable to do anything to help?" she demanded. "Do you realize what you are asking of me, to stay here and wait?" His eyes flickered downward in response.

"If you love me, let me go with you," she whispered. "If you must die, let me see what it is for and know it isn't futile."

He looked at her unable to answer. Commander Nihl stepped to within a few paces of them and said, "Surchatain." Roman turned his head. "Our horses are being shod for the trip. We need to know which animal you wish to take."

Roman gave Ariel to Deirdre and silently left her in the archway. "I had not noticed your showing preference to any particular horse since the bay died," Nihl continued as they walked to the stables.

They stopped at a sturdy fence which enclosed a dozen milling horses. "These are the best of our proven animals, according to Olynn," said Nihl. "The black gelding is calm and sure-footed. The sorrel is particularly fast. The piebald has been trained to run smoothly with an archer."

Roman looked them over. "What of the white?" he inquired, nodding toward a sleek Andalusian with a delicate head and finely curved neck. It stood on the far side of the pen, head up, nostrils flared, observing the men.

Nihl arched a brow. "I don't know why that one is in here. He's not been gelded, and he's hot-tempered. But most intelligent and unmatched for courage."

"What is his name?" Roman asked, rounding the pen to have a closer look at him. The horse's eyes followed warily.

Nihl paused. "He has been tagged Bastard."

Roman glanced at Nihl with a wry smile. "I'll need a fighter—have him shod. But the old name won't do, since he's the Surchatain's horse. From now on he is Fidelis." As he left the pen he added, "And have shod the black gelding."

Deirdre sat by the window in a sitting room of soft, pleasant colors, working on her stitchery. All thoughts were painful now, and this at least was some distraction. She dropped her work to take in the horizon, set aflame by the setting sun, and let its beauty comfort her.

A housemaid entered with a bow. "Surchataine, dinner waits."

Deirdre passed a hand over her tired eyes. She could not face him at the table tonight. She could not bear to dine with him while thinking it the last time, and pretending all was well. "Please tell the Surchatain I am not well enough to attend. Please—give him my deepest apologies." The maid bowed and left.

Deirdre rested her elbows on the windowsill and bowed her head to pray. "Dear Lord in heaven . . ." but all that would come out was a wave of sorrow and longing. So she abandoned the attempt and merely watched the glowing horizon darken.

The maid appeared at the door again. "My lady," she said, twisting her hands, "forgive me, but the Surchatain says you shall come down for dinner."

Deirdre stood a little abruptly. "We shall obey him, then, shall we not?" she said with a touch of bitterness.

With the maid at her heels, Deirdre swept into the banquet hall and bowed to Roman, already seated. He nodded tightly. The guests stood until she had taken her chair and Roman waved for the serving to begin.

The maids placed steamed red snapper before them, but Deirdre ignored it. "Eat, Deirdre," said Roman, as he delved into the dinner. She picked up her fork and poked at the fish.

"You need to eat, Deirdre," Roman said in a lower tone, "for our fare on this trip will be much less substantial."

Deirdre looked up with a gasp. "You mean—"

"You may come with me." He tried to look disgruntled, but could not mask the love in his eyes.

"Roman!" She threw herself on him with such force that his great chair creaked ominously. "You won't regret it, Roman, I promise!" she cried, kissing him abundantly. Kam glanced questioningly at Nihl, who shrugged. The other guests smiled discreetly.

"Before you rejoice, Deirdre, listen a moment," Roman said severely. She sat back down in her chair with her best student posture. "This trip is likely to be not only dangerous, but uncomfortable. We'll be

30

riding all day and sleeping on the ground and eating what little we can pack. And once we get to Corona, we may find ourselves fighting or captured. It will not be a pleasure trip, Deirdre!"

She waited before answering, pretending to consider the gravity of her choice. "That does not matter. I must be with you."

"Then you shall." The way he said it was almost a threat, but Deirdre began her dinner again in buoyant enthusiasm.

"Surchatain." The holy man near the end of the table stood.

"Brother Avelon?" Roman nodded toward him with gentle respect.

"As you leave on this undertaking, I have this to say to you:" he raised his goblet, " 'The Lord bless you and keep you; the Lord make his face to shine upon you, and be gracious to you; the Lord lift up his countenance upon you, and give you peace.' "

Twenty chairs scraped back and twenty people stood at once, lifting their goblets. "Hear, hear!" And they drank their goblets empty.

Roman looked around the table and quietly responded, "Thank you."

CHAPTER 3

IN THE MORNING Deirdre awoke feeling something was amiss: Roman was gone. She leapt from bed, muttering, "Surely—!" Throwing open the door to the outer room, she saw a housemaid sitting and stitching. The Surchataine's sudden appearance caused her to bolt up and cruelly prick her finger.

"Ow! Surchataine—" The finger went to her mouth as she flung herself to a bow.

"Has Roman left?" Deirdre demanded.

"No, Surchataine—he is seeing to the gear. I am almost finished with your clothes, my lady." She held up a pair of brown trousers, like those the soldiers wore.

"My clothes?" Deirdre lifted a trouser leg with interest.

"Yes, my lady. Surchatain Roman instructed that you be outfitted with functional clothes." She pointed to a lightweight shirt, a doeskin shortcoat, and a standard army cloak.

"How clever!" laughed Deirdre. "And how necessary." She shed her nightdress, taking the underlinens the maid handed her. Then she pulled on the trousers. They were unaccountably tight around her waist, and the maid frowned.

"My lady . . . I am sorry . . . I thought I had the correct measurements." She fumbled with the drawstring waist as she muttered apologies.

"No, never mind, they are adequate," Deirdre insisted quickly, brushing her away. "The shirt?" The maid helped her put on the rest of the clothes.

Deirdre swept from the room in her uniform, feeling competent to face anything. Her long blond hair was gathered back from her face in a simple band. In a moment of excitement, she had even considered chopping her hair short. But she knew such a drastic move would send Roman into a fit—the aggravation of which he did not need at present.

She arrived in the courtyard to see the horses being saddled and packed. Roman held Olynn by the shoulder, speaking confidentially to the big, blond, smooth-faced Captain. When Roman saw Deirdre, he paused in mid-sentence. Olynn turned his eyes to her, then bowed his head to avoid embarrassing her with an unmannerly smirk.

Deirdre bounced up to Roman and announced, "I am ready."

"So I see," he answered, smiling.

"Where is Lady Grey?" she asked, scanning the animals.

Roman shook his head. "Lady Grey is too old to carry you on this trip, Deirdre. I've selected a younger, stronger horse for you."

"Oh?" She felt as if she were abandoning a lifelong friend. Roman walked up to the black gelding and stroked his shiny neck. "This one is yours today."

She patted the animal's fine head and he nosed her hand for a treat. "What is he called?"

"You will have to name him," he said, then turned as someone questioned him about the water bags.

Deirdre smiled at this privilege. The soldiers took the horses' names seriously, believing that a name contributed something very real to a horse's temperament and personality—or vice versa. She silently began sifting through prospective names. However, the bustle of preparation distracted her so that she could not think of an acceptable name immediately. Instead, she threw herself into overseeing the packing of the gear.

Due to the patience of those who knew what they were doing, the animals were soon loaded and ready to ride, in spite of her help. They jangled their bits impatiently, sensing excitement.

Roman scanned the group of well-wishers standing by, then turned to the Counselor. "Basil, I leave you charge of Westford. I know she rests in good hands. If you have any difficulties, I have left written directives with Brother Avelon."

"Surchatain." Basil bowed, but Roman extended his hand and Basil grasped it as if reluctant to let him go. In like manner, Roman gave farewells to Reuel and Olynn.

"Remember," Roman told Sevter when he took his hand, "I have left sealed instructions with Avelon in the event of a crisis—or a confrontation." He glanced at Troyce, who stood at a distance from the party.

Gusta carried up a silent, wide-eyed Ariel to Deirdre. "Ou, Ariel," she breathed, hugging him. He wrapped his little arms around her neck.

"Mother and father must leave for a while. We will be back, Ariel. Gusta will take good care of you," she reassured him. Seeing his stricken face, she reconsidered for the first time her going.

"Go too," he pleaded.

"No, baby; we can't take you," she said tenderly, at which he egan to cry. *Now I know how Roman feels,* she thought ruefully.

"Ariel, stop!" Roman said sternly. The child's lip quivered and he put a fist to his eye. Roman took him from Deirdre and held him in arms of iron. "You must stay here, Ariel. You are the Chatain. You must be strong."

He pressed his mouth close to the child's ear and whispered, "I know sometimes you just have to cry. But go to your room and cry alone. God will hear—that's enough. And He will never use it against you. I love you, son. I love you so."

Roman set Ariel on the ground and faced him toward Gusta. The boy marched stolidly to her and turned to calmly see his parents off. Deirdre looked in amazement to her husband. "Whatever did you tell him?"

"What he needed to hear." Roman smiled just slightly, grasping her waist to help her mount. He swung up on Fidelis while Kam, Colin, and Nihl mounted their horses. Roman gestured a farewell to the palace and the scouting party departed through the front gates.

Behind them in the courtyard, Basil stood staring after them with anxious eyes. Troyce, seeing him, asked, "What troubles you, Counselor?"

He blinked. "Nothing, really. Only that Surchatain Galapos left in such a similar manner for Goerge . . ." He let the sentence die away under Troyce's steady gaze.

The party crossed the stone bridge spanning the Passage and took the broad northbound market road at a good clip. Newly paved with clay brick, it invited fast travel. And this kind of morning inspired great endeavors, being sunny but not hot, green and dewy and clear. But such seasoned soldiers knew better than to let the weather dictate the success of their mission.

They galloped steadily without conversing, so Deirdre returned to the problem of naming her horse. He was a pretty black, with no white at all but a small star on his chest. He had a smooth gait. How about . . . ?

"Surchatain," said Nihl abruptly, and everyone looked to see what had drawn his attention. Sitting on the side of the road was an old woman draped in widow's black. She did not look up at the approaching party, but sat staring at nothing in front of her.

Studying her, Roman held up his hand to stop the party. "Are you in need, woman?"

"I am a widow. I am in mourning." She stated the obvious with simple deliberateness.

"What do you require, lady?" Roman asked again.

"Mercy," she said.

Kam cocked his head and Colin's transparent face conveyed a youth's judgment of her mental condition.

"In what form, woman?" Roman asked patiently.

"How will you give it?" she returned, looking up at him for the first time.

Roman reined back. "I have no time for your riddles. I trust this will provide what you need." He dropped his leather money bag to her.

She said, "It will come back to you." He glanced at her, then spurred on, the party with him.

"Crazy old woman," muttered Colin. Deirdre turned back to look. The woman was gone. Deirdre craned her head in the other direction, but saw no sign of the widow.

Aside from this exchange, the first day of their adventure turned out to be rather dull. They traveled so efficiently through the day that they arrived early at Outpost One, their lodging place for the night.

In the time since being breached by Tremaine, the gates had been repaired and the fortress itself refurbished. It now housed a thousand soldiers as comfortably as any inn. They were still dispatched to patrol the border, but had seen no fighting for many months now.

The scouting party approached the forbidding southern face of the outpost as the guards in the watchtowers shouted down greetings.

34

Rounding the corner to the northern gates, Roman cast a peevish glance at a huge apparatus sitting off to the side and serving no purpose but to house birds and foxes.

He had sent more men to work on that battering ram than any other single project, but it so far refused to yield up the secret of its construction. The crafty Tremaine had built it with baffles and locks to prevent anyone but his own soldiers being able to move it and use it. All of Tremaine's men who had attacked the outpost had died here, and Roman's men had been entirely unable to take the ram apart to transport it to Westford for safekeeping.

Roman could have ordered the ram destroyed, but such a war machine was too valuable. They had tried moving it intact, but no matter how many horses they harnessed to it, it stubbornly bogged down in the hardest road, even with stones and planks placed under its wheels. The fact was, it would not be moved or disassembled, and Roman would not give up and burn it, even with it sitting ominously before the outpost's own gates.

Over against it, standing at the other end of the gates, was one solitary post which remained of the first gates the ram had destroyed. Secured to the top of the twenty-foot pole was Tremaine's glittering golden robe which Galapos had tossed to hang there. Roman had decreed that as long as the gates stood, that robe would remain as a shining memorial of the divine deliverance from Tremaine's mighty army.

The scouting party entered the outpost courtyard and gave up their horses to the care of stablemen, then progressed toward the dining hall. On the way, they were met by Captain Clatus: "Surchatain! You arrived so much sooner than I had expected. I was preparing an honor guard to meet up with you—"

Roman waved lightly. "Don't be concerned, Clatus; you're not at fault. I am rather pleased with our fast horses and the improved roads."

Clatus turned to escort them in stride. "The messenger who came yesterday from Westford claimed he made it in four hours, according to the sundial. Devoy is such a liar, though; I wouldn't say that to an honest man's face." He poked a nearby soldier in the ribs. "I suppose Captain Colin was right in arguing that the cost to improve the roads was justified. Even the local villagers are pleased—they've named the northbound road 'Roman's Highway.' "

Deirdre thought that was excellent, but Roman hardly smiled. "They were not so honoring at the last tax day. They love my roads and the protection of my army, but they'd as soon hang me as pay their legal dues for those amenities."

Colin laughed with a snort and Clatus nodded ruefully. Then they all entered the dining hall, where soldiers jumped up from the benches to stand at attention.

Roman's group sat down to plates of roasted capon—rather tough meat for tender palates. Before attending to the information being directed to him, Roman glanced at Deirdre, and saw her serenely devouring a good-sized leg. "As you were saying, Clatus?" he smiled.

"Yes, Surchatain—Jud and Vernard returned just yesterday from scouting around Corona. I thought you would want to hear from them firsthand." Roman nodded as he ate and Captain Clatus sent a soldier with a summons.

At this point, Clatus paused to watch Deirdre. "Surchataine," he murmured respectfully, and she smiled on him in satisfaction at being where she was.

The soldiers sitting near the captain exchanged questioning glances, and several pairs of shoulders were raised. Roman told Clatus, "The Surchataine asked to come, and I felt she would be useful to me on this trip."

"Of course, Surchatain," agreed Clatus, and there was a lull.

The men standing near the table parted as Jud and Vernard nudged them aside. Roman indicated they should sit as he said, "Tell me what you observed in Corona."

They instinctively glanced at each other. Jud answered, "High Lord, we did not even get into the city."

"Do not call me High Lord. Why didn't you get into Corona?"

"It almost seems to be in a state of siege. There are guards at every thoroughfare entrance, searching carts and questioning everyone who tries to enter. We also saw them confiscating weapons. Something murky's afoot."

Roman chewed pensively. "What did you observe of these guards? Were they uniformed? And how were they armed?"

"Yes, they were uniformed," Jud answered emphatically. "In red. We could not see their crest at a distance, but they looked to be in the Order of the Bloodclad."

Roman stared at the scout. Tremaine's Order of the Bloodclad had been the model for Surchatain Karel's armed guard, the Cohort—only Karel's order had been but a shadow of the Selecan original. The Bloods were selected from Tremaine's vast army on the basis of strength, intelligence, and—most importantly—cruelty and imaginative bloodlust.

Vernard added in a subdued tone, "They carried heavyweight broadswords, typical of Tremaine's kind."

Roman shifted his gaze to Vernard. "Have you any idea what they number now?"

Vernard shook his head. "No, Surchatain. The man we had on the inside is there no more." Roman cocked a questioning brow. With reluctance, Vernard explained, "We found his body one morning nailed to the city wall. We stole it during the night and buried him."

"How is it you let him be exposed?" Roman asked in reprimand.

"Surchatain, we used great caution—we never spoke with him in person, but used a code of rock arrangements outside the city wall. There is no earthly way he could have been found out! But his last message to us was something we could not understand—about eyes in the night. Eyes watching him in the dark," muttered Jud, and Vernard nodded.

"It was the next day we found him nailed above the rocks, and the code read, 'The eyes saw him, and have seen you too,'" Jud added. "That's when we left."

An uncommon stillness fell on the hall. "That's uncanny," someone murmured. Deirdre felt the hair on her neck stand up.

"Surchatain," Vernard said bluntly, "we don't take to the idea of your going there. What's your army for, if not this?"

Roman stared past Vernard's tense face. His reply was quiet but unshaken: "Two armies fighting within the city would destroy any innocent lives left. Something is there only I can deal with." He lowered his eyes and shifted infinitesimally toward Deirdre.

She gripped the fork in her hand. "You must let me go, Roman. You gave your word."

He looked at her as if wounded by an unjust accusation. "I would not go back on my word to you," he said, though it appeared he wished he could.

After they had eaten, Roman motioned for the members of his party to take their mugs and come with him. They went up the outpost's narrow passages to the suite which had been prepared for Roman. The soldiers they met in the corridors stopped and held a salute until they passed by.

Roman herded them into the Surchatain's suite, then deliberately bolted the doors. He faced the group with heavy words weighing on his mind, and took a moment to think them through before speaking.

"It seems I have taken too lightly the problem in Corona," he opened. "The Lord has just now given me a glimpse of what we actually face. I see now why you were all compelled to come with me—you too, Deirdre. You are all strong believers. And I see that our only hope of success—that means coming away with our lives—lies in our going under the protection of the Lord. I want you to join me in asking for His power to cover us." He paused to see that they were all of one mind.

He knelt, and they followed suit, kneeling in a circle facing each

37

other. Roman placed his palms on the floor in front of him as a brace and said, "My Lord Jesus Christ, we have come at your summons to root out whatever evil this is growing from Corona. Lord Jesus, if we came amiss, I ask that you prevent us from pursuing this mission. But if you indeed bid us go, Lord, I ask that you go before us in power, and direct our steps to accomplish your ends.

"Lord Jesus, let my life and the lives of these be precious in your sight. Empower us to deliver Corona from the grasp of this new tyrant and take it captive to you. And while Deirdre and I are away from our son, protect him by the power of your name. Our eyes are on you, Lord. Amen."

Deirdre and the men repeated, "Amen." As she looked up into her husband's taut face, a surge of love passed through her. Over the years she had seen Roman grow stronger and deeper, and, in some mysterious way, more vulnerable, with a compassion defying reason.

They stood. Nihl calmly picked up his mug to drain it, appearing not reluctant to take on this challenge. Kam pensively crossed his arms on his chest.

Colin broke the quiet. "Surchatain, I thought I should tell you . . . while I was serving under my father, during the alliance with Galapos, we had some experience with the Bloods."

"Yes?"

"We had one outpost on the border of Seir and Seleca, north of the Fastnesses, which was overdue in sending a report. We feared they might have had an early clash with Tremaine, so we took scouts through a hidden mountain pass to check on the outpost.

"Coming out of the pass, we found the body of one of our soldiers impaled on a post. It was set in the ground like a signpost at the secret entrance to the pass. Going further, we came upon a second body, headless. Still further, we found another man, also tortured to death. Then another and another—they were laid out in a trail for us from the pass to the outpost.

"We saw from a distance that the outpost had been taken. Plundered, burned, and ground to rubble—I'd never seen such thorough destruction. At what had once been the entrance, a broadsword stood rammed into the ground. It bore Tremaine's crest of the Order of the Bloodclad."

The group silently pondered this. Colin continued, "It does not excuse my father's actions, but—it was after this that he agreed to betray Galapos. That secret pass leads from the mountains directly into Ooster."

"I'm sure he saw no other option, with his capital in peril," Roman mused.

38

"If they have resurrected the Bloodclad, then what is our plan against them, Surchatain?" asked Kam.

Roman straightened, running a hand through his thick black hair flecked with grey. "I don't know yet," he said flatly. "But don't worry. The Lord Jesus is mightier than any number of Bloods, and we are following in His shadow. Let's get some sleep now."

The others exited to their quarters, and Roman lay wearily on the mattressed bed, rubbing his forehead. Deirdre undressed and lay beside him, reaching over to caress his temples. He closed his eyes. She kissed his forehead, his nose, his stubbly chin, then she firmly planted her mouth on his.

"Deirdre, this is not a good time," he murmured, lightly stroking her back. Undaunted, she lay across his chest to kiss him. "You are incredibly demanding," he mumbled. She loosened his shirt laces, drawing it off over his head, and he rolled over to embrace her.

CHAPTER 4

IN THE EARLY DAWN, the outpost's officers stood by as Roman's party received their freshly groomed animals from the stablemen. "If you won't let us accompany you, then what we'll do is post a watch outside Corona for you, Surchatain," said Clatus. "Day or night, if we see you coming out, we'll have someone there to meet you. Don't forbid me that."

"That would be welcome," Roman replied. He pressed the Captain's hand. "So watch for us."

They started off on the grassy plain at a brisk canter, but the horses were frisky and wanted to run. In the cool freshness of the early morning, the party could not help but cast long glances at the eastern sky, with flashes of the awakening sun bursting up from the horizon through the clouds. As they galloped, the horses scattered the crystalline dew, leaving a trail of prints on the glossy green grass.

With increasing daylight, the Fastnesses appeared more clearly before them in the distance—silent, deep green sentinels watching all the little humans scurry back and forth through them on their great campaigns.

The riders let the horses run off their excess energy, then slowed to a more suitable pace for travel. Still, they did not seem inclined to talk—not even Deirdre. They were inwardly preparing for whatever they might soon be standing against.

When, later, they exited Falcon Pass, they diverted their course to climb a short way up a gradual northern slope. From there, they could see much of the road and the surrounding countryside for miles, almost to Corona.

"What do you see, Kam?" muttered Roman, squinting into the distance.

Kam, who had generally the sharpest set of eyes in the army, shielded his face from the sun and scanned the straight northern road. "Nothing," he said at last, shrugging. "I can't pick out any uniforms at all. There doesn't seem to be anything on the road—strange, for this time of day."

Roman took the reins to lead his horse back down the slope. "There may be a deceptively simple reason for that."

They rode out of the Fastnesses in formation, with Deirdre on the inside. When they came within view of a village they slowed. A small field grew wheat scattered among weeds. A hut stood back a way from the road, but there were no animals around it.

The scouting party cantered into the village, which was vacant. "This place has been deserted for some time," noted Kam, nodding toward the village well overrun with ivy.

"Umm," murmured Roman, looking. "No sense in stopping here, then."

"We might see if we could water the horses," Colin suggested. He slid from his mount and ripped away some ivy to peer down into the well. Then he lowered a bucket on a rope by hand to bring up water. He stuck two fingers in and tasted it. "It's good," he said, so they all brought their horses up to drink.

As Deirdre dismounted, something on the ground caught her eye. "Oh look," she said to no one in particular. "Some little girl left her doll behind."

Stooping, she picked up an eight-inch clay figurine. Colin smiled at her but Roman was talking with Nihl and did not see. So she remounted, holding the doll.

"There's something about this place I don't like," muttered Roman. Then suddenly they all jumped at the sound of enraged barking. A large dog bolted from behind a hut and pounced toward Deirdre, its teeth bared, and foaming at the mouth.

40

She screamed as it leaped. Nihl drew his sword and slashed the dog's throat in one swift motion.

It fell back and lay quivering. They stared down at the scruffy dog, unsure it was dead. Nihl, irritated at the apparent miss, severed its head with a stroke. Still it quivered.

Kam urged, "Let's get away from here," and they all quickly went to their horses without argument.

As they spurred out of the village they immediately met a strong northerly headwind which blasted dirt in their faces and whipped their clothes. The further they tried to ride, the harder it blew, until they could no longer ride into it. Squinting and sheltering his face, Kam cried, "What is this? A gale in June?"

"I don't know!" shouted Roman. He said something else that went unheard, for the horses began slipping down, backing up toward the village. They were forced to turn tail to the wind and let it drive them in retreat to the abandoned village. As soon as they passed the first hut, the wind abruptly died.

They stopped dead still. Hardly breathing, they shifted only their eyes to look around the desolate place. "The dog is gone," said Nihl.

The sudden angry barking chilled their hearts. Around the corner of the hut came the foaming dog. A thick red line matted the hair in a circle around its neck, and its head lolled as if the neck were broken, but still it snapped and barked as it charged Deirdre.

"Watch out!" shouted Kam, grabbing Deirdre. Roman and Nihl threw themselves from their horses at the same instant, drawing their blades. While Nihl slashed the dog's throat a second time, Roman broke its back with a blow. It fell, quivering.

"What is happening?" breathed Colin.

Roman clenched his fists and cried, "Lord Jesus, what is causing this?" Suddenly he stared at Deirdre, who was clutching the clay doll. "What is that?"

"This?" she faltered, as he strode over to her. "It's just a doll I found."

"Here?" he asked, taking it.

"Yes—" she startled as he crushed it to powder in one hand.

The dog stopped quivering. Roman brushed off his hands. "Don't pick up *anything* from the places we pass through," he said tersely.

"What was it?" she gasped.

"They are called *anakim,*" answered Nihl. "Village gods. Spirits confined to an image of wood or clay. They are supposed to be indestructible."

"Do you know of these things?" Roman asked, climbing back on his horse.

41

"Only in the form of mountain folklore. Polonti do not concern themselves with such things."

"At least it gives us a clearer idea of what we are up against in Corona," Roman said. He reached over to squeeze Deirdre's shaking hand.

The second time they exited the village, the air was calm. Resolutely, they resumed the trip to Corona.

As they traveled into the day, they met no one else. There had been numerous travelers the day before, while they were within Lystra's borders. "This road used to be crowded with merchants," observed Colin.

"Whatever is happening in Corona has apparently put an end to that," remarked Roman.

The group came to another dead village, and passed through at a uniformly fast pace. Beyond it, they encountered a part of the road that was encased in forest. They plunged without hesitation into its shadows.

Deirdre had never felt at ease in forests, for they hid all manner of unfriendly creatures. One could get lost so easily, too, without being able to see the sky. She remembered a night long ago when she had lost herself in the woods beyond the palace at Westford. Just being able to see the night sky through the early spring branches had calmed her. Then Roman had stepped through the trees . . .

"What is it?" queried Kam, for Roman had drawn up on the reins.

The Surchatain was waiting, listening, while Fidelis danced around. "I don't know," he murmured. "I thought I heard something." He shook his head uneasily and allowed his horse to bound forward again. The ride continued into a denser part of the forest, dark as twilight.

Nihl raised his head with a jerk. "I hear it. It sounds like laughter."

"No, like weeping," said Roman, frowning. They unconsciously sped their pace.

"It's something howling!" exclaimed Kam.

"No, it's moaning," Colin contradicted him excitely.

Deirdre strained to listen. "I don't hear anything," she complained.

The horses lengthened their stride to a run. "It's coming closer!" Kam warned.

"Wait! Stop!" shouted Roman, and they reined in their panting mounts. "It's senseless to run until we know what it is!"

They held their breath, listening. "That?" said Deirdre. "Is that it? You silly men, that's the wind in the trees!"

Nihl dropped his head and Kam went red in the face. Colin coughed

42

and glanced at Roman, who lowered his shoulders with a relieved laugh. "Look at us! Brave warriors—running from the wind!" They had a good laugh at themselves, then continued at an easy canter.

By late afternoon, they entered the pasture lands surrounding the city. Here they were somewhat encouraged to see some sheep and other signs of life. The market road, which had been dirt for miles, gave way to the smooth, paved thoroughfare leading up to the city gates— a remnant of the days of glory under Tremaine.

On the edge of the thoroughfare, they stopped, looking toward the gates. At an hour when the city should have been bustling, the gates were shut tight. "This is not right," muttered Colin. "Even the scouts who were here two days ago mentioned traffic going in."

"Perhaps they are under curfew," suggested Nihl.

"But we have not met anyone coming or going, Commander," argued Kam.

"Not on this road," acknowledged Roman. They silently studied the lifeless gates.

"What do we do, Surchatain?" asked Kam. "Ride up to the gates and demand entry?"

Roman stared ahead without answering. From her knowledge of him, Deirdre could see he was inwardly inquiring of his High Lord.

"Well, why not?" he decided. "Deirdre, to the inside. Men, hold your swords ready. Let's go." He tapped Fidelis lightly with his heels, and the horse took the lead prancing. Roman held his sword down by his thigh, but still in sight.

They clop-clopped steadily toward the gates. Tensely, they scanned the wall for lookouts. *Clop, clop* and the gates loomed larger before them. When they were within ten feet, there was a startling creak and the gates opened.

Twenty mounted Bloods filled the city entrance forbiddingly. One of them, wearing a sash of authority, spurred from the gates to Roman. "State your name and your business," the Captain of the Bloodclad demanded.

"We are emissaries from Lystra, who wish an audience with your Surchatain. I am Roman," he answered with unruffled composure.

The Captain smiled in amusement and looked them over, especially Deirdre. "Is she a gift for the Surchatain?"

Roman opened his mouth and uttered, "She is an emissary also, under my protection."

"Yes?" the Captain sneered at him. "Well, emissaries may not enter with weapons. You must leave them with us to come into the city."

Roman slowly handed the hilt of his sword to the Captain, who took it, then gestured at him: "Dismount." Roman did, and the Captain waved two Bloods forward while he turned to Nihl, extending his hand in a silent demand for his weapon.

Meanwhile, the two Bloods searched Roman, rifling his clothes and saddlebags, and taking a dagger from his belt. Nihl gave up his sword to the Captain with visible reluctance and likewise submitted to a search. The Bloods removed a knife from Nihl's belt, another from his boot, and the money pouch from his saddlebag.

While Kam and Colin were being searched, the Captain of the Bloods turned to Deirdre, smiling broadly. "Dismount."

As she did, Roman said, "She is not armed."

Ignoring him, the Captain reached out to open her shortcoat. But Roman reached him in one stride and put a prohibitive hand on the man's chest. "*She is not armed.* Will you answer for abusing an emissary to the Surchatain?"

The Captain opened his mouth, glaring, but another Blood spoke in his ear. He glanced at Roman and Deirdre, then hissed, "You'll get an audience, fool, if you're sure you want it!"

He spun back to his horse as Roman, exhaling, lifted Deirdre into her saddle. Then the Order of the Bloodclad surrounded the party to escort them in, and the city gates groaned shut behind them.

As they rode toward the palace, Roman glanced about the streets. Some odd changes had taken place since he was last here. The only people who were out of doors had Bloods accompanying them. A Blood stood at the doorway of almost every shop and house. For the most part, the buildings themselves were neatly maintained, but something about their façades nagged at Roman until he put his finger on the difference.

Each shopfront carried one of two symbols—a black cross or a red circle. Most by far had the red circles. Those that had the black crosses had something of a shabby look about them: broken facings, damaged signs—the marks of vandalism.

The escorted group turned up the impressive thoroughfare to the palace and Deirdre let out a low moan. On her first visit here years ago, this street had been lined with mulberry and maple trees. But now, in place of the trees, stood large wooden crosses, on which hung citizens of the city—some dying, some already dead. Nailed above their heads were the same black crosses Roman had noticed on the shopfronts.

Deirdre bowed her head, tears streaming down her face, as they powerlessly passed by the suffering and dying. Roman's and Nihl's faces were flint; Kam was crimson and Colin pale.

They drew up to the magnificent gates and the Captain motioned them off their horses. As the mounts were led away, Fidelis balked, rearing. One of the Bloods yanked angrily on his bridle and Roman ordered, "Fidelis! Go." The animal grudgingly allowed himself to be led away, working his sore mouth.

The Bloods wordlessly herded the party up the steps to the great doors, which were opened to them. Apprehension rolled over Deirdre as they entered the audience hall. It was all there, all the same—the stunning mosaic covering the expanse of floor, the shifting angles of the paneled walls, the golden chandeliers above with hundreds of candles. As they approached the throne, she noted that, although it and the carved lions which supported it were gilded, the jewels were gone.

"Wait here." The Captain jammed a finger toward the floor before striding out. The party certainly did not attempt to run away, but quietly waited, evaluating their surroundings. Roman and Deirdre looked at each other, and, for some reason, her heart constricted violently.

CHAPTER 5

FOR THREE QUARTERS of an hour, Roman's group stood in the audience hall awaiting the Surchatain. The only movement they made was to shift as their legs grew stiff. Nor did they talk to one another, with so many unfriendly ears nearby. The stares of the Selecan soldiers discomforted Deirdre, but she made her back iron to them and kept her face toward the vacant throne.

Footsteps from a side entrance drew their eyes. An honor guard of Bloods stalked in and stood aside. A man in a swirling golden robe entered through their lines, ignoring their salutes, and seated himself upon the throne.

At first Deirdre did not really see him, her attention being diverted by the robe. It was indeed patterned after Tremaine's, which now hung at the outpost's gates, but was somehow less brilliant. Then she saw that it was not pure woven gold, but gold strands interwoven with bright yellow ones to make a facsimile of the original, using a fraction of the gold.

Roman bowed and his companions did the same. As Deirdre was raising herself, the man spoke, bringing her head up with a start: "Who are you and what do you want?"

It was not such an unreasonable question, but Deirdre had to grimace awfully to keep from laughing. There before her on that mighty throne was a chubby little imp of a man with a pouting face and a nasal, whiny voice. From the start of their trip Deirdre had unconsciously held the imposing image of Tremaine as the man they would meet here, so that the contrasting presence of this man was almost too much of a shock.

Before Roman could respond to his question, the Captain of the Bloods stepped arrogantly in front of him and bowed to the man on the throne. "Most High Lord Tremelaine, this is Homan, an emissary from the Surchatain of Lystra."

"Lystra?" Tremelaine curled his lip. "What does he want? Speak up, man! Are you dumb?"

Roman inclined his head. "Surchatain, the Surchatain of Lystra wishes to know your intentions in mobilizing your army."

Tremelaine grinned. "Ooh, he's scared."

"He wishes you to be aware that an attack on Lystra or her allies would not be prudent."

Tremelaine chewed on his thumbnail, studying Roman with a malicious glint in his eyes. "He must not value you much to send you to me with that message."

"I came of my own desire to serve my High Lord," Roman answered.

"Well now that I have you here, what shall I do with you?" Tremelaine fretted happily. "Berk," he turned to the Captain, "what shall I do with them?"

"Flay them on the rack and send their skins to Lystra as your reply," answered Berk immediately.

"Oh yes! That would be fun!" Tremelaine chortled. Deirdre broke into a cold sweat. "Oh no," he pouted, reconsidering. "Then he would attack us and we're not ready for him yet. No, no, no. What shall I do?" In nervous excitement, he sprang up from the throne and began to pace.

"I must think!" he cried. "Put them in prison while I think." He stopped before Roman, who looked down on him by eight inches. "Put *him* in the pit."

Roman and his companions were taken out of the hall and down a long corridor to a heavy wooden door. Deirdre, beside Nihl, saw his eyes shifting continually to take in every detail of this route. Berk unlocked the door and one of the Bloods pulled it open to reveal the first few steps of a long, dark, damp flight leading down to the dungeon. Roman was pushed to descend it, followed by a guard with a torch. The other prisoners went after, a guard treading heavily behind each.

One side of the stairway was fully open, and they descended into something of a cave, the wall on their right being wet and slimy. Deirdre heard the echoes of dripping water. She felt her way slowly down, wondering how Roman could walk blindly down into utter darkness, for the guard's torch behind him did not illumine the steps in front of him.

They went down and down, sixty steps or more. Then she felt Roman pause and the guard shove him ahead. They had reached the bottom. Here, the prisoners were pushed against the mossy wall while chains were brought and fastened on their wrists and ankles. In the dancing torchlight, Deirdre could see four tunnels intersecting twenty feet from the stairway and leading diverse ways.

More guards came down the steps. Four took Colin and Kam down one tunnel and four took Roman and Nihl down another. But only one Blood was deemed necessary to take Deirdre toward a third tunnel.

The guard who took her stopped close to the intersection, just beyond sight of the steps. He unlocked a black wooden door which had a small window covered with rusty iron slats. As he opened it, he paused to grab Deirdre by the neck and kiss her. She gagged at his stinking breath. "I'll come for you later," he whispered gruffly, then locked her into the rocky cell.

After the guards had shoved Nihl into a cell, they took Roman farther down the same tunnel. The dirt floor gave way to mud, which sucked at their boots as they went. The ceiling dropped lower, until Roman and some of the guards had to stoop to go on. The farther they went, the harder it was to breathe in the dead air.

Finally they came to the end of the tunnel—a blank rock wall. One of the Bloods reached down and pulled up a creaking trap door, revealing a black hole less than four feet across. He shoved a rope into Roman's manacled hands. "Hold this, if you can."

Without warning another Blood struck Roman in the back and he toppled into the hole, grasping the rope. It slipped a bit, burning his hands, but he managed to hold on and get his feet below him as they lowered him about twenty feet into a pit the size of a well. When he hit the mud bottom, the rope was jerked up from his hands. Then what little light there was vanished as they dropped the trap door with an echoing crash.

Roman leaned tentatively against the oozing wall, listening to his own breathing. He stretched his hands out before him and felt the opposite wall. Gingerly, he extracted his shackled feet from the mud bottom and braced them against the wall. He leaned his head back, waiting for quietness of spirit. Then he said, "Lord God, this is my battle. Please get them out of here."

Deirdre crouched in her cell, holding her breath. In the darkness, she intently listened to the scurrying scratches of a rat on the dirt floor. When she felt a furtive nibble on her boot, she stomped with inspired force and winced to feel a small body crunch beneath her heel. She kicked the rat up against the other wall and sat again, holding her knees.

In moments she heard the distant creak of the dungeon door. Another moment later she saw snatches of torchlight through the iron slats. Footsteps approached, then stopped at her door, and a key scraped in the lock. When the door swung open, she blinked in the torchlight, which revealed that the guard had returned as promised.

He set the torch in a sconce outside, then reached down and pulled her to her feet. She brought up her chains and smacked him in the face with them. He slapped her in retaliation, swearing.

Impatiently, he drew out a key ring from his belt and unlocked her hands and feet, tossing the chains aside. He threw her up against the rock to kiss her roughly. She struggled, twisted, and scratched, but was no match for him in strength.

Suddenly he yelled and jerked away from her, grabbing at his pants. As he hopped about, screaming and slapping, Deirdre saw a bulge in the back of his trouser leg. The seriously injured rat, blinded by pain, had found its way up his leg to vent its rage.

Deirdre instantly leapt to the sconce and seized the torch. When the guard lunged after her, she wheeled and slammed the torch down on his head. She tore the key ring from his belt and rushed from the cell. Slamming the door shut, she locked it.

She paused in the corridor to grip the torch tighter, shutting the guard's cries out of her ears. Then she rushed down the passage where she had seen Kam and Colin taken. She ran from door to door, urgently whispering, "Kam! Colin!"

A low groan answered her from one cell. She unlocked its door and wrenched it open. But a strange man came out, staring dazedly at her. Hardly hesitating, she drew him after her, whispering, "There are others I must find. Come quickly."

Thin and hollow-eyed, he took her arm. "My wife and daughter are here somewhere," he croaked.

"We'll find them also," she said, swiftly moving to the next door.

She held the torch to the slats and saw Kam's head bounce up.

Deirdre opened the door for him to stumble out. "Surchataine—!" he began to mutter, but startled at the sight of the prisoner behind her.

As she unfastened Kam's manacles, she briefly explained, "We are cleaning house." The stranger kept a slight distance from them, as if uncertain whether he should go at all. He then evidently decided he should, but did not stay close enough to hear their whispered conversations.

They found Colin a few doors down. When she freed him, he grinned, "I knew Roman was justified in bringing you."

They peered through every door of that tunnel for the man's wife and daughter, but they were not there. Deirdre began to fear that she would not find them, and looking for them was eating up precious time. But the haunted look in the stranger's eyes shut her mouth to suggesting they not bother.

Back at the intersection of tunnels, Kam anxiously whispered, "Where is the Surchatain?"

"He and Nihl were taken this way," she said, turning confidently down a passage. But the first door they looked in held a woman. "Mara!" the man rasped, embracing the pale, fragile woman. She twisted in surprise at the newcomers around her. She wore no fetters, as neither had the man. Deirdre quizzed her, "Where is your daughter? Do you know?"

"Down this way," she whispered. Before she could say more, the man buried her face in his shoulder.

The next two cells in the direction Mara had indicated were empty, but the third held Nihl. He stepped out as if he had been expecting momentary release. "Deirdre the Liberator," he murmured, watching her take off his chains. "Will you always be freeing me?" She grinned up at him and he said, "We must get the Surchatain. He is not in one of these." He paused to assess the strangers behind Colin, then stalked straight down the passage without the torch, stooping as the roof dropped.

Following, Deirdre stopped at every door to peek through the slats. At one she halted and jammed the key into the lock to release a girl a few years younger than herself. The girl looked so astonished to see Deirdre that she did not seem inclined to come out until her father reached in and took her. She wore no fetters either.

From there, they cautiously trod through the shrinking passage until they found Nihl at the end, standing over the open trap door. "We need rope," he said. "We cannot get him out without rope."

"Roman!" Deirdre gasped, falling on her knees to look into the

49

hole. "Are you down there?" The torch showed him far down at the slimy bottom, shading his eyes as he looked up. "We're going to get rope to get you out!" she shouted.

"Deirdre!" he exclaimed, weak with relief. "Thank God! Get Nihl. Nihl!" His voice echoed up the pit.

"Surchatain," Nihl answered, leaning over Deirdre.

"Nihl, I command you to get the others out of this palace immediately. You must not waste time trying to free me. I order you to get them out now!"

"Roman, no!" Deirdre cried as Nihl straightened. "No, we won't leave you," she insisted. The Commander took her arm to draw her away as he let the trap door down. "Nihl, no! How could you?" she wept, beating on him. "I order you to get him out!"

Nihl gazed at her and even in the wavering torchlight she could see agony in his eyes. "I cannot, Surchataine," he said. "His order supersedes yours. He knows what he is doing."

"No," Deirdre shuddered with weeping, clinging to Nihl. "I beg you not to leave him down there. I beg you."

Nihl took the torch and held her in his other arm, turning to lead them out of the passage. Kam coughed repeatedly and Colin brushed tears from his face, but they retreated from the pit, the rescued family mutely following.

At the intersection of passages they stopped, facing the stairway. Nihl mused, "Somehow, we must get past that door, and—"

"No," said the man hoarsely. "There is another way. Come with me."

With no time to spare for debating him, they followed as he led them down a wide passageway extending straight out from the stairs. They trooped through this tunnel for several hundred feet, passing intersections and branches. Always the stranger bore to the right.

They came to an apparent end. In the face of the wall before them was a small shuttered door four feet off the ground. The man opened it to reveal a square crawlspace which inclined upward.

He explained to Nihl, "This tunnel leads to a hidden entrance just outside the palace walls. It may be blocked up; it most certainly is watched. But there is no other way we can escape."

"I will go first," Nihl said, "the Surchataine behind me." Deirdre, numb and pale, shifted her blank eyes to him. "Colin, follow her, then you three, and Kam in the rear." The others lined up as Nihl lowered the torch to the dirt floor and snuffed it out.

Deirdre felt him climb into the hole, then Colin nudged her. With a last moan for Roman, she put up her knees to climb after Nihl. Colin came close behind.

50

They edged up through the narrow shaft like a column of ants. Clutching handfuls of dirt in attempts to gain ground, they climbed on hands and knees up the sixty-degree incline. Deirdre brushed the side of the shaft and felt a support beam, dangerously splintered from the weight it held. If their way was blocked ahead, the confines of the tunnel made it nearly impossible to back up or turn around. She was assailed by a mocking certainty that they would perish in the escape Roman had ordered.

Farther up the shaft, the air deadened so that they began to gasp for breath. Deirdre already felt the perspiration trickling down the side of her face. The blackness around her was so impenetrable that she doubted if light alone would ever restore her vision. Once or twice she stopped, unable to move a knee forward. But each time Nihl reached back to take her hand and pull her along until she could go on her own.

At last Deirdre succumbed to the airless blackness and collapsed. But then the tiniest waft of cool air reached her face. Nihl dragged her up a few more feet and the draft grew stronger. She raised her bobbing head and got up on watery knees.

Nihl stopped, panting, "There is a door here." He tested it. "It is locked on the other side."

"Of course," Deirdre murmured. "We are trapped in this hole. We will die here."

Nihl did not hear her, or did not respond. He was twisting, attempting to turn around in the narrow tunnel. "Back up," he whispered.

"What are you doing?" she asked. Rather than answer, somehow he reversed his position and now lay on his back with his feet against the door. He curled up, placed his arms against the sides of the shaft and directed over his shoulder, "Colin, brace my back." Colin squeezed up next to Deirdre and they both leaned against Nihl's solid shoulders.

He drew his knees back to his chest, then rammed his heels into the door. It broke open with a resounding crash. Nihl rolled out, braced to fight.

No one was there. Nihl spun around, making sure. He stood in a small dry stream bed thirty feet outside the palace walls. The forest was just a step further. Deirdre began to climb out of the tunnel mouth, but Nihl motioned her to lie where she was.

Crouching to conceal himself, he surveyed the wall to see if any lookouts had detected the disruption in the night. His eyes moved from bartizan to casern window to tower, but he could discern no movement from these sentry posts.

Surprised, but satisfied that their escape had gone unnoticed, Nihl bent to lift Deirdre out of the hole into the fresh night air. As the others came out, Nihl studied the entrance. No wonder the Bloods had not bothered to guard it—it was incredibly well camouflaged. Those exiting the tunnel appeared to be springing up out of solid earth.

When Kam was out, Nihl shut the door, removing the broken, rusty lock. They rearranged the brush over the hole so that it sank back to invisibility. Then they ran for the trees.

In the pit, Roman crouched, breathlessly staring straight ahead. Suddenly he relaxed and breathed, "They are out. Thank you, Father. Thank you." Then he dropped his head and wept.

CHAPTER 6

THE SCOUTING PARTY, minus one, but with three new additions, stopped in the murky forest to collect themselves. Deirdre grasped the arm of the man who had led them out of the labyrinth. "Who are you? Where do you live?" She could see only his shadowy figure.

He answered, "I am Graydon. Does the name mean anything to you?"

She shook her head, responding, "No."

"I am the brother of the man who sits on the throne and calls himself Tremelaine."

Deirdre did not reply for astonishment. He continued, "These with me are my wife Mara and my daughter Magdel. What we have to tell you would keep us here till morning, and I must first show you how to escape. Come." He took a step, gesturing.

But Deirdre put a hand on the shoulder of Nihl, close beside her, and whispered, "What do you think?"

He paused a beat, then said, "We should see what he has to show us."

Deirdre told Graydon, "We will see what you have to show us."

"Then come," he urged, agitated.

52

They followed him through the black trees. Deirdre, still shaking, held on to Nihl with her left hand and Colin with her right, wondering now why she had so stubbornly demanded to come on this trip.

When they emerged from the forest they stayed near the trees, which sheltered them from the revealing moonlight. Fifty yards ahead was the city wall, guards patroling atop it. "We are still within the wall?" Deirdre murmured, confused.

"Yes," whispered Graydon. "This forest is merely the Surchatain's hunting grounds. Getting out of the city will be very difficult for you, but it can be done. Straight ahead, where the moon shadow of the tallest tree points to the wall, there is a hidden breach in the wall at the base. You must slip through one at a time exactly as the guards pass each other directly overhead—they cannot see you then. Outside, the shadow of the wall will hide you as you move along it, out of sight. Go quickly now."

"No," said Nihl bluntly, and Graydon became very still. "We will not leave Corona without the Surchatain," said Nihl. "I have fulfilled his command, but now we must rescue him." Deirdre gratefully squeezed his hand.

"I thought I heard you use that title in the dungeon. What province are you from?" frowned Graydon.

"Lystra," answered Deirdre.

"Then the one in the pit is Surchatain Roman?" Graydon exclaimed.

"Yes," Deirdre said uneasily.

"Oh, woe, woe," moaned Graydon. "What Tremelaine will do to him is unspeakable!"

Deirdre swayed on her feet. Nihl put his arm around her and said, "I do not believe Tremelaine knows he is the Surchatain."

"No?" queried Graydon. "Perhaps there is hope, then. If you will not leave without him, we must find a place for you to stay—and I think I know where—with others who are in danger from Tremelaine. Then we can get you all out of the city at once. Come now." He took a path along the edge of the trees back to the heart of the city, the Lystrans following warily.

They wove down into the city streets, skulking in the shadows of the buildings as they watched for Bloods. Graydon took them down a side street and stopped at the rear door of a shop. He knocked a tattoo on the door. After a few moments, Deirdre heard a slight rustle within. Patiently, Graydon knocked again.

A peephole in the door slid open, then a muffled exclamation was heard. A scraping bolt was drawn back and the door opened. The seven slipped inside.

"Lord Graydon!" whispered a man holding a candle. "I had thought never to see you again! And Mara—Magdel—" he greeted them urgently. "Who are these?" he asked in some alarm, lifting the candle. Deirdre noted he was dressed like a tailor but was somewhat rumpled—evidently he had dressed in haste. He was a slight, wispy man with a scared expression she soon accepted as habitual.

"Orvis," Graydon said wearily, "we need a hiding place. Go ask Vida to bring meat and drink." Graydon was moving over to a table, which he lifted and set aside with Nihl's help. Graydon tossed a floor covering to one side and bent to pry up a trap door in the wooden planking. As he swung down to a ladder, Orvis handed him another candle.

Below, the party found themselves in a fifteen-by-twenty-foot food cellar, lined with shelves holding stone jars and stuffed gunnysacks. Graydon took a seat on the floor, and the others sat with him.

The ladder creaked as down it puffed a beefy woman in nightdress and bonnet. "It is you, my lord!" she gasped. Graydon jumped up and spoke in her ear. She nodded, glancing sidelong at the Lystrans. From above, Orvis used a length of twine to lower a basket with victuals and a jug. "Mara! You look starved!" Vida declared, setting the basket in front of her. Mara smiled gratefully as she reached for the bread.

Orvis joined them, tentatively eyeing the scouting party while they passed the jug, beef strips, and bread. Graydon swallowed and said, "Orvis—Vida—these good people freed us from prison. They come from Lystra, though why I do not know."

Deirdre said, "I am Surchataine Deirdre. This is Commander Nihl, the Second Kam, and Captain Colin. My husband, Surchatain Roman, remains in that prison. He came in response to a plea from Polontis to quash the threat your new Surchatain is becoming." Orvis and Vida stared open-mouthed. "Now tell me what he has been doing to this city," demanded Deirdre.

Graydon sighed, as if wondering where to begin. "Polontis has reason to be concerned. Tremelaine is fashioning Corona into a war state. His goal is the unification of the Continent under himself, and I fear he will accomplish it."

"How can he—by gathering an army from Corona?" Nihl asked incredulously. "There are not nearly enough fighting men."

Graydon shook his head as if Nihl had no understanding. "He does not need many men. He has other resources." Nihl skeptically cocked a brow. Graydon explained, "He has learned to tap the powers of the beyond."

There was a chilly silence. "You mean, he is a sorcerer," said Deirdre.

54

"Of the most dreaded and powerful kind. Even I could not stop him."

Deirdre's eyes widened. She and Nihl glanced at each other. "Are you a sorcerer?" she asked carefully.

"I was," Graydon answered, "but am not now, nor had I always been. Up until nine months ago, Galen—that was his name before he changed it—Galen and I ran a glassblowing shop here in Corona. Then one evening he came in with an old book he had found lying in the street. It was full of interesting little spells and runes. We tried one or two at the beginning of the book—simple love potions and rainmaking, that is all—but how surprised we were to discover that they worked!

"At once, it became a contest between us to see who could work the stronger spells. It was—how can I describe the feeling of power? To know secret things, to have wonderful visions and sensations pouring through my body—to grow stronger and stronger and feel that nothing was beyond me—" He cut short, speechless in rapture, then saw that his audience was gaping at him.

Quickly collecting himself, he continued in a more subdued manner, "We progressed rapidly through the book—learning to inflict diseases on our enemies, make objects move of their own, and even conjure up the dead. That is how Galen met and grew enamored of Tremaine, whom he emulates, as you must have noticed.

"There was one last spell that eluded us, however—how to make the powers of darkness obey our command. That is where the real power lies. We both knew it. We wrestled continually to gain mastery of it before the other.

"He gained it first; I still do not know how. But one day he walked triumphantly into my house and commanded, 'Take him up and show him who is lord!' I felt myself thrown up into the air and bounced like a puppet on strings. From that moment on, not even the smallest spell had any power on my lips.

"Then, he swiftly took control of Corona and changed his name. He seized me and my family and put us into prison to play with us as he wished. But he concentrated on gathering an army with the help of the dark powers. Once he is ready, I assure you no power on earth will be able to withstand him."

Here Graydon paused, considering something that had just occurred to him. "Recently, though, he has been agitated. He knows that somehow the Surchatain of Lystra is a threat to him. But now, with your Surchatain in his grasp, Tremelaine will do away with him and progress to his goal."

Kam interjected, "You don't know Roman. He was sent by God

to get rid of this madman, and he goes in the power of the Almighty."

Graydon bit his lips. "The last I saw of your Surchatain, he was helplessly trapped in the pit of the dungeon."

This no one could argue. After a disheartened silence, Deirdre asked, "What is Tremelaine doing to the people here? What is the meaning of the symbols on the shopfronts?" Roman was not the only one who had noticed them.

Graydon inhaled. "Before Tremelaine can march out of Corona, he must remove all resistance to his power here. Thus he marks and divides the people into those who are with him and those who are not. The red circles are the conformers; the black crosses are those who refuse to kiss the beast. They are executed along the thoroughfare according to a very neat schedule."

" 'Kiss the beast'?" wondered Deirdre.

"Being accepted by Tremelaine involves a willingness to give allegiance to the powers as he stipulates," said Graydon. "It involves much bloodletting and certain incantations. Most, who refuse out of fear, he simply executes. But those who refuse on principle, he destroys by a special show of power. I hear it is quite spectacular."

Deirdre shuddered, not doubting that Roman would be one saved for the spectacle. She asked Orvis, "Are you a black cross, then?"

"We are scheduled to be executed in three days," Vida said calmly, even proudly.

"Crucified," added Orvis in both dread and relief.

"We had no choice," said Vida. "We were friends of Galen's nd Graydon's before all this happened. We saw what that power does, so we agreed to die rather than give in to it."

"You will not die," Deirdre said suddenly. "We are going to get you out of this and when we do, you are going to see that the power of the Lord is greater than this—this dark power. First, though, we must gather everyone in the city who has been tagged with a black cross."

"We'll send messages," agreed Orvis. "But you'll find it's only a handful."

"So be it," she said. They stopped talking to eat a moment. Some inconsistency nagged at Deirdre, though. Finally, remembering the throne and the robe, she pinpointed it. "Graydon, if these dark powers are as mighty as you say, then why hasn't Tremelaine accumulated even a portion of Tremaine's wealth? The robe he wore was not pure gold. The throne was not jeweled. And he doesn't even control Corona yet. What is his lack?"

Graydon shrugged, "That is part of the process, as he calls it. You must know that it took Tremaine years to amass his power. Tremelaine has been on the throne only six months. He has been promised all of Tremaine's might and possessions and more, once he breaks the Surchatain of Lystra."

"Promised? By whom?" Deirdre asked.

"The dark powers."

"Is he commanding them? Or are they commanding him?" she demanded.

Graydon's face twitched slightly. "He thinks he is in control, but he is not."

Staring into Graydon's eyes, Deirdre saw that his soul was still in prison. She leaned back weakly, closing her eyes. *Lord Jesus, help us!*

Roman jerked his head up as he roused from tormented sleep. One foot had slipped down into the muddy bottom. He pulled it up stiffly, feeling a sharp sting. Reaching a hand to his calf, he found a leech up his breeches leg. Gingerly, he detached it and squashed it between his fingers.

He moved his head around on his stiff, aching neck. He summoned moisture to his dry tongue, then braced his arms against the wall of the hole to try once again to climb out.

Pushing up with his manacled hands and feet, and scooting along his back, he made it several feet before sliding back down to the bottom. Evidently, it would be necessary to scrape the slippery moss off the wall before he could gain enough traction to hold his body weight. Determinedly, he set himself to try again.

Then a thought covered his mind like a net. What if he did climb out? What then? How would he be better prepared to confront Tremelaine? Wasn't he concentrating on the wrong thing here? Now, he had opportunity, and privacy, to use the time preparing most formidably for this challenge. . . .

He relaxed his limbs to rest them and gave himself fully to intense prayer.

At the same moment, Deirdre woke from a half-sleep. It was not yet dawn, but there were footsteps passing through the parlor where the Lystrans lay stretched out on the floor. By the light of the low-burning fire on the parlor hearth, she saw Kam snoring gently. Glancing over her shoulder, she saw Nihl's eyes watch the owner of the feet leave the parlor, then close for more sleep.

Deirdre rolled onto her back, tired but unable to sleep any longer. Quiet voices from another room drifted into the parlor. She sat up, and Nihl raised himself on his elbow. "I believe the other black crosses have come," he whispered.

"Let's allow Kam and Colin to sleep," she returned as she got to her feet.

Deirdre and Nihl opened the parlor door. In the eating room, twelve Selecans looked up with suspicion and fear from where they sat.

Orvis rose, facing the Lystrans. "These are all that remain," he said, spreading his hands. To the townspeople, he explained, "These are two of the Lystrans who have come to rescue us. This is the Surchataine Deirdre and the Commander Nihl. They say they are going to get us out of Corona."

In one motion all heads turned toward Deirdre and Nihl. One man said, "How are you going to do that? Do you know how tightly the city is guarded?"

Another man, very pale, said, "I am due to be executed this morning. When they do not find me at my house, they will come to every black cross until they find us all here. There is no way out."

Deirdre inhaled deeply, taking in those frightened faces, groping for an answer. Nihl was silent. In desperation she cast up a feeble plea: *Lord, what now?*

Then she straightened and said, "You will not die. The Lord will deliver you. But I never said we would get you out of Corona. First, we are going to take you to a safe hiding place."

"Where?" demanded the first man. "There is no place the Bloodclad won't find us!"

"Yes, there is," she smiled. "The palace."

There was a stricken silence, then the first man exploded, "Witch! you are mad! You—"

Nihl could not endure that. He crossed the room in two strides and yanked the man up by his collar. "You will show respect to the Surchataine," he breathed into his face. The fellow shrank back into his chair.

"Take your choice," Deirdre said calmly. "You can come with us or stay here. But we know of a secret entrance to the palace. We can hide you in the dungeon until we can infiltrate you into the Bloodclad. You will have a chance to fight Tremelaine yourselves and be a part of his overthrow. Even if you *were* to die, wouldn't it be better to die holding a sword rather than hanging on a cross?"

Nihl stood back and smiled. The townspeople looked around at each other dubiously. Graydon stood, saying, "Though it means returning to that pit of hell, I will go with you—I and my family. I will fight what Galen has become however I can."

Orvis said, "Vida and I will go." Vida nodded vigorously. One by one, the people expressed their consent, even the first man.

Deirdre said, "Quickly, then, gather all the food and water bags you can carry. We must be out of this house by dawn."

Deirdre helped them pack provisions from Orvis' cellar while Nihl awakened Colin and Kam. In minutes, the townspeople were lined up at the door, ready to leave. Kam and Colin pushed their way up to Deirdre. "Back to the dungeon?" Colin asked bleakly.

"Roman should have known we would not leave him," Kam said in satisfaction.

"Ready now?" she inquired, scanning the group. "Do you have the rope?" she asked Nihl.

"Yes," he said, smiling tightly.

She nodded, almost lighthearted. "Graydon, if you will, take us back the way we came."

He stepped up, hoisting his pack, and they opened the door into a night that was rapidly fading to grey.

They threaded through the streets as one or two shop windows lit up with candles; then out of the city toward the cover of the hunting woods. They ran through the forest, for dawn was imminent.

At the edge of the trees, they stopped in view of the dry stream bed. "There is no better time," murmured Deirdre, tensing her shaky legs.

"I will lead as before, the Surchataine behind me," Nihl said, adjusting his pack. "The rest of you cross over one at a time. Kam, you come last." Then the Commander leapt like a roe the few feet to the stream bed.

At that instant the Bloods had discovered the dungeon cells were vacant but for one weak and injured guard.

Roman startled awake as the trap door crashed open and blinding torchlight cascaded down upon him. He covered his eyes and tried to look up at the same time. "He is still here!" shouted one voice. Another farther away answered it.

Then a rope was tossed down, slapping him in the face. He grasped it and walked up the side of the pit, slipping mostly, while they pulled him. Gaining the top he fell, unable to stand, so they jerked him to his feet. The light from their torches was unbearable. Blind and chained, he stumbled between them up the passage to the steps.

Here, he almost had to go on all fours, still unable to straighten. He hardly noticed the nagging of his hunger and thirst for the screams of protest from his back and legs.

They arrived at the dungeon door and the opening of it was like entering heaven. The light of morning blinded him all over again, but now he could walk, somewhat.

Unseeing, he counted the number of steps and turns and stairs to

59

form a mental map of where they were going. By the time they arrived at the Surchatain's suite, his vision had returned.

The Bloods knocked. Tremelaine's unmistakable voice cried, "Enter!" The Bloods brought in their prisoner to stand before the Surchatain.

Tremelaine turned in a swirl of his robe, eating breakfast from a tray of delicacies before him. Roman's stomach wrenched with need. "So you alone remain!" Tremelaine declared in a tone of exasperation and satisfaction. "Did you know your companions escaped and left you behind, Homan?"

Roman did not answer, and steadfastly kept his eyes off the tray. "Are you hungry?" Tremelaine asked sneeringly. He picked up a pastry and walked over to hold it under Roman's nose. "Would you like this?" He held it there a moment, and Roman's eyes began to water.

Tremelaine dropped the pastry to the floor and ground it under his heel. "You may have it now."

Roman's eyes cleared immediately at this challenge. He did not so much as glance downward, but kept his gaze on Tremelaine.

"Eat, dog," snarled Tremelaine, "or I will not give you a crumb or a drop while you are in my prison."

You will have to starve me before I allow you to rob my dignity from me so easily, Roman answered in thought.

"Such pride!" sneered Tremelaine, as if he had heard every word. "Shall we let that go unpunished? We shall not! So what shall we do with you? I suppose it does not matter," he added, his thoughts taking a turn. "When your companions return to your Surchatain and tell him my response, he will attack us anyway. But do you know what?"

Tremelaine stepped toward him with gleaming eyes, reveling in an exciting secret. "I want him to! I have been given the power I lacked, and I am ready now! *If* your friends can escape the city alive to make a report, then when the Surchatain comes with his army—oh, will he be surprised!" Here Tremelaine exploded with chilling laughter.

Perspiration appeared on Roman's scarred brow. Tremelaine quieted suddenly and studied him. "That still does not answer the question of what to do with you. You are proud and dangerous and you must be punished. Men like you must never be allowed to go freely about the streets. Others should be warned . . ." He paused in sudden inspiration. "Oh yes! You'll carry a warning!"

He gestured to the guards, "Bring him to the Teaching Room!" Then he practically skipped into an adjoining room. The two smiling Bloods shoved Roman after him.

The door to the next room was standing ajar. Roman halted at the threshold while dread welled up from his feet to his throat. Within the room was a remarkable assortment of torture devices, each one gleaming and evidently primed for use.

Roman lowered his eyes, feeling himself slipping away under extreme stress. But in his mind there came the picture of a man in anguish on a cross and these words: *Because I live, you will live also.*

He raised his watering eyes to see Tremelaine busily stoking a fire in a furnace. Humming, he rummaged through a selection of brands before choosing one and placing it in the fire. He ordered the guards, "Take off his shirt and coat."

They removed his manacles and yanked the clothes from his upper body, then replaced the chains. While Tremelaine waited for the iron to heat, he scolded Roman, "You must be marked, so everyone will know what an arrogant fool you are. Now let me see . . ." So saying, he scrutinized Roman for a branding spot.

With the scars on Roman's forehead, shoulder, and back, Tremelaine was hard pressed to find a satisfactory place. Then he leveled his eyes at Roman's chest and decided, "Here—dead center. Over the heart."

Grinning, he returned to the furnace and drew out a glowing red cross, shaped like the ones on the shopfronts. He bore it toward Roman, ordering, "Hold him."

The guards took his tense arms and Roman closed his eyes. He felt the heat first, then the most searing, maddening pain he had ever experienced. He wrenched, choking back a scream, biting his mouth till the blood came and the iron was taken away.

Roman was on his knees, half-conscious, with the smell of his own burning flesh in his nostrils. But he faintly heard Tremelaine say, "Take him back to the pit until I want him again."

They yanked him up and dragged him out. All the way down, he was aware of nothing but his own heart throbbing *pain, pain, pain* . . . The darkness closed over him again as they entered the dungeon.

Then they were standing over that horrible pit, and someone shoved a rope in his hands. "No," he murmured involuntarily. When they pushed him this time, he could not keep his hold on the rope, and he fell the last ten feet to the mud bottom. He landed with a sickening thud and quickly sank up to his knees. The door was slammed down and he was again alone. The sides of the hole seemed to press in, crushing him, and for a time—minutes? hours?—all was black.

The darkness, the mud, the pain, the hunger and thirst! His chest began heaving. "I—can't—endure this—Lord God! I can't—"

Then he instantly stilled, hearing something above. He pressed his face to the slimy wall, wondering how he could maneuver Tremelaine

61

into giving him a quick death. The door above slowly opened, and torchlight poured down. He did not look up.

"Roman?" a sweet, familiar voice whispered. "Roman, are you all right?"

He raised his face apprehensively, fearing himself caught in a delusion of madness. "Deirdre . . . ?"

"Oh Roman!" Seeing him shirtless, she leaned over the hole in urgent concern. "Have you been hurt?"

He laughed quietly, shaking tears from his face. "Not badly, my love. But—what are you doing here?"

"We did get out, Roman; Nihl obeyed your command. But we came back here to hide—I don't have time to explain it now—"

Roman urgently interrupted, "Deirdre, you must not leave the city to bring an army yet!"

"We won't, Roman. And we're going to get you out. We have a plan: Nihl is going to get a Blood's uniform for you first . . ." She was doing something as she talked which caused her to lean away from the hole momentarily. "Until he comes"—she now began lowering something on a rope—"we thought you might need some nourishment." He caught a basket which held bread, dried beef, and a bottle of sweet wine.

Trembling, he loosed the rope from the basket so she could draw it out, then he leaned back to look up at her. He could see nothing but her head haloed by torchlight and a golden braid of hair hanging down. "I love you, Deirdre," was all he could utter.

"I love you, Roman." The echoes of it somehow eased the throbbing pain. "We'll return directly with a uniform," she said, lowering the door gently.

Roman consumed everything in the basket, then dropped it in the mud beside him. He tore his feet from the sucking bottom, propping them up on the wall to wait.

In scant minutes the door opened again and a rope was thrown down to him. But when he came over the top of the hole, he found himself in the company of six Bloods. They escorted him without a word out of the dungeon and back up to Tremelaine's quarters. There was something slightly different in their manner toward him—it was not deference so much as fear or uncertainty.

They brought him directly into the Surchatain's suite without knocking. As they entered, Tremelaine whirled and screamed at Roman, "I know who you are! You are the Surchatain of Lystra!"

CHAPTER 1

"WHY HAVE YOU come here? What do you want with me?" Tremelaine screamed at Roman.

"I would ask the Lord to wipe you off the face of the earth, but He has His own plans for you," Roman replied.

Tremelaine began to tremble violently. "Take him!" he shrilly ordered the guards as he flew out before them. They shoved Roman to follow Tremelaine back down the stairs to a pair of doors off the audience hall. The Bloods pushed Roman into the room after Tremelaine and then also entered themselves, shutting the heavy doors behind them.

It was a small, dark hall resembling the chapel at Westford. But instead of an aura of peace, there was an ominous intensity. Incense hung in the room like a heavy veil. Peering through the smoke, Roman fought to subdue his drumming heart. For at the front of the hall, gleaming golden and awful, was an eight-foot statue of a beast with the head and wings of a hawk and the body of a man. The image of the ultimate predator, its clawed hands were outstretched in a posture of demand. On either side of it burned two large censers.

Tremelaine stood before the hawk-man, throwing handfuls of powder on the censers. The flames burst up momentarily. He turned back around, feeling his power, and gestured.

The guards pushed Roman forward. The overpowering smell of blood and incense nauseated him. Standing beside Tremelaine, Roman looked up at the monster and thought, *So this is where all the gold is.*

"You think you are some mighty man to come here alone and try to usurp me," Tremelaine sneered. "But now you will see what Power you are up against. Watch before you die!" He whirled to the statue and prostrated himself before it. Roman felt an upheaval of disgust.

"O great Milcom, feared and worshiped, see this foolish mortal who comes to defy you! This is the man you warned me about, and now I have placed him in your hands!" Tremelaine raised himself to his knees to throw powder up to the clawed fingers in a symbolic gesture. "I call on you to show your terrible power against this puny man!"

Tremelaine rose, arms uplifted. The guards next to Roman backed away from him, as if they knew what was coming. "O great Milcom!" shouted Tremelaine, stretching higher, "send fire upon this man!" He jumped aside, pointing toward Roman, who startled. The guards covered their faces. And—

Nothing happened. A bit of powder remaining on one censer popped, but that was all. Several silent seconds passed, and the guards uncovered their eyes. Tremelaine stared, a look of confusion creeping into his face. Roman cocked a brow. "I don't think he heard you."

"Silence!" Tremelaine snapped, but his brow was damp. "O great MILCOM!" he shouted, his voice tinged with desperation, "send the FIRE, I say!"

The guards flinched, but all was still, as before. Roman could not help smiling. "Perhaps he is asleep," he jabbed. "How can you tell with a lump of metal?"

Infuriated, Tremelaine wheeled on him. "You will pay for your insolence! On your knees before Milcom!"

"No," said Roman.

Tremelaine gestured angrily, and the guards put their swords to the back of Roman's neck. "Kiss the feet of Milcom," Tremelaine hissed, pointing downward at the blood-splattered, clawed toes, "or I will feed your flesh to him one strip at a time."

"The Lord Jesus judge you and your damned idol," answered Roman.

Suddenly the fire on the censers roared up wildly. The men fell away from it. The flames grew and joined across the body of the idol. As if feeding on it, they climbed to singe the ceiling rafters.

The humans were driven further back as the gold of the statue began to glisten, then melt. The dreaded beast began sagging. The arms fell. The head toppled. The heat intensified till the four men were pressed against the door, but their eyes remained locked on the spectacle.

The torso crashed down from the legs into a pool of gold, but the fire was not sated. It burned until a river of molten gold streamed out toward the men.

In a panic the guards shoved open the doors and ran out, with Tremelaine stumbling on their heels. Roman stepped out, watching over his shoulder as the last lump of gold was melted and the flames finally died.

"Stop, stop!" Tremelaine cried shrilly to his fleeing guards. With the greatest reluctance, they did. "Take him—take him—" floundered the Surchatain, but his guards did not look at all inclined to obey.

As Roman stood chained and still, Tremelaine quickly regained control. "Take him back upstairs to the Teaching Room. Chain him there."

The Bloods warily took Roman's arms. They led him to the Surchatain's chambers, totally unnerved by the slight smile on his face. Now,

64

when they brought him over the threshold to the torture room, he did not even blink. They chained him to the wall and he smiled. His eyes were full of the vision of the burning god, and the peace of the power of his God consumed his heart like the fire. What meaning did pain and death have now? *He* was here!

After securing the prisoner, one guard ran from the room, but the other paused, fearfully peering into Roman's face. Then he too backed away and fled.

Deirdre crouched with the townspeople as they hid themselves in the darkness of a cell on the far end of one tunnel. Nihl alone was gone, to procure a uniform for Roman first, then the other men. As they sat waiting, touching each other for reassurance, they heard marching steps and saw glimmers of light.

"They've found us! They're coming—" one woman began to cry out before someone clapped a hand over her mouth. They waited tensely, but the steps quickly faded down another corridor. In a few moments the steps resounded, then were heard no more.

Deirdre thought apprehensively, *They've either added someone, or . . . taken someone away.* But they awaited Nihl in perfect stillness.

In a surprisingly short time they heard his faint, cautious steps as he felt his way to their cell. "Nihl?" she whispered.

"Surchataine," he answered.

"You have one already?"

"A Blood lingered on the steps after the others had gone. I fear he fell."

Deirdre reached out to feel the bundled-up uniform he carried. "Good! Did you see why they came?"

"No," he said uneasily. "Let's get the Surchatain."

While the others remained in their hiding place, Deirdre and Nihl felt their way down the tunnel till the sconced torches left at the intersection by the guards gave them enough light to walk more surely. They removed a torch and carried it down Roman's tunnel.

Nihl lifted the trap door and breathed out an oath. Deirdre closed her eyes. "He is gone," she said without looking.

"They took him out from under us. We should have released him immediately. Why did they come at just this moment?"

Deirdre sagged. "Oh, Roman! What shall we do, Nihl?"

He closed the trap door. "Infiltrate as quickly as possible. We may still save him."

They took the torch back to the cell. "The Surchatain has been removed," Nihl announced quietly to the others. "But we will carry out our plan. I will dress in this uniform, and use every opportunity to get more and locate the Surchatain."

"No good," said one Selecan gruffly. "They'd spot you in a minute. You're Polonti, and there are no Polonti living here. Not a one."

Nihl looked down at the uniform in his hands, and Deirdre murmured, "If that is so, then even Roman would not pass unnoticed. And by now, I fear too many would recognize him."

"Then who will wear the first uniform?" asked a Selecan timidly.

"Let me wear it, Commander," urged Kam.

Nihl handed it to him. As Kam shed his Lystran uniform for the new one, he muttered, "Only problem is, how do we recognize each other in these rags? I'm not sure these fellows"—he nodded toward the townspeople—"would know me nor I them as Bloods." He pulled on the coat, and straightened. It was a little tight in the chest, but not unreasonably so.

"Here," said Deirdre, fingering a medal dangling from the chest pocket of the shortcoat. "This has a bird's head on the front side. Wear it face down—that will be our signal." Kam nodded, turning it over.

When Kam was dressed, Nihl said, "I will go with you to see if we can get you out the door into the palace." They opened the cell door into the tunnel.

"Kam." Deirdre stopped him. "God go with you—and please find Roman."

He halted, staring at her, and she did not know what she had said that made his eyes wet. But he took her hand and kissed it in a silent pledge, then he and Nihl left with the torch.

They took the stairs and stopped at the barrier of the door. "Well," muttered Kam, "as Roman said at the gates, why not just knock and demand entry?" Nihl lay flat on the stairs a few steps below him. Kam began pounding on the door, shouting, "Hey, man! Hey, you!" He continued to pound and call until there was a scratching in the lock and the heavy door miraculously creaked open. Two Bloods stood glaring in the doorway.

"What's the meaning of leaving me down here?" Kam demanded, flicking his eyes to see if anyone else was nearby.

"How'd you get left?" one growled.

"How? Come here and see!" Kam insisted, stepping back. They entered the stairway cautiously. Nihl reached up and yanked the ankle of the first while Kam nudged the second from behind. The two Bloods fell from the open-sided stairway before they could even cry out.

Kam stepped over the threshold, whispering back to Nihl, "There's you two more, Commander. I'll leave the door unlocked until someone notices." Then with a salute and a pat on the blank face of the medal, he sauntered out.

In the palace at Westford, Basil sat in the library amid documents and maps and ledgers, intently scratching out a letter with his quill pen. Finally, he laid the quill aside and carefully blotted the ink. Then he melted wax in a small pool at the bottom of the paper. Removing the golden seal from a chain around his neck, he stamped the letter with the authority of the Surchatain. The Counselor blew the wax cool, then rolled up the parchment and affixed another seal at its edge.

Basil sat back, tapping the scroll in his palm. Then he rose and opened the library door to press the letter into the hand of the courier outside. "See that this is put into the hands of the emissary from Qarqar to deliver immediately to his Surchatain." The courier saluted and trotted away.

Basil remained in the doorway, thinking. With that letter, he had executed the last of the Surchatain's explicit instructions regarding the emissaries Roman had seen. Now, the Counselor would be faced with hearing and responding to the emissaries in the Surchatain's stead. It was a heavy responsibility he did not particularly desire, nor was he entirely comfortable with Roman's unhesitating confidence in him. He had seen too much duplicity in his lifetime, and wondered if deep within himself was the capacity for betrayal.

As if pretending he did not know where he was going, the Counselor took the corridor at a troubled stroll. For the hundredth time he came to the door of the nursery and looked in. Gusta had just brought Ariel in from a romp with the hound's puppies and was struggling to wash him in the marble washbasin.

At the sound of the door the nursemaid turned to see the Counselor, then shook her braids. She was a healthy girl with a silky complexion and hair as blond as Deirdre's. Gusta left Ariel to splash in the water and came to the door, scolding Basil, "You worry too much, Counselor. I forever see your head at that door."

"I know, Gusta," he sighed. "Only—do not leave him alone, not for an instant, until his parents return."

"This child is my charge, Counselor," she said, offended. "You do not need to remind me to watch him. I would sooner die than neglect him."

"I know, dear," he nodded, patting her rigid shoulder. "I know how trustworthy you are." With no more reason to stand in the doorway he backed out, nodding cordially. From there, he went directly to the courtyard, where a unit was practicing with the pugil sticks.

He scanned the grounds until he found Olynn, then raised a beckoning hand. The Captain ambled over. "Counselor?"

"Captain Olynn." Basil put an arm around his shoulders to speak quietly to him. "I wish you to post one of your most reliable men in a constant watch at the nursery door. Not directly in front of the door, mind you—I do not wish to irritate the nursemaid—but down the corridor a few paces. Also, the nursemaid and child must be continually watched over when out of the nursery—at a distance, of course. Change the men frequently so that she does not see the same man nearby all the time. Begin the watch immediately, and report to me anything out of the ordinary—only to me."

"Certainly, Counselor," assented Olynn, eyes widening slightly. "May I ask, has something come to your attention which prompts this measure?"

"Not specifically," Basil admitted. "But with the Surchatain and his lady both gone, any precaution regarding the child seems prudent."

"It will be done," Olynn assured him, then motioned a soldier over to give him the order.

Basil reentered the palace, his mind somewhat eased. Coming toward him in the corridor was Sevter, so he paused genially.

"Counselor," Sevter bowed in familiar respect, "may I have your approval to order ten new threshing sledges?" He held out a requisition for Basil's scrutiny.

"If you feel they are needed, Sevter," replied the Counselor, scanning the paper.

"Badly. We have seven now, which barely got us through the harvests last year. They are rotting and rusting from years of careless storage, and with the fields we've planted this year, they will not hold out through the wheat harvest alone." As he spoke, he scratched his curly red beard in unconscious earnestness.

Basil nodded, half smiling. "It is ironic that after Surchatain Galapos gave away so much land to the peasants, acquisitions returned to us double the farm land the Surchatain previously owned. But plenty brings its own problems. Can the smith handle such a large order of sledges?"

Sevter confidently replied, "I have already spoken with him. He is prepared to order the iron from Qarqar and hire on extra help to complete the job, upon your approval."

"Good," said Basil. "That will work out well. The smith need not even order the iron himself. I have just finalized a treaty with Qarqar to supply us iron and copper."

"And gold," added Sevter absently, rolling up the paper.

"No," frowned the Counselor. "Just iron and copper. How is it you thought they were to give us gold?"

Sevter raised his eyebrows, perturbed. "Not gold? Lord Troyce said the emissary had agreed to gold—"

"Not in my presence!" snapped Basil. "Summon Troyce to my chambers!"

Basil stalked up to his suite and waited, pacing angrily. When Troyce knocked and entered, Basil demanded, "Did you speak with the emissary from Qarqar?"

Troyce glanced down. "Yes, Counselor."

"And did you demand gold of him to consummate the treaty?"

"Yes, I did. I came upon information that Qarqar has a large store of gold which they keep in secret. I have even verified its location— in Hornbound, buried in graves at their old cemetery, the Abode. If we cannot march in and take it, I felt it would insure our position over them to at least see they paid us tribute."

Basil inhaled to gain his temper. "You have grossly overstepped your authority. The Surchatain left word to require of them copper and iron at a fair price. He specifically ordered that they are not bound to pay tribute. It is not your position to speak with emissaries, and if you do so again, I will be forced to censure you."

Troyce's smooth face tightened. "The Surchatain did not know about their horde of gold. I myself discovered it only with great effort and risk, when the Surchatain did not see fit to track down their weaknesses."

"Whether or not he knew about the gold is not our concern. We are to carry out his stated wishes. When he returns, you may give him what information you have, but you will not presume to make such decisions yourself. Do you understand?"

Troyce pursed his lips at Basil's tone, but bowed. "Yes, Counselor."

"You are dismissed."

When Troyce had gone, Basil sank into a cushiony chair. Elbows braced on the table, he rested his forehead on his twined fingers and murmured, "Good God! Help me keep control of this place!"

The remainder of that day Roman hung on the torture room wall, watching the day pass through the narrow window across the room. After spending those long hours in the pit, he found reassurance in being able to see the sky. Unfortunately, the light also enabled him to study in detail every machine around him.

He was frankly amazed at the ingenuity of their design, to elicit the most pain without killing. He could not discern exactly how some were used—he could only guess. And he knew that if Tremelaine had opportunity, he would use every one of them on him.

At that point he diverted his eyes again, determined not to preoccupy himself with those machines. He was still in the hands of his Protector, who would not allow any evil to overcome him beyond endurance. He must cling to that, to the knowledge of His goodness and power, which had been demonstrated to him over and over again—

The door to the corridor began to inch open. Roman watched it intently, feeling his convictions drain away like the sand sucked out by the tide. A Blood tentatively poked his head in the door, and, seeing Roman, startled and smiled. Then immediately he was gone again.

Roman waited, but nothing more happened. It was strange behavior for a member of the Bloodclad. He acted as though he wasn't supposed to be here at all . . . Roman leaned back against the wall, thinking. Then he dropped his chin to look at the brand on his chest, still tender and throbbing. And suddenly he swelled with gladness to carry it—*for I bear on my body the marks of Jesus.*

He rested, watching the sunlight gild the spikes of the machine closest to him.

CHAPTER 8

KAM CROUCHED in a small storage room with Colin and another man, all of them dressed as Bloods. "I found him," breathed the third man.

He paused to swallow his excitement and catch a breath while Kam demanded, "Where, Lew?"

"Adjoining the Surchatain's chambers is a torture room he calls the Teaching Room—everyone knows of it. He posts drawings and descriptions of all the devices in it, so the black crosses will know what's ahead for them. I thought right off your Surchatain had been taken there—so I looked and there he was, chained to the wall. I am sure it was him."

"Has he been tortured?" Colin asked weakly.

"He's been branded on his breast," answered Lew. "But other than that, he looked alert and well."

Kam narrowed his eyes in concentration. "Are the keys to his chains in that room?"

"No," said Lew despondently. "Not that I saw. I have no idea where they would be."

The three were a moment in searching thought. "*Something* must be done," muttered Kam. "Lew, you said you've seen drawings of these machines?"

"Yes. Detailed drawings, with annotations."

"Then you know how they work?"

"Yes," answered Lew reluctantly.

"Would you also know how to disable them?" pressed Kam.

Lew's face opened with delight. "Yes! But we need tools."

Colin took Kam's arm excitedly. "There's a tool bin just down the corridor!" To Lew: "What do you need?"

"A hammer, a chisel, a blade, and perhaps a gimlet, for now."

"I'll get them." Colin jumped up. "And meet you back here."

Roman twisted his head from side to side to relieve the cramp in his neck, then let it drop and closed his eyes. Waiting quietly had been easy the first hour or so, but now that the time for Tremelaine's return was advancing, it was harder to keep his mental composure. He had prayed so much he no longer knew what to say.

That door, the one to the corridor, began to move. Roman gazed at it as if the power of thought could keep it closed. But through it stepped a grinning Blood with a black beard. Shocked, Roman murmured, "Kam."

"Surchatain," he whispered, saluting. With Colin close on his heels, he quickly crossed the room to ascertain Roman's condition.

"Kam—Colin—you're in grave danger here." Roman jerked his head up as Lew entered and knelt beside the rack.

"We'll only be a moment," whispered Kam. "Surchatain, you must try to recall—did you see what they did with the key to your chains?"

"The guard took it with him. It hangs on a chain from his belt."

This displeased Kam and he scowled. "Have they given you food or drink?"

"I've had only what Deirdre brought me," Roman said wearily. There was a sharp clang as a handle fell from the rack Lew was working on. "What are you doing?" Roman asked Kam.

"What we can, Surchatain," he winked. Then he and Colin each took a tool to dismantle the working parts of the machines, under Lew's direction. They removed the hinge pins from the iron maiden and set the door delicately back on empty hinges. They frayed the

71

ropes of another machine to a thread. Roman watched, increasingly heartened, as they moved from piece to piece, wreaking destruction.

Colin stopped before the furnace. "What are we to do with this?"

Kam's brows gathered. "Throw the brands in it." Colin gingerly opened the door, gathered up an armload of branding irons, and dropped them clattering within.

Kam stood before the Surchatain as Lew worked on the last machine. "If they're intent on torturing you, they'll still find means. But this should frustrate them a bit till we can free you." He paused to reach up and jerk on one of the chains that held Roman. It was most secure.

"Meanwhile," Kam growled, "we'll see about getting you more grub." He stepped back and saluted. Roman nodded, somewhat stupefied.

"Surchatain." Colin also saluted, then whispered, "You're not alone. We're in the shadows around you." After that the three counterfeit Bloods stealthily exited.

Roman pressed his back to the stone wall, taking great breaths. "Thank you, Father. You do care."

As Colin, Kam, and Lew strolled down the corridor, they were arrested by a sharp command: "Halt, you three! Present yourselves!"

They about-faced to see the Captain of the Bloods. "What are you doing up here?" he demanded.

"Sir!" Kam said crisply, hiding well his fear that the Captain would recognize him, "we were checking out reports of escaped prisoners!"

Captain Berk sneered, "Not here, stupid! In the town! Present yourselves to the Ninth Division to search houses!" He stopped, waiting.

Kam remembered the salute he had seen the Bloodclad give Tremelaine in the audience hall, so he gave it now. Colin and Lew instantly followed suit. The Captain stalked away.

The three marched downstairs with an air of ruthless determination. But they turned into the corridor leading to the dungeon and slipped into the storeroom. Colin sank up against the door. "We must be more careful about appearances. If we look like we're doing something, we might not get called down."

Kam shrugged, thinking. "That's always a danger. It's clear we will have to split up, though. Colin—you post yourself as guard in the upper corridor, to keep an eye on the comings and goings to that torture room. Watch closely for that key! If the Captain asks you why you're there, tell him the Surchatain ordered it. Lew—you see if you can get more provisions and uniforms to those below."

"What of you, Kam?" asked Colin.

"Why, I'll do as the Captain ordered," he replied genially. "I'll attach myself to the Ninth to see how I can foul up their operations.

If I'm able, I'll meet you in the dungeon tonight after dismissal." The three clasped hands in fervent camaraderie before Kam and Colin slipped away.

Lew sat back down glumly in the dusky storeroom. How was he going to get more uniforms and provisions? Sure, they needed to stockpile food because they did not know how long they would have to hide down there. But where did they keep food in this huge palace? The kitchen? And where was that?

Pondering this, he leaned into a burlap sack. Then he caught a very faint scent. Growing excited, he untied the sack and plunged his hand into a mixture of nuts and dried fruit. "Dunce, this is a food cellar!" he muttered.

He lifted the sack, and his eye dimly caught something beneath it. Bending, he took up a discarded servant's dress. "Maybe someone can make use of this." He stuffed it under his arm and peeked cautiously out the door. Then he strode to the dungeon door, earnestly praying not to be seen.

Kam stalked out to the grounds wearing his toughest face. A unit of soldiers on horseback was just returning to the stables. Tied to a nearby post a horse stood idle, thoughtfully provided for Kam's use by a careless owner. So the Second quickly loosed its reins and hopped up on it, then merged with the forty men as they dismounted and stabled their horses.

All of the horses should have had assigned stalls, but Kam observed the men putting them anywhere, so he led the horse to a vacant space and untied the saddle cinch as he listened to the talk around him. "Why all the fuss over those Lystrans?" one Blood was muttering in complaint. "Since they were only emissaries, why not let them go? Why does that crazy ape on the throne want to start a war with Lystra?"

"Best hold your tongue—the Surchatain hears things like that. No one can hide from him," a Blood nearby warned him.

"No? Those Lystrans have done it."

"Shhh!" whispered the other, agitated. "They'll be found, and when they are, you'll see them hanging along the thoroughfare. No one can fight Tremelaine—not even his brother. So don't try it."

"Hmmph," snorted the first, unconvinced. "I still say he's full of wind."

The Captain of the Ninth barked into the stables, "Make it quick, you cripples! Chow!" The men curried the horses a few strokes, then joined the others hustling out. Kam fell in with them.

They marched to the soldiers' dining hall, where they jostled for places in line to grab plates of mush and bread. Then they jostled for places to sit at long tables and benches. The huge hall, built to accommodate many soldiers, made the number of men here now look pitifully few. Kam estimated there were no more than two hundred.

He sat near some other Bloods, who were glumly eating. "This is garbage," muttered one. "Have you ever eaten such garbage?" he asked Kam, who shrugged.

The fellow looked more closely at Kam. "I don't know you."

Kam gave him only a sidelong glance. "I don't know you either, and I want to keep it that way," he said sullenly.

"Huh," the soldier grunted disparagingly. "You can count on it." He turned back to his companions, and Kam was able to eavesdrop on their conversation without being dangerously drawn in to it.

He listened to them talk about, of all things, the weather. It had been hot and dry for five weeks running, and this fact concerned them very much. "If we don't get rain soon, my sheep are going to choke on the dust," complained one. *Sheep?* wondered Kam.

"You say," agreed another. "I'll be lucky to harvest a fourth of my rye." *Rye? Sheep? Are these men the dreaded Bloodclad?* Kam mulled.

As he listened to them talk more, he realized, no, they were not the Bloodclad—not like those under Tremaine. These were simply farmers who had been pressed into service for lack of real soldiers. They were not so much concerned with conquest or killing as with maintaining their fields and feeding their families.

Kam shook his head. The fearsome Bloodclad, it turned out, were no more awesome than any other conscripted army. They were a sham, like Tremelaine's "gold" robe. Whatever was to be feared here, it was not them.

Dinner over, Kam ambled out with the rest of the men to find a spare bed in the ample barracks and learn what more he might.

Half an hour after Lew had gone down below, the dungeon door opened again. Out stepped a girl wearing a servant's dress. She paused to put on a saucy air, then strolled down the corridor toward where she knew the dining hall and kitchen were.

At the door leading into the dining hall, Deirdre put her eye to the crack before opening it. This hall was paneled with seamless sheets of glass on silver, making the whole room a colossal, flawless mirror. It was sparkling, yet unnerving and confusing to guests, as Deirdre knew from her visit here years before. No doubt that was the reason Tremaine had it constructed so.

There were no guests in the hall yet, only servants putting out dishes

74

and candelabra. Deirdre came in and a maid glanced up. "Captain Berk sent me down for a tray," Deirdre said carelessly. "He's got someone in his room and he doesn't wish to be bothered to come down, if you understand me," she added, rolling her eyes and praying that Captain Berk would not choose to appear in the hall any time soon.

"I hate that filthy Blood," whispered the girl, then glanced at Deirdre, wondering how loose her tongue might be. But she shrugged and took Deirdre into the humming kitchen.

"What does he want?" the maid asked, pulling out a serving platter.

Deirdre glanced down the work tables. "The veal and potatoes, the boiled onions—and two bottles of wine."

"Two?"

"As I said, he has someone with him," Deirdre tossed off. She stood by as if bored while the maid filled the tray. The girl was quick and lithe, with almond-shaped eyes and light brown hair that curled around her face in ringlets. Something about her appealed to Deirdre, so when she took the platter from the maid's hands, Deirdre said, "Thank you."

The maid knitted her brows. "Who are you?"

"Goldie." Deirdre's old servant name returned to her immediately. "And what is your name?"

"Izana," the maid replied.

Deirdre did not wait for any more questions. She took the tray and clay bottles down the corridor to the dungeon door, which she opened just enough to set one bottle on the landing behind it. Then she carried the tray up the stairs toward the living quarters, watching for Colin standing guard in the corridor.

When he saw her, his eyes widened to circles. "Is Roman in there?" she whispered, nodding to the door across from him.

"Yes—but *don't go in!* Tremelaine and two Bloods just went in there!"

Tremelaine stood glaring up at Roman. "I cannot find out the reason for your coming," he said in his nasal whine. "There is a dark veil around your purpose that won't open to me. But one thing is clear— you are at my mercy. And I intend to make you plead for it on your knees to me!" He stabbed a finger at the iron maiden. "Open it!" he commanded the Bloods.

Captain Berk unlatched it and swung the door open. But it swung right off the hinges and fell to the stone floor with an ear-shattering clang.

Tremelaine and the Bloods jumped. In wordless astonishment, they gazed at the incapacitated maiden. "Idiots! Idiots!" shouted Tremelaine as the Captain raised his hands helplessly. "The rack, then!"

They unchained Roman from the wall and laid him on the rack, fastening his wrists and ankles in its fetters. As one Blood took the handle, Tremelaine glowered over Roman, "It will be a pleasure to hear your bones crack."

The guard began turning and the gears began moving. But just as steadily, they began slipping. With every notch forward they slipped a notch back, so that as much as the soldier cranked, all he could do was tire his arm.

"Turn, fool!" ordered Tremelaine.

"I am, Surchatain!" the soldier answered, breaking into a sweat.

With an oath, Tremelaine yanked him aside to look down into the workings. "The teeth have been broken," he seethed. Turning on the Captain, he demanded, "Execute the man responsible for maintaining these machines!"

"Yes, Surchatain!" said Berk desperately. "But—" He was thinking of sabotage, knowing the machines to be in recent good condition. But then it occurred to him the methods the Surchatain would use to find the culprit. Berk strangled the rest of his sentence.

"On the rope!" decreed Tremelaine. Urgently, the Bloods unlocked Roman from the rack. They stripped the rest of his clothes from him and put him face down lengthwise on a thick coarse rope, suspended a yard high between two wheels. The rope sagged from his weight as his wrists and knees were pulled to the floor and strapped down. The rope now ran tightly from one wheel down his front and out between his legs to the other wheel.

"Draw the rope," Tremelaine commanded. "And don't stop until it severs him in two. Which will not be for many hours," he grinned unpleasantly at Roman.

This time the Captain took the handle of the back wheel and began cranking. The rope started to move, scraping and burning. Roman sucked in his breath with the pain of it while a panicky thought flashed by: Had they gotten to this machine, or overlooked it? He could not remember.

Abruptly the rope snapped, sending Roman to the floor. He lay on the cool stone, breathing thanksgiving.

"AAARRGHH!" Tremelaine went into a screaming fit that exceeded anything Roman had ever seen, even from Deirdre. He ran cursing from one machine to another, kicking them and tearing them apart with his bare hands. Then he strode through the door, calling back over his shoulder, "Bring him!"

The Bloods unlocked Roman, hoisting him up. They took him naked out into the corridor behind Tremelaine. Roman saw the serving girl with the food tray and the guard in the corridor, but did not so much as blink. The girl gasped and the guard went ashen. Tremelaine and his soldiers never glanced at them.

They took Roman through corridors and up stairs, in full view of anyone who happened to be around. Roman kept his eyes straight ahead, trying to make his heart stone to the indignity, but praying continually that they would reach a place of cover.

They ascended a long flight of steps which ended at a narrow door. The Bloods opened it to reveal the roof of the palace—the highest point in the entire city. The view from here of the sun setting on the horizon was magnificent.

Roman was led to a tall pole set within six feet of the crenelation at the edge of the roof. Using a short ladder, the guards strapped his hands above his head and his feet to the base of the pole, stretching him so that he stood precariously on tiptoe.

"See how tall you are now, big man!" sneered Tremelaine. "Where is your mighty God now? When I am done with you, you will beg to serve me! What do you say to that?"

Roman looked down on him silently. "Still too proud to answer! Then I will give you time to think on it. Days!" Tremelaine spun in his yellow-gold robe and went back into the palace with his guards and the ladder.

Alone in the purple twilight, Roman tested the leather straps, finding them unyielding. He rested his feet against the pole to make himself as comfortable as possible, ignoring the spasms in his calves. He kept watching for sentries patroling the roof, but never saw one. Apparently they were unneeded this high up.

He heard a slight rustle behind him and froze. Something was set on the ground, then a soft hand touched his side. "Oh, Roman!"

He wrenched to look into her tear-filled eyes. "Deirdre, please get away. *Please* get yourself hidden. The only thing worse than what they can do to me is what they would do with you!"

"I'm getting you down from here," she whispered through gritted teeth, drawing Colin's knife from under her dress. But she could not reach his wrists. "I'm going back for Colin," she said.

"No! Deirdre, listen to me," he said in a voice low with urgency. "You *must not* endanger yourselves to rescue me. You would *not* be able to get me through the palace unnoticed." She got that look of heedlessness on her face and he hissed, "Deirdre! If you never obey me again, do this for me now."

She weakened, with a look of pain. He went on, "It will be well, Deirdre—God is here. I don't know exactly what is taking place; somehow, it's a test of wills. I do not know why, but it is important that I submit to this—that I not be distracted from my purpose here," he said on a sudden insight.

She wrapped her arms around his taut body, pressing her face into his chest. "I can't bear to see you like this."

"Give me up, Deirdre," he said tenderly. "I had to give you up, once."

She wept, kissing his chest, as she could not reach to kiss his lips. "Can you eat and drink?" she moaned, anxious to stay near him as long as he allowed.

"Yes," he said quickly. So she bent down for the platter and bottle she had carried up. She fed him every last piece of meat and potato and onion, then held the bottle up for him to drain. That need filled, he looked down on her with clearer eyes. "Thank you, my love."

She started to cry again. He said, "Deirdre, there is one more thing. *Do not* try to come to me again—you are bound to get caught. Instruct the others not to come to me. Concentrate on rescuing the townspeople who are in danger and keeping yourselves hidden. Do you understand?" She raised miserable eyes to him. "Deirdre, I ask this of you not as your husband but as your sovereign. Will you obey me?"

She breathed brokenly, "Yes, my lord." He smiled, relieved. She embraced him a final time, then slipped back into the palace to descend to the dungeon.

CHAPTER 9

DURING THE NIGHT, Roman nodded off as weariness overcame discomfort. In the early morning, the radiance—and exposure—of the rising sun on his left brought him to full consciousness. He watched the growing light, feeling increasingly vulnerable. He forgot entirely what he had said to Deirdre the night before and began earnestly working the weathered leather straps.

He heard the door bang open and loud voices. They drew nearer, laughing, and he stiffened. "Ho—have a look at the good Surchatain!"

Three Bloods stood around him, leering and shaking their heads. They were disheveled and repulsively drunk, obviously straight from a night-long revelry. One Blood was still swilling from a jug.

"Ain't you a pretty sight?" gloated one, striking him savagely. Roman gasped, recoiling. The Blood leaned back on his fellow, laughing, and staggered a little on the rooftop slate, slick with early morning dew.

The soldier with the jug emptied it, then tossed it carelessly behind him over the crenelation. He wiped his mouth on his soiled sleeve, eyeing Roman. Grinning at an idea, he pulled out a knife and pointed it at Roman's throat, then drew it down to his target, saying, "We are going to have fun with you today." The other two, propping each other up, roared at the promise.

Drowning in fear, strangling on helplessness, Roman sent up an anguished inner cry: *Lord—will you stand off and let them torture me?*

Say it aloud, a silent voice urged.

He hesitated, muddled. What good would it do to say it aloud? But when the Blood with the knife put it to his skin, he lifted his face and said, "Lord Jesus, must I be tortured?"

The Bloods looked at him in surprise. The one holding the knife stopped and drew back a pace, watching uncertainly. But nothing happened, so his face filled with laughing derision and he sneered, "You'd better pray to *me,* Surchatain! I'm the one who's going to torture you!" He lunged playfully at Roman, leading with the knife point.

In lunging, though, he stepped in a pile of bird droppings and slipped, one foot shooting out in front. He reflexively caught his balance on the other foot, which skidded on the dewy slate, propelling him backwards again. He thrust the first foot back to catch himself, but again slipped.

At this point, seeing him dangerously close to the edge, the others quickly sobered. But by the time they reached for him, his last fatal step and slip had neatly flipped him over the crenelation of the wall. The other two looked down, transfixed, as his scream faded. Roman closed his eyes.

The remaining Bloods gazed at each other, then simultaneously turned to stare at Roman. Without a word, they carefully went around him and darted back into the palace.

The morning sun shone down brilliantly on Roman, now alone again.

Tremelaine rose from the bed on which he had passed a sleepless night. Something was persistently troubling him, and he did not know what it was. All he knew was that it involved that man on the roof—and what Tremelaine should do about him.

He nervously draped himself in some fine brocades and gold chains, then ripped them off as he changed his mind about which of them to wear. Growing increasingly distraught, he finally yanked furiously on his hair and clothes. "I surrender! I am coming!"

He ran from the chambers down the long corridor to a door at the end. Fumbling, he pulled a key from his tunic and unlocked the door. He paused to light one candle before shutting and locking the door behind him.

Tremelaine stood in a small, windowless room. All it contained was an intricate design of clay tiles, which shall not be described, laid in the wooden floor. He placed himself in the center of the sigil and called on a name, crying, "I am here as you commanded! Now what shall I do with him?"

There was a faint ripple in the candle flame, but nothing more. Tremelaine clutched the candlestick in desperation. "I was wrong not to come before! I confess it! Now tell me what to do with him!"

Kill him. The candlelight wavered.

The Surchatain started to pace, but remembered himself just in time and did not step out of the lines of the sigil. "I don't think I can," he whimpered. "You saw what he did to the figurehead you ordered made. The swords of an army we could turn with a word, but him alone, unarmed—"

You must kill him.

"Can't I just—put him in prison forever?" he asked tremulously.

Your prisoners escaped. He will too. He must die.

"I'll leave him on that pole to die. It won't take long now—he's had nothing to eat or drink," Tremelaine suggested encouragingly.

No. Ak erving girn had en feeding him.

"What?" frowned Tremelaine.

Heb ak en bed by an gervin birl! And a terrible rush of frustrated wind shook the frightened ruler.

"I cannot understand you!" cried Tremelaine. "But I will do as you say! I swear it! I will kill him!" In fearful urgency, he spun to the door and dropped the key. Groping, he recovered it and shakily jammed it into the lock, still on his knees. In terror, he bolted from the room.

Outside, the sun rose higher in the cloudless summer sky. Even this early, townspeople were wiping their brows and saying, "It's bound to be a hot one today!" And high up on the roof of the palace, one figure hung fully exposed to the burning rays, unable to sit or even shade his eyes.

80

In the courtyard far below, Kam the Blood rolled out with the other soldiers to present himself for the second day of the search. Kam had arrived too late yesterday to search with the Ninth, but today he fell in easily, scowling with the worst of them.

From the soldiers' dining hall, where they suffered through slop for breakfast, they were ordered to the stables. There each man saddled his own horse. Kam looked around and immediately spotted Roman's white Andalusian, tied with a short rope in a pen. He took up saddle and bridle and headed toward the stallion.

"Good luck with that bastard," growled a Blood. "He won't be ridden."

"I'm meaner than any half-broke horse," Kam answered, glowering at the animal. But he approached it quietly, whispering, "Easy, Fidelis. You know me. Easy, boy."

As he slipped the bridle over its nose, he ran his hand down the sleek neck and noticed whip marks. "Your master's had a hard time of it too, boy," he muttered.

Once mounted, he directed the jittery animal toward the gathering unit. They cantered out the front gates into the thoroughfare.

The first thing Kam noticed was that the crosses beside the road were empty. He grinned inwardly. Either there were no more marked people left to crucify, or Tremelaine was too preoccupied with other matters to bother with them.

The soldiers stopped at an intersection, where the Captain of the Ninth directed a line of men down each street. Kam's group, four men, split up on their street, two going down the north side and two searching the south.

Kam and his fellow Blood dismounted at the first house they came to. It was a wainwright's shop, with a red circle on the wide double doors. Without warning the Blood entered the house and Kam followed.

They bypassed the shop and went directly upstairs, where they surprised the wainwright's family at the breakfast table. The householder stood. "What—?" The Blood paid him no mind but began to search through the rooms, overturning furniture and breaking open doors. Kam went to another part of the house, making a great deal of noise while doing as little damage as possible.

When through in the house, the Blood went back down to the shop and began searching it. He threw aside wagon wheels, axles, and planks, narrowly missing the wainwright who stood anxiously by. Kam listened as he pretended to search further.

When the place was thoroughly ransacked, the Blood turned on the bewildered family, demanding, "Have you seen strangers, or Graydon and his wife and daughter?"

81

"No," uttered the wainwright in perplexity.

"There's a cross waiting for anyone who aids them," the Blood informed him, jabbing a finger into his chest. Then he and Kam stalked out.

They advanced to the next door, that of the ironsmith's house, also with a red circle. Clanging sounds of a hammer came from the lower-level shop, so they went in.

There the ironsmith was already at work, sweating over the intense heat of his furnace. He glanced at the pair of soldiers unconcernedly.

"Have you seen Lord Graydon or strangers about?" demanded the Blood. (Kam noted that this was the second time he had heard someone refer to Graydon by a title, and he wondered why.)

"You'd better check Orvis the tailor's shop," drawled the ironsmith, taking a bar from the furnace to examine it.

"We have," said the Blood, stepping closer. "Why do you say that?"

"He sent word to my wife night before last, in the middle of the night, to come to his shop. If Graydon's gone, that's where he went."

The Blood snarled, "Why did you not inform us of this before?"

The ironsmith turned deliberately to the Blood with such a twisted, cruel face that even the soldier dropped back. The smith held the glowing bar in tongs toward the two and uttered, "What Orvis and Graydon do is their business. What I do is mine. But my wife did not ever get there."

The Blood said coolly, "We will inform Captain Tarl." He and Kam almost fell over each other trying to get out of the shop.

They returned to Captain Tarl and gave him the ironsmith's report. The Captain called the rest of the men together to charge the tailor's shop. With upwards of forty men searching the house, it did not take long for them to discover the trap door in the kitchen.

The Captain descended into the cellar, then came up again scowling, "They probably were here, and took provisions when they left. Then what?"

Kam waited appropriately, as if thinking this through, then ventured, "If they took provisions, they must have been intending to travel. We certainly would have found them by now if they were still in the city, so they must have escaped, somehow. But who knows where they would be heading?" He did not want to seem to have all the answers.

"The emissaries were from Lystra," the Captain replied. "If they did get out, that's where they went. We'll search the wall now for signs of escape."

This dismayed Kam somewhat, for he feared the lack of evidence would discredit his theory. But at least examining the wall would remove them from the tales of treacherous townspeople.

To Kam's amazement, when they approached the city wall, the Captain of the Ninth took his division straight to one particular part of it. Removing brush and loose stones, the men uncovered a hidden tunnel at the base of the wall, all in a very routine manner.

The Captain poked around the tunnel for telltale signs of passage, then spoke to several of the guards stationed at the wall. As the men waited, Kam realized with a start that this was exactly the spot Graydon had indicated the night they escaped the dungeon.

Captain Tarl returned to his men, grumbling, "They swear the only ones to come through have been townspeople, but I think they are idiots and have let the Lystrans escape under their noses."

Somehow, this did not add up to Kam. "Stupid guards to sit by and let townspeople get out," he muttered to a nearby Blood.

The other sneered back at him, "You're stupid, if you think that. I can tell you've never done guard duty. They catch them on the outside of the tunnel. Saves the trouble of crucifying them, and they divide up the valuables of those they catch. Clean and quiet."

Kam chuckled in apparent appreciation of this cleverness, but inwardly his stomach was rolling.

The division returned to the palace to inform Captain Berk of what they had found. Kam lingered in the stables, grooming and feeding Fidelis, to observe the results of their report. Word was passed along that the guards who had been on the wall the night of the escape were being taken out to the thoroughfare to be executed.

Kam chose that time to slip to the dungeon and make his own report. As most of the soldiers went around front to watch the scapegoats being strung up on the crosses, he found clear going to the dungeon door. He trod cautiously down the slippery steps, then took a torch from the intersection and proceeded to the end cell of the hiding tunnel. When he reached the door, he whispered loudly, "It's Kam!"

Deirdre immediately stepped out into the tunnel and waved him in, relieved. "We still jump at footfalls," she said. "What have you been able to do?"

He told the group quickly about the house-to-house search and his own discovery: "They called off the search at a hidden tunnel in the wall. The Lord was with us, to prevent us trying to use that means of escape. Graydon, are you aware that they knew about the tunnel all along?" Kam asked accusingly.

Graydon paled. "No—of course not. We almost went through it ourselves."

"Why do they call you 'lord,' anyway?" Kam pressed suspiciously.

"I am the Surchatain's brother. I had some honor before he imprisoned me," Graydon answered defensively.

"Never mind that," Deirdre interrupted. "What of the search, Kam?"

The Second resumed, "They think we escaped through that tunnel and got past them somehow. I'll try to learn now if they intend to pursue us outside the city."

"Good!" exclaimed Deirdre. "Then you are sure they are no longer searching for us in Corona?"

"Yes, I'm sure," said Kam. "But we must not try to leave yet. They know about Orvis' cellar, and anyone who sees us in town may betray us."

Graydon quickly agreed. "It seems coming here to hide was a wise move. But I cannot believe Galen is unaware of our presence."

"How could he be aware of us?" Deirdre asked, startled.

"Why, the dark powers tell him everything he needs to know. They must know we are here. And if they know, he knows. It is that simple." This calm statement froze their hearts.

"That doesn't make sense," Deirdre argued. "If he knows about us, why would he let us run freely? Why would he let me see Roman, and feed him? Why wouldn't he recapture us and torture us too?"

"I do not know," answered Graydon despondently. "But what's to prevent his knowing?"

"What's to prevent it!" exclaimed Deirdre. "God's to prevent it! Can't I make you understand that we are under God's protection? He won't hand us defenseless to those dark powers. Roman knows that, even as much as he is suffering."

"What *are* they doing to Roman?" Kam asked hesitantly.

"They've lashed him naked to a pole on the roof of the palace," she answered dully. "But he told me he can endure it, because he knows there is a reason for it. He also forbade me—or any of you—to try to reach him again."

"Why?" demanded Kam.

"He fears we'd be captured," she said. "And I promised to obey him."

In spite of her gravity, Nihl smiled, realizing what a momentous accomplishment that was. "We will clothe him with prayer," he responded softly.

High above them, Roman sweltered as the summer sun reached its apex. Its direct rays made the slate beneath him sizzle. Whenever he opened his eyes, he saw the air around him rippling with the heat. He could hardly swallow for the dryness, though sweat ran unimpeded down his face and body. *How long, Lord? How long will you leave me here? Why are you doing this to me?* He sagged in semiconsciousness, his strength drained dry.

At the palace in Westford, Troyce passed by the nursery door and saw the guard posted there. He paused in concern. "What are you doing here?"

"Standing at sentry, Administrator," the guard replied, saluting.

"Why? Who ordered it?"

"Captain Olynn, sir."

"Well, you have no business here," Troyce said brusquely. "I suggest you go attend to your responsibilities."

The guard shifted. "I was ordered here, sir. My responsibilities are to execute my orders."

"And I outrank Captain Olynn," Troyce irately countered. "I say you will leave." The guard bowed slightly and retreated down the corridor. The first thing he did was search out Captain Olynn.

Troyce watched the soldier until he turned the corner. Then Troyce opened the nursery door and stepped inside. Ariel, supposedly napping, was sitting up in the center of the bed, busy shredding the netting around it. He smiled up at the administrator.

Troyce stood by the bed, hands folded contemplatively, and watched the child. Whatever thoughts he had were disturbing, for his expression grew troubled.

A side door opened. "Lord Troyce—what is it you need?" inquired Gusta deferentially. She came to the bed to lay Ariel back down and scold him.

"Peace of mind, my dear," Troyce answered. He turned abruptly and left the nursery.

Roman. He jerked his head up and blinked with sweat-covered eyes into the blinding sky, then dropped his head again. *Now I am hearing things. I will go mad before I die.* He laughed a little, with parched throat and tongue. *Yes—where is my mighty God?*

Roman. "Wha'?" His head bobbed up again and his heart thumped. He moaned, "Oh, where are you, my God?"

In communication expressed directly to his inward being, he received: *I told you I would never fail or forsake you. Do you believe me?*

He began to sob, but had no moisture for tears.

Do you believe me?

"Yes," he said thickly.

Do you believe that whatever dangers you face, I am there also; and wherever you are taken, I go with you?

"Yes," he gasped.

Will you give me my right as Sovereign to send you and use you? Will you obey me, Roman?

"Yes, yes!" he moaned. Drooping, he mouthed, "You are God. You are sufficient." The words were barely whispered in his physical depletion.

There was no reply. But in moments, he groggily discerned a change, though at first he could not tell what it was. Then he perceived through his closed lids that the sun was not so bright and burning.

He opened his eyes a crack. The sky *was* darker, and growing more so by the second. He gazed heavenward. Thick clouds were gathering with incredible speed, growing darker as they merged. He heard the rolling of thunder through the skies. A moment more, and he felt a drop on his forehead; another on his shoulder. Lightning erupted from the black clouds.

Suddenly, the skies burst to let the torrent fall. Roman's racked, thirsty body sprang to respond to the downpour. He threw his head back as rain soaked his hair and ran down his bearded face. The delicious refreshment tickled him, bringing him to laughter.

Then he could cry. Drenched with restoration, he wept out his gratitude.

Within the palace, it had grown uncommonly dark for midday. Tremelaine stood at a window, wringing his hands as he watched the rain. "I have no choice," he muttered. "It must be done. It must be done now."

He drew a gilt-handled dagger from a jeweled sheath, then paced down the corridor to the rooftop stairs.

He ascended them at a shaky run. A bolt of lightning crashed nearby outside, possibly on the roof. The shock flattened him against the stairwell wall, causing him to gasp for breath and clutch his chest. But he clenched the knife in his fist and continued up the stairs.

When he unlatched the rooftop door it crashed open, almost knocking him back down the stairs. It banged against the wall behind him as he stood on the landing, squinting into the rain.

The figure on the pole still hung there, but Tremelaine staggered to hear him laughing and singing hoarsely. Roman could not have turned enough to see someone at the door, but as it was, he was not even aware of the other's presence.

Sighting between Roman's shoulder blades, Tremelaine lifted the dagger with both hands and came toward him. He stopped at Roman's back, his victim still unaware. Tremelaine squeezed the blade handle in his dripping hands and brought the knife up over his head.

Then a white-hot, deafening lightning bolt seared down between the two men, scorching Tremelaine's hands and throwing him backward.

That is, Tremelaine thought it was a lightning bolt, until in falling away he looked up to see a terrible flaming warrior raising a mighty sword to crush him to nothingness.

Tremelaine fell down screaming. Roman wrenched around to look, but could not see. Still screaming, Tremelaine crawled on all fours back to the door. He fell whimpering down the stairs, then wildly threw himself into the room at the end of the corridor, crying, "You saw it! I could not do it! What can I do with him? What, what, what?"

Bring him here.

Tremelaine stopped dead. Then he threw his head back and howled with laughter. "I cannot even approach him and you want me to bring him here! Ha, ha, ha, ha!" He was abruptly silenced as the wind lifted him and shook him fiercely.

It is in your power to bring him. Bring him to me!

Tremelaine was set back down and thrust from the room. He landed at a run and raced up the stairs and through the door to the roof, where the torrents had slackened to a gentle, caressing rain.

He retrieved his dagger from where it had fallen earlier and cut the bonds around Roman's feet as the other watched him warily. Then he shinned up the pole to cut his hands free. Roman fell, rubbing his wrists. But he quickly straightened and eyed Tremelaine with an unwavering purposefulness.

"Come!" Tremelaine grabbed Roman's arm to pull him along. Puzzled, Roman allowed him. Tremelaine dragged him down the stairs and to the open door of the little room, where he thrust him inside, then slammed and locked the door.

CHAPTER

ROMAN HELD himself still in the dense darkness of the small room, feeling the intense presence of evil. The sigil of tiles in the floor began to glow like burning embers. Roman stepped away from it, watching it throb brighter and brighter. As it did, the floor beneath him began to tremble, vibrating the walls. He pressed his back to the shivering wooden door.

87

Bursting up from the floor came a great gusting wind which lifted him up and battered him against the door. In the midst of the wind roared a savage voice: *On your knees, mortal, before God!* And the wind flung him to the floor face down.

From deep within him came the stillness of an imparted thought: *My sheep know my voice.* Roman raised himself with great effort against the wind. "You are not God, whatever you are."

Ah, ha ha ha ha! Came rolls of wicked laughter which attempted to pierce him through with arrows of terror. *Worship or die, mortal!* the voice demanded.

"He said, 'You shall have no other gods besides me,' and I will not," Roman gasped.

The wind threw him backward to the floor with such force that it knocked the breath from him. When he opened his eyes, he saw hovering over him the very image of the golden idol—only alive and moving now, spitting blood, clawing at his chest. Roman squeezed his eyes shut, stifling a scream.

Die, human! You are helpless before me! the voice beat on his very soul.

"I am," Roman whispered weakly. "But He said He will never fail me or forsake me, and the Lord Jesus always stands by His word."

There was a sudden, profound stillness. Roman felt instant release. Then he heard an unearthly scream such as he had never heard before. Instinctively Roman rolled into a corner and flattened himself against the floor. Just as he did, the wind roared wildly past him, seeking escape. It blasted the locked door off the hinges and threw it ten feet down the corridor as it rushed out.

Roman raised his head and looked out to see Tremelaine lifted up and carried by the wind to a window at the far end of the passage. Screaming, the little man was hurled through the window, crashing through thick leaded glass.

Roman staggered to his feet and stumbled down the corridor to the window. Far below in the wet courtyard was the Surchatain's broken body. Shouts and a shrill trumpet alarm brought Roman's head around.

He dashed into the Surchatain's chambers and rifled through the wardrobe, looking for something he could wear. Piled at the bottom he found some dress uniforms which had evidently belonged to Tremaine and were awaiting alterations to fit Tremelaine.

With immeasurable relief at being dressed again, Roman yanked on silk trousers edged in gold, and black leather fur-trimmed boots. Nonetheless, he shook his head in disgust as he pulled on a fussy brocaded shirt with puffy sleeves, for he had always despised finery.

On his way out, he deliberately avoided the large, bronze-framed looking glass, but something beside it caught his eye. Roman reached down to pick up a magnificent gold and leather sheath, and from it drew the finest steel sword he had ever seen. Its ebony hilt bore the word *Azrael.*

"Whoever you served before, Azrael, you will serve me now," smiled Roman, strapping the sheath on his hip. He took up the sword, admiring its perfect balance, then grasped the door handle. He paused. "Lord God, you have truly been with me in everything; go before me now."

He threw open the door and ran toward the stairway. Two Bloods appeared from the stairs, drawing their weapons as they approached. Roman swung his sword in a scintillating arc, striking their blades and throwing them off balance. They toppled down the stairs and he followed in leaps, jumping the last four steps to the floor.

Another Blood appeared around the corner and Roman raised Azrael again. But the Blood held up his hands, exclaiming, "Wait! Wait! I'm Lew, one of the townspeople from the dungeon!"

Roman lowered the sword. "Then let's go below and get the others."

In the confusion of the alarm, most of the soldiers had run to the courtyard. Upon seeing the Surchatain's body, Captain Tarl had led them up to the rooftop. As Roman and Lew ran unobserved to the dungeon corridor, the Bloods bolted up the stairway.

The two edged with cautious speed down the dungeon stairs, then Lew grabbed a torch and led Roman down the passage. They threw open the door to the cell, and the fugitives within leaped up.

Deirdre gasped, "Roman!" For his appearance this time was as much a shock as before. He was glittering and gorgeous, the delicate materials aglow against his burned brown skin.

Before anything else, he took her to him and kissed her. The others gazed in speechless amazement at him. Roman loosed her a little and directed the group, "Follow me quickly. I am sure the Bloods have gone up to the roof, where I was bound. We must get weapons and attack while they are still up there."

Nihl, Colin, and Lew jumped forward. "We have some swords already," Colin said. "There are more in a niche off the audience hall."

They began to move out, and Roman glanced wryly at Deirdre. "I do not suppose I could convince you to stay down here with the women."

"Not the smallest chance," she replied sweetly.

Orvis rose, fastening his vest. "Will *you* stay here, Vida?" he asked hopelessly.

"Indeed not, my lord," she answered, glancing at Deirdre. "For I do believe I'm a better fighter than you."

Roman grinned slightly and glanced around. "Where is Kam?"

"He has infiltrated the Ninth Unit," answered Nihl. "We must watch for him."

Roman redirected stern eyes toward the townspeople, particularly the seven men who stood against the cell wall. "Come quickly. We must catch them on the roof."

The others looked quickly at Graydon, who said, "We are not fighting with you."

Roman turned to scrutinize him but Deirdre burst out, "Graydon! Why not?"

"We do not recognize his authority over us," Graydon answered, crossing his arms.

Deirdre opened her mouth but Roman put a restraining hand on her arm. He began, "Tremelaine is dead—"

"I know," interrupted Graydon.

"Then stay here if you wish," Roman said coolly. "But when I am through above, I will come back down and kill you. Because if you do not fight with me, I must assume you are against me. In this battle, there is no neutral party."

He turned up the tunnel with long strides, Nihl and Colin flanking him. Deirdre, Lew, Orvis, and Vida trotted behind. Colin voiced what Nihl knew better than to ask: "Surchatain, how shall we seven fight against the whole Bloodclad?"

"Eight, with Kam," Roman replied. "And ten thousand times ten thousand with the Lord." Colin nodded unsteadily, but Deirdre ran forward, fired with anticipation of great happenings.

Out in the corridor they found the niche Colin had mentioned, and everyone took a weapon. Deirdre selected a half-sized blade she could handle, though not with great skill. Vida took a slender saber and tested it knowledgeably. Deirdre looked on admiringly, feeling a sudden desire to tell Vida how well she could handle a bow.

Then Roman led them swiftly up the stairs. They flew down the corridor to the rooftop stairway. They had ascended halfway when the door above opened and the Bloods, having found the roof empty, began descending. Nihl drew up alongside Roman, and the two of them blocked the stairway completely.

Seeing them, the Bloods charged with their long, heavy blades. But in the confines of the stairway, no more than two abreast could fight. The two Bloods who led the attack got in each other's way trying to strike, whereas Nihl parried while Roman lunged, and the two Bloods fell. The second two were disadvantaged by having to maneuver over their fallen comrades, and they fell also.

One Blood above attempted to throw his sword like a javelin at

90

Roman, but Nihl knocked it clattering against the wall; disarmed, the Blood fell back. After a few more minutes of frantic battling and useless repositioning, Captain Tarl called a retreat back up to the rainy rooftop.

Nihl began to charge up after them, but Roman grabbed his arm. "Wait! It's better for us here—" He twisted to those below. "Does anyone know if there is another way down from the roof?"

He was answered by dumb silence. Then Deirdre exclaimed, "I know how to find out!" She gave her dagger to Vida and raced down the stairs.

She ran nonstop to the kitchen on the first floor, then stopped to gain some wind and put on a more casual air. She entered the kitchen to see all the servants gathered at the windows, looking out into the courtyard and talking excitedly. Deirdre overheard: "Who could they be going after?" "The escaped prisoners, surely—" "But who was on the roof—?"

Deirdre had come intending to draw Izana aside and pump her for the needed information, but then she had another idea. At that moment Izana turned from the window and saw her. The maid frowned, pointing at Deirdre, "You are a stranger here. Who are you? Do you know what is happening?"

Deirdre said, "I am Surchataine Deirdre of Lystra. My husband Roman, the Surchatain, has deposed Tremelaine and now asks your aid. Is there anyone here who wishes to fight with him against the Bloodclad?"

The kitchen servants, four men and six women, stood gaping at Deirdre. Then one little old man, the head cook, raised his fist with a shrill battle cry: "AAIEE! To the fight!" He lunged forward, the others behind him.

They would have bolted pell-mell past Deirdre had she not seized the old cook, crying, "Wait! Roman needs to know how many ways there are up to the roof."

"Two," said the old man. "Only two." He had sharp eyes and short, spiky white hair. His face looked like tanned leather laid across high cheekbones. His jaw jutted out with determination—no stranger to conflict, he.

"Come show him quickly, then." Deirdre led them at a run to the rooftop stairs.

"Roman!" she panted, reaching Vida at the rear of the group.

He looked down in mild alarm. "Deirdre—who is with you?"

"The kitchen servants. They wish to join you!"

"Long live Surchatain Roman!" cried the old cook, raising his fist again.

91

"Thank you," said Roman, peering down. "But is there another passage up to the roof?"

"Yes sir!"

Roman came down the stairs, instructing, "Nihl, come with me. Colin, you and Lew block this doorway." Then to the cook: "Show me quickly."

"The only other way up is on the far side of the palace," rasped the old cook. "We have to go through the courtyard to the east tower. It's a straight run on the roof, though."

"Quickly, then," urged Roman. The feisty fellow whisked them to a door leading to the open courtyard, where they paused. "They did not all go to the roof, did they?" muttered Roman, scanning the grounds.

"No sir!" said the cook. "Several divisions rode out in a big rush. Went south, I heard."

Roman and Nihl glanced warily at each other, but Nihl reasoned, "The outpost is well defended."

In the slackening rain, they traversed the yard to the east tower. "This way," pointed the cook. They followed him down a short corridor to a tightly winding iron staircase.

As they climbed to the top, they heard banging sounds echoing down. Rounding the last bend of the stairs, they saw one Blood lying motionless on the landing and another striving to hold the rooftop door shut against the pounding of those behind it.

At the sound of their footfalls, the Blood jerked his head around and grinned. "Surchatain—good to see you—didn't know how long I could hold them back."

"Kam, you are an excellent fellow," muttered Roman, while the cook brought an iron bar from a corner and slid it in place against the door.

Kam exhaled, wiping sweat from his forehead. "Think they'll be able to hack through it?" he asked, looking over the iron-banded hardwood door.

"No sir, not this one," assured the cook, patting it proudly. "Not for a long, long time."

Kam arched a brow at him. "Who are you, sir?"

"I am Titian," he answered, drawing up his entire five feet.

"We already owe much to this man's courage," said Roman. Titian took on a positive swagger. "I am thinking," Roman added as they walked away from the commotion behind the barred door, "that it may spare us fighting to simply lock the Bloods up on the roof. Nihl, you and Kam go back to that first stairway. See if you can bar that door also."

"Where do we meet you, Surchatain?" asked Kam. "The dungeon?"

"No—not yet. I'll give those below time to change their minds," replied Roman. Kam hesitated, not understanding him, but Roman was already considering something else: "For now . . . Titian, can you find us something to eat?"

"Can I!" he declared. "The best roast beef you ever tasted, with thick brown gravy, and fresh-baked white bread—"

"Just—show me," Roman interrupted, putting one hand on Titian's shoulder and the other on his own empty stomach.

"We'll meet you in the kitchen, then," said Kam.

"Yes. Once you secure that door, bring the others there to eat, and we'll decide what our next move should be," Roman said. Nihl and Kam saluted as they sprinted away.

Titian took Roman back to the deserted kitchen and emptied a roasting rack from the fireplace onto a worktable. Roman stood over him as he began slicing thin strips of tender pink meat. Then he filled his emptiness with beef while Titian brought out bread to slice and a bottle of wine.

In between mouthfuls, Roman asked, "How long have you been here, Titian?"

"I served Tremaine eight years, and every Surchatain after him," he answered.

"Who besides Tremelaine?" asked Roman. "Rollet?"

"No sir. Tremaine's son Rollet never ruled as Surchatain. He just led a worthless band of renegades."

"Then who ruled before Tremelaine?"

"Lord Graydon."

"Graydon?" Roman repeated. The name rang familiar. "Was he in prison?"

"Aye."

"How long did he reign before Tremelaine deposed him?"

Titian laughed wryly. "He was never really deposed. He's a clever one, hey?"

"What? How so?" demanded Roman.

"Why, somehow he got wind of your coming, and put his brother on the throne as a dummy—a puppet. Graydon still pulled his strings from prison."

"But—the crucifixions—the black crosses and the Bloodclad—"

"That began with Graydon organizing a bodyguard and marking the town dissenters publicly so he'd be able to watch them easier. But when he let little brother have the throne, Galen went crazy—changing his name to Tremelaine, making the bodyguard into the Bloodclad, and executing everybody. Graydon never tried to stop him. I think he was more concerned about throwing you offtrack than controlling Galen's wild-brained notions."

Roman continued to eat out of sheer need. He felt sick at the realization that his friends had evidently been sheltering their own enemy. "Do the townspeople know all this?" he asked evenly.

"No sir. As far as they know, Graydon really was deposed. When he divined your threat some four weeks ago, he and Galen staged a little confrontation, and baby brother took over—he always had a hankering to play the part. Lord Graydon let him do whatever he wanted, as long as he carried out Graydon's orders from prison. The people hate Galen, but not Graydon."

Roman chewed thoughtfully, then asked, "How do you know all this?"

"I got good ears," Titian winked, tapping the side of his head. "And I'm in all the right places."

As Roman finished eating, Nihl entered with the others. "The door is locked and barred, Surchatain," he said.

"I saw that it could be," Roman nodded, "but didn't see the bar."

"Lew found it, and the key—" Nihl was explaining, when Deirdre ran up to Roman and put her arms around his middle, still overwhelmed at the sight of him. He held her, smiling, while the others helped themselves to plates of beef passed around by Titian.

Deirdre said, "Roman, Vida told me something you should hear. Graydon—the man in the dungeon who defied you—ruled before Tremelaine took control. He lied to us about it. Vida said he told her he wanted to discern our purpose before revealing himself to us."

"I have learned more than that," Roman responded. "According to this good man, Graydon has not ceased ruling, even from prison." Titian then repeated to the others all he had told Roman.

"So you see, Lord Graydon is still Surchatain," Roman summarized. "*He* is the one we came to depose."

Kam spat, "I *knew* he wasn't straight! He took us like blind merchants!"

"He tried to," Roman remarked thoughtfully, "but instead he lost control of Corona. No wonder he refused to fight with me—he is trying to regain power himself."

"The liar—the deceiver!" sputtered Vida. "He called himself our friend! And had you not escaped from prison and come for us, he would have allowed Galen to execute us, too!"

Orvis feebly shook his head. "I never could understand how Galen managed to overthrow Graydon—Lord Graydon was always the smarter of the two."

"What is certain now, Surchatain," Nihl said with characteristic Polonti coolness, "is that we *must* kill Graydon."

Roman nodded grimly. "First, we must insure he doesn't release the Bloods on the roof. All he has to do is get by us and get to either of those doors to let them out."

"Surchatain," interposed Lew timidly, "if you let me have a look, I may be able to jam the hinges on the doors so they *can't* be opened."

"Good," said Roman. "Go now. And Colin—go with him, in case he runs into trouble on the way." As Colin and Lew went out, Roman wiped his hands and instructed, "The rest of you that wish, come with me to face Graydon." No one remained in the kitchen after Roman stalked out.

So with an army of fifteen, Roman descended to the dungeon once again. They took torches and went to the hiding place at the end of the passage. The cell was empty. They split up then, and searched every cell in every tunnel. Graydon and his handful of townspeople were long gone.

The searchers met at the intersection, every face turned inquiringly toward Roman. He nodded toward the stairs: "Back to the kitchen, then."

On their way, they met up with Lew and Colin returning from their mission. Colin reported gleefully, "This man has the keenest knack I ever saw for ruining things mechanical!"

Roman smiled and Kam slapped Lew on the back. They filed into the kitchen, then sat on tables and benches to rest. Laying his sword aside, Roman asked Colin, "Did you meet up with anyone?"

"No," responded Colin, his face growing serious. "No servants or guards. No one."

"When the Bloods found Tremelaine's body outside, most of the servants took that as their chance to get away," Titian informed them. "We would've too, if your pretty wife hadn't invited us to your party. But they don't have much hope of actually getting anywhere."

As he listened, Roman looked contemplatively out the courtyard windows to the quadrangle, lit orange with the glow of the dying sun breaking through the clouds. "What now, Surchatain?" asked Kam.

"We wait. And rest," Roman said, putting his feet up. "Graydon must return to challenge me. The Lord is giving us opportunity to regroup before then. Titian, take a man and find bedding for us to sleep here—I believe this is the handiest place for us. Kam, you take the first watch, then Colin, then Nihl, then wake me for the last watch."

In short order, Titian and the other servant returned with quilts and pillows which they passed around for all to make themselves comfortable. Izana took a blanket, and with deliberate carelessness, placed it a few feet from Nihl. He glanced at her. "I . . . feel better sleeping near someone who knows how to use a sword," she explained lamely.

He smiled slightly. "Then stay beside me."

"I will." She moved her blanket up next to his and lay down.

Deirdre and Roman settled down on a fluffy quilt in a corner of the kitchen, and night spread softly around the walled-in group.

CHAPTER 11

AS ROMAN SAT on the blanket, his back to the wall, Deirdre leaned on his chest. Caressing the shimmering brocade shirt and toying with the golden fagoting in front, her fingers inadvertently brushed the brand on his chest. He flinched slightly. She loosed the fagoting to kiss his breastbone tenderly in penance, and he stroked her hair.

"You are beautiful," she whispered.

"You didn't say that when I was hanging on that pole," he returned smiling.

"Even then, you were beautiful," she said slowly. "So very . . . very beautiful." He looked down at her in the shadows, caught by her earnestness. "I remember your being whipped on the post for me because of my disobedience over that horse, and how beautiful you were then, though I did not see it as clearly as I do now."

He pressed his lips to her forehead, wanting to divert her. "Just wait until we get out of this and return to Westford," he whispered. "Then I'll go back to being mean and ugly."

"No," she said. "You are too heavenly."

He felt mildly disturbed. "Adore God, Deirdre. Not me," he said gently.

"How can I help it, when there is so much of Him in you?" She buried her head defensively in his neck.

He opened his mouth to argue the point, then recalled a time when he had wished for this devotion from her more than anything in God's whole realm. Now that it was given him, what was he trying to correct? He knew she was not in danger of worshiping him, especially when

96

their lives did return to normal. This was no time for reproval, but just for accepting her love.

He bent his face down to kiss her, then gripped her in his arms. She sighed contentedly. "I remember also," she continued, "a time when I dreamed to be loved by someone very powerful, who would love me above everything he had. I was too blind to see you standing right beside me, doing just that."

"That was when you were at the Fair with Laska," he recalled.

"How do you know that?" she wondered, raising her head.

"You talked about it, and I overheard you."

"You loved me even then, didn't you?"

"Oh yes," he said, tightening his arms around her.

"I wish I had known," she breathed into his neck.

"Oh no," he smiled, shaking his head. "You were too young."

She grinned up at him, but the waning light did not reach into their corner for him to see. So she brought his mouth down to hers to feel her happiness.

Not very far away, Graydon sat alone at a table in a dark room, meditating. When he opened his eyes, he called quietly, "Captain Berk."

The officer appeared at the doorway, tentatively extending a candle to illumine the other's back. "Here, Lord Graydon."

Graydon did not turn to face him, but merely asked, "How did the Lystran Surchatain kill Galen?"

"He threw him out the second-level window at the end of the corridor, my lord."

"The one that is leaded and paned?"

"Yes."

"That is not possible," Graydon murmured. "No human strength could perform that."

"Well, it's sure he didn't jump through it!" Berk snorted, stepping just inside the room. It was uncomfortable talking to someone's back. But Graydon still did not turn around. Berk continued, "That is the window he came out of, though. My men and I were in the courtyard when it happened."

"And that is when you chose to run," Graydon snidely observed.

"How could we know you were still alive?" Berk asked defensively. "And we came when you summoned. Now, what are you going to do about the Lystrans?"

Graydon folded his hands in contemplation. "Surchatain Roman has taken it upon himself to challenge powers beyond his understanding. Therefore, he must be destroyed by means other than human." Berk

97

stood very still. "Leave me now, Captain. I have much to do."

"Of course, Lord Graydon," Berk shrugged.

"And Captain," Graydon added, his back still to Berk, "remove that silly amulet from your neck. It does not protect you without the proper words."

Berk paled, putting a hand to the charm under his shirt. "Yes, my lord," he mumbled, backing out.

Graydon placed his hands on the table before him and began to utter strange words. Eyes closed, he waited. Then into his mind came the picture he wished to see. It was dark and shadowy at first, but gradually focused to reveal two sleeping figures.

The man in the silk brocade was the Lystran Surchatain. Graydon observed him sleeping deeply, shifting only to tighten an arm around the other figure resting on his chest—the Surchataine Deirdre.

Graydon directed his vision to see that they were in the kitchen of the palace, and to see all the others sleeping, except for one Lystran on watch. The guard was gazing through the kitchen window, but then blinked and glanced around the black room as if suddenly uneasy.

The sorcerer directed his mind once again to the unconscious Surchatain. Then Graydon reached out both hands in front of him and brought them together as if clenching something between them, while he focused his mind on Roman.

The Surchatain stirred and Graydon clasped his hands together more tightly. Roman's breathing deepened to a rasp and his face grew anxious in sleep. Graydon pressed his hands together with all his strength. Just as Roman began making choking noises in his throat, a cold wash of something spilled heavily over Graydon, knocking him from his chair like a forbidding slap from a powerful hand.

As Graydon lay stunned on the floor, his vision showed him Roman breathing easily again, settling back into undisturbed sleep, before it vanished as behind a slamming door.

Graydon lay where he had fallen, breathless and mystified. At last he struggled to his knees and climbed back onto the chair. "I will have to find another way," he muttered, then paused at the perception that, perhaps, he should not. But a savage voice jolted him: *You must! It is commanded you!*

Graydon obediently stretched his hands out and began saying words.

In the pitch blackness of the kitchen, Roman awakened at a voice in his ear: "Surchatain." He raised his head. "You instructed me to wake you for the last watch," whispered Nihl.

Roman eased the sleeping Deirdre from his chest, then rose and

98

took up his sword in the darkness. He followed Nihl to the open kitchen window which looked out into the courtyard.

The night luminaries bathed the neat, hedged yard in soft silver light. The cobbled paths and stone archways, still shimmering with moisture, gave the deserted grounds an air of peacefulness and security.

Roman scanned the grounds yawning. "You may go rest now, Nihl."

"I don't wish to," Nihl answered. "I want to hear what happened after Tremelaine took you from the torture room."

In whispers, attended by questions from Nihl, Roman related his experiences while tied to the pole on the rooftop—the drunken Bloods, the rain; then Tremelaine's taking him to the little room and what transpired within. "When I said the name of the Lord," Roman concluded, "whatever was in that room shrieked and blew the door off its hinges. It picked up Tremelaine, carried him to the window, and . . ." he trailed off, watching the courtyard.

Nihl turned to look. "What do you see?"

"Someone in the shadows." They watched a moment, but saw nothing.

Nihl resumed, "What then happened to Tremelaine?"

"He was thrown through the window to the stone pavement fifty feet down. He was quite . . ." Roman broke off again, staring across the courtyard.

This time they both saw him. A figure was loping across the grounds toward the kitchen with sword raised high. Nihl dived through the open window; Roman grasped the casing and vaulted out feet first. They extended their blades as a formidable warning.

Heedless, the intruder lunged wildly toward them. His erratic gait suggested broken bones or mental imbalance. As he drew closer, muttering and slavering, Roman's mouth went dry, for he recognized him.

"Stop!" warned Nihl. The man reared back as though to strike a death blow, but Nihl swung his blade in a sure and fatal stroke to his throat. The attacker fell, quivering. Nihl looked down at him bemused, knowing the blow had been well placed. But the man on the ground would not lie still as he should have.

Then Nihl and Roman watched in near terror as his palsied hand grasped his fallen sword. His eyes popped open, and he jerked to his feet like a puppet on strings. Again he lifted his sword. Nihl violently rammed his blade into the man's belly clear to the hilt and twisted it back out. Again the body fell, quivering.

Nihl stood over it, breathing very hard, gripping his sword. Roman, who had been immobilized by the proceedings, leaned weakly against the wall and breathed pleadingly, "Lord Jesus." The body went still. They watched it, and it stayed still.

Nihl, gazing at it tensely, muttered, "That looks like . . ."

"It is Tremelaine," said Roman.

"But . . . I thought that . . . he . . ."

"He could not have survived that fall. Certainly not to come attack us later."

Nihl turned to gaze levelly at Roman. "The dog in the village," he said simply. Roman met his eyes without breathing. "But—" Nihl went on slowly, "are there *anakim* here?"

"Nothing so easy as that," answered Roman. "But from the same source." He looked down at Tremelaine's body for a moment, as if wishing to ascertain without touching him whether he were truly dead.

"Nihl," he said, taking hold of the Commander's arm, "there is no need to mention this to the others." Nihl nodded, shaken.

Roman inhaled deeply, then reached down to grasp the body under the arms. "What are you doing?" demanded Nihl.

"I am going to bury him."

"I will do that," insisted Nihl.

"No. You stand watch over the others. Let me do this. Only . . ."

"I will send you protection in prayer," Nihl responded. Roman smiled weakly and began dragging the body away.

Deirdre awoke shortly after sunrise. She reached for Roman but he was not beside her. Sitting up, she saw Nihl talking quietly with Kam near the window. The others were stirring, rolling up blankets and excusing themselves from the kitchen.

Titian was already standing before the large stone hearth, stirring up the cinders. A servant carried in a gunnysack and dropped it on the worktable. Titian began emptying it of summer fruit to add to the smoked ham and bread already on the table. As Deirdre gravitated toward him, she caught the lush scent of ripe peaches. Titian winked and handed her an especially large one.

After savoring it, Deirdre remembered that she had been going to look for Roman. She took peaches to Nihl and Kam, asking, "Where is Roman?"

They took the fruit, Nihl bowing his head to her and Kam saying, "Thank you, Surchataine." But they did not answer her question.

"Where is Roman?" she repeated.

After a moment's hesitation, Nihl answered, "He left to see to a small task. He will return soon."

"What is he doing?" she persisted, alarmed at Nihl's evasiveness.

But before Nihl had to choose between lying to her and disobeying the Surchatain, Roman walked through the kitchen door, brushing dirt from his hands. "You are becoming a real morning bird, Deirdre," he joked tenderly.

She let her breath out in relief, not even attending to his teasing remark. "Where were you?" she asked, handing him the fruit.

"Scouting around the grounds," he answered as he bit into a juicy peach. He ate, then added, "There is no one around the palace. The gates are wide open. It's almost as if the people fled from a coming disaster."

"Of course they have," Titian said amiably, putting out more bread and pouring drink. "Who wants to be caught in between two powerful Surchatains fighting it out?"

Roman gathered his brows and asked, "Why then have you cast your lot with me, Titian?"

The fellow looked up with twinkling eyes. "Because you're on the offensive," he said, poking a finger into Roman's chest. "And you're going to win."

"How do you know that?" pressed Deirdre, smiling.

"Because you're either crazy or you really have the power to beat old Graydon. And you don't look crazy to me."

Roman turned his head to smile wryly at no one in particular. "Thank you, Titian. You're a real encourager."

The band of eighteen warriors ate as the morning sun spilled into the kitchen. "This is such a beautiful place," murmured Deirdre. "It is a shame that it has been ruled by such awful men."

"We thought we had a good one in Graydon," Orvis reflected despondently. "We had been working so hard to make Corona into something decent again, and Graydon promised to lead us that way. Now, it's hard to tell who is honest and who is not."

"You can be confident in Roman," said Kam stoutly.

"We are confident in the Lord," Roman answered quickly. "Left to myself, I've already seen what I can do—nothing." He shook his head over the months he had spent here in Corona, fruitlessly searching for Deirdre.

"But what now?" asked Orvis. "Do we just wait here for Graydon to come back? How long do we wait?"

"I don't know," answered Roman. "I just don't know. For now, Colin, you and Lew go check those rooftop doors and make sure they are still secure."

"Surchatain." They saluted as they left.

While they were gone, the rest sat or stood around the large work table. Roman scratched his new stubble of a beard and thought aloud, "What we do now depends on Graydon's next move. I can only pray the Lord gives us the resources to deal with whatever he throws at us. Unless something is brought to our attention, I see nothing else we can do at present but wait."

Roman paused, assessing Orvis. "It might help to know more about him."

Deirdre added, "Yes. Vida, how much of what Graydon told us at your house was the truth?"

"Well, some," she responded uncomfortably. "He and Galen did find the book, and did compete to work spells. Then suddenly they were both living at the palace—Graydon sitting on the throne and calling himself Lord Graydon. Galen was supposed to be his administrator, or something, until they concocted that plan of putting Graydon in prison. I wonder why he allowed you to escape the dungeon and take him with you?"

Nihl said, "He had to play the part, at first. He did not know who we were, nor why we were in prison. By the time he discovered that, we were out of the dungeon and he was outnumbered."

"You remember," added Kam, "the first thing he did was take us to the wall to show us how to escape. It's a good thing we didn't try it, because the Bloods knew all along about that hidden tunnel. If we had tried to get out, they would have slaughtered us like cattle."

"When we refused to leave, what could he do? To take us to a place with a red circle would have betrayed the truth about him at once," continued Nihl, studied intently by Izana as he spoke. "Then the Surchataine's idea of coming back to the dungeon trapped him further. He could not reveal himself then, for he had already told us too many lies. It seems he was maneuvered into helping us, though we were ignorant of it at the time." He paused, leaving open the question of who had manipulated Graydon.

"Do the ones with him now know he ruled from prison?" asked Roman. Nihl looked questioningly at Orvis.

"There is no reason they should!" answered Orvis. "*We* would not have known, had you not told us."

Roman deduced, "Then Graydon is leading the townspeople that remain, and possibly a number of the Bloodclad." No one argued this.

Kam observed, "If Graydon can blame you for the death of Galen, then he might incite the people to storm the palace and hang you."

"If Graydon blames Galen's death on him, the townspeople are likely to give Seleca to your Surchatain in gratitude," Orvis snorted.

"Which is to say we still cannot predict what he will do," concluded Roman, resting on his elbow.

About this time Colin and Lew returned. "Surchatain, the doors are fast. We listened, but could hear nothing beyond them," Colin reported.

Roman nodded, staring into space. "I suppose it would be prudent to post a watch at the front entrance. It is pointless to prevent his

102

coming, but at least we need to know when he does. Kam, you go first. And try to keep yourself out of sight."

After the Second left, no one else shifted from his seat or took his eyes off Roman. "I assume then," resumed Roman, "that Graydon has been practicing sorcery also?"

Orvis said, "Yes. And he was good at it. Now, with Galen dead, he can only be stronger. Are—are you a sorcerer, Surchatain?" he asked timidly.

"In no way," Roman answered, repulsed. "I am a Christian."

Orvis did not appear particularly relieved, but that seemed to exhaust the questions for the time being. They settled back somewhat uneasily to wait.

In the same dark room he had been in the night before, Graydon paced edgily near a small cauldron on the table. Even in daylight, the room looked no brighter than it had at midnight. There seemed to be a haze occluding what little light filtered in through the boarded-up window. Yet there was no fire in the room to account for the haze.

Graydon paused over the cauldron and glanced at the door. He was apparently waiting for something vital. He sat in the chair to rest, but then sprang up as if prodded by a hot iron and began to pace again.

At last he wheeled expectantly toward the door, and within seconds he heard rapid footfalls. Berk entered. "I brought all that you ordered, Lord Graydon—"

Graydon jerked the canvas satchel from his hand and poured out the contents, some alive, on the table. "Now get me fire quickly," Graydon ordered.

Berk glanced around, confused. "But there is no hearth—"

"Just a torch, man!" shouted Graydon as he began dismembering something wriggling and tossing the pieces into the pot. He stopped, placing a hand over his eyes as if to prompt his memory. "I must get that book," he mumbled to himself.

Berk privately gave him a murderous look as he left the room, but returned immediately with the torch. "Why the haste?" he muttered, not liking all these weird orders.

"He is not . . . doing what I had anticipated. He is becoming . . . dangerous. . . . He must be stopped at any . . . cost," murmured Graydon disjointedly as he concentrated on what he was doing.

Berk grinned, "What're you going to do to him?"

"I can't touch him!" whispered Graydon, abruptly staring up at the wall. "Why? What is blocking me? I must go deal with him myself." He returned to assembling the ingredients in the cauldron.

103

"How?" asked Berk.

"Stop questioning me! Go arm your men immediately."

Berk stepped out with a wary glance over his shoulder and saw Graydon passing the torch over the pot. The Captain shut the door. In the corridor he paused, sniffing, and turned to see heavy red smoke curling out from under the door. He ran.

In the palace kitchen, the group sat waiting for the unknown to dictate their actions. The servants entertained themselves while they waited with a crude gambling game of shells and nuts, but the Lystrans seemed on guard, clustered around Roman. Izana wandered from the group of servants to sit near Nihl, and smiled at him. Titian, too, divided his attention between the game, the door, and Roman.

Suddenly they all heard the faint echoes of an explosion. They jumped, looking around, then upward. "That came from above," said Colin. "Do you suppose—?"

But then Kam appeared breathless at the kitchen doorway. "Surchatain—Graydon approaches with the Bloods behind him!"

"Arm yourselves quickly," Roman instructed, standing. As Deirdre stood, he turned to her. "Deirdre, I *command* you and the other women to hide yourselves in the nearest storeroom."

She opened her mouth from habit, then slowly shut it. She, Vida, Izana, and the other five women slipped out of the kitchen and plopped themselves into a small storeroom.

That left ten men against Graydon and his Bloods, however many there were. Roman unsheathed Azrael and said aloud, "Lord God, please go before us and fight for us." Then they left the kitchen and strode to the audience hall at the front of the palace.

As they entered the hall, Nihl gestured urgently to his left. The Bloods under Captain Tarl who had been trapped on the roof were descending the stairs in a fury. Kam took a step back to look through a corridor window, and saw, across the courtyard, more Bloods pouring from the east tower.

Then through the main door of the audience hall came Graydon, with Captain Berk and the remainder of the Bloodclad behind him. Roman's group stopped in the hall, facing Graydon. The sorcerer held up a restraining hand to Captain Tarl and his men coming from the stairs. The Bloods from the east tower entered the hall behind Roman and halted there. Roman's men were completely surrounded.

CHAPTER 12

GRAYDON GLANCED at the Bloods encompassing Roman's group to make sure he knew they were all around him. Then he told Roman, "It was not wise of you to come here. Yes, you defeated Galen, but he had become weak and eccentric. I gave your companions the chance to escape alive, and they would have, but for you. You should never have come."

"I had no choice but to come," answered Roman. "I came under orders."

"And now you will die," Graydon said. Seeing the faces of the Bloods surrounding them, several of those with Roman thought that a fair conclusion.

"Not until I have accomplished what I was sent to do," Roman replied with rocklike certainty.

"Should I throw up my hands and let you kill me, then?" asked Graydon, amused.

"I do not wish to kill you," Roman said. "But you must renounce the dark powers you serve and be done with them."

Graydon's face twitched slightly. "I do not serve them. They serve me."

"You are quite mistaken. That is what your brother Galen thought also. And they killed him when he was of no more use to them."

"This talk is worthless, Lord Graydon!" Berk exploded. "Kill him now!"

Roman did not take his gaze from Graydon. "The dark powers use anyone who allows them to. And they destroy everyone they use."

Graydon's breathing began to deepen. "You don't know their strength," he rasped. "They do not let go so easily."

"The power of the Lord Jesus is greater. How do you think I survived all that Tremelaine tried to do to me?" Roman asked pointedly.

Graydon's eyes widened. For a moment he stared at Roman, daring to consider that what he said was actually possible. There *must* be another force interfering with the dark powers, else this Lystran would be dead many times over now. At this moment the unprecedented thought came to Graydon that he had the choice to say no.

Then from above came a rumbling. Those in the audience hall felt the mosaic floor beneath them shivering. To the last man, they looked in mounting fear up the stone stairs.

Faces drained white to see rolling down the stairs a thick red fog. Neither vapor nor liquid, it oozed down the steps, trailing a fine red mist.

Suddenly it condensed tightly and shot like a projectile toward Graydon. The men around him saw it and dodged. But it closed around Graydon's head and then seemed to disappear. Graydon's look changed to fury and he lifted his sword, commanding, "Kill them!" The Bloods charged Roman's band.

The ten backed up in a circle as they were assaulted on all sides. While the Bloods closed in on them, slashing with their broadswords, Graydon stood aside and watched. The small band had to fight desperately just to parry the strikes of so many blades. Roman knocked one Blood's sword into the Blood next to him, and Nihl used the disruption to finish him, but still another Blood instantly replaced him.

The circle grew tighter, as some of those who were unskilled fighters fell back. A servant dropped his sword in despair, falling down, and Roman felt the rush of air from a swinging blade behind him.

But then there seemed to be a distraction on the outer edge of the Bloods. A number began slipping and falling. As they caught hold of each other, more were pulled down. Then one Blood screamed, "The mist! The red mist is coming back!"

In a blind panic, Bloods began shouting and stumbling for the doors. They were falling down, jumping up, falling again, lunging out. In only a few moments the hall cleared of Bloods. Graydon stood alone, blinking blankly, as though he had just awakened. "Surchatain! Seize him!" gasped Nihl.

Roman took hold of Graydon's coat and raised his sword. But as he gazed at the sorcerer, he slowly lowered his weapon and released him. Graydon escaped the hall.

Titian muttered, "Well, I'll be a horsetail. Look at that." He was staring down at a vast scattering of dried beans all over the floor. Peeking and grinning around the corridor were Deirdre and the other women, holding empty gunnysacks.

"They're gone!" she shrieked jubilantly, running carefully around the beans to embrace Roman.

He received her, shaking his head. "Now how did you think of that?"

She laughed, "It was Vida's idea!"

"Surchatain," Nihl began hesitantly, "why . . . why did you let him go?"

106

Roman carefully sheathed his fine sword. "It was revealed to me that I must not kill him. My fight is not with him. He is only a slave, not the master. Somehow, he must be convinced to willingly renounce the dark powers."

Nihl looked disturbed, not agreeing at all, but put away his sword. Izana impulsively stepped toward him. He looked at her, turned his eyes away, but then turned to look at her again.

Roman walked over to the stairway and faced it as if it were an enemy. "There is one thing I see that we must do right now." He glanced back at the group. "Kam, you and Colin take the others back to the kitchen and wait for us. Nihl, you and Deirdre come with me. We're going to shut one door of entry that those powers have here."

As Roman led the two up the stairs, Deirdre asked, "Roman, what door are you talking about?"

"There is a room which Tremelaine evidently used to summon the dark powers. I believe that is where the red mist came from. Somehow, we must render that room useless." Roman brought Nihl and Deirdre past the wrecked door still lying on the floor of the corridor.

They stopped three feet from the black entrance to the sorcerer's room and peered within. "What is it that we should do, Surchatain?" whispered Nihl.

Roman did not immediately answer, for he was reliving the awful experience he had in this room. A great reluctance came over him. *Oh, forget it. There's nothing in there now. I have too much else to worry about. . . .*

He shook his head emphatically. "We must go in, and—" *You had better not. Remember what happened last time?* "—and destroy the pattern on the floor, made of tiles—" *That thing will come up at you again! And what about Deirdre?*

He took in a deep breath and closed his eyes. "Lord Jesus, surround us with your protection." He turned to Deirdre. "Do you still have your knife?"

"Yes," she said, wondering.

To them both, Roman said, "There is a design set in the floor. We must obliterate it by prying up the tiles and breaking them or throwing them out. As we do, you may see or hear some frightening things. Just—ignore them, and keep your attention on what you are doing. The Lord is our shield."

They entered the room and knelt, feeling in the darkness for the tiles in the wooden floor. Nihl found the first and dug it up with his blade. At once there was a ripple in the air and a hollow, laughing voice called out a once-familiar, almost-forgotten name: "Drud! Filthy drud! No woman would have you! You'll always be a slave!" Nihl set his jaw and fiercely ripped up another tile.

Deirdre nervously touched a tile and yelped, putting her fingers to her mouth. "It burned me!"

"It can't hurt you. Dig it out," Roman said sternly. Obediently, she wedged her blade under it and popped it up. Then she gasped as the image of her beloved nursemaid, Nanna, now three years dead, appeared in the room. Weeping, Nanna put her hand to a terrible bleeding gash in her midriff and pleaded, "Darling, don't! You are hurting me so!" Deirdre hesitated, but then quickly lowered her head and forcefully pried up tiles.

Roman had located tiles at the far edge of the sigil and was destroying them with ruthless efficiency. The floor began to shake and a gust of air blew up. It sat Deirdre back on her heels, but Roman noticed it had not near its earlier potency. "Stop it!" he ordered.

The air stilled. The three pried up tiles with renewed courage. Then a faint, wavering image appeared before them. Roman looked up before he thought.

It was the image of the little girl he had freed while searching the slave markets, the one he had thought at first to be Deirdre. She held out pleading hands to him and begged, "Don't kill me again. Please let me stay."

"Kill you—again?" he murmured.

"Ignore it!" said Nihl.

"Do you know what happened to me after you released me? Some renegades found me. Do you know what they did to me?" As she began to describe how horribly they had abused her, Roman's blade dropped from his limp fingers.

"Roman, don't listen to it!" Deirdre urged, shaking him, but his face was fixed in horror to think that he had been responsible for another's suffering. Not knowing what else to do, Deirdre and Nihl tore up tiles as fast as they could. Roman sat weakly and unwillingly listening to the pitiful tale.

The image grew fainter; the voice distant. Finally, as Deirdre and Nihl found and broke up the last tiles, the vision vanished with a sigh and all was still.

They took hold of Roman's arms and pulled him from the room, benumbed and pale. "Roman, you know that was not really the girl. You *know* that was one of the dark powers trying to dismay you!" Deirdre exclaimed, holding him.

"Yes, Roman," Nihl added with quiet intensity.

Roman stirred and blinked. "But . . . but what if that really happened to her?"

"They are lying, Roman! They would say anything to discourage you!" Deirdre argued.

"I still do not know what happened to her."

"Whatever happened to her is not your responsibility—" she began, but he turned on her passionately.

"Yes, it is!" he exploded. "*I* released her, but *I* would not ward her!"

"She would not let you!" Deirdre shouted back. "You must not torment yourself over what happened three years ago!"

He shook off her grasp. "I never should have even been there. How could God forgive me, when I turned my back on Him? What possesses me to think He has any use for me now?"

Deirdre looked over to Nihl in desperation. He observed quietly, "By asking that, you are ignoring most of what has happened in the time since then, and all of what has happened here.

"We all fall. We have all turned our backs on God. I became a slave through pride and ignorance, and the Surchataine was enslaved because of her disobedience. But our sorry condition drove us back to God, and now all that remains of our chains is the memory of the Lord unlocking them. We have found that He is not thwarted by our mistakes—haven't we, Surchatain?"

Nihl and Deirdre watched Roman with compassion as he swallowed and nodded. He murmured, "But I will always carry with me the burden of not knowing what happened to her." Then he put his hand on Deirdre's forearm. "Please forgive me. I must never raise my voice to you."

She squirmed. "I am guilty also. Forgive *me.*" She slipped a hand under his arm and gave her other to Nihl. Thus linked, they wearily returned to the stairs.

Arriving in the kitchen, they found the group seated quietly around the worktable. Colin turned from the courtyard window as the three entered; the others raised their heads expectantly.

Nihl hesitated near the doorway, pretending not to notice Izana's steadfast gaze. But abruptly, as if pushed, he walked over to her. She stood very close, looking up steadily into his face while she said something to him. He missed much of the conversation that followed . . .

Roman was saying, "That's one problem resolved," which made his companions stir in relief.

"No more red mists?" asked one servant anxiously.

"Not from that room," Roman assured him. The Surchatain paused, holding a goblet which Titian filled from a stone jar.

"What now? Do we wait some more?" another servant asked, a shade frustrated.

Roman was silent a full minute. "Vida," he said.

"My lord?" she started.

"Vida, you mentioned something about a book that Graydon and Galen worked spells from. Was it a sorcerer's book?"

"Yes, Surchatain."

"Do you know if Graydon brought it to the palace with him?"

"No, I do not," she said, apprehension crossing her face.

"He did, but it's not here now," Titian interjected. "Little brother put hands on it and hid it somewhere while Graydon was down in the dungeon. I don't know if Lord Graydon ever knew it was gone."

"Do you have any idea where he might have hidden it?" Roman asked.

"Not I," Titian said with certainty.

Roman asked, "Orvis, do you or Vida?"

Reluctantly, Orvis admitted, "There are a few likely places I can think of . . ." He did not say the last word: *Why?*

Roman drained the goblet and answered the unasked question. "That is another door we must shut. If Graydon is ever to be made to renounce the dark powers, we must shake their hold on him. That book must be destroyed."

Orvis gave a start. "Do you know what you are saying? Do you know what's likely to happen when you touch that book? In God's name, why don't you just kill him and be done with it?" Orvis' voice rose to a hysterical pitch.

Roman lowered the goblet with a thud. "Because if I kill him in God's name, I'll be bringing judgment down on my own head. God has commanded mercy and I *will* obey!"

Orvis flinched at the rebuttal, too clearly seeing that he had mistaken Roman's restraint for weakness. Levelly, Roman explained, "I know, one step at a time, what I am to do here. And I know that the Lord is more powerful than anything bound in that book. You may come with me to search for it if you don't hinder me. Otherwise, just tell me where it might be hidden." He stopped, waiting for a response.

Orvis glanced up at Vida, but there was no pity in her eyes. He sighed, "I'll go. I'll show you. We both are with you, and we won't hinder you, shaking though we may be." Vida nodded, not appearing to shake much at all.

Roman smiled grimly. "Under the circumstances, I could not ask a firmer allegiance from you. Kam," Roman glanced around for the Second, who leaped up. "Are there any horses left in the stables?"

"Yes, Surchatain."

"Then let's go." The entire party filed out of the palace to the pens by the stables.

110

Roman spotted Fidelis at once, and took up a rope to catch the jittery animal. He clucked sympathetically upon seeing the lashes on his neck and haunches. Kam overheard him scolding the horse: "You're going to have to lose your stubborn ways, or keep getting beatings . . . like me." Kam had to smile.

Colin found Deirdre's black gelding and his own horse. Nihl located his spirited Arabian, but Kam and the others had to settle for the inferior Selecan animals.

As Deirdre mounted, she observed with interest that Nihl was lifting Izana onto a horse. Nihl left the maid behind to ride abreast of Roman, so Deirdre took the opportunity to canter up beside her. An irresistible inspiration struck. Deirdre cocked a brow and murmured, "You are certainly fortunate to have caught the Commander's attention. He is not easily impressed."

Izana's eyes flicked up shyly at Deirdre. "Does he—have a woman at home?"

"No one that he has committed himself to. Of course, Roman depends so heavily on him, I dare say he has not felt free to give himself to anyone else. I always thought that such a waste . . ."

"He is so dark," Izana murmured.

"He is Polonti," Deirdre said proudly, adding, "Roman is half Polonti."

The maid gazed ahead at the pair of men. "Are they always this bold?"

Deirdre also looked ahead, pausing to choose her words carefully. "They have learned," she said slowly, "to pursue what is important without flagging."

Izana was silent, and the aggressors rode out through the palace gates.

CHAPTER 13

BASIL SAT on the throne in the audience hall of the palace at Westford and announced to the people gathered there, "In the Surchatain's absence, he has instructed me to hear your petitions and answer them as I decide. He has given me the authority to carry out my judgments, so I would advise you not to test me." Captain Olynn, standing to the right of the throne, straightened in support of this.

Basil continued, "Is there anyone here now who has a request of me?"

One man came forward and bowed. "Counselor, I am Axel, a farmer. We have been hearing that the Surchatain is never coming back. Is this true?"

Basil glowered. "Of course not! He has been gone but a few days, and you people let your imaginations fly like the wind. He would not have gone had he no confidence in what he was doing."

Another man asked from the crowd: "If he doesn't come back, who will rule?"

"*I* am ruling until his return. And if anyone thinks differently, let him ask the standing army—any one of the thousands!" Basil retorted. The people were quiet.

After the audience, Basil took Sevter with him to the ironsmith's shop to give their order for threshing sledges. They left the palace on foot to walk the short distance to the smith's, talking in subdued voices as they went. Basil mused, "The apprehension of the people disturbs me. Why would they take Roman's leaving as a sign of abdication? He has been gone before."

Sevter glanced around thoughtfully, but his mind was not on anything he saw. "Rumors are flying. I don't know the source, but something is stirring their fears."

Basil stroked his beard, opening his mouth to reply, but then stopped in midstride. He was staring down at a child sitting off to the side of the road, playing quietly by himself. The child was intently watching two interlocking silver rings spin endlessly with perfect balance and rhythm.

Basil bent down and stopped the rings' spinning. The boy's head

112

came up. The Counselor took the gimmal, saying, "Young man, will you take me to your mother?"

The boy got up and led the two men to a neat wooden house on one of the better streets. "Mama," he said, opening the door.

Without looking up, a servant scrubbing the floor replied, "She's in back, boy." As the boy took Basil and Sevter through the house, a maid glanced up and bounced into a startled bow.

Out the back, they found the boy's mother tending a small but fragrant herb garden. "Mama," said the boy, running to pull on her sleeve, "they want to talk to you."

She bowed apprehensively, but before she could speak, Basil held up a reassuring hand. "No reason for fear, my lady, we simply wish to know where you obtained this toy," he said, showing her the gimmal.

"We bought it from the silversmith, Counselor Basil."

"DuCange?"

"Yes, Counselor."

"When?"

"Yesterday, my lord."

Sevter shifted uneasily. Basil pulled out a purse and gave her a few coins. "I will pay you for this, as I must take it. But I will warn you that Surchatain Roman has declared the sale of these sorcerer's rings illegal. You must not buy another."

"I will not, Counselor," she gasped. "I did not know—!"

He nodded distantly. From there, he and Sevter went directly to DuCange's shop. They found him at a table, directing his apprentices on the crafting of a cup. He eyed their intrusion with obvious irritation.

Basil said without preface, "DuCange, I am giving you opportunity to defend yourself. Have you been selling these, contrary to the Surchatain's order?" He held up the gimmal.

DuCange bristled, "Yes, I have been selling them, contrary to no order. The Surchatain's hasty word on that has been rescinded."

"By whom?" Basil asked in astonishment.

"Lord Troyce," DuCange answered confidently.

Basil pressed his lips together to select his next words judiciously. "Troyce does not have the authority to overturn Surchatain Roman's decrees. Instead, I will carry out the Surchatain's warning to you: You are hereby banished from Lystra. I will give you one hour to gather your family and your tools, then I will send soldiers to escort you to the border."

He turned away, but DuCange sputtered, "I appeal to Lord Troyce!"

Basil wheeled on him, as furious as Sevter had ever seen the gentle Counselor. "Troyce is no source of appeal! He is answerable to me,

113

and as of this moment, he is no longer administrator!" He stormed from the shop back toward the palace, entirely forgetting the threshing sledges.

Sevter followed him, muttering desperately, "Troyce knows better than to defy the Surchatain. There must be some misunderstanding."

"Summon him and Captain Olynn to me in my chambers," Basil instructed coolly, with a sidelong glance.

Sevter paused, seeing it. "At once, Counselor. But—do not doubt my loyalty, just because I also came from Goerge."

Basil nodded. "You are trusted—until I have reason to believe otherwise."

Perturbed, Sevter left to carry out his orders.

Olynn arrived in Basil's chambers first. "Counselor?" he saluted.

"Captain, in one hour, I want you to take a unit of soldiers to escort DuCange and his family into banishment."

The Captain hardly blinked. "Yes, Counselor."

Olynn did not ask for an explanation, but Basil inquired, "Were you in the audience when DuCange asked the Surchatain permission to sell the gimmals?"

"Yes, Counselor."

"Then you heard Surchatain Roman's reply to him."

"Yes—he threatened him with banishment if he sold another one."

"Sevter and I have discovered that he continues to sell them, with permission from Troyce," Basil informed him. "So I want you to execute the Surchatain's command regarding him."

"Certainly, Counselor," the Captain answered him. Then a shadow crossed his face. "I forgot to tell you—yesterday, Lord Troyce pulled the guard I had posted at the Chatain's door."

"What?" demanded Basil.

"Oh, I posted another," Olynn said hastily. "I thought not much of it—figured Troyce was just lording it over the soldiers a little. But in light of this, I suppose you should know."

Basil's eyes fastened on the Captain, then he said in a low monotone: "I wish you to attach a spy to monitor Troyce's doings. Select the most experienced, who can operate in utter secrecy. He is to report to me nightly, here."

Olynn bowed. "You can rely on me to have it done as you wish, Counselor. I'll stake my rank on it."

Basil cocked a calculating brow. "You have, Captain."

When Olynn opened the door to leave, they saw Troyce standing behind it. Olynn did not bow to him as he passed by. Basil said, "Come in and shut the door, Troyce." The administrator did as he was told.

Basil took a moment to order his thoughts, then asked, "Is it true you gave DuCange permission to sell the gimmals?"

"Yes," Troyce answered easily.

"Were you not aware of the Surchatain's ban on them? I had notices posted in the market square."

Troyce shrugged, averting his eyes. "I have authority over trade matters. The Surchatain himself gave me that authority."

"That does not extend to overturning his decrees," Basil answered calmly. "No one has the authority to do that—not you, not me, not even Surchataine Deirdre. That is the law; you know that. Why have you deliberately broken the law?"

Troyce assessed him with an unnerving confidence. "Some laws are in need of revision. The people should not be unduly bound to an unwise decree from the Surchatain."

Basil rumbled dangerously, "You are advocating treason."

"Certainly not," said Troyce. "Simply reform."

Basil eyed him, seeing with stark clarity Troyce's clever plan: to quest for power by stirring up groundless discontent among a fat and spoiled people. Yet Basil also saw that stern measures would merely strengthen Troyce's cause. Censure and banishment would release him from service to Roman so that he could speak freely against the Surchatain and, moreover, give substance to his complaint. Basil could already hear him crying, *See how the Surchatain punishes honest men for seeking fairness!*

Patiently, as if instructing a child, Basil told Troyce, "Because you are continually overstepping your authority, I believe you have not learned the meaning of loyalty to the Surchatain. So, I am temporarily removing you from your post as administrator, and placing you under Sevter as secretary. I will issue an official decree to that end. When Sevter reports to me that you are behaving responsibly, I will consider reinstating you."

Troyce gazed at him with eyes slightly widened, but otherwise his face was a mask. When he did not reply, Basil said, "You are dismissed."

Troyce turned on his heel and left the room, neglecting to bow.

Roman's party rode up the deserted thoroughfare of Corona, scanning side streets and shops as they passed by. There was certainly not a person to be seen. "Have all the people left?" muttered Colin. No one answered him, for the answer was in evidence all around them.

They stopped in the market square beside the well and watering fountain. Roman directed, "Kam, go check the city gates. Carefully.

Return at once if you see Bloods." The Second clucked to his horse and spurred out of the square.

In a house several streets away, in the same dismal room, Graydon sat on the floor rocking back and forth, staring into space. After being routed by Roman's handful, he had come back to this room for solace, but had found something else waiting for him instead. He suddenly laughed in a high-pitched, unnatural voice and then, just as suddenly, stopped. His expression changed to that of a little child's; he folded his hands and recited, "Four to a barrel, six to a bin, eight to a bushel, when will you come home again?"

Then he collapsed over his knees in a fit of weeping, but an instant later sat up at attention, his mind and body pliable as fresh clay. "Yes, he is doomed," he said loudly, as if in response to a statement. "Yes, I will watch." He took to rocking again as the door banged open to admit Captain Berk.

"You lost them all, Graydon," spat Berk. "They ran like rabbits. Where's all this power you have, sorcerer?" he demanded sarcastically.

Graydon stilled his rocking. "Bring me a mirror," he said in a voice low and hollow.

"A mirror? Why?" Berk asked rebelliously.

"Bring me a MIRROR!" repeated Graydon. He did not move from the floor, but the force of that last word flung Berk out of the room and slammed him against the corridor wall. Berk scampered away. But, out of fear, he soon returned, carrying a large looking glass. This he propped up on the wall in front of the rocking sorcerer.

Graydon gestured at the mirror, mumbling something Berk did not understand. Then the Captain gasped to see the mirror cloud over, then clear again to present an image. It was of Roman and his companions standing with their horses in the market square . . .

They were watering the horses as they waited for Kam, though the animals did not need it, and no one spoke except in whispers. The silence pressed threateningly around them.

They heard the *clop clop* of Kam's horse before they saw him, and by the time he appeared in the square, he was met by seventeen expectant or anxious faces. He broke the spell of stillness with his booming voice: "Surchatain, you won't believe this, but the gates are standing open and there's not a Blood in sight."

"I'd believe anything, at this point," replied Roman. "Now, Orvis— where do we look for that book?"

"The first place would be their old shop and house," decided Orvis, and he guided them down a side street.

116

They pulled up to a small, dingy shop with a broken door. The group left their horses and Roman stepped up to the door. He pushed it open on creaking hinges.

He crossed the threshold into a dusty, long-vacated front room. Most anything of value had been removed from it. Orvis and the others filed in behind Roman. Someone went to a window and broke open the boards covering it.

Roman pierced the persistent, eerie deadness of the air, directing, "Everyone split up and search anywhere a book might be hidden. Pry up the floorboards and test the walls."

The group dispersed, and soon the busy sounds of search were heard from every corner. Deirdre stayed in the front room of the shop with Roman. He was not searching yet, but looking, surveying—taking in the walls, the ceiling, the floor—and as Deirdre knew, inwardly praying. But then he gave his head a brief, befuddled shake and began stamping the floor, listening for hollow sounds.

Deirdre busied herself picking at the wooden planks of the walls. There was really no place to hide a large book that she could see, unless it was within the structure of the house itself. She pried off a plank to expose the mud bricks of the wall. Curious, she chipped at it with her knife until she had dug through to another piece of wood.

This find excited her, so she dug earnestly at it until suddenly it fell off and she saw daylight through the hole. Embarrassed, Deirdre glanced around, hoping no one had seen her demonstrate her ignorance of how houses were built.

She moved on to other planks, knocking and poking. Everyone searched most diligently. But, after half an hour, Orvis reluctantly approached Roman and said, "Surchatain, I do not believe it is here. We have looked everywhere."

Roman responded, "All right, then. Where else did you think it might be?"

Orvis lowered his brows. "Well, Galen and the innkeeper were friends. It might be hidden at the inn."

"To the inn, then," Roman said simply.

Deirdre heard mumbled, "Are we going to search the whole inn?"

Someone else shrugged in reply, but Titian turned on the complainer and said scathingly, "Tuss, you're so blasted lazy, it's a marvel I could ever get you to work." Tuss reddened and glanced toward Roman in front, but the Surchatain just smiled ahead slightly.

They arrived at the inn, finding it vacant as well. Roman directed them, "Titian, you take several and go to the south wing. Nihl, you take a few to the north. Deirdre, you and the women search the kitchen and dining areas. Kam, you and the rest go through the courtyard

and stables. Except Colin—you'll come with me to the storerooms."
Each went as instructed and began to search again.

Roman and Colin went through the storerooms one by one, rummaging through feed sacks and plunging their arms into barrels of grain. They poked sticks into wine vats and dug through crates of spoiling fruit. Finally, they resorted to overturning every large container in sight to reveal the contents. This method dislodged numerous little creatures but nothing like a book.

By the time Roman and Colin had finished digging through all the storerooms, the others were beginning to return from their assignments. They met in the dining hall. "We did everything but tear down the walls," said Kam. "It's just not here, Surchatain."

Roman stood thinking. "Or not where we can get to it."

"Roman, I'm hungry," pleaded Deirdre, and the others shifted restlessly. They were all tired of this unprofitable effort.

He nodded in resignation. "We will continue later. Back to the palace." He turned to go and the rest followed, relieved.

On their way back through the entryway of the inn, they passed a large, beveled looking glass which hung on the wall. Deirdre glanced in it to smooth a blond lock, then gasped and grabbed Roman's arm. "There it is! Sitting out on the table!"

They whirled to a small table across from the looking glass. There was nothing on it. Roman glanced quizzically at Deirdre. "But—" she protested, turning back to the mirror, "there it is!"

They looked. Sure enough, the looking glass showed the table holding a large, worn, leather volume. But the table itself held nothing. In unison, they looked back and forth from the mirror to the table. Roman passed his hand all over the table top and felt nothing but wood.

He took the mirror off the wall, which was plain and smooth behind it. "Tear up that wall," Roman directed Kam, who in turn sent Lew to a tool bin so they wouldn't dull their swords unnecessarily.

Roman held the mirror and looked down into it. It reflected him and the others around him truly. It reflected the walls and a view of the dining room without error. But whenever it was pointed toward that table, it showed the book.

Lew, meanwhile, returned with an axe and knocked a man-sized hole in the clay-and-wattle wall. A rat scurried out, drawing shrieks from a few of the maids, but that was all the wall hid.

Roman held the glass facing the table and told Deirdre, "Put your hand on the table again." She did, and the looking glass showed her placing her hand on the book. "Try to pick it up," he instructed. She did, but, of course, came up with empty air. She tried again and again,

118

watching in the mirror. It reflected her somehow missing each time she tried to grasp it.

Orvis muttered, "That figures. It's a sorcerer's book. It's bound in the looking glass by a spell."

"Is it in the glass or on the table?" queried Roman.

"In the glass, to be sure. I should have remembered—that's a favorite spell, to put things in mirrors, making them look as if they're in the room."

"Do you know how to get it out of the mirror?" Roman asked him.

"No. Only a sorcerer could do that."

"Well then, if we destroy the mirror, will we destroy the book? Or make it inaccessible?" posed Roman.

Orvis looked at him and there was a breathless silence. "I don't know, but it's bound to bring evil on the one who tries it," he finally whispered.

Roman cocked his head and looked down into the mirror. "You think so? What will happen if I try it?"

"I—do—not—know," Orvis repeated, fear causing every word to come out staccato.

Roman held the mirror a moment longer, but his mind was already set. "Very well, then."

He set the looking glass to rest against the wall, and firmly took the axe Lew had brought from the tool bin. Roman planted himself in front of the mirror and the others dropped back. Then he lifted the axe to smash it to pieces.

At once the mirror clouded, and sparks and flashes danced across its surface. Then an inhuman voice issued from it: *Touch this glass, and you will see hell!*

Roman did not even blink. He brought the axe head down upon the glass with a mighty crash.

CHAPTER 14

AT FIRST the mirror did not break. But it began to shudder—slowly at first, then with a force that seemed to make the walls of the entryway heave. Roman stepped back, bracing himself to strike it again if necessary.

But suddenly the mirror *imploded*. Roman was sucked forward. And then he was gone. His companions stood dumbfounded, staring at the broken glass. Deirdre came to life and screamed, "Roman!" Falling on her knees before the frame hung with mirror shards, she groped all around the floor and wall. He had simply vanished.

"Roman, oh Roman," she moaned. Nihl put a shaking hand on her shoulder and knelt before the looking glass. His fingers tightened. "Look," he whispered. The others pressed around to see.

Reflected in the jagged pieces of glass, they saw Roman lying prostrate in a dark pit. And they saw all that was around him.

As he came to, groggy and shaken, Roman raised up on his elbow and opened his eyes. At first he could see nothing, it was so dark, but gradually a weak red light illumined his surroundings so that he could see—nothing.

All was a gloomy, nether region of shapeless, empty land. He was lying in the bottom of a shallow pit that reminded him somewhat of a trap for stupid animals.

He brought himself to his knees, struggling to breathe, for the air around was noxious and stinking. The deeper he inhaled, the more he felt the need for air in his stinging lungs.

Then a sound reached his ears—*tramp, tramp, tramp, tramp*—it was faint at first but quickly grew loud. His heart faltered and he could not rise further, listening as the ominous sound grew and filled his ears. *Tramp, tramp, tramp, tramp*—the relentless approach of a massive army.

Run! Escape! But he had no power to run. Only with great effort could he stand and look up out of the pit. He *was* a helpless, stupid animal, trapped and waiting for destruction to come.

Suddenly the marching stopped. And then the ridge of the pit filled with forms which looked down on their quarry—immense, black forms

120

with faces so twisted and deformed as to sicken him. But Roman did not even have the power to look away.

They descended en masse into the pit. The first to reach him threw a sticky rope, which wrapped around his neck to drag him along. They just absorbed him into their march as they continued through the pit and up the other ridge toward their destination.

Roman stumbled along in the midst of them because he was helpless not to. He was utterly overwhelmed by the force they exerted, sucking up everything in their path, heedless. The terror of their presence should have made him faint mercifully away by now, but at this moment, he was strangely numb. Escape was meaningless. Destruction was certain. He plodded on, blind and unthinking . . . *lost.*

Then one of the black forms turned its hideous face toward him and opened its mouth, exhaling a cloud which engulfed Roman's head, stinging him fiercely. As he raised his arms, trying vainly to sweep it away, he saw that it was actually a swarm of tiny winged creatures with human faces. They stung him with streams of cursing, accusations, and mocking laughter, and no matter how he wrenched and swatted, they tenaciously clung about him.

Suddenly he realized that he was able to see them because the red glow had become stronger. And he was sweating profusely. He peered ahead and saw the source of the light—a huge lake that burned with ferocity from shore to shore. It was a lake of leaping flames, red and cruel and unquenchable. He dropped his arms from fending off the forgotten swarm, because he comprehended with fresh horror that the army was marching straight to the lake—*into* the lake. And he was inextricably caught up with them.

The heat became unbearable, and still they marched forward, determined nothing would stop them. Roman's mouth and eyes dried to crustiness, and he felt his hair singe. The vanguard before him reached the shores and plunged into the waves of fire, screaming in agony, but going on.

Roman was dragged gasping to the edge. As he looked down at the flames with no hope or breath to rescue himself, he whimpered weakly, "Oh, Lord Jesus . . ."

His foot went forward to take him into the lake but landed on rock instead. His other foot came up to join the first on the rock, and he stopped. The swarm of tiny creatures about him dropped crackling and sizzling, and the hordes passed by him in their blind plunge into the abyss of fire. He startled to see Captain Berk go by him, clawing and screaming, to be consumed in the flames. But Roman, standing on the safety of the rock, no longer even felt the heat of the blaze. Gazing about, he saw several other captives also standing on the rock.

He felt compelled to look up, and saw a gorgeous sky of purple and mother-of-pearl. Across it, in a wide panorama, he saw presented to his eyes a scene of a man hanging on a cross, being taunted and stabbed. Black forms resembling those that had dragged Roman to the pit were flocking around the man like vultures. As he watched the scene, Roman perceived a terrible battle taking place between the apparently helpless victim and the black forms—a battle that shook the earth and darkened the skies above it.

Then the man on the cross hung his head and died. But rather than defeat, his death seemed to indicate something else, for the black forms began falling like lead plummets, falling a great, immeasurable distance into the lake of fire below.

The man was taken down from the cross and sealed into a rock tomb. Roman witnessed the sun setting, rising, setting, rising, and then the man bursting from the tomb in brilliant splendor and power.

Roman wept as he watched, recognizing the spectacle. The Man who had been crucified now filled the sky, wielding might and compassion like weapons of war. After winning the great battle, He was now able to extend His strong arm downward to the captives suspended in the fire and say, "Come up from there."

Roman felt himself lifted from the rock and drawn skyward. The others on rock were drawn upward also. Upward and upward, higher and higher—the red heat and noxious fumes faded, overcome by shimmering light and clean, pure air.

Catching his breath with giddiness, Roman felt drenched in life and wild, unrestrained joy as the Victor drew him closer to Himself. And there were other things surrounding Roman as he ascended—lush green landscapes and fertile fields; crystal rivers and gardens blazing in colored glory; and a city, a great city, with walls and gates of precious gems.

All these he only quickly glimpsed, for there was another impression which overwhelmed him as he soared heavenward—the gratitude for a rescue so spectacular; the indebtedness to a Rescuer so powerful; the determination to cast himself at the feet of the Crucified once he ever stopped ascending. One thought seared through the surging tide of adoration: *So this is what it means to be saved.*

At once he was stopped. Or rather, held at a pause. He did not know on what he stood or where he was, but around him were many others, standing as he was. They were surrounded by such a complexity of sights and sounds that Roman was unable to perceive it all. The impression he received was one of purposeful, exuberant activity.

There was music, and singing, which made his chest swell with emotion. There were colored lights dancing all about him, too. Iridescent and shimmering, they were tantalizingly elusive—impossible to focus

122

on but impossible to ignore. As Roman watched them with the wonder of a child, trying to discern meaning in their movement, he realized with a start that they were *alive*, and dancing with what could only be spontaneous joy.

He was distracted by someone nearby exclaiming, "Adele!" He turned to see a ragged old man embrace an indescribably beautiful woman in fulfillment of what must have been years of longing and patient hope. Roman pondered how much love could make her take the dirty old fellow so passionately into her spotless white arms. Then he saw others being greeted by more of these white-clad, shining people, whom they seemed to know intimately. He began to wonder if, perhaps, there were someone here he knew . . .

Then he saw her at a distance and gasped, "Mother!" She looked so very young and glowing, with raven-black hair, and in spite of the distance between them he could see clearly the expression on her face. She was smiling at him the way she used to when he brought a frog or a bunch of wildflowers home for her approval. But she would come no closer, as if it were understood that she could not—and he did not know how to cross over to her.

Then, as if silently summoned, all eyes turned in one direction to see thick dark clouds. It seemed that they had been brought up close to a brewing thunderstorm. The dancing lights held themselves to an excited vibration; the singing paused on a low, sustained note.

Roman stared spellbound at the clouds, his heart palpitating with anticipation. There was something—Someone—hidden in the covering of cloud, and the yearning to be allowed to see beyond it was excruciating.

As if in answer, the clouds began to break, and white light flashed out at the parting seams. Roman sank to his knees under the weight of expectation.

The clouds burst apart, showering light. Roman raised his hands to cover his eyes, but found the light did not blind him. It throbbed lifelike around him, emanating from a Man standing in prominence, surrounded by a great number of superior beings who were prostrate before Him.

Weakly and timidly, Roman peered through the light, which to his horror revealed him naked and dirty before the shining beings around him. Burning with shame, Roman reached down to cover himself, but saw that his hands were dripping with blood. Moreover, he was not just dirty, but stained with filth. He rubbed his skin anxiously, desperate to be clean, but what soil came off revealed foul, oozing sores and scars of disease.

Then the Man, Purity Himself, stretched out His hands to him—

to *Roman,* who, cringing, allowed himself to be touched. The hands that touched him were the only feature of the Man he could see clearly. They were scarred, front and back, with puncture wounds and torn flesh—the price of Roman's rescue. But as he gazed at those hands, he heard the Man say, "Welcome, Roman."

Welcome? I? Filthy and diseased? He gestured despairingly at his wretched condition. But in looking down, he saw that his skin now was clean and healthy. He was no longer naked, either, but clothed in a gleaming white tunic, as were others of this crowd. This he recognized as having been accomplished merely by the Man's touch.

A moment before—or was it an eternity ago?—Roman had thought the horror of hell unbearable. But the transport of the Redeemer's welcome exceeded it on the opposite end of the spectrum to an infinite degree. Roman fell on his face in speechless worship.

The Man caused Roman to rise and told him, "This is not your hour, Roman. That will come soon enough. The others need you now." The thick clouds merged again to separate Roman from the beauty of His presence, and Roman began to descend.

"No!" he cried, struggling. "No! No! Let me stay!" He screamed his disappointment as the dancing lights vanished.

But there was a hand on his shoulder, and his beloved Commander Galapos said, eyes twinkling, "Get past your stubbornness and obey your Sovereign, my boy." Roman hazily saw his father Eudymon somewhere near Galapos and also, standing close by, someone he felt he had known a long time—someone supernatural who had protected his life countless times. . . . Then there was nothing.

"Roman . . . oh, Roman . . ." He heard a sweet, soft voice from a great distance. Then he felt himself being rocked in tender, feminine arms. A delicate hand stroked his hair from his face, and soft lips were pressed repeatedly to his forehead.

He felt all this as consciousness returned to him. Before opening his eyes, he heard himself say clearly, "I understand."

There was quick movement around him. He looked up into Deirdre's beautiful, anxious face, and she whispered, "What, Roman? What do you understand?" Nihl, Kam, Colin, and the others were pressed closely around.

Roman gathered his brows, raising himself weakly. "Someone was telling me I was not ever in danger of being thrown into the lake of fire, because I had already confessed Jesus. All that happened was just a demonstration of what had already been accomplished."

He then realized this would need explaining, and twisted in her arms to tell her rapidly, "Deirdre—I woke in a barren, dark land, where I couldn't see or breathe—" but she was already nodding.

Nihl said, "Surchatain, we saw you in the mirror. We saw it all—the pit, the army, the fire—"

"But Roman!" interrupted Deirdre, "When you were taken up to the light, what was it that you saw? We saw you stop, and the expression on your face! But we could not see what you were seeing, and then the image vanished."

Roman feebly answered, "I saw heaven, and . . . I saw the Lord."

Several pairs of widened eyes glanced around. "What . . . what did He look like?" Deirdre asked carefully.

He blinked. "I can't tell you; I don't know. I could not see His face. I can only recall the unbearable beauty, the light, and the love . . ." Just saying the words brought back the sensations that weakened him all over again. "I could never tell you adequately what I saw—I haven't the words. I only know that there is not enough adoration in the world to match His worth."

There was a moment of wondering silence, then Roman began shakily to rise. Nihl and Kam bumped each other in reaching out to help him.

Roman halted, swaying. "What became of the book that started all this?" he murmured.

Nihl pointed to a heap of smoldering ashes on the floor near the fractured mirror. The odor of the pit rose faintly from the dying ashes. Roman smiled crookedly. "That He also accomplished. I saw hell, as the dark powers promised, but they did not tell me I would see heaven also." He added, "We can go eat now," and Deirdre laughed weakly.

They returned to their horses in the inn courtyard and mounted, the whole group of them mute. On the thoroughfare leading to the palace, they heard running hoofbeats and reined up their horses.

They listened, scanning the streets they could see, looking for the rider. Then Kam shouted, "Ho!" and they all saw Graydon galloping up a side street toward them, alone.

As he reached them, he threw himself from his horse and fell toward Roman on Fidelis. Nihl pulled his sword but Roman motioned to him to put it down. Fidelis reared slightly as Graydon clutched the saddlebow, sucking in erratic breaths. His face and hands were red, as if slightly burned, and Roman was astonished to detect the smell of the pit also on his clothes. The group watched him tensely.

"I saw it," Graydon said between breaths. "I alone saw it and lived. The dark powers opened a companion mirror for us, intending to show me your destruction in the fire. Instead, I saw you placed on the rock by another power that intruded when you spoke that name. And then the fury of the dark powers broke out through the mirror upon us— Berk, beside me, was burned alive where he stood. And I was pulled forward into the march of death. I myself was walking into those flames!" He shook Roman's saddle in his attempt to make Roman understand the horror of it.

"I said the name of Jesus as you did," he continued, leaning on the horse. "I don't know where I had heard it before. Yet I never imagined there was such power in a name—never knew that He was waiting for me to say it, for He placed me on the rock also! Why? Why would He do that?" Graydon shouted. Roman gaped, unable to answer.

"And there—on the rock—I saw the dark powers clearly for the first time. Horror! What hatred, what blind, vicious rage—against *me*. But on the rock, the power of the name I spoke made them release me. Nothing else could have. And I awoke before the broken mirror, alive and free. I had forgotten what it was like to be free. I was directed to come surrender to you. Here I am. Do what you will. It does not matter anymore."

Having said all this, Graydon blinked up at Roman, and Roman motioned slightly. "Get back on your horse and come with us." As Graydon limply obeyed, Roman took up Fidelis' reins, frowning. This was certainly victory, but such an unexpected one, and somehow unsatisfying to him.

Demanding mercy for Graydon had been a fine theoretical exercise, but the actual doing of it was not so much to his liking. He had assumed all along that the Lord would do away with Graydon as He had Tremelaine, and Roman need only stand aside and watch. So what was he to do with Graydon now?

Roman glanced back at the other Selecans. They looked indifferent, sullen, some even angry at the mercy extended Graydon. And in perfect honesty, Roman felt the same. That admission awakened him to the reason for his dissatisfaction: *He does not deserve to be spared.*

But before he could work up a good strong righteous indignation, a chastising thought came clearly, as from an old friend who knew him well: *Neither, my boy, do you.*

Roman looked over his shoulder at the defeated sorcerer, and he remembered the Master's acceptance of himself, dirty and diseased as he was. Judging by the look on Graydon's face, he, too, was thoroughly aware of his state before the Lord. If Roman were more acceptable, it was only because of what the Lord Himself had done. There was a

126

reason He had said, "Whoever comes to me I will never drive away"—no one came to Him righteous, or remained with Him without being made righteous.

They took the thoroughfare at a measured, thoughtful pace. Kam caught sight of someone watching them from behind a building, but thought it not important enough to mention. Deirdre was the first to break the silence, asking gently, "Graydon, where is your family?"

"They fled with the others, after our confrontation in the hall. I do not know where they went."

"Perhaps they will come back now," she said encouragingly. He lifted his shoulders in resignation.

Upon their arrival at the palace, a few servants took the horses to the stables while the rest of the group sat down around the large table in the mirrored dining hall. Without being asked, Titian took several servants with him into the kitchen to bring out meat. Watching him leave, Roman received a spark of illumination in his befuddled brain.

"Surchatain Roman," Graydon interrupted his thoughts. "I have surrendered to you. I ask you now what you intend to do with me."

"I?" responded Roman, easing back in his chair. "Why, nothing." Graydon's eyes took on a gleam of hope. The others looked up, shocked. "You are not my problem," said Roman. "Your Surchatain will decide what to do with you."

"Not you, sir?" asked Graydon, the gleam dying. "I have given Corona to you."

Roman firmly shook his head. "I do not wish to annex any of Seleca . . . yet."

"One of your officers, then?" posed Graydon, glancing over the Lystrans.

"No," said Roman. Nihl, Kam, and Colin seemed relieved.

"Who is left?" demanded Graydon. "Surely not one of the townspeople!" But the townspeople leaned forward in interest.

"No," admitted Roman. By now everyone was baffled. Roman smiled and stood as Titian entered the hall and put a platter of cold mutton on the table. "Titian," Roman said in a tone commanding him to stand at attention. "I proclaim you acting Surchatain of Seleca. I give you control of the palace, land, and people. Do you accept the charge to rule Seleca by my laws, answering to me, with all the wisdom God has given you?"

Titian's white brows arched up in surprise, then he grinned broadly and bowed very finely. "Your servant accepts the charge, Surchatain." The others in the hall sat dumbfounded.

Roman added, "I will send you advisors to give you aid where you lack. And if anyone refuses to serve under you, I will regard it as an offense against myself."

Nihl smiled and murmured, "Well done, Surchatain Roman."

Kam also apprehended the genius of the move, in that Roman's highest criterion for selecting a governor was loyalty, and Titian had already proved it when he had stood to gain nothing. Kam recalled, "Surchatain Galapos often said that only those who had served as the lowest should serve as the highest. Well done, Roman."

"I have some to commend to your service, Titian," Roman continued. "Your own folk, Lew and Vida and Orvis, have proved themselves useful. I think you should attach them to your service in high positions." Titian cocked his head toward the three, who remembered themselves enough to bow to him.

Even Orvis looked Roman straight in the eye and said, "You have made me believe. I'll do whatever you say."

"There is your Surchatain," Roman told him, indicating Titian. Orvis inclined his head just as seriously to the former head cook.

Then Roman said, "Titian, your first responsibility is to decide what to do with your former lord." All eyes followed as he pointed to Graydon.

Titian squinted at the perspiring defendant. "Surchatain Roman would not kill you when he had the chance, and I won't be the one to put your neck in a noose now. But is it right for you to go free among these folks you were going to let Galen crucify?" Graydon began to wring his hands.

"I think it's best to send you off, Lord Graydon," continued the new Surchatain. "Take your horse and be on your way. You are banished from Corona."

Graydon bowed to Titian, relief vivid in his face. He turned to go out through the audience hall, but met up with one of the servants entering, who said, "There's a mob on hand outside—don't know where they all came from. But they're demanding that Graydon be crucified." The servant looked at Graydon as if he thought that entirely appropriate.

But Roman leaped forward and took Titian's arm. "Time to introduce you. Graydon, take your horse out the back way. The rest of you, come out front with us. Carry your swords."

As the group fell in place to escort them out and Graydon melted back, Roman had a final word. "Graydon!" The other attended, but did not look him in the eye. "The Lord has been extremely gracious to you—had it been up to me, I would have killed you. But He demanded that you be spared. Remember that. He will not tolerate your ever returning to the dark powers."

128

A look of abhorrence crossed Graydon's face, and he shuddered. "I understand," he whispered, then he was gone.

"I wouldn't worry over him, Surchatain," remarked Titian. "He's a broken man."

Roman nodded, thinking, *But a broken man can come back stronger than ever, for evil or for good.* He shook off the thought and steered Titian into the audience hall, pointing toward the throne. As Titian seated himself, a group of townspeople burst into the hall, led by several of the Bloods. Roman stepped up before them and they halted.

"Where is Graydon?" demanded one Blood, rope in hand.

"Graydon has been deposed," announced Roman. "I have set in his stead a new Surchatain, Titian. And anyone who refuses to serve under Titian will answer to me." Roman walked over to place himself squarely in front of the Blood with the rope. "Will you serve peaceably?"

"Titian?" echoed the soldier in disbelief.

The new Surchatain stood. "Pindar, stop striking sparks when you need to be cleaning ashes. Now hold your tongue and listen. I want you to go around to every house and collect those circles and crosses and bring them back and pile them up in the front courtyard. Get those rascals behind you to help dig up those crosses along the thoroughfare and pile them in the courtyard, too. Cass, you and your brother go up to that torture room and bring down all those machines—throw them out front with the rest of the garbage."

"That will take all day and all night!" protested Pindar, but he had forgotten the rope in his hands.

"Then you had better find some of those fellows in the Third and Fourth that ran off and make them lend some muscle!" snapped Titian. "Tomorrow morning we will send the Surchatain of Lystra home with a pretty bonfire. Well?" he cracked.

"Surchatain!" exclaimed Pindar, saluting. The mob suddenly dispersed into a work party carrying out orders.

Roman looked back at Titian in genuine surprise. "You handled that rather well."

Titian winked, "If I can make a kitchen crew work, I ought to be able to move any mule." The others in the group studied Titian with new and subdued respect.

Roman sighed, tired. "I suppose that does finish our task here. Only . . . Kam, I want you and Colin to remain until I send advisors to replace you. Tomorrow, Deirdre, Nihl, and I will leave for Westford. Questions?"

At first, no one spoke. As they stood there, Deirdre happened to glimpse Izana on the edge of the group. The maid did not speak or shift, but Deirdre saw the yearning in her eyes.

Deirdre also looked at Nihl standing beside Roman. He was as unmoved as the Fastnesses. She wanted to kick him, but instead sent up a quick prayer for illumination on his behalf.

Nihl blinked. "Well, if there are no questions—" Roman was saying, as he sheathed his sword.

"Surchatain," Nihl said suddenly.

"Nihl?" Roman gave him full attention and waited.

"Surchatain, I . . ." he seemed to have some difficulty pulling the words out. Roman watched him patiently, without prodding. "Surchatain, I ask permission to take Izana with us to Westford." This took everyone but Deirdre by surprise.

Roman shut his gaping mouth to regain a stately appearance, and said gravely, "Well, that depends. You know how I feel about my soldiers wenching, especially my officers. What do you intend to do with her in Westford?"

"Don't abuse me, Surchatain," said Nihl, peeved. "Of course I will be honorable and—marry her."

Izana's eyes took on a meltingly warm expression, but Roman and Nihl exchanged a quick look of understanding. "You have permission, my brother," Roman said quietly, in a tone almost of gratitude.

Izana crossed the room and embraced Nihl's neck. Deirdre shook his shoulder, exclaiming, "I know you will be happy, Nihl!" He murmured thanks to her, but held Izana.

"Well," Roman cleared his throat, "if no one has any other surprises . . . Surchatain Titian, will you show us guest chambers now? I believe we have seen enough of the dungeon and the kitchen."

130

PART TWO

WESTFORD

CHAPTER 15

BASIL SAT in his chambers late that night, poring over the ledger of palace expenses. Repeatedly, he shook his head, flipping back over a page or two, then scratching out sums and subtractions with his quill pen. "That is not right," he murmured, scrutinizing a figure in the ledger. A page later, he gave another shake of his grey head and a firmer: "That is *not* right."

He straightened and strode to the door. To the courier standing outside, he ordered, "Summon Sevter and Troyce to me immediately." As the courier left, Basil returned to the desk to tap the thick ledger in agitation.

He waited an unreasonable length of time, growing more and more irate at the delay. Finally, Sevter entered with a quick knock, the courier and Captain Olynn behind him. "Counselor—" Sevter bowed breathlessly, "I am here at your summons—"

"Troyce seems to be gone, however," Olynn interrupted, determined to give the report himself. "The man we had watching him did not even realize he was not in his chambers," he added, red-faced.

Basil froze for just an instant. "Give a silent alarm to hunt for him as a fugitive," he ordered with frosty calm. "Sevter, come with me now." Captain Olynn and the courier raced down the corridor in one direction; Basil and Sevter shot down the other.

The Counselor and the overseer came to the nursery door. Pausing to take the torch from the corridor sconce, Basil muttered tightly, "No guard." They pushed open the door, which was unbolted. The two tiptoed to the bed of the Chatain and drew back the curtain.

The bedding was mussed and empty. With constricted hearts, they ran to the nursemaid's adjoining room. It also was vacant. The two men whirled to stare at each other with eyes full of dread. Then Basil commanded, "Find Captain Olynn and change my order. He is to sound a first alarm and every man is to turn out to search for Troyce and the Chatain Ariel."

Sevter bolted out. Basil stood in the empty chamber, raising his fists to heaven in anguish and crying, "Lord God, take my life before you allow Troyce to slay the Chatain!"

Troyce stealthily led the nursemaid, carrying a sleepy Ariel, out the back gate toward the forest. This gate had been recently reconstructed by Roman to increase its security. He had narrowed it so that only one horse and rider could pass through at a time, and had faced it on the outside with stone which matched that of the wall so perfectly that, when closed, it could not be discerned as a gate at all and could not be opened from without. Roman had meant to limit its use to that of an emergency exit—which was exactly the use Troyce made of it now. As he passed through it with Gusta, he propped it open ever so slightly with a small rock.

"Where is the guard that is supposed to be stationed here?" Gusta whispered edgily.

"I do not know," responded Troyce, who a few minutes earlier had sent the guard to investigate a fictitious corpse in the courtyard. "Men neglecting their duty is a sign that rebellion is at hand. Basil has won over so many to his cause, I fear the revolt could occur at any time."

The trumpet of alarm from the palace startled them both. "What is the alarm for?" she gasped.

"There—it means Basil has begun to strike! I got you out barely in time!" he breathed in relief, not entirely feigned.

"Where are you going to hide us?" she asked as they ran for the black cover of the forest.

"In a comfortable little house, well hidden," he answered reassuringly. In the dark, he felt for the dagger under his cloak.

"I must know where it is, or I cannot go," she argued. "And I must send word to Olynn. He is a trusted friend who would not betray the Surchatain."

"I told you, no one can be trusted! Basil has convinced so many of the soldiers that the Surchatain is not returning, how do I know Olynn is not one of them?" He was trying to keep her close by his left side, but every time he gently took her arm, she drew away from him.

"Because *I* trust Olynn," Gusta replied. He halted, taken by surprise. The tone she used implied a confidence based on friendship—certainly

134

a greater confidence than what she had in Troyce or his position.

The time had come; the future of Lystra was at stake. What must be done, must be done now. He drew out his dagger, urging, "Gusta, listen to me!" In the blackness she would never know what happened.

But from a tiny patch of moonlight that somehow found a straight path through the thick branches overhead, she caught the glint from his knife. Instantly she ran with the child. Troyce shot after her, and was lifting the dagger to her fleeing back when his foot caught neatly under the gnarled root of an old tree and he sprawled headlong. He quickly raised himself again, listening for her steps.

Silence, but for the wind in the trees. He turned his head to listen in the other direction. An owl hooted mournfully. She must have stopped and hidden somewhere close by, hoping he would pass her over in the darkness.

He opened his mouth to advise her of the futility of escape, but then thought better of it. "Gusta, wait, my dear! I drew my knife because I fear the wolves in this forest! You know about the wolves, don't you? Please, let me take you to a place of safety! You may walk behind me if it will ease your mind, but don't expose the child to the dangers of the forest!"

He paused to listen. There was a rustle to his right. He went that way, leading with the dagger, but it was only a night creature scuttling away into the underbrush.

He tried again: "Gusta, you cannot go back to the palace. The first man you meet may be one of Basil's hired assassins! And how will you send word to Olynn without Basil hearing of it? If you do not trust me, Gusta, the Chatain will die at his hands!"

Troyce stopped to listen once more, but now what he heard was the sound of searchers penetrating the forest. "They are coming now to kill him!" he whispered urgently as a last shot, before turning back toward the palace in frustration.

But now here was a problem. He could not get back in without being seen. How would he explain his presence in the forest, with the babe and nursemaid gone? The searchers were closing in.

He turned his dagger inward and ripped a hole through his coat and shirt. Then he clenched his teeth and gashed himself in the side— not deeply, but enough to bleed impressively. He lay down and propped the dagger through the artificial hole, then waited for the searchers to find him.

They did, very soon. With torches and swords they came thrashing through the forest and almost stumbled over him. Troyce heard loud exclamations and commands: "What the—!" "It's Lord Troyce! He's been stabbed!" "Send a report to the Captain, quick—here, Seth, help me lift him. Easy, now." They carried him moaning to the palace infirmary.

As the voices and footfalls faded, Gusta quietly rose from her hiding place and ran with the frightened child deeper into the woods. She had not been able to hear exactly what had made the soldiers take their torches and leave. Possibly, Troyce had been able to divert them away from her and the child—in which case, he must have been telling her the truth.

She wavered in her flight while Ariel clung to her neck. What if he were right, and the Counselor *was* attempting to take power? Basil *had* seemed preoccupied with knowing the child's whereabouts every moment. But surely Olynn could be trusted . . . couldn't he?

Olynn and Basil had always been staunchly loyal to Surchatain Roman. Did two such men change overnight? Or were they only now showing what they had always been?

Gusta stood in the agony of making a blind decision on which her and Ariel's lives precariously hung. One thing was clear: Someone was a traitor, and if she returned to the palace without knowing who, she would likely walk straight into a deathtrap.

But Troyce was right on one account—the forest was a perilous place to hide. Which was worse, to face wolves or traitors? In such a dilemma, Gusta at once did the most reasonable thing; she began to sob. Ariel whimpered, "Go home, Gussa. Pwease go home." She silenced herself and stroked his head to reassure him.

Then she remembered dear Surchatain Galapos and the medallion he had bequeathed to the child before going to his death in Goerge. Galapos had said God delivered those who called to Him for help. She had heard many stories of such deliverance—of Outpost One and of Roman's travels in Corona. But those were other times, other people. Here, now, how could God help her?

She heard a stick crack behind her and she jumped. She could only gasp out, "God help me—" as she saw the shape of a large animal gathering to spring.

Gusta wheeled to run, powered by a surge of terror. In the denseness of the night she ran blindly, one hand outstretched to warn of trees. She ignored branches slapping her face and briars catching her nightdress. She lost her slippers to twigs and roots but ran on unslowed, heedless to anything but saving the child. At every step she felt the animal pouncing behind her, barely a body length behind, chasing her to exhaustion.

She struck one foot on a sharp rock and almost tumbled down.

136

The beast took that opportunity to spring, and she veered to the left to escape. Pressing Ariel's head tightly to her shoulder, she continued to run sightlessly through the treacherous woods.

Stop. She did very suddenly, in time to slip feet first down the steep bank of an unseen ravine. She slid rudely on her rear, clutching Ariel to her chest, until she landed upright at the bottom. Overhead, she glimpsed a black shape leaping across the ravine in misguided pursuit.

Gusta shook with exhaustion and relief, leaning against the side of the ravine. Ariel raised his little head and calmly requested, "Do again." She laughed and cried weakly, kissing his face.

Something moved beside her and she leaped up with a startled cry. A hand grasped her arm but she was too weak to struggle. An old voice crackled, "Come with me."

Gusta twisted her arm free to feel a wrinkled, bony hand. That did not seem too dangerous, so she allowed the person to lead her through the ravine. It sloped upward as they walked, and then abruptly came to an end. But the person reached out and opened a door. Gusta stood blinking into a little candlelit room containing a table, a chair, a bed, and even a cozy fire. A window opened up the ceiling of the room, which was latticed with roots supporting it and descending downward.

The nursemaid entered in a stupor, then turned to look at the one who shut the door behind her. It was an old woman in widow's black. The woman carefully removed her cloak as Gusta watched silently. Then the widow eyed her and asked, "Are you in need, child?"

"I—I am running for my life and the life of this babe!" Gusta blurted as if the widow should have known. In her agitation, Gusta never thought to explain the situation at the palace which put them in the forest at midnight.

"What do you require, child?" the old woman asked serenely.

"Help!" Gusta exclaimed.

"In what form?" the woman asked.

"Why are you questioning me like this?" Gusta cried. "Can't you see I need help? Are you going to help me, or must I beg for it?" Part of her frustration lay in not knowing what to ask the woman to do for her.

The widow studied the distraught nursemaid with unruffled detachment. "It appears to me you need to be hidden and taken to safety."

"Do you know Lord Troyce?" Gusta asked on a sudden thought.

"I know him, but he does not know me," the widow replied, and Gusta was somehow relieved. The woman, meanwhile, was turning down the modest bed and plumping the straw pillow. "Sleep out the night, and I will go make arrangements," she said.

Gusta watched bemusedly as the old woman again donned her cloak and stepped back out. Then, because it seemed the most logical thing to do, the muddled nursemaid climbed wearily into bed with Ariel already asleep in her arms.

At the palace, Troyce had been laid in an infirmary bed and a physician called to tend him. Some of the soldiers stood by as the physician dressed the wound, then Basil stalked into the infirmary, Olynn and Sevter at his sides. "Where did you find him?" Basil asked a soldier.

"At the edge of the forest, Counselor. Lying wounded on the ground."

Basil asked the physician tightly, "How is he?"

"Not badly injured, Counselor. It appears to be just a glancing strike."

Then Basil looked down on the patient and demanded, "Where is the Chatain, Troyce?"

"You tell me, Counselor!" Troyce spat sarcastically. To the soldier by the bed, Troyce said, "I saw the good Counselor here trying to sneak the child and the nursemaid out of the palace. I followed him and accosted him in the forest, whereupon he turned and attacked me." The soldier raised his face in disbelief.

Basil went livid. "You are lying!"

Olynn coolly interrupted, speaking to Troyce: "That is not possible. The Counselor summoned me from his chambers to find you gone and the Chatain gone."

"Of course he planned it to look as if I did it! Don't you realize he is trying to usurp the Surchatain?" exclaimed Troyce.

"Traitor! How dare you accuse me?" sputtered Basil.

"Who is in a better position to take control, with Surchatain Roman gone?" Troyce suggested bitterly. The soldiers began looking dubiously at the Counselor.

"You are out of line, Administrator," Olynn said coldly. "As acting Commander, I have had opportunity to observe both you and the Counselor in the Surchatain's absence. Only *your* actions have been suspicious and irregular."

Troyce turned his eyes to the Captain. "Of course," he posed, "Basil cannot take power by himself. He must have the help of the army."

Now Olynn went red and drew his sword. "I should kill you for suggesting I would betray Surchatain Roman!"

But a soldier put a restraining hand on his chest. "There'll be no killing—yet," he said in a commanding tone. Olynn gazed at his fellow in surprise at the suspicion.

"Wait," urged Basil. "Wait. Do you see what he is doing? He is dividing us against ourselves. Let us not touch him, then. Our first

138

concern is to find the Chatain, then when the Surchatain returns, he will hear and decide between us."

"Well, that sounds fair, Counselor," said another soldier, "but suppose only you know where the Chatain is?" All the soldiers in the room looked at Basil now.

Then Sevter spoke up with calm, earnest restraint. "Hold, now. Shea was standing guard at the Counselor's door. You all know he is honest and reliable. Let's ask him if the Counselor ever had opportunity tonight to do as Troyce suggests. Or if any of the guards saw him leave with the Chatain and the nursemaid."

Troyce smiled, grateful that he had strategically engaged the guards along their escape route in other apparently pressing duties. And none of those men was standing in this room now. "If the good Counselor cannot arrange to get out of the palace unseen—or deliberately unnoticed—he's not very smart, for a counselor."

The soldiers stirred visibly. Sevter, Olynn, and Basil stared at each other in rising desperation. One fellow looked down at Troyce and drawled, "You're full of accusations, Lord Troyce. Have you any proof of what you say?"

"You ask for proof, when the child's life is in danger!" exclaimed Troyce.

"Listen, men!" ordered Olynn. They turned to him coolly. "Before he left, Surchatain Roman gave the Counselor command of the palace. Don't you know the Surchatain has the utmost faith in him to leave him with that responsibility? If we're to obey the Surchatain's final command, we must listen to the Counselor."

This time Troyce was shrewdly silent. A soldier observed, "Anyone can turn traitor."

"Yes," said Olynn quietly. "But if you condemn the wrong man, the Surchatain will have your head."

"If he returns," a man muttered. One soldier slipped out of the tension-filled room, and went to locate Captain Reuel.

Basil suddenly announced, "I will voluntarily hand over power to Troyce on one condition: that we unite first to find the Chatain. If Troyce is loyal as he says he is, surely he will not refuse to do that."

The soldiers turned back to Troyce, some nodding. He stretched in the bed, wincing to emphasize that he was wounded, and countered, "You can say that because you have already killed the Chatain."

"No!" exploded Basil.

"Then produce him!" challenged Troyce.

"I cannot, unless you tell me where you have taken him!" shouted Basil.

"It's a test of power, then," interposed one soldier. "Choose who you'll go with, men." He himself stood by Troyce's bed. Others joined him, but one came to stand by Basil and the room quickly divided.

"No!" cried Basil. "No! We *must not* allow ourselves to be pitted against each other—" But swords were already drawn and clashing.

CHAPTER 16

GUSTA AWAKENED from pleasant slumber as morning light came dancing down through the skylight. She blinked a moment, lost at first, then remembered their midnight flight and snapped her head around to her side. Ariel was sleeping deeply, eyes closed tightly in fatigue, forefinger in his mouth.

She sighed in gratitude, which made her recall that she had begun to ask God for help when they were attacked by that animal, whatever it was. Well, almost attacked. Chased to death, nearly. Chased . . . straight to this ravine and safe shelter.

The door opened and in came the widow woman, still wearing the black cloak. As she hung it neatly in its place beside the door, Gusta wondered if she had been out the whole night. The woman put an old, chipped flagon on the table and one cracked cup. Gusta rose from the bed as the widow poured the cup full from the flagon and held it out to the girl. She drank down clear, sweet spring water, then roused Ariel enough to make him drink some of it before his head bobbed down to his chest.

Their hostess put half a loaf of days-old bread on the table and said, "This is all I have." It was not an apology, just a statement of fact. Gusta knew better than to offend her by refusing it, so she ate a decent amount. But she could not wake Ariel sufficiently to feed any to him.

Gusta promised the woman, "You will be repaid for your kindness to us."

The widow said, "Take the child and come." Gusta carried the soundly sleeping Ariel and followed her.

They stepped through the door into the ravine, lit by spots of morning light filtered through the trees. They climbed up natural steps leading out to level ground, and Gusta looked around curiously as they walked

140

across the roof of the room. It appeared to be normal, solid ground on the edge of the ravine. She even had difficulty locating the skylight, but finally decided it was somewhere among the roots of a young birch tree.

The widow took her in a straight path through the woods without any word of explanation. Gusta had no notion of where they were going, or even where they were now, but it seemed pointless to question the woman after her unforced hospitality. If the woman had meant to do her any harm, she surely would have done it while they were sleeping.

Gusta went with her through crackling leaves and fragrant undergrowth until, unexpectedly, they came out of the trees to intercept the paved northbound market road. Gusta blinked in confusion before realizing that they had never been far from the palace. The widow stopped and looked southward down the road expectantly.

A moment later a peasant farmer driving a creaking, one-horse cart came within view. He pulled up beside them and nodded to the widow, then reached out to help Gusta climb up with Ariel. As she sat, somewhat baffled, the peasant clucked to the horse to start up again, waving to the widow as if confirming something understood between them.

Gusta stared at him, then wrenched around to say goodbye to the poor widow and assure her again of reward. But the woman was gone. So the nursemaid turned back to assess the peasant—who seemed to be a simple man, with an open, honest bearing and casual goodwill. "Where are we going?" Gusta asked him.

He cocked a speckled grey brow back at her. "Ya don't know? The widder paid me well to take ya to Outpost One."

Outpost One . . . ? Of course! Whatever was happening at the palace, she knew Captain Clatus and his men would die if necessary in defense of the Chatain. And the Captain would know better than anyone how to reach the Surchatain. Then Gusta startled, "The widow *paid* you? With what?"

"What this here was full of," he answered, showing her a fine leather money bag with an imprint of a shield bearing a cross and a lion. "I'm a man of my word. Since I been paid in advance, I got to get ya directly to the outpost, so ya just sit back and ride easy till we get there."

As that very morning broke with splendor over the palace of Corona, Roman, Deirdre, Nihl, and Izana saddled their animals in the rear courtyard, preparing to leave. Colin stood by, unhappily shifting from foot to foot.

Kam came out of the palace with a puckered grin. "Surchatain, they've got a nice little pile out front ready to be lit. Servants are

141

cleaning up the place and posting notices about the change in rulers. People are coming back from nowhere."

Roman nodded, smoothing the horse blanket. "Any sign of Graydon's family?"

"Not that I have seen," Kam replied.

As Roman pulled tight the cinch, Fidelis raised a rear hoof threateningly. Roman slapped a warning on the haunches and the hoof went down. Continuing to Kam, "If they come back, you will have to escort them out of Corona also. We must not leave any temptation for Graydon to break his banishment. But they are not our main concern. I am leaving you here to supervise Titian, and see that he does not get carried to extremes with his new power. Stay in the background, though—if matters get out of hand, I want you able to get yourself out of it. If I have to, I will come back. But if I do, it *will* be with an army and I *will* annex Seleca."

Roman broke off to lift Deirdre onto her saddle, and she appreciatively stroked his freshly shaven face. He never forgot that she preferred him cleanshaven.

As he swung up on the prancing Fidelis, he added, "Colin, I want you to supervise the army—what remains of it. I want you to concentrate on changing their attitude from being Bloods to that of a disciplined standing army. As I told Kam, you're to do this from the position of an informal advisor. If they won't heed you, come back to the outpost. I will send Nihl and enough of his men to convince them to change."

Nihl nodded at the mention of his name, though for once he was not attending exclusively to Roman. For Izana had obtained (with Deirdre's conniving) a shiny, ginger-colored dress, close-fitting and provocatively cut. Nihl's proud Polonti demeanor cracked slightly as he boosted Izana to her saddle; he did it with the adroitness of someone who had never seen either a horse or a woman before.

Roman observed them, then turned to Deirdre and muttered, "I blame you if I have lost my Commander."

"Me? Why?" she exclaimed innocently.

"You are a woman. That is reason enough," he answered gruffly, with an incongruous twinkle in his eye.

As the four of them rode toward the front gates, with Kam and Colin walking alongside, Titian appeared with a number of people carrying torches. The new Surchatain was dressed in the fine clothes Tremelaine had altered for himself (and which matched the brocade and silk Roman still wore, having been unable to find any remains of his uniform).

Titian saluted Roman, who dismounted. Then Titian said grandly, "Surchatain Roman, you brought this about"—gesturing to the pile

142

of crosses and contraptions ready to be burned—"so we ask you to do the honor of setting the first flame to it." He held the butt of a torch out to Roman.

"Gladly," Roman agreed, taking the torch. He walked over to the pile and set fire to the dry wood of a cross near the bottom, then tossed the torch up to the top of the heap.

With a roar, the crowd moved in and set their torches to the pile. Immediately it was engulfed in flames.

Smiling, Roman backed up to the horses; then told Titian, "I am leaving the Commander's Second and a Captain here to help you re-group. They have their instructions as to what I expect of them. They are to have the freedom to carry out their orders however they feel necessary, answering only to me. You'd best advise your people to cooperate, for if they don't, I'll forget everything I said yesterday and come back with an army."

"If you have to do that, I'll be the first to open the gates to you," promised Titian.

Roman grinned, "I believe you would." He joined the other three on horseback, and they paused to watch the bonfire a moment before departing. The crowd around it was chanting and singing as it blazed. Atop the pile jutted a burning cross, and beneath it was the lid of the iron maiden. Something about the sight caused the brand on Roman's chest to throb, and the sight blurred in his watering eyes.

Deirdre exulted in the spectacle of the bonfire. Somehow, no matter how awful the pain and the hurt, the Lord made the healing of it that much sweeter than she could have imagined. She surveyed the crowd of townspeople, marveling again at how God seemed forever able to multiply good to reach as many as were suffering. It had even reached Graydon . . . Though he had meant to lead them out of prison to their deaths, if it not been for his showing the way, they would never have escaped. Perhaps that was one reason Graydon had found mercy.

She lingered on the mystery of this thought, still looking over the crowd. But when she caught sight of one particular girl, Deirdre's thoughts lost some elevation. The girl was scrutinizing the Lystrans, especially Roman. As she was behind him, he did not see her. Once or twice she turned away as if to leave, but each time she came forward again, eyes fixed on Roman.

Deirdre could not help feeling relieved when Roman decided it was time to depart and clucked to Fidelis. But in sudden determination the girl ran straight up to Roman on his horse and placed her hand on his thigh.

He startled, reining up Fidelis. The girl said nothing, only gazed

143

up at him. Emotion filled his face as he stared down at her. Then, to Deirdre's absolute chagrin, he reached down and lifted the girl in a fervent embrace. She squeezed his neck, pressing her lips to his cheek.

Deirdre lowered her eyes, her face burning. Nihl glanced at her, then down, visibly disconcerted. Then he jerked his face up in sudden understanding.

Roman lowered the girl back to the ground, and she skipped off into the crowd. He inhaled, closing his eyes a moment before twisting around to those behind him. Nihl nodded at him, smiling imperceptibly, but Deirdre refused to raise her eyes. Roman reached over to take her hand. She pulled it away.

"Deirdre," he said softly. She forced herself to meet his eyes and was shaken to see tears tracking down his brown face. "It was the girl I freed from the traders. The one I thought was dead."

"Oh . . . Roman . . ." she murmured, more ashamed of herself than relieved for him. "I am so glad—"

He grabbed her with one arm and pulled her out of the saddle to kiss her. "After all this time, I am glad to see you are still jealous over me!" he grinned roguishly.

Deirdre flushed, as a number of people were watching, and protested, "My lord—let us be discreet."

Roman returned her to her saddle, laughing, "You? Discreet?"

"Roman!" she exclaimed, shocked. He laughed again, and Nihl smiled, glancing impulsively at Izana to his left. The look she returned to him confirmed in his mind that asking to bring her had been no mistake.

So the homeward-bound party spurred out of the city at an eager clip—Roman on Fidelis, Deirdre on the still-unnamed black gelding, Nihl on his Arabian, and Izana on a Blood's horse which Nihl had appropriated. The morning was aglow with victory; the recent events, which had seemed impossibly evil while in progress, now appeared to have been planned all along to demonstrate the greatest Power in the universe, ruling with the greatest love.

They traveled rapidly. The horses seemed bent on racing each other abreast down the wide, smooth road. When the party did stop for a rest at midmorning, Deirdre sighed, "Oh, I am so anxious to see Ariel. I miss him so! I hope everything is well at the palace."

"Of course it is," Roman answered confidently. "What could happen in a week?" Inwardly, however, he did feel a nudge of concern that they had not encountered Clatus' promised watch outside Corona.

They drank from their water bags, and Deirdre squirted a bit into her horse's mouth. As he lipped it, she patted his nose. "There must be a good name for you somewhere," she murmured. "Poor ol' no name. No name. That's it!" she laughed. "No Name. I like the sound of it."

Roman smiled briefly at her, then said quietly to Nihl, "I wonder what Bruc of Polontis will make of what we have done in Corona."

Nihl thought it over, watching Deirdre and Izana talk. "It will utterly baffle the Surchatain. And then, if he thinks himself able, he will attack Corona himself."

"Do you think?" Roman started.

"It is likely, unless he has weighty reasons not to. 'Strike while your adversary is down, lest he rise again to kill you.' "

"Then I will have to give him reason not to," Roman said darkly.

"Would you attack Polontis?" Nihl asked evenly, glancing at him sidewise.

"Not willingly. I have not forgotten that your brother Asgard still serves Bruc."

"It was his choice to return to Polontis," shrugged Nihl. "He is a soldier, and knows the dangers of war."

"Can you influence him to maintain peace?" Roman asked hopefully.

Nihl considered it a moment. "No," he said flatly.

"Then what else am I to do to keep their armies from killing each other, and everyone caught in between?"

"I don't know. We should ask ourselves whether you *can* keep them from attacking each other."

"Obviously, I cannot," Roman said in disgust, reaching for the saddle. "Unless . . ." he put his foot in the stirrup and threw a leg over ". . . I annex them both."

By late afternoon they came upon the plain north of the outpost, and a half hour more brought them within sight of the fortress. Approaching, they heard a trumpet sound a call to arms. "Clatus' watch has spotted us," Roman grunted in satisfaction.

But no honor guard came out to meet them, and they were within a hundred yards of the outpost before they were even seen. As they reined up at the gates, a sentry took their horses and saluted, abashed. Another led them inside amid a great rush of preparation. The newcomers were confounded.

Then Captain Clatus rushed up, exclaiming, "Surchatain! You have the timing of a hawk!"

"What is happening here?" Roman demanded.

Then Deirdre cried, "Ariel! Gusta!" For they had appeared behind Clatus—Gusta in her nightdress and Ariel tired and dirty. There was confusion for several moments as they all greeted each other with kisses and embraces, all talking at once.

Finally Roman shouted, "Silence! Order!" They all stilled. "Now, Gusta, what are you doing here?"

"Surchatain," she said tremulously, "there is revolt at the palace. We fled for our lives."

Deirdre's knees gave way and she staggered, holding Ariel. Roman's face hardened. For a moment he could not speak. "Led by whom?" he then asked in a gravelly voice.

"I am not sure," she blurted. "By either Troyce or Basil. They have been at odds the entire time you've been gone. Finally, last night Troyce took us from the palace because he said Basil was plotting to kill your son and take over the throne. I ran from him in the forest, because I did not wholly trust him. But then I heard an alarm from the palace, and—we fled rather than return there. I do not know who is fighting for you and who is against."

"How did you get here, Gusta?" Deirdre gasped.

"Well, that is a strange tale. There was this old woman—this widow who lives hidden in the forest. . . . She sheltered us last night, and she paid an old farmer to drive us here. We arrived only minutes ago."

There was a moment of breathlessness, then Roman spat angrily, "Where does it end? Now I have to attack Westford!"

CHAPTER 17

"HOW ARE WE going to attack Westford?" exclaimed Captain Clatus. "You yourself have made it impregnable!"

Roman looked coldly outside the gates. "Not against a battering ram."

At first no one dared speak. Then Nihl said, "Surchatain, you and I and everyone else have been trying to move that machine to Westford for almost three years now, and have not succeeded."

"We haven't needed it before now," he answered, turning on his heel. They all followed him outside to survey the war machine, serenely formidable amid the tall grass and ivy.

"Deirdre," Roman said abruptly, and she jumped. "You are looking at this with fresh eyes. How do we get it apart?"

"I have no idea!" she protested.

"Just look it over a moment," he insisted.

Baffled, she stepped up to the monster, placing a tentative hand on it. Soldiers began gathering around to watch, but Roman waved them back a ways. Still, they observed closely as Deirdre gazed up at the beams and joints, the rusting metal screws and the mammoth, pointed end of the ram itself. She felt overwhelmed by this unreasonable demand of Roman's and the cynical stances of the soldiers. *Lord, I know nothing about this,* she pleaded. *What do I do?*

"What is this?" she asked, moving her fingers to a metal loop protruding from the main support beam.

"It is a cotter pin," answered Roman. "It secures the drive rope to the base."

"Oh." The rope had long since been removed. The pin was sitting across a six-inch slit in the beam. She tried to twist the pin to align with the slit, but it would not move.

Deirdre ran her hand over the crossbeam, feeling for weakness, but it all seemed as solid as if it had been hewn from one tree. She kept returning to the cotter pin, though. She started to twist it the other way when Roman advised her, "The pin must be stationary—" But suddenly it dropped into the slot with a click.

There followed a rapid series of clicks and snaps, and then the machine sagged with a groan. Nihl reached up and pulled on a crossbeam, which came off in his hands. The disturbance of balance caused several other joints to fall apart. With quick precision, the soldiers had it completely disassembled in minutes.

Deirdre stood off to the side and gazed on in satisfaction, not to mention relief. Captain Clatus approached her scratching his head. "Surchataine, I don't know how you did that, but—well done. I must have pushed and pulled on that cotter a hundred times."

"I asked the Lord what to do," she said honestly. "You know I had no knowledge about it myself." He furrowed his brow and walked away, glancing back once or twice.

Roman came up and squeezed her waist. "Somehow, I knew all along that would happen. I prayed over it countless times, but He would not reveal its secret to me. When you tell the soldiers you had no knowledge about it yourself, they believe you."

Nihl walked over to report, "The men are dressing out in full battle gear—all but five lookouts, who will stay here. I have a unit hitching up the battering ram now. We will be ready to move at your word."

Deirdre sighed, "I suppose you are going to insist I stay here."

"No," replied Roman. "You and Ariel and Gusta must come with us. Since we are taking almost all the soldiers, I dare not leave you here unprotected."

Gusta, standing nearby with Ariel, bowed her head obediently, but looked profoundly weary at the idea of turning around and making another seven-hour ride back to Westford. Ariel's head was bobbing like a newborn pup's. Deirdre murmured, "I wish we still had Tremaine's fine carriage here."

"We do have a carriage," Roman answered, lifting his face. "Not that one, but a good one we use to transport emissaries." He sent a man to harness it up. "By the way, Clatus, what became of the watch you were going to post outside Corona?" Roman casually asked the Captain at his side.

"We had two men hidden in the forest by the thoroughfare day and night," Clatus said rapidly, "but day before yesterday they hied themselves back here to report soldiers storming from Corona. We fortified for an attack, but got the Chatain and then you instead."

"No sign of the Bloodclad? Any of them?" asked Roman.

"No, Surchatain, not a one. They must have been charging elsewhere."

Roman mulled this over, wondering if that many soldiers had turned renegade at once or if they had simply quit and gone home. The number he had seen return to Corona was nothing like the number that must have fled.

While the Lystran soldiers gathered into formation, Deirdre, Gusta, Ariel, and Izana climbed into the cushioned carriage, where Ariel immediately dropped his head and slept. A soldier assigned by Roman sat in front to drive.

As twilight fell, the front gates opened again and Roman led out the outpost thousand, Nihl at his side. The carriage started out behind them, but dropped back in the ranks as the mounted men passed them. At the extreme rear, specially harnessed horses pulled the pieces of war machine on wheels.

They rode at an attack pace—just as hard as the horses could endure. As rudely as the carriage bumped and jolted, Ariel never woke. Even Gusta dozed off for weariness, so Deirdre and Izana comforted themselves by mischievously comparing notes on the two men who led the ranks.

Their pace did not slacken as nighttime darkened the landscape around them. They rode with the fury of determination, and Deirdre could only surmise what was going through Roman's mind as they covered the miles toward treachery at home. She felt strangely detached from it as she laid her head back on the cushions and one hand on her precious sleeping child. As long as Ariel was safe in her care, let the turmoil come to a head. God was in command.

Halfway to Westford, Deirdre was blinking sleepily when by the pale moonlight the vanguard spotted a lone horseman pounding full speed toward them. Roman called a halt. The rider spurred up to the Surchatain, recklessly reining his frothing mount around. "Surchatain Roman!" he gasped, winded.

"Captain Reuel! What is the situation at Westford?"

"Surchatain—" Reuel swallowed "—the Chatain has disappeared, and—"

"He is here, with us," Roman interrupted.

"He is? Thank God!" Reuel said. Then he paled like a dead man. "Oh, no. Oh my soul," he moaned.

"Speak up, Reuel!" Roman demanded in agitation.

"Surchatain, the Counselor Basil is about to be hanged for the murder of the Chatain."

Roman gaped at him. "On whose order?" he sputtered.

"On the witness of Lord Troyce."

"Gusta—?" Roman wrenched in the saddle to look for her. Word was passed through the ranks until the soldier driving the carriage brought it up to the front, then leaned back to tap the dozing nursemaid. She sat up, startled.

"Gusta," demanded Roman, "say again what happened at the palace."

She blinked rapidly, trying to wake up. "Lord Troyce woke us and took us from the palace into the woods."

"Did Basil threaten you?"

"No, not directly. Troyce said the Counselor was plotting to kill your son. But, now that I think on it, Basil was the one always posting guards over him."

"A snake has been at work," Nihl quietly observed.

Roman brought his attention back to Reuel. "Who sent you?"

"I came on my own, in secret. After the Chatain disappeared last night and the Counselor was thrown in prison, a few of us went out again to search, hoping to find the boy and clear Basil. We didn't. So today, Troyce declared the Chatain dead and himself emergency ruler of Lystra."

"He has no legal basis for doing that!" growled Roman.

"No one seems to realize that," Reuel pointed out disgustedly. "And anyone who speaks against Troyce brings suspicion on himself. So we few agreed that I would summon help from the outpost, while they kept watch on Troyce."

"You did well to come," said Roman, "but is Basil still in prison?"

"Yes, and Olynn and Sevter with him, for they backed him. I suspect they will also share the gallows. That was the final push to send me out the gates—when word leaked out that Basil was to be executed tonight at midnight. That's typical of Troyce, to do it in the middle of the night without the town's knowledge, for Basil is more popular among the people than he is. We could go along with Troyce playing lord until we had a chance to uncover the truth, but not with him executing the Counselor."

"The truth is about to break open Westford," Roman promised grimly. "Turn and ride." As they took up the road to Westford again, Roman shouted across to Reuel, "Does the army follow Troyce?"

"They don't know who to follow," he shouted back. "The palace is in chaos."

"Indeed, what could happen in a week?" Roman muttered savagely to himself.

Basil sat on a bench in a gloomy cell, staring at the stone walls. A torch in a corridor sconce cast deep, dancing shadows on the stones' pocked surfaces. "I am an utter failure," he announced to them suddenly. "A remarkable, spineless failure."

There was a stir in the cell opposite him. "You are overly harsh on yourself, Counselor," Olynn's voice said. "I never saw such a bold liar as Troyce. When the men won't even listen to me, their Captain, you know we're up against something too clever for us simple men."

"They took Sevter from his cell when he asked to talk to Troyce," Basil mused. "I wonder what he wanted to tell Troyce."

"They are from the same country, originally. Perhaps Sevter goes to reason with him."

"Or join him," Basil said flatly. "I trusted those around me much too freely, and now I will receive my just recompense."

"Troyce cannot succeed in this," insisted Olynn. "What do you think the Surchatain will do with him when he returns?"

"Reward him," Basil answered bleakly. Olynn shut his mouth, finding that to be an unnerving possibility.

A guard let Sevter into Troyce's chambers. The administrator turned to greet him, downing a goblet of wine. "It appears I will not be under you after all, Sevter."

Sevter pleaded, "Lord Troyce—what are you doing?" Out of habitual respect, Sevter used the title which Troyce had not possessed since leaving Diamond's Head.

"What am I doing?" Troyce seemed perplexed by the question. "I am taking control of a country in crisis. I am going to save it, and make it what it should have been from the beginning."

"What it should have been!" exclaimed Sevter. "What more could it be?"

150

"Sevter, you are as blind as Basil!" Troyce set the goblet down with a thud. "I have been sitting back and watching Roman govern for two years now. And all I have seen are missed opportunities and careless discipline. This province could be twice the size it is now, but he let those chances for easy acquisition slip away. He could have extended our power throughout half the Continent, but he refuses to take the initiative and be aggressive. I can no longer sit back and watch the chance for Lystra's greatness pass by."

"*You* are the one who is blind, Lord Troyce! And I think it is not Lystra's greatness you seek, but your own! The Surchatain *is* expanding the province in a careful, controlled manner. He expands without war and bloodshed, and keeps order by benefiting the acquired areas. You forget what Lystra was when he came into power—nothing! That he has built it up to what it is now is astounding."

"I can do better," Troyce stated.

"How?" demanded Sevter. "By treason, and the murder of innocent men? And what will you say to the Surchatain when he comes back knocking at your front gate?"

"Sevter, you wound me. Is it treason to rescue a country from an incompetent ruler? Look at what Roman did: he not only went himself to Corona, but he took the Surchataine and his top officers, leaving Basil in control. Basil!" Troyce's tone was one of angry disbelief. "I knew I must act then, and act quickly, or the country would perish."

Sevter was silent, groping for a foothold of sanity on which to reach him. "After Galapos was hanged by Sheva, I heard you with my own ears swear a declaration of loyalty to God and to Surchataine Deirdre. Would you dare go back on that oath?"

Troyce looked hurt. "How am I betraying my oath to her?"

"You will answer that when you tell me what you have done with her son," Sevter replied.

At this Troyce's pained expression disappeared, replaced by a face that was frighteningly serene. "Men in power learn to do what is expedient, Sevter," he uttered.

"Then breaking your oath means nothing to you?" demanded Sevter. "Roman and Basil consider their word to be as binding as chains, and you despise them for it, yet you consider murder an act of honor! You are a deluded fool, *Lord* Troyce!"

Troyce gave a half-smile at Sevter's sarcastic use of his title. "I forgive your unkindness, Sevter. I will not even think of it while you are swinging from the gallows."

"You learned well from Sheva, Troyce," Sevter remarked bitterly.

Troyce merely opened the door and spoke to the soldier standing

151

outside. "He still refuses to swear loyalty to Lystra," Troyce informed the soldier gravely. "Return him to the dungeon."

On the way down to the prison, Sevter said to the soldier, "Troyce is manipulating you all to gain power for himself. Don't you see that?"

"Who are we to obey, then?" the soldier asked defiantly. "You?"

"Obey the man Surchatain Roman left in command: Basil," Sevter responded earnestly.

"And what if he did murder the child?"

"Ask the men who it was that put a continual watch over the Chatain and the nursemaid. Ask them who followed through with every instruction the Surchatain left behind. Was it Troyce—or Basil? Then let them decide for themselves who is saying the truth. But for the sake of peace, don't execute anyone until you're sure of guilt—for what if you're mistaken?" Sevter left off while the soldier opened the dungeon door and took him down a corridor.

As the soldier shoved him into a cell, Sevter shot, "And ask the men whether the Counselor has ever been shown to be a liar by anyone. Or Olynn—a Captain among you—left as acting Commander by the Surchatain! Was Roman mistaken to trust all three of us—or just Troyce? Ask them!"

Olynn and Basil had come to the doors of their cells to listen. The soldier glanced their way, but reserved the weight of his attention for Sevter. "I will speak to the others," he grunted, then left.

Sevter grasped the iron bars across the small window of the cell door as the soldier's footfalls faded. From his cell nearby, Basil said, "Forgive me for doubting you, Sevter."

"Be assured Troyce intends to hang me along with both of you," Sevter answered bitterly.

"I should have seen it coming," lamented Basil. "There was rebellion in his every move. Why didn't I act on it at once?"

"You did," defended Olynn. "But who of us saw he was waiting for a chance to take power? Not even the Surchatain."

They were silent. Then Sevter said weakly, "God, Westford is crumbling. Help us . . ."

An hour later the tramping of boots brought them to their cell doors again. The doors were unlocked, and stolid soldiers took the men out. By the attitude of the soldiers, the prisoners knew no reprieve had been given. "How shall you tell the Surchatain you hanged your Captain, Sebastian?" Olynn asked one of them scathingly. The soldier stared straight before him, expressionless.

The prisoners were brought out to the courtyard, which was lit in the midnight blackness with torches carried by soldiers. Standing in their midst was the newly constructed gallows. Basil was distraught and yet strangely amused to see it. None of the soldiers serving now remembered how to build a sophisticated gallows with a trapdoor platform; the best they could put up was a simple pole and crossbeam from which a rope hung. The condemned would be fitted with the noose while sitting on a horse, then the horse would be taken away.

The soldiers' ignorance in the building of gallows spoke well of Roman's peaceful rule, but bode evil for Basil. It meant he would die slowly from suffocation rather than quickly from a broken neck.

Almost everyone in the palace had turned out to watch the spectacle. They filled the courtyard and walkways, and leaned out of palace windows and balconies. The buzz of their questions filled the air, as few knew who was to be punished for the Chatain's disappearance. The palace gates were shut for the night, so no townspeople were present, but even the sentries had left their posts to observe the courtyard proceedings.

Troyce rode up before the gallows and raised his hands, although there was already quiet around him. He proclaimed, "Because of treason against the Surchatain and the murder of the Chatain, this man Basil is sentenced to die by hanging. For betrayal and treason, these men Olynn and Sevter are sentenced likewise. Proceed to execute justice!" Astonished murmurings surfaced everywhere as soldiers took hold of Basil.

Observing from a high palace window, one official turned to another. "The law says a man shall not be executed on the same day he is condemned, except by order of the Surchatain, doesn't it?"

"Yes," said the other.

"And Troyce has not legally been proclaimed Surchatain, has he?"

"No."

"Well then—someone should stop them!" said the first.

"Good!" said the second, his elder. "Will *you* go down and tell the army they must wait until morning to hang them?"

The first said no more. Meanwhile, Basil was set on a horse, his hands were tied, and he was led to the gallows.

Suddenly a trumpet blast and shouts were heard faintly from outside the front gates, on the other side of the palace. "Someone is demanding entry," remarked some observant folks. "It is the townspeople," some others decided, and turned back to watch the noose fitted around Basil's neck.

The shouts and blasts from beyond the gates intensified. "Ignore the distractions!" ordered Troyce, for the people were beginning to stir, looking around.

"Perhaps it's the Surchatain returning," someone said hopefully.

153

"In the middle of the night? Don't be stupid," another answered. But a few of the soldiers slipped away to have a look from the sentry posts in the gates.

"Have you any last words?" Troyce questioned Basil. The Counselor just stared at him mutely. "So be it." Troyce rode away from the gallows, wheeled, and raised his hand. The people in the yard were torn between witnessing the hanging and attending to the increasing uproar at the gates.

Troyce slashed his fist downward and a soldier pulled Basil's horse away. He slipped from it, writhing on the rope. At that instant the soldiers who had gone to the gates came running back into the courtyard. "It is the Surchatain!" they yelled. "Surchatain Roman is at the gates! Come help us open the gates!" For it was a highly prized defensive feature of the gates that they could not be opened by fewer than ten men.

"No! It is a lie!" cried Troyce.

An arrow whizzed through the air, neatly slicing the hanging rope. Basil fell to the ground, gasping and coughing. Sebastian stepped up with his bow and said, "No one's to be hanged till we open the gates."

"Traitor! You set this up to gain control yourself!" accused Troyce. Another soldier drew his sword on Sebastian and the army turned on itself, soldier against soldier.

The handful of soldiers who had gone to the gates ran madly among the fighters, shaking them and insisting, "Stop, fools! The Surchatain is outside! Help us open the gates to him!" But in the heated confusion, the men who wanted to could not separate themselves from the fighting.

Then a crash rippled the air. The soldiers paused, looking in bewilderment toward the front gates. Another crash sounded, accompanied by the groaning and creaking of wood. Another crash, with the sound of splintering. The fighting subsided as those in the courtyard, stupefied, watched what they could not see.

On the final thrust, the heavy gates burst open, sagging between the iron and stone supports. An army poured in, knocking aside debris, as the spectators in the yard nervously clutched their weapons.

Roman, clad in the shimmering brocade and silk, spurred into the midst of the gaping, silent crowd. He scanned them furiously, taking in the gallows, Troyce—and Basil, removing the noose from his neck. "Who is in rebellion, that you would not open the gates to me?" he shouted. "Let him challenge me to my face!"

No one dared come before him at once, but the soldiers began looking at Troyce. Finding himself the object of increasing attention, he came forward and threw himself on the ground before Roman. "High Lord,"

154

Troyce moaned, "we are in terrible difficulties without your leadership. There has been treachery among us, for the Counselor Basil, whom you trusted with control of Westford, has murdered your son in an attempt to take power!"

"How do you know this, Troyce?" Roman asked in a low, dangerous voice.

A thousand people were absolutely motionless as Troyce raised his face to the Surchatain, thinking quickly. He had told the men he had seen Basil take the child. As far as he knew, the babe and nursemaid were still in the forest somewhere. He cast a glance behind Roman and saw only soldiers. But he saw that Polonti Nihl sitting on his horse near Roman, smiling in an infuriating way.

Troyce stood upright and declared, "I saw him take the babe and the nursemaid into the forest. They have not been seen since." Basil dropped his head with the resignation of the condemned. *I will not escape again.*

Roman gestured to the side without turning around. Through the soldiers behind him came the carriage with Deirdre, Izana, Gusta, and Ariel. Exclamations arose in one voice from the crowd.

"Say again: Who took you from the palace, Gusta?" Roman asked in a loud voice, eyes on Troyce.

"Lord Troyce," she answered distinctly.

One by one, faces turned toward the administrator. "What have you to say, Troyce?" asked Roman.

"I have committed no crime," he said, defiantly lifting his chin. "My hands are clean of blood."

Roman jerked his head, throbbing with anger. "Only because you were prevented from doing as you wished. But you are such a thorough liar, I think you have even deceived yourself into believing you are innocent. But you have saved me some trouble— " he glanced ominously toward the gallows.

"I charge you with treason and the attempted assassinations of the Chatain Ariel, his nursemaid Gusta, and the Counselor Basil. By my authority as Surchatain, I sentence you to die on the gallows you have built. Do you have anything to say in your defense?"

"I have done nothing to deserve death!" Troyce sputtered.

"Your own words have condemned you," Roman replied.

"I appeal to Surchataine Deirdre!" Troyce cried. Roman's fiery glare intensified, but Deirdre sat stonily silent as she clutched her child to her, refusing the appeal.

"Olynn." Roman motioned to the Captain, who stepped out from between ashen soldiers, taking the rope they held. He made Troyce mount the hanging horse and tied his hands behind him. Then he led the horse with its desperate rider to the gallows while Sevter replaced the rope.

When Olynn put Troyce's unwilling head through the noose he protested, "You are about to murder a guiltless man!"

"That's what I kept trying to tell *you*," Olynn said. "Now you are the one no one believes, Troyce."

As the Captain continued preparations for the hanging, Nihl abruptly spurred up before the gallows. The administrator bit his lip. "Nihl, my friend—"

"I consider that you are now being paid back for the part you played in the death of Surchatain Galapos," Nihl said. "Your heart never changed and you never regretted his murder. Your aim has always been to advance yourself, whatever the cost to anyone else. It is right that you have been exposed for what you are."

Troyce gazed at him, then shouted, "Drud! You are filth!"

Roman lifted his hand and dropped it forcefully. Olynn slapped the horse on its haunches and it bolted. The crowd watched, tense and reserved, as Troyce's accusations were forever silenced.

After sufficient time, Roman motioned for the body to be removed. Then he waved Basil forward from the crowd. "Counselor."

Uncertain as to what was coming, Basil limped up to Roman, who was still seated on Fidelis. Roman observed the rope burns on his neck and inquired, "Do you need the physician, Counselor?"

"No, Surchatain," he answered in a wavering croak. "Your appearance was most timely." Then he opened his mouth to explain to Roman his failure, his lack of firmness in dealing with Troyce, his loss of the Chatain, and the ensuing chaos.

But Roman forestalled him by asking, "Who else rebelled against you?"

"Why—no one," replied Basil, surprised.

"They were going to hang you on Troyce's word alone?" Roman asked in astonishment.

"Well—" Basil faltered, looking back to Sevter for help.

"It was a strange situation, Surchatain," interposed Sevter respectfully. "Troyce's lies cast so much suspicion on everyone, no one could be sure who was telling the truth."

Roman looked in wonderment over the sheepish men. "Are you telling me *no one* thought to consult the written directives I left with Avelon?"

"Your directives!" Basil and Sevter stared at each other. "No, Surchatain," murmured Sevter. "In all the upheaval, we . . . forgot . . ." Roman sighed in disgust.

156

"What . . . was it you directed?" Basil inquired lamely.

"Among other things, that if conflicts arose between you, Avelon was to act as judge," responded Roman. "And where is he?" Heads turned, looking for the holy man.

"Asleep, probably," someone answered from the crowd, and there was a weak ripple of laughter.

Breathing out, Roman dismounted and delivered a rapid-fire string of orders: "Olynn, have the men dismantle the gallows tonight. Sevter, in the morning, you are to begin directing the repair of the gates—I want you to redesign them so that they are not so easy to batter down. Clatus, return with your men to the outpost tonight. Basil, meet me in the library at sunrise. The rest of you—go back to bed."

There was a rush and a jumble as the spectators did what they had been told. Nihl, however, took Izana by the hand, and they went to awaken Brother Avelon out of a sound sleep to mumble a marriage blessing over them.

CHAPTER 18

AFTER THE brief refreshment of a few hours' sleep, Roman sat in the library with the Counselor. The Surchatain pressed his fingers to his throbbing brow and said quietly, "Now tell me what happened here."

Basil began with the day of the party's departure, relating the steps he had taken to carry out Roman's orders and the conflicts with Troyce over DuCange and the emissary from Qarqar. Basil particularly made a point of telling him about the hidden gold at Hornbound. When Roman failed to register surprise, Basil wondered if somehow he already knew of it.

Then he told the Surchatain of his concern over Ariel's safety, and his final act of removing Troyce from his position as administrator. Ashamedly, he also informed Roman of the financial discrepancies he had uncovered in the ledger of palace expenses. This was an area in which Basil had direct oversight of Troyce.

Roman listened without interruption as Basil finished, "Then when

157

Troyce tried to hang me, and you arrived pounding on the gates, Sebastian shot me down. Some of the men were insisting that you stood at the gates, but there was such disorder—" he broke off, putting his head in his hands. "I do not understand how such a situation could have developed."

Roman tapped pensively on the desk. "Don't blame yourself. I am ultimately responsible for what happens here. It seems I left to subdue trouble in Corona while ignoring it in my own palace."

"I assume then that your mission was successful," Basil said, anxious to change the subject.

"Yes, beyond anything I had expected. I will tell everyone at dinner what the Lord did there. For now, show me the judgments and transactions you completed while I was away."

With great relief to be back in his normal administrative role, Basil brought out the books and laid them open before Roman.

Toward the end of a two-hour session, Roman straightened at a knock on the door. "Enter."

Deirdre peered around the door. "Counselor—forgive me. Roman, I just learned something I must tell you." He cocked his head, pointing to a chair across from Basil.

"Gusta told me all that happened after Troyce left them in the forest. She was found by a very poor widow who lives hidden in a ravine. The woman gave her and Ariel a bed for the night, then paid a peasant to drive them to the outpost. But this is the strange thing— the widow paid him from one of your money bags! He showed Gusta the bag—she is sure it had your imprint."

Roman thought this over, then shook his head, unable to reason it out. Deirdre continued, "Remember the widow we met along the road to Corona? Didn't you give her your money pouch?"

"Yes." Roman startled in remembrance.

"I described her to Gusta. She thinks it was the same old woman! Gusta said she was living in wretched poverty—but apparently she gave the whole bag to the peasant in payment for carrying Gusta and Ariel."

"She said it would come back to me," he mused. "I wonder how she knew . . . ? Well, we cannot let that pass unrewarded. See if a soldier is at the door." Deirdre stood and opened it, motioning. A solemn-faced messenger stepped in, very erect.

"Summon Sebastian to me," Roman ordered. The messenger saluted and raced off.

"I think you'll have no problems with discipline for some time," muttered Basil.

158

"Sebastian is the one who shot you down from the gallows, is he not?" inquired Roman.

"Yes."

"Then he is the one I'll use." They waited a time, while Deirdre smoothed her fresh dress and studied Roman appreciatively. He glanced away, smiling at her transparency, and Basil, seated across from her, suddenly found something on the floor which engrossed him.

The messenger came to the door with Sebastian. He was not big, as soldiers go, but he had sharp, intelligent features and a quick stride.

As Sebastian bowed, Roman said, "The Counselor tells me you are the one who saved him from the gallows."

"It was not right to execute him like that, Surchatain," he answered. "I had decided in my own mind not to let anyone be hanged unjustly, and I knew some others felt the same. We're not the simple sheep Troyce thought, especially since the Commander had warned us to watch him. It was more a matter of finding proof that he was lying."

"Good thought," commended Roman. But Basil angrily reflected, *You could have taken that stand* before *I was strung up.* "In the future, however, I am sure the Counselor would appreciate your support before you build a gallows," Roman added, and Basil startled. Sebastian inclined his head.

"Now," Roman went on, "I have a task for you. The Chatain and his nursemaid were given shelter in the forest by a widow living hidden in a ravine. I want you to find that widow and bring her to me. Gusta will give you directions to find her."

Sebastian bowed. "Consider it done, Surchatain."

As he was leaving, the kitchen mistress appeared at the door. "Surchatain Roman and my lady—welcome home," Merry said, bowing. "We have prepared a special midmorning meal that is ready for you now."

Deirdre smiled warmly at her and Merry appeared anxious to say more, but Roman had stood and was saying, "Very good. Basil, please go down and be seated. Deirdre and I will be down directly."

Basil closed the door behind him as Deirdre turned inquiringly to Roman. He walked around the desk and took her in his arms. Brushing her forehead with his lips, he murmured, "How blessed I was to have you by my side in Corona—weeping over me, bringing me meat—and now you look more beautiful than I have ever seen you."

"There is a reason," she whispered, waiting for that to sink in while he kissed her neck.

"Oh?"

"Yes." She guided his hand suggestively to feel the firmness of her abdomen. He caressed her an instant, then froze.

He opened his eyes. "You are pregnant?" he demanded, his voice rising sharply.

"Yes!" she laughed.

"Deirdre—" he gasped, "how long have you known?"

Her grin faded when she saw his shock. She faltered, "Well, I suspected for some time, but did not really know for certain until today, when I saw the midwife . . ."

It was too late. He had stepped back in anger and dismay. "You knew, and did not tell me before we left to go to Corona!"

"If I had told you, you would not have let me come! And weren't you just saying it was good that I came?"

"That is not the point!" he sputtered. "You had no right to endanger the life of my unborn child, as well as Ariel's, for your stubborn adventure. You had no right to deceive me!"

Deirdre gaped at him, unable to comprehend his anger. "You know my reasons for coming, and they were not for adventure! And where does the value of *my* life fit into your outrage?"

He stopped, inhaling deeply. "That comment was not worthy of you, Deirdre." She bit her tongue. No, it was not—she knew how often he had placed her life above his own. She began an apology, but he interrupted: "You shall not sit with me at dinner today. Go to our chambers and wait there. I will have your meal sent up to you."

"Roman, let me—"

"Go!" He would not hear her out, so she fled the library and ran down the corridor in angry tears. Brushing past the startled soldier at the door of her chambers, she threw herself onto the great downy bed and sobbed fitfully, "How dare he treat me like that—ordering me to my room like a child!"

The humorous thought came faintly to her that the measure was appropriate, considering her present behavior, but she deemed herself too wounded to laugh it off.

"If he does not care for my company today—so be it!" she declared dramatically, rising. She swept out the door, past the perplexed soldier, into the corridor.

There she paused. She could not leave the palace, but she did want to get away—and yes, to defy his order. So she ran to the small courtyard garden, which she had tended with her own hands. She plopped onto the little bench amid the heavy sweetness of gardenias, putting her head forlornly in her hands.

You're doing it again. The thought came to her clearly, in a tone of chiding humor. "What?" she startled up. *Pouting when you should be rejoicing.* "What have I to rejoice over?" she murmured bitterly.

160

"Roman is angry with me." *How quickly you forget all the Lord has done!*

She sat back, almost unwillingly reliving the incredible course of events in Corona, and the power of the Lord demonstrated there. "Oh, Lord," she moaned, "why do I do things that anger Roman, even though I love him so? You've done so much—why can't you change me?" She waited, listening, but there was no response to her query.

She surveyed the garden again. The sweet bushes surrounded her, but they gave her no pleasure. The roses, always her favorite, were blooming in full radiance, but somehow this just depressed her further. "Where is the joy you promised, Lord?" she asked dejectedly. Again, there was no reply, but she was not expecting one.

Well, now she had a choice. She could stay here and sulk in the garden, or she could return to her chambers where Roman had sent her.

Sighing, she stood. It seemed pointless to do anything but obey Roman, even when he seemed unreasonable. Listlessly, she left the garden and trudged the corridors to her chambers.

As she came to her door, she met an empty-handed kitchen maid. "My lady, the Surchatain requests you to come to the table."

Deirdre nodded and followed her down. Roman had relented, which she should have guessed. That presented her with another choice, harder than the first. As they drew near the banquet hall, Deirdre's stomach tightened to hear the voices and laughter. She wavered, but knowing what had to be done, she set her mind to do it. It would not be easy in front of all of them.

The activity stilled somewhat as she entered, and the guests rose. Roman turned in his great chair toward her. Seeing the look of hopeless resignation in his eyes, she knew all that was necessary to regain his favor was to sit and smile at him. But that would no longer suffice.

She knelt beside his chair. "Forgive me for my disobedience, my lord," she said clearly.

One would have thought all the tongues in the hall had melted away for the sudden quiet. Roman gaped at this first-ever public apology. Then his face changed, and he glanced around the table as if he were burdened to say something he knew would embarrass him. He cleared his throat, extending his hand to her. "You are forgiven, my love. Please, sit—I could not bear your absence."

She sat, but he still looked as though he had something to say. "It was wrong of me to punish you, Deirdre. Your loyalty is not a fault," he said softly. "I was just so—surprised, and afraid for you. I feel that now, at my time of life, it is important for me to—to protect my offspring . . ."

He then looked up and announced lightheartedly, "The Surchataine is carrying our second child."

Those at table came to life with congratulations and expressions of delight. When these had died down, Basil said, "Surchatain, I am consumed with curiosity to know what took place in Corona!" Other voices clamored in agreement.

Roman, his confident self again, shifted back in his chair to a storytelling posture. Before he began, however, Deirdre glanced down the table toward the Commander. Sternly, she asked him, "Nihl, where is Izana?"

He jumped at her question, then his color deepened. "I—had not asked permission for her to sit with me, Surchataine." Deirdre cocked a threatening brow.

"You may seat her at this table, today and hereafter," Roman said with a half-smile. As Nihl rose from the table, Roman added, "That is, if you are enjoying your married state." Nihl stumbled a little in leaving his chair. That telltale slip brought down on the Commander a barrage of friendly teasing that did not cease until he had hurried past the door.

When Nihl returned with Izana, she was given a chair next to him. Roman led the table in a toast congratulating the pair. Then as servants brought out braised lamb, rye bread, and blueberry tarts, Roman began to recount to them all that had transpired in Corona. Sevter produced a quill and parchment to take notes for the history books.

Roman quickly related accounts of the Bloodclad and Tremelaine. He described the torture room and the branding, and loosed his shirt to show the brand on his chest. As he progressed to accounts of Graydon and his duplicity, Sevter scribbled feverishly, scratching out lines in places. When Roman described the supernatural occurrences surrounding the mirror, Sevter finally dropped the quill and listened open-mouthed with the others.

Roman told of leaving Kam and Colin in advisory positions to the new Surchatain he had appointed; then of meeting up with Gusta and Ariel at the outpost. He told how Deirdre had found the key to unlocking the battering ram. "When we got to the gates and no one would open up, I chose to use it."

"And how grateful I am for that," interposed the Counselor. "I was almost a dead man!"

"Not as close as you feared, Counselor," Reuel said quietly. "Some of us never doubted you."

Olynn stood abruptly, slapping the table as he took up his goblet. He extended it toward the head of the table, declaring, "Surchatain Roman and Surchataine Deirdre: May you reign long in peace and

162

prosperity. Welcome home!" The guests stood enthusiastically to join the toast. Roman nodded and Deirdre smiled benignly.

When all had finished eating, Roman rose and said, "Brother Avelon, I think there can be no better time to go to the chapel and thank the Lord for His deliverance once again. May we have the Scripture reading early today?"

"If you will come, then now is when we will have it," Avelon said. The guests followed him to the chapel and a boy ran to ring the tower bells, summoning others to hear.

As the people poured into the small hall, Avelon stood before them with the great book of Scriptures, finding the Psalm for the day. He raised his head, and Roman remarked the special aura that came upon him when he took his place on the dais to read from that Book.

"Brothers and sisters in Christ, we gather today to thank the Most High Lord that the Surchatain has returned in victory, and has restored peace to Westford. Remembering our gratitude for those returned safely to us, we continue our reading from the Psalms." He held up the book, cleared his throat, and read:

> I love the Lord, for he heard my voice;
>   he heard my cry for mercy.
> Because he turned his ear to me,
>   I will call on him as long as I live.
>
> The cords of death entangled me,
>   the anguish of the grave came upon me;
>   I was overcome by trouble and sorrow.
> Then I called on the name of the Lord:
>   "O Lord, save me!"
>
> The Lord is gracious and righteous;
>   our God is full of compassion.
> The Lord protects the simplehearted;
>   when I was in great need, he saved me.
>
> Be at rest once more, O my soul,
>   for the Lord has been good to you.
>
> For you, O Lord, have delivered my soul from death,
>   my eyes from tears,
>   my feet from stumbling,
> that I may walk before the Lord
>   in the land of the living.
> I believed even when I said,
>   "I am greatly afflicted."

And in my dismay I said,
    "All men are liars."
How can I repay the Lord
    for all his goodness to me?
I will lift up the cup of salvation
    and call on the name of the Lord.
I will fulfill my vows to the Lord
    in the presence of all his people.

Precious in the sight of the Lord
    is the death of his saints.
O Lord, truly I am your servant;
    I am your servant, the son of your maidservant;
    You have freed me from my chains.

I will sacrifice a thank offering to you
    and call on the name of the Lord.
I will fulfill my vows to the Lord
    in the presence of all his people,
in the courts of the house of the Lord—
    in your midst, O Jerusalem.
Praise the Lord.

Basil quietly uttered an intense "Amen!" Deirdre turned to Roman to comment on the reading, but saw that his face was stricken with wonder. Every line of the Psalm had brought to his mind scenes of the pit, the chains, the idol, and the relentless deliverance of the Lord. The astounding relevance of the words left him suspended somewhere beyond himself, in a realm where Intelligence rules with purpose and no pain is unnoticed or unshared.

He lowered his head, unconscious of the tears building in his eyes and escaping down his face. That such superhuman effort would be exerted on his behalf, at such a cost, awed him to utter humility. Who was he to be the concern of the Almighty?

Nihl turned, and, seeing Roman, stilled. Others began to turn and look. Roman, not noticing, went down on his knees and Deirdre joined him. Nihl promptly knelt, too, as did Izana. In a widening ripple the gatherers kneeled.

Roman spoke from his heart: "Lord God, you delivered me also. You made your word good and saved me from death and hell, though all their power was bent on destroying me. You delivered me! Even when I doubted, even when I despaired, you were still working out your purpose. Lord God! I am helpless to understand the reason for

164

your love, but oh how I benefit from it! How I praise you, my God, for you are so very good."

He stopped, swallowing. Deirdre leaned her head on his solid arm and he took her with him from the silent hall.

That evening, when they slept, Deirdre woke in the dead of night. She must have awakened from a dream, because she awoke in the most intense state of joy she had ever experienced. It was as palpable as rushing water. She was surrounded by it, or suspended in it, absorbing it into her being. The reason for it escaped her, and the inexpressible sensations faded as she came to full consciousness, but it left behind the undeniable imprint of reality.

She lay still in the darkness, fully awake, watching and listening. But all she heard was Roman's rhythmic breathing beside her. What was it? What did it mean? she groped. With a rude start, she recalled her childish complaint for joy. She had lacked it, and He had given it—at least, a taste of it.

But, in honesty, she had to concede she had received it before this moment. The look in Roman's face when she had asked his forgiveness, and what he had given her in love beyond that . . . It seemed that when she had acted upon what she knew was right, then the joy had begun to creep in. It had come slowly at first. But then, as she followed up one obedience with another, it had compounded itself, rolling along, gathering into an unstoppable force which at last had to break out in her sleep.

And Roman . . . she reached over to touch him in the darkness, picturing the black hair mussed over his brow, and the brown face etched with fine lines of care. . . . Every victory that he had won had followed on an act of obedience to his High Lord. For eight long years he had stayed faithfully with the dreary task of guardianship— and won her for a wife. He had refused to let Galapos fight without him at the outpost—and won Lystra. Now, he ruled as a powerful Surchatain who had battered even the gates of hell in the name of the Prince of Peace.

She rolled over on her back, still thinking. That was why Roman— as her mentor Josef had—put such importance on knowing the Word: so he would know what was obedience and what was not. And in the obedience rested the power.

With such power available to him—why, Roman was invincible. The Continent lay open before him.

Deirdre closed her eyes with the weight of the thought, but did not sleep for hours afterward.

165

CHAPTER 19

THE FOLLOWING DAY, Roman sent two advisors, whom Basil had recommended, to replace Kam and Colin in Corona. At the open audience in the morning, he sat patiently while the townspeople aired the grievances they had been saving up for his return.

"Surchatain, I just don't know how long I can keep a good temper while these boys run wild through my shop, day in and day out; I've tried locking the doors, but as hot as it gets during the day you know I can't keep my doors shut and locked while I'm trying to work, so that won't do; then I collar them and throw them out, and they just keep coming back, getting in my tools, playing with the leather, and how is a man to get an honest day's work in with those kinds of distractions? And . . ."

Roman blocked out the droning for a moment, sighing inwardly. He glanced at Nihl to his left, and the Commander looked as if he were sleeping on his feet. Resentment began building in Roman over the continual petty demands made on him as Surchatain.

Then he recalled that just a few days before he had been in a pit with little hope of seeing daylight again. What would he not have given to be right here, sitting on this throne, even to hear the people make their endless complaints? No, now he knew better than to squander opportunities the Lord gave him for patient service during times of ease.

". . . now they've taken to snatching scraps, and I had to wallop one youngster before he would turn them loose—"

"I understand they are interfering with your work. That is not good," Roman finally interrupted. "But it's obvious they like you, and they're interested in what you are doing. It seems you have ready-made apprentices, if you will take it upon yourself to teach them. I am sure their families will gladly pay the apprentice fees. I will send a soldier with you to explain to the boys that the only ones who will be allowed in your shop from now on are apprentices." He waved to a guard.

The tradesman nodded his balding head thoughtfully. "Yes, yes, I suppose that would work. Well, thank you, Surchatain; you're a good man to pay mind to the difficulties of your people, though you should, for we pay enough in taxes . . ."

166

Roman nodded in dismissal and eyed the guard, who led him out still talking. "Who is next, Counselor?" he asked, determined not to show his impatience.

"The emissary from Qarqar, Surchatain."

Roman turned in perplexity as the emissary made his way to the front and bowed. "You should be in Hornbound by now, reporting to your Surchatain," Roman observed.

"My lord, after the conflicting terms given me by you and by your former administrator, I sent my companions back, but stayed on myself to see what would happen here," the emissary said with surprising frankness. Roman's face changed slightly. The Qarqarian continued, "There is no doubt now as to the power you hold. We are prepared to offer you whatever you require in tribute or taxes."

Roman opened his mouth to reply but the emissary forestalled him. "There is no need to pretend you do not know about our hidden gold. Your administrator discovered it. I will not deny it. That puts Qarqar in a vulnerable position. So I must do whatever is necessary to protect her. What will you demand to leave us in peace?"

"I wish to abide by our original agreement. I will not require tribute of you," said Roman. He did not like emissaries dictating a course of action to him. Nihl was watching the emissary through narrowed, distrustful eyes.

The emissary hesitated as if not fully persuaded, then bowed deeply. "So. Consider us your humble servants and allies, Surchatain."

"I will call on you if I need you," Roman answered. "You are dismissed."

The emissary bowed again as he backed out, and Roman stood up, stretching. After six interviews this morning, the crowd had thinned out. "This audience is concluded for the day," he said, nodding to Basil and Nihl.

On his way out of the hall, Roman directed a soldier, "Find Ariel for me, and bring him to the stables. Be sure to tell Deirdre where he'll be." He had suddenly decided it was time for Ariel to have a pony.

He went out to the back courtyard, but the din of construction in the front brought him around to see what progress was being made in repairing the gates.

Sevter met him with a drawing on parchment in hand. "Surchatain, here is what we have designed for the front entrance—double gates, separated by a hold of twenty feet. The battlement spans the hold between the gates, as you see, so that if the outer gate were somehow breached, the intruders would be caught in a trap for the archers above.

We will also run iron sheeting fifteen feet down into the ground just within the outer gates as a defense against tunneling."

"Excellent, Sevter," murmured Roman, looking over the plans. "I think this deserves some additional reward."

"Surchatain, I am humbled," Sevter said sincerely. Roman made a mental note as he left the yard to recommend Sevter to Basil for the post of administrator.

At the stables, he asked the stableman to round up the gentlest ponies. By the time the soldier arrived bouncing Ariel on his shoulders, Roman had selected a young Celtic pony for his son. "Ride a horsey!" Ariel chortled, lunging from the soldier to his father.

At this point Deirdre appeared, smiling curiously to see the pony being fitted with a small saddle. "What are you doing?"

"Ariel is going to ride by himself today," Roman announced. Ariel clapped his hands with the thrill of it as Roman set him in the saddle.

"Isn't he rather young yet?" she asked anxiously, leaning against the railing to stroke the pony and test his temper.

"No," said Roman, smiling at her clouded face. "I will walk beside him." He put the reins in the little hands, instructing, "Now, Ariel, pull them gently the way you want him to go. Pull back—easy!—when you want him to stop. See? Let me lead you." Taking hold of the bridle, he led the pony around the pen while Ariel perched like a proud warlord.

Deirdre watched smiling, but something prescient about the scene caused her smile to stiffen. Roman walked the pony around the circumference of the pen, encouraging and praising Ariel as they went, but the vision flashed before Deirdre's eyes of the young man riding out in full battle regalia. The thought that he would one day win great victories and accomplish noble goals made her catch her breath.

When they had come full circle, Roman glanced at her, grinning, but his face fell to see her wide-eyed expression. Mistaking her look for fear, he said, "Deirdre, what is it now? Am I not taking enough care?"

"Yes." She reached over the rails to embrace his neck. "You are a good and loving father, as I always knew you would be."

"I had hard practice for it, teaching you," he said distractedly, one hand on her and the other on the bridle. Ariel kicked the pony, demanding, "Go!" and Deirdre released Roman so he could lead the pony around once again.

That afternoon, Sebastian found Roman with Basil in the library and requested that he come downstairs to the foyer. Deirdre and Gusta met them there, also at Sebastian's request. "Surchatain, and my lady, I have been searching throughout the forest with a number of men to

168

find the widow, as you ordered. I've found several candidates, and I ask you to tell me whether any be she."

He gestured toward a line of five ladies in old, worn clothes standing in the foyer. They were all elderly and obviously poor. "Gusta, do you recognize any?" Deirdre whispered.

"No," she shook her braids. "No. None of these is the widow who helped us."

Deirdre lifted her hand to dismiss them but Roman stopped her. Addressing the first widow, he asked, "My lady, how do you live?"

She eyed him proudly, gathering her tattered cloak about her. "I fend for myself, young man."

He nodded respectfully, then asked the others as a group, "Do any of you have children to care for you? Any family whatever?" No one answered him directly, but two shook their heads.

Roman turned toward Sebastian, thinking. In a low voice he told the soldier, "Register them to receive a stipend from the treasury in the amount Basil approves. Then inquire of Sevter to see what work they can do around the palace—anything at all will do."

Roman faced the widows again. "We have need of more workers in the palace, if you are willing. Sebastian here will show you what needs to be done." Before they left, Roman threw Sebastian a final directive: "When you are done, go out and look some more."

After they had left, Deirdre flung her arms around Roman. "You are so good!"

He smiled tightly. "I half wonder if that widow was really what she appeared to be. But in looking for her, I've seen a need I can't turn my back on. We will continue to search till we find her, or until we run out of widows."

Deirdre's arms were still twined around his neck, so he leaned down to kiss her lightly. "So, when are you due?" he asked.

"Midwinter," she replied, then informed him, "And no matter how often you ask me that, it will not change much."

He looked down on her imperially. "Do you charge me with impatience?"

"I? Never, my lord." She made her face that practiced picture of innocence, but harbored a mischievous glint in her eyes. "Roman!" she exclaimed in inspiration, "Take me to the lake!"

He leaned away, moaning, "Oh no. Deirdre, I can't. I have so much work to attend to—"

"Go too! Go too!" demanded Ariel from nowhere. They turned around to see that Gusta had brought him down from the nursery. "I go too!"

"Please take us—only for a moment," she pleaded.

He sighed. "I could never hold my ground against you, and now I am outnumbered!" Deirdre took the grinning Ariel and in resignation Roman led them to the stables.

"I want to take Lady Grey," she said. "I missed her on our trip."

"As you wish. I suppose she can still make it to the lake. She could walk the path blind," he remarked. Deirdre glowed in triumph, and Roman fetched the horses. As he saddled them himself, waving away the stableman, he glanced sidelong at his grinning family. "You two were cut from the same quarry," he muttered.

Deirdre carried Ariel on Lady Grey while Fidelis highstepped with Roman. The Andalusian seemed to think they were headed off on another adventure, for he began to prance sideways in his eagerness to run.

The willows of the familiar grove were larger and greener, the lilies blooming more profusely than ever before. Roman dismounted, not even bothering to tie Fidelis, and Deirdre let Ariel down into his arms. The child's legs were working in a run before they ever touched the ground. "Stay near us, Ariel," Roman ordered, turning to help Deirdre off.

She slipped into his arms and they sank down into the soft grass under the willows, her satin dress crumpling in their embrace. She murmured, "I have a confession to make."

"Tell me all," he said, lifting his face.

"Once, when you were my guardian, I thought of kissing you here under the trees, just to see what you would do."

"You did not bother to wait for the privacy of the grove," he chided. "You kissed me on top of a hill, in view of all Lystra. Remember?"

She flushed, protesting, "Oh, I was just a child then!"

"Old enough to get me into trouble." He prevented her reply by means of a lengthy kiss.

She opened her eyes suddenly. "Where is Ariel?"

He lifted up on one elbow to look around. "Nearby, I'm sure; we have only been here a moment. Ariel!" There was no immediate reply.

Deirdre nudged Roman over and sat up. "Ariel!"

They stood, scanning the peaceful grove. Then in unison: "Ariel!"

At the same time they both looked toward the lake, and saw the little red-brown head bobbing in the water. "Roman!" Deirdre screamed.

He had already lunged for the lake, breathing, "Lord Jesus—please—" He dove into the water and reached his son in one stroke. He lifted out the child, limp and blue-faced.

Deirdre fell to her knees, gasping in anguish. The cherished dream she'd had of her son riding out to battle fell apart before her eyes. Roman turned Ariel upside down, slapping his back again and again. Water ran from the child's mouth, but he did not respond.

Roman brought him up to shore and laid him on the grass with a father's face of agony. On all fours, he brought his head down to the little chest, shaking in silent sobs. Deirdre sat in uncomprehending shock.

Roman raised himself to his knees abruptly. "Lord God!" he choked. "I do not understand why you have done this—but—everything I have came from you, and is yours. If you must have Ariel now—he is yours. Who am I to question you?" He pounded the ground with his fists. "Who am I to question your love? Oh, Father," he moaned, falling back to the turf.

Then they heard the slightest little cough. Roman jerked up, seizing Ariel and slapping his back. Deirdre fell forward with a cry. The boy gasped, and coughed, and then sucked in his breath and came around crying fitfully.

His color returned, and went further to an angry red. His parents clutched him between them, shaking as hard as he. "Thank you. Oh thank you," Roman repeated weakly.

They numbly carried Ariel to the horses, while he continued to cough up water. Roman cradled him in one arm as he helped Deirdre up with the other. He set Ariel firmly in the saddle before her. Deirdre held the child, weeping in relief, while she stroked Roman's dripping head.

He leaned weakly against Lady Grey. "How careless . . . how stupid of me—"

Deirdre placed her trembling fingers against his lips. "I will not hear that from you. I was as much at fault. God gave him back to us, so—*please* don't flog yourself. I can't bear it." He took her fingers and kissed them passionately, then mounted, his face drained and stony.

They took the path to the palace at a subdued walk. The sun was a large orange ball dropping to the horizon on their right, splashing the sky and clouds with exuberant color. Glints of light shot through the nearby trees to stripe Fidelis with bands of gold.

Roman said quietly, "The Lord has just now shown me something. I had been so full of plans for Ariel—to train him and educate him into the most intelligent warrior on the Continent. I had not stopped to consider that God's plans for him may differ from mine. I may make my plans, and I may train Ariel as best I can, but I must not forget that God is his High Lord and not me. I must let God be God."

171

He paused, dropping his head. "And yet—oh God! I am so grateful you showed me this without taking him from me now!" Roman rubbed his eyes as if weary of the tears, and Deirdre squeezed Ariel tightly.

CHAPTER 20

THREE DAYS LATER, Kam and Colin returned from Corona. They arrived in Westford at the time of the evening meal, so Roman waved them into the dining hall to eat as they gave their report. "We stopped at the outpost a few hours, Surchatain," Kam said as he sat. "We heard of the trouble you found waiting for you. Whew! What a homecoming!"

"That was quickly resolved," Roman said calmly. "What is the situation in Corona?"

"Things were humming, as long as we were there," Kam answered as he helped himself from a pot of venison stew. "That fellow Titian has taken the reins and made things run. Send the bread this way, Colin."

"By the by, I had thought there were no Polonti in Corona," remarked Colin.

"You saw some?" queried Roman.

"Yes, two, as we were leaving. They followed us a ways," Colin answered.

"How were they dressed?" asked Nihl.

Colin shrugged, "In common workmen's clothes. Not uniforms."

"Armed?" asked Nihl.

"Not conspicuously, but they could have been. Why, Commander?"

Nihl shifted away from the table. "There *were* no Polonti living in Corona—of that I am sure. As for those two that you saw, I am willing to bet my post they are spies."

"From Bruc, I assume," Roman said.

"Almost certainly."

"I suppose, under the circumstances, I would send spies also, to find out for myself what is happening. Which is just what we will

172

do. Nihl, dispatch two of your men to Polontis—are Bruc's headquarters still in Eledith?"

"As much as we know."

"Then send them off immediately. With the mountains, it will take four days for them to even reach the city."

Nihl left the table. Roman then looked around distractedly. "Where is Deirdre?" No one answered. He turned to the serving girl who had just refilled his goblet. "Tell her to come to the table." She bowed and backed out.

While they were waiting, the conversation lapsed. Roman stroked his forehead, full of weighty choices and plans contingent upon information yet to be received. A soldier entered from the foyer and whispered, "Surchatain, one of the townspeople requests your ear."

"I will hear him at the morning audience tomorrow," Roman replied.

The soldier hesitated. "That is what I told him, Surchatain, but he insists it is urgent."

"All their problems are life-and-death matters," Roman said with a touch of disgust. "Send him in," he sighed.

In a moment the soldier brought in a rudely dressed, bushy-headed tradesman who turned here and there to look all about him as he came.

"Who are you, and what is your need?" Roman asked testily.

The man stumbled a bit on the thick rug and bowed ungracefully. "Surchatain, my name is Orenthal. I am a weaver." He paused to gaze at the table.

"What do you need?" Roman repeated, watching the door for Deirdre.

Orenthal turned his attention back to Roman in earnestness. "Surchatain, I came to warn you. In the dining hall at the inn today, I heard a stranger hire a man for a great deal of money to kill you—he paid in gold." The guests at table sank into utter stillness.

"Oh," said Roman, unimpressed. "I suppose they just arranged it in the hearing of the whole hall."

The serving girl he had sent for Deirdre entered the hall alone and Roman questioned her with his eyes. "Surchatain, my lady says she does not feel well," the girl told him in almost a whisper.

Roman inhaled, irritation building within. He knew the games Deirdre could play, and he did not feel a bit like playing them now. "Tell her to come down *now.*" He glanced back at the weaver and picked up his spoon.

"Sir, the discussion I heard was in whispers, very low. I was a good twenty feet away, and there was no one else around. But something about that hall—in certain places, your voice carries. I heard them as

173

clearly as I hear you now. The stranger was dressed finely in a red robe, like an official. He had an accent, too—clipped his words."

"He is describing the chief emissary from Qarqar perfectly, Surchatain," muttered Basil.

"The other fellow, the one he hired—I didn't know him. But he seemed familiar with the area. Got out before I could catch him." Orenthal stopped, having had his say.

Roman looked up disinterestedly. "Thank you for your report. You are dismissed." The tradesman shrugged and bowed. On leaving, he screwed his head around to observe more of his surroundings.

Roman continued to eat, ignoring the startled silence around him. Finally Basil ventured, "Surchatain, I believe that report bears some investigation. What do you intend to do?"

"Nothing," said Roman.

This resulted in another uncertain silence. "Your reasons for disregarding such a pointed warning must be compelling, Surchatain," Kam observed.

Roman sat back impatiently, glancing at the door again. "I can hardly believe Qarqar intends to assassinate me. And with all the enemies I have faced, and will face, I will not hide in the palace on account of a rumor."

Then Deirdre entered the hall. She came to the table and sat quickly, as if she did not trust her legs to hold her up. "Deirdre!" murmured Roman, staring at her white face. She did not answer, apparently not hearing, and made a pretense of picking up her spoon to eat. But a sudden spasm of pain jolted the spoon from her fingers, and she grasped the edge of the table.

Roman needed to see no more. He jumped up, lifting her in his arms, and she held tightly to him. "Doctor, to our chambers," he instructed the physician at the table. "And summon the midwife." After Roman took her out, the diners began leaving the table in subdued anxiety.

As they quickly filed from the hall, Nihl appeared in the doorway, his brow knitting as he found himself going in against the stream of those coming out. Basil placed a hand on his shoulder to tell him of the sudden and foreboding events.

Roman carried Deirdre up the stairs and laid her on the bed. When her breath came, she sobbed, "It was wrong of me not to tell you about it before we went, Roman, and now I am being punished for it."

"Stop that, Deirdre," he said sternly, tensely unlacing her dress. Already the blood was seeping through the layers of skirting. "You

174

know that is not right. God acts only in love toward us." He tried to smile comfortingly, but his face was full of dismay. She moaned and lay back.

The physician entered, and at his back the midwife. He looked at Deirdre and ordered the midwife, "Bring clean water and cloths." She directed herself out promptly. Then the physician just stood looking down at his patient.

"What can you do?" Roman demanded.

The physician blinked rapidly. "Very little, I fear. If it were only slight bleeding, we could give her an herbal potion to stem the flow. But with that much blood, she's miscarrying, and there is nothing that can be done to stop it." He added, "We should leech her, to draw off the black humors that have caused her to miscarry."

"No!" Deirdre cried.

Roman glared at him. "With all the blood she is losing, you want to drain more from her? That is senseless, doctor."

The physician straightened defensively. "The use of leeches is declining in enlightened medical circles, true, but they do have their benefits."

"To physicians, who charge for them," Roman said scathingly, then turned as the midwife entered.

"Here, love," she said soothingly, placing cloths under Deirdre's hips, then sitting on the bed to stroke her abdomen. "You'll be fine," she murmured. "You weren't too far along . . ."

The physician was arguing, "Now Surchatain, if you want me to help her, you must follow my advice."

"I will not allow you to put those bloodsuckers on my wife," Roman responded angrily.

"If you don't—" the doctor began a warning, but the midwife abruptly got up, put a hand on the doctor and one on Roman and steered them outside.

"Continue your argument out here," she ordered. "Leave her in peace, and she will be better." With a curt nod to them, she went back into the chambers and shut the door.

A little while later, a humbled Roman quietly reentered and stood at Deirdre's bedside. The midwife watched him with a sharp eye and he nodded meekly. Taking Deirdre's hand, he asked, "Are you in pain?"

"Some," she admitted feebly, not daring to tell him how much lest he relent about the leeches. He held her hand, trying to think of something comforting to say, but the disappointment in his face at their loss spoke clearly. Her eyes filled with fresh tears. "Roman, I am so sorry—"

He would not let her continue. "As long as I have you, that is all that matters. The Lord gave me you and Ariel. I am content." She reached up to him to wrap her arms around his strong brown neck, as she had done since childhood.

She pressed her face into his leather shortcoat, inhaling its muted, earthy scent. From that moment on, something about it remained with her to arouse uncommon feelings of warmth and yearning whenever she scented leather. Perhaps it was connected with what he murmured next: "First Ariel nearly drowning, and now this. How fragile a thing our life is . . . How careful I must be to use the time I have with you, for in a moment, a breath, the moments are swept away . . ."

They watched Deirdre closely afterwards, to see if she would develop a fever, but she did not. By the second day the pains had subsided and, over the objections of her maids, she insisted on going about her daily routine. Their worrying over her normally would have pleased her, but now she grew impatient with their coddling and unwilling to allow herself such solicitous care. Her new toughness was largely due to Roman's evident fear that he would lose her suddenly; so for his sake, she determined herself to be well.

For Roman's part, the relief he felt when he first saw her up and dressed caused him to flood her with renewed attention. In spite of his appointments and responsibilities, he began seeking her out during the day to take her away from the palace. Further, his manner of doing that became almost devious.

A fortnight following Deirdre's miscarriage, he summoned her away from her sewing to meet him at the stables. Mysteriously, he had requested her to wear a simple villager's dress he had sent up to her room. As she put it on, she immediately thought of the time when as her guardian, he had dressed her this way for a mandated trip to Corona. "Now, what's on his scheming mind?"

When she arrived at the stables, she found Lady Grey and Fidelis tied to posts with rope bridles, but no saddles. Intrigued, she took Lady Grey's rope, looking about for Roman. She did not see him right away, until he came around the corner toward her. Whistling.

Deirdre squinted in disbelief. He was sauntering with a pack flung over his shoulder, wearing absolutely tattered peasant clothes. A soldier he passed came to a dead stop, staring, then collected himself to salute. Roman returned a casual salute, still whistling.

Roman drew up beside her and winked sideways at her bemused smile. "When was the last time you rode bareback, rose?" he asked. She blinked.

He lifted her up on Lady Grey, and she nervously grasped the rope bridle. "I don't remember *ever* riding bareback! Roman, what are we doing?"

He jumped up easily on Fidelis. "Going riding, like we used to." They rode out of the yard, Roman's shirt flapping open in the wind, while startled courtiers gazed after them. A bulky, knotted neckerchief covered the telltale brand on his chest.

"Where are we going?" Deirdre laughed.

"Oh, to the hills," he decided, taking a westward tack. They crossed over the road and passed through part of the town. When they did, Deirdre realized the reason for the clothes: no one gave either of them the slightest attention. Roman, anonymous and unhindered in his disguise, was momentarily free of the burdens of being Surchatain. For the present, he was no more a target of the people's demands, complaints, and criticisms than any other peasant on the street.

They passed a soldier who didn't salute because he did not even notice them. Roman smiled. "It's working," he whispered.

But a young boy playing on the side of the street looked up, calling, "Hello, Surchatain Roman!" as if to say, "Fine day, isn't it?"

Deirdre glanced around in sudden uneasiness at being recognized in such a state. But a woman reached down and cuffed the boy, saying, "Hush your nonsense!" And no one paid him any mind.

Roman sent the boy an acknowledging wink which asked him to keep their secret. Vindicated, the lad smiled to himself and continued playing. From there, Roman and Deirdre took a side road out of town and galloped across the open meadow where she had first learned to ride. Then he brought her to the foothills.

"Up this way," he said, leading her on a path through trees and low bushes. Summer glowed around them in full green splendor. The spring rains had been generous and the summer sun kind, so everywhere they looked there were clusters of wildflowers and bushes laden with berries. Fidelis trotted habitually kicking out his hoofs, so Deirdre kept Lady Grey a safe distance from him.

"Roman!" She pointed to their right. "Blueberries! Have you a basket?"

"I happen to have brought a small bag," he said smugly, drawing a burlap sack from his pack. They slipped off their horses to gather their find.

"Ooh, they're ripe," she exclaimed, popping several in her mouth. "They fall right into your hands."

"So I see," he replied, casting a glance at her stained fingers.

Noticing his glance, she mischievously returned, "Here, try some," and scooped up a handful to thrust into his face. But he caught her

177

arm, shaking a finger at her and chiding, "No, no, little girl."

She struggled to plant them in his face anyway, but he held her arm, smiling, until she had to break out in laughter. His smile faded slightly, and her laughter subsided. She stopped struggling. He released her arm to hold her waist and pull her close. His lined, solemn face took on that aspect of vulnerability she saw only at certain moments, and he gathered her up in a strong embrace.

The blueberries fell around their feet, forgotten. He laid her down in the grass, the sweet scent of honeysuckle around them, the crystal blue sky above.

Hardly a moment later there was a rustle behind them and a startled "My soul!"

Roman turned to see a matron with a berry basket, drawing her skirt up away from them. "Pardon, lady," Roman said hastily, lifting himself off the blushing Deirdre.

"How disgusting," the matron bristled.

"Pardon, lady," Roman repeated, his voice harder. "She is my wife."

"Really," the matron sniffed. "The Surchatain would whip you if he saw such behavior."

Deirdre and Roman stared at each other in surprise. "Why do you say that?" asked Roman.

"Everyone knows how strict he is. And you nasty peasants are the worst!" She left in a dignified huff.

Deirdre burst into laughter, but Roman bent to pick up the blueberry sack with a troubled air. "Roman, you can't be embarrassed by that silly old woman!"

"No," he said. "Not embarrassed. I just wonder where they get such a harsh view of me."

"Because they don't know you well," she answered, playfully putting his arms back around her.

He smiled. "I suppose, of anyone, you know me best."

"And I intend to know you better," she murmured, nibbling his lip. He let the sack drop again.

When they returned to the palace, they were met by Nihl. The Commander hardly glanced at their apparel, but said, "Surchatain, the men are preparing the grounds for the games. They will be ready to start tomorrow morning. Surchataine," he added belatedly, inclining his head.

"Oh good!" Deirdre exclaimed, looking out toward the yard where workmen were constructing a raised platform.

The games were a series of combative and athletic competitions Roman had instituted to encourage training among the soldiers. The events were archery, pugil sticks, horsemanship, spear throwing, wrestling, running, and stone hurling, with large sums of gold going to the winner in each game. A soldier could enter as many contests as he wished, and a special award was given to the man who won three or more.

Roman excelled in the games, of course, and the first year he held them he had won in pugil sticks, archery, and horsemanship. (Nihl had beat him out in wrestling; Captain Reuel had won the foot race in full battle gear; and a Polonti named Wence had taken the prizes in stone hurling and spear throwing.) Roman had turned his awards back over to the treasury and after that had foresworn competing again himself. As much as the men protested otherwise, he suspected judgments had been unconsciously weighted in his favor.

"Well, Nihl," commented Roman, "I will look forward to seeing what you can do this year."

Nihl turned up one corner of his mouth. "And I you, friend."

Roman shook his head. "Not this year, my brother. This year I will not compete; I will judge."

"I know you don't mean that," Deirdre said firmly.

The following morning, Deirdre found herself an advantageous spot on a balcony overlooking the grounds as the games began with pomp and pageantry below, colorful banners curling in the wind. The trumpets blasted a call to attention, and contestants lined up before the judges' dais at the end of the yard.

Roman walked up to the dais and raised his hands to quiet the excited crowd, then he began opening announcements. Deirdre could not hear him, as the dais was at the opposite end of the courtyard, but now and then his remarks were interrupted by bursts of cheers from the crowd—evidently in reaction to the value of awards this year.

Deirdre noticed a large number of townspeople had come to watch. Some enterprisers among them had set up refreshment stalls offering beer, cheese, and small pastries. She noticed too the giggling girls who had clustered together to cheer their favorites.

At the end of his little speech, Roman gestured toward the balcony where she sat. The soldiers about-faced to salute her with a shout. Deirdre smiled and lifted her hand.

The opening rounds of the games began. In one roped-off corner of the courtyard, the first two opponents faced each other with pugil sticks. Another area had been chalked with measuring marks for the stone throw. And the first round of horsemen reported to the stables to race the course of hedges and ditches.

Roman left the field. Deirdre was scanning the grounds for him when a sudden motion rocked her chair. Roman had grasped it as he sat down beside her. "I will watch the games with you from here until I have to go back down to judge the archery," he said.

179

"Roman, I want to see you compete," she protested, stroking his face.

He pulled his chair closer with a theatrical sigh. "My love, I am just getting too old for this."

"Don't say that! It's not true!"

He cast a sidelong glance at her as he settled back. "But it is, Deirdre. The younger men are quicker, and spring back easier. I can't tell you how difficult it was competing last year."

She stared ahead in stubborn denial, so he leaned forward and took her fingers. "Deirdre." He turned her face toward him. "Look at me. While you have grown up, I have grown older. Don't you realize this spring made eleven years that we have known each other?"

"Eleven years . . . ?" Could that be?

"Soon, you'll be mistaking me for grey-headed Basil!" He sat back with a laugh. She smiled too, until the inevitable end of that thought struck them both. "And soon, Deirdre, Ariel will take up my sword and shield—"

"No," she pleaded. "Don't start on that again, not now. Please— let's just watch the games." She stretched her hand to him and relenting, he kissed it, while cheers went up from the crowd below at a long stone throw.

CHAPTER 21

TWO DAYS LATER, in the midst of the continuing games, Roman was standing at the archery lines observing when an errand boy tugged on his shortcoat. "Surchatain, the Counselor sends for you. He says it is urgent."

Roman turned with reluctance. "Where is he?"

"In your chambers, sir." That raised Roman's brows. It must be important for Basil to intrude into the Surchatain's chambers.

When Roman opened the door to his receiving room, he saw Basil standing over a winded messenger. "Surchatain—" Basil met him and closed the door in one swift motion.

"What is the urgency?" he asked, looking to the messenger. The soldier stood and saluted, but the Counselor answered before he could.

180

"Surchatain, this man is from Outpost One. He reports the spies you sent to Polontis arrived at the outpost early this morning."

"This morning! From Eledith?"

"Yes, Surchatain—er, no, Surchatain." The man swallowed to gain his breath. "They did not make it to Eledith. On the way, they encountered an army marching due west, toward Corona. The vanguard carried Bruc's banners."

In his anger, Roman slapped a nearby couch so hard that the messenger jumped. "When I catch Bruc, I will—" Roman opened the door and told the boy outside, "Have Fidelis readied for me."

Basil advanced a step as the boy ran off. "Surchatain, we can send to have done whatever you wish."

"We must intercept that army before they reach Corona. And I need to hear the scouts' report firsthand at the outpost." Roman let off to belt on his sword, take up a money bag, and conceal a small dagger in his belt.

"Will you take the Commander with you, then?"

Roman paused, then shook his head. "Nihl has a good chance of winning at the pugil sticks today. I don't want to take him out of the games."

"I am certain he would consider this a higher priority," Basil insisted, his voice rising slightly.

Roman all but ignored him, striding out the chambers, but Basil and the dazed messenger followed. "Be certain to tell Deirdre where I have gone," Roman added over his shoulder.

"Surchatain—who shall go with you?" Basil demanded.

"I need no escort to the outpost, Counselor," Roman returned testily. He stepped into the foyer and the guards opened the great doors to him.

"Roman!" Basil shouted. "This is foolhardy!"

Roman glared at him, and the messenger behind the Counselor wilted, but Basil stood his ground. "I am not yet infirm to the point of needing someone to protect me," Roman said coldly.

At this point Fidelis was led up to the steps and Roman mounted with a vigorous leap. Basil grabbed the reins, groping for a convincing argument, but Roman merely nodded to him and kicked in his heels. He passed the inner gate instantly and was through the outer gate before the echo of hoofbeats had faded.

Sighing and muttering, Basil retraced his steps to the interior of the palace, where he stopped a passing maid. "Where is the Surchataine?"

The maid bowed. "Counselor, I believe she is on the balcony overlooking the archers."

He found Deirdre there, leaning on the stone rail as she watched the competition. She turned at his approach and smiled. "Basil, did you know I used to be rather good at archery? I wonder, if I practiced, how long it would take to get back into form . . . ?"

"Surchataine, I am afraid I have news that will not please you," he said with an air of resignation.

"What?" She gave him her full attention.

"We have received a report that Lord Bruc is advancing to attack Corona. The Surchatain has just departed in haste—alone—for Outpost One."

"Oh no," she moaned, leaning heavily on the railing. "Must he handle every problem himself?"

"Evidently, yes," he shrugged. "Please excuse me, Surchataine." She nodded, and he went to the pugiling ring to find Nihl.

But Basil was stopped on the way by Olynn. "Counselor—come arbitrate for us." The Captain took his arm and started toward the stone throwing arena.

"In a moment, Olynn. First I must find the Commander," Basil began, but voices were rising in the courtyard.

"Silence!" Olynn shouted. "The Counselor will make a judgment, and his decision is final." Then three contestants began presenting their complaints at once.

Basil waved his arms distractedly. "Stop, stop. I can't possibly understand you. You, first—what is your trouble?"

"He's using a different stone that throws easier," the man protested, pointing to his fellow.

"They are the same weight and roughly round, as the rules require," argued the second.

"But it's smaller. It hefts better."

"You should have used it then, when you had your turn." The other responded angrily to this and they began shouting again.

Basil interjected, "You will all throw again, using the same stone. In the future, you will throw only stones that have been matched fairly by the judges. Now, Olynn, excuse me. I must find Nihl." Basil took his leave of the contestants, who were still arguing, and walked through several yards to the pugil ring.

Commander Nihl had just stepped into the ring and taken up his pugil stick, as had his opponent. Basil gained the ringside as the match began, but he merely watched from there. It was best to let them finish, once started. If he attempted to interrupt and call Nihl aside, his opponent could legally take advantage of the distraction to win the match. With purses at stake, that kind of thing happened. Basil could not help smiling, however, when he saw Izana on the other side of the ring, watching anxiously.

The two contestants circled, gripping their oaken pugil sticks, which had thick leather pads on each end. The men were well-matched, about the same height and weight. For a time they just gauged each other and feinted, then Nihl followed an upward feint with a sharp lower blow. His opponent caught it narrowly, using the impetus to return a blow, which Nihl warded off smartly.

The other tried an upward lateral to the throat and Nihl ducked. Spinning, he caught his opponent in the back with the right pad. The fellow staggered, but used the opportunity to jab his pole in between Nihl's knees, tripping him. Nihl fell, rolled, blocked a blow, and swept his pole to bring the other down with him. Meanwhile, the spectators cheered and hissed lustily at solid blows and feints.

Basil shifted. The match was drawing out into a long one, owing to the skill of the competitors. His eyes flicked to a portion of the north market road visible beyond the palace walls. Roman was probably justified in his confidence in traveling it alone, but Basil was never one to take unnecessary risks, especially in light of the weaver's warning. Nihl would likely agree.

A sudden shout from the onlookers around him brought his eyes back to the ring. Nihl had delivered a sound blow, but the other recovered to continue fighting. As it went on, Basil grew decidedly edgy.

Finally Nihl solidly decked the fellow, who raised a hand in defeat. As Nihl sagged out of the ring, Basil rushed through the crowd and pulled him away, urging, "Come immediately."

Nihl followed him, panting and wiping his face on a cloth thrown to him. ". . . Counselor?"

"We have received a messenger from Outpost One who says that an army has been sighted traveling due west from Eledith."

"To Corona," Nihl remarked dully, shaking his head. "I feared it."

"The Surchatain has just left for Outpost One. If you ready yourself quickly, you may catch him on the road."

"Why did he leave without me?" Nihl asked, starting toward the palace.

"Pride," Basil answered immediately.

Nihl glanced at him before racing up the stone stairs to his chambers.

Within a quarter hour Nihl was astride his Arabian, waiting as the great front gates swung slowly open for him. It was almost a full hour after the Surchatain's departure, however. As Nihl spurred out into the roadway, he suddenly yanked his horse to a stop, staring down the road.

Baffled, Basil ran out of the gates to look down the road himself. And his heart went cold as they watched Fidelis, riderless, leisurely trot up to the gates. The horse allowed Basil to take the reins and stroke him numbly. He was unmarked and uninjured.

Nihl said, "If the Surchatain has had an accident, he cannot be far. I will look." He spurred off without further conjecture.

The Counselor sent Fidelis to be stabled, then stood at the front gates to wait. He stood as the clouds passed by and the sun moved westward. He stood as the sentries changed the guard for night duty and a query came from Deirdre: Was he going to eat tonight? He sent back a polite request to be excused.

Then, one rider galloped up. Nihl. He dismounted at the gate and wordlessly gave the reins to an errand boy. Reluctantly, he brought his eyes up to meet Basil's. "I found nothing," Nihl whispered in defeat. "Nothing."

Basil gazed at him, sick with despair. Without a reply, he took the Commander's arm and led him to the banquet hall where Deirdre and her guests were eating. As the Counselor and Commander solemnly entered, Deirdre turned and said, "Well, will you eat now?" Then, "What is wrong?"

Basil bowed. "Surchataine Deirdre, Surchatain Roman has disappeared. In his stead, until he is found, I appoint you to rule Westford."

Deirdre paled to a sickly grey. "What . . . what has happened to him?"

"We do not know, Surchataine. He left, as I told you, for the outpost, but his horse has returned without him. The Commander was able to find no clue as to what befell him. The first action I suggest is to have searchers comb the forest along the highway."

Kam stood. "Surchataine, I will see to that immediately." He left without waiting for her nod, and Olynn left with him.

"Surchataine," said the Commander, "when you are done with your meal, there are matters we must lay out before you."

Deirdre put her cloth aside and left the hall with Basil and Nihl.

After Roman had ridden out the palace gates, he intercepted the paved market road and took it north. He had traveled this road so many times that he hardly attended to his surroundings, his mind being weighed by numerous concerns. There was, however, one section of the road that was famous as a bane to travelers. It ran through thick trees which often hid wolves or robbers. Roman unconsciously sped Fidelis down this stretch, for he knew that faster travelers made harder targets.

As he rounded a curve, he came upon a white cloth lying in the middle of the road. It was just a dropped neckerchief, but it brought Fidelis to a dead stop. Roman was muttering to himself and urging Fidelis to go around it when his ears caught the telltale whiz of a flying arrow behind him.

He ducked too late. The head of the arrow pierced his shortcoat and planted itself in his back. He fell from the saddle to the brush at Fidelis' hoofs, and there he lay.

PART THREE

CALLE VALLEY

CHAPTER 22

ROMAN LAY face down in the dirt at the side of the road, the arrow that felled him protruding from his back. Fidelis stood nearby nosing in the grass.

The slender shadow of a man fell across the Surchatain's still form. The man stuffed a white neckerchief into his pants, then reached down and ruthlessly jerked out the arrow. There was no cry in response.

He bent to touch the body, or take something, but was startled by a not-far-off sound in the bushes. So he quickly gathered the Surchatain's leather money bag and ebony-hilt sword and grabbed for Fidelis's reins.

The horse shied away. Cursing under his breath, for the rustling was nearer now, he chased after the horse. But Fidelis kicked out his hoofs and trotted off.

With a last glance at Roman's form, the man departed.

Moments later, a peasant girl carrying a bread basket stepped out of the forest onto the road. She was about thirteen years old, with a heart-shaped face and wide-set brown eyes. A dingy scarf covered her thick brown hair.

She took to the road and began walking along it, approaching Roman. She did not see him, however, for those wide-set eyes were hazily focused on her daydreams rather than the road ahead. So it was only when her foot caught under his knee and she fell sprawling across his body that she discovered him.

"Ugh!" She scrambled up, wiping blood from her arm. Then she looked down on him curiously. "Must be one of the soldiers. Good thing he's dead." But seeing that blood was oozing from a wound in his back, she bent her ear to his mouth, then jumped up. "He's not dead—he's *alive.*"

189

This discovery made her scowl. "I have to finish him, then. That's what Pax would do. That's what I should do." She had no weapon, so she searched around him for one, but failed to find the dagger hidden in his belt.

"Well . . ." She rose uncertainly. "I'll just leave him here to die, then. No one cares for those stupid soldiers. They just live like rulers and lord it over regular people. Pax will be glad to hear about him, dying in the road like a dog." She picked up her basket and began walking away. "Dying like a dog," she repeated to herself, as she took a step.

Involuntarily she looked back at him. "You can just die," she said spitefully, and took another step.

But with each step her feet seemed to grow to the ground. She cast another glance back at him, and could not turn away again. The pressure was not eased until she came to stand over him once more.

"I can't leave you here," she said suddenly. "Someone may find you and help you. I have to make sure you die. I have to take you to my brother Pax—he'll make sure. He'll be pleased to make sure." So she took his arms and dragged him from the road into the forest.

She dragged him a ways, though he was heavy and she had to often stop and rest. But she kept at it—over briars and poison ivy, through woods where there wasn't even a sheep path. Finally, panting, she brought him to a mean little hut in the midst of the trees. A small garden in back and a thatched overhang for animals were all that distinguished it. She dragged him through an excited gaggle of curious geese, then through the main room of the hut to a crude lean-to attached to the back wall. There, she maneuvered him into a face-down position on a rough cot.

She checked his breathing again, thinking that the rough trip might have killed him. There was breath in him yet, though it was short and fast. "Pax will be home tonight," she announced to him. "You'll be a dead man for sure when he gets here." He made no more response than any dead man would.

His blood-soaked leather shortcoat glistened in the afternoon sunlight, which spilled in through a tiny window onto his face and back. The girl watched him quietly, studying his strong features and thick black hair. He was pale under a normally brown complexion. She touched his hand, and found it cold. She moved her fingers to touch his face, then jerked her hand away as if caught in a wrongdoing.

She sat beside the cot, chewing her lip and watching him bleed. "If you die before Pax comes home, he'll be angry," she said. "He would want to do it himself. I had better keep you alive till tonight." She quickly stripped off his shortcoat and shirt. She daubed the shirt

190

in a nearby bucket of water and washed the blood off his back to find the wound. It was in the middle of his left shoulder blade. It must not have opened his heart, but how it bled!

Folding the leather into a compress, she stood over him and pressed it onto the jagged puncture. She held it there, pressing down with all her strength to stop the flow of blood.

After a few minutes, her arms grew tired and she let up on the compress to see if the bleeding had stopped. No—the blood poured out again as soon as she released pressure. She quickly replaced the compress and leaned on it, longer, until she had no strength left and had to ease up. The blood flowed again.

She pressed on it once more, feeling a rising apprehension as the sun dropped in the sky. Her brother would be home soon. She had to finish this before he came home . . .

She lifted her feet from the floor to lean her full body weight on the compress. She leaned, pressing steadily on his back, as the sky grew steadily redder. Finally, she carefully removed the compress, sure the bleeding had stopped by now.

Breathlessly, she watched the small wound stay closed. Then it opened to release a trickle again.

"Blast!" she shouted. In frustration and rising panic, she slapped the compress back on the wound and threw herself on it, trembling with the fatigue of effort.

Seconds later she heard her brother's voice outside the hut: "Effie!" Her insides wrenched in distress. She lifted herself up and threw a coverlet over the injured man, spilling out in a passionate whisper, "You're going to die and there's nothing I can do about it!"

Pax entered the hut just as she came into the main room. He was a strapping young man, maybe nineteen or so, with unruly brown hair like hers and hints of an straggly, immature beard. "Effie, you worthless snip, where is my dinner?" He slumped onto a stool at a crude table.

"It's just warming up, Pax," she whispered, running to the kettle on the hearth to stir the long-forgotten stew.

"Get it on the table!" he ordered, slamming something down beside him. Numbly, Effie ladled out a bowlful and put it in front of him. She lit a candle from the fire and placed that on the table too. That was when she saw the fine leather money bag beside his bowl.

"What is that?" she pointed to it.

He startled up and slapped her hand away. "Greedy snip! Leave that alone!" He jerked it off the table and it fell open, spilling a shower of gold coins to the floor.

"Pax!" she gasped in disbelief. "Where—where did you get all the *money?*"

He fell on the floor to gather them back into the money pouch, which carried an imprint. "I work, don't I?" he spat at her. "And if you touch any of this, I'll kill you."

"Oh no, I won't," she murmured, then stood back against the hearth as he sullenly ate.

It was dark now, but for the fire in the grate and the candle on the table. Pax finished his supper and took the pouch with him to a cot against the wall. Then Effie ladled out some stew from the kettle for herself. As she sat to eat, he watched her warily, tying the money pouch around his middle. Then he lay down carefully on top of it.

Effie cleaned her bowl and put a cover on the kettle. Saying, "Goodnight, Pax," she picked up the candle and turned toward the lean-to.

"Oh no!" He sat up suddenly. "No you don't! I know what you're scheming!" The candle quivered in her hand. "You think to wait till I'm asleep, then slit my throat for this money!"

"No, Pax!" she protested.

"You sleep right down here on the floor beside me, where I can keep an eye on you," he demanded.

"Pax—" she whined.

"Lay down! Here!" he shouted.

She spread a blanket on the dirt floor beside his cot and snuffed the candle. When he heard her lie on the floor, he grunted and settled down.

Although Effie soon heard him snoring, she did not dare get up from the floor. But in her mind's eye she saw the blood trickling stubbornly from the wound. She rolled over and pressed her face in the blanket to muffle her weeping.

After a tormented night, Effie awoke when Pax kicked her as he rolled out of the cot. "Get up and get my breakfast," he growled.

She leaped up and grabbed a bucket. Rubbing her swollen eyes, she stumbled to the well outside while hints of morning streaked the sky. When she brought the water in, she almost dropped it upon seeing him stepping toward the lean-to room. "Pax!" she screamed. He jerked around.

"Pax—that—that water is dirty. I brought you clean water."

He grunted and took the bucket she tremulously held out to him. As he washed, she mixed the lard and wheat flour into dough, then patted out cakes. She tested the walls of the fireplace oven, finding it warm enough from the overnight coals, and slapped the cakes against the walls of the oven to cook.

192

Then she poured him ale from a jug while he counted out the money pieces at the table. Effie watched him sidewise, but could not see how much gold he had. It looked to her like more than fifty pieces.

She brought him the cakes and he ate. Effie thought he looked rather like a turtle with his head scrunched down between his shoulders. A snapping turtle, she thought. Then he stood, swallowing the last bite as he gathered the gold into the pouch. "I'm leaving for a few days, Effie. You keep yourself out of trouble, or when I come back I'll whip you good."

"Yes, Pax," she whispered.

He turned to go, but paused. She watched his feet, fearing he needed something from the other room. But he reached into the pouch and tossed her two coins. "Here."

"Thank you, Pax!" she exclaimed, more in relief than gratitude. She scurried to pick them up, but once his back was turned she let them drop again. Effie watched him tread away into the forest, as he had no horse. She waited, watching, afraid that the moment she left the door he would return. But he didn't.

With a quietly pounding heart, Effie approached her secret in the lean-to. At the doorway she stopped and closed her eyes. He was dead. She knew it. She knew he had bled to death during the night. All she could do for him now was bury him. Her eyes began to water, but she scolded herself, "Stop that now!" and went in.

He was so pale, almost grey. The wound was no longer bleeding. Of course not—dead men don't bleed.

She reached out to his neck and felt his flesh warm yet. Then her fingers felt the weak, rapid throb of his pulse. Unwilling to believe it, she sat for minutes with her fingers on his neck. Each heartbeat surely must be his last. But they stubbornly persisted.

He was alive. Not only that, but he was alive because of her. Worthless Effie had saved a stranger's life. She leaned her head weakly down on his right shoulder and wept.

After a little while she stilled, continuing to rest her head on his back. She listened to the faint *puh-pomb, puh-pomb* of his heartbeat, drawing a kind of strength from it.

Effie lifted her head with a little shake. Why should she care so? She did not even know his name. But she could not be rid of the persistent sense of excitement over what she had done. Timidly, feeling as though she were being watched, she lifted the bucket of bloody water to empty it. As she carried it outside, she might have sworn someone followed her, speaking strange, voiceless encouragement in her ear: *Things will never be the same for you again.*

193

Deirdre awoke that morning from despondent, lonely dreams. She reached over to Roman's side of the bed, and its cold emptiness stung her. She rolled onto her face, moaning, "Oh my God, why have you done this to me? What has become of him?"

She lay in bed, unwilling to pray and unable to sleep, until a serving girl brought a tray of breakfast to her. The maid set the tray down to open the draperies, and Deirdre hid her eyes from the wash of light. "Please go away," Deirdre murmured.

"Surchataine," the maid bowed, and her soft voice communicated depths of sympathy. But she had a message to deliver: "Counselor Basil asked to meet with you after you have had breakfast."

Deirdre lay unmoved a moment, then slowly pushed up on her elbow. "I will meet him in the library in half an hour," she said. The maid bowed and glided out, leaving the tray.

Deirdre bowed her head on her arm. "I cannot do this, unless you help me. I am weak, and scared, and lonely . . . How can I stand unless you hold me up?" Sighing, she reached for the tray.

In exactly half an hour the door to the library opened. The Surchataine entered and nodded as the Counselor and Commander Nihl rose. The first thing she said was, "Did the scouts find anything along the road last night?"

"No, Surchataine," answered Nihl. His brown Polonti face, impassive and rugged, gave no hint of what he felt at losing a ruler who called him brother. "We have just now sent teams to the nearest villages to search and question the people. Someone must have seen something, or know something."

"Should we . . . let it be known that Roman is missing?" she asked dubiously.

"That information has already spread far and wide," said Basil. "What we must do now is put you on the throne at open audience this morning and leave no doubt that you are ruling."

She sat weakly, and Nihl and Basil also sat. "I simply cannot understand what might have happened to him. Roman just does not fall off horses," she muttered.

Basil's thin shoulders drooped, and he ran a hand over his smooth grey hair. "It appears he should have heeded the weaver's warning."

Deirdre's face came up. "What warning?"

Basil and Nihl looked at one another. "You did not know of it?" Nihl asked.

"I should have realized Roman would not tell her," Basil said. "Surchataine, the night you miscarried, before you came to the table, a weaver from town requested an audience with the Surchatain. He reported that he had overheard an assassin being hired to kill Roman."

194

Deirdre paled. "You think that is what happened?"

Basil did not answer, so Nihl said dispassionately, "It seems likely. If so, it was a very clean kill."

"You think . . ." Deirdre struggled, "you think he is dead?"

"We must assume it, Surchataine," answered Nihl, gently now. "To protect ourselves, we must act on the assumption that he is dead, and hope privately that he is not."

Deirdre put her head in her hands, overcome. Nihl and Basil sat by quietly, empathizing with her in her grief, but also anxious for the state of Lystra. At this time, of all times, they must have someone of strength on the throne, for the smell of weakness would bring predators out from every corner of the Continent.

Nihl knelt beside her chair. "Surchataine," he said sternly. She looked at him with surprised, teary eyes. "We must have your word to send an army to Corona. Bruc must be prevented from attacking it. What is your word on this?"

Floundering in sorrow and ignorance, she gazed at him. But from habit she sent up a weak impulse of prayer in this most severe trial.

The tears stopped flowing. She still gazed at Nihl, but her look had changed to one of concentration. "No," she said. "You will not send an army; you will go. Take with you a unit of Polonti volunteers— only Polonti. Go stand at the gates of Corona and tell Bruc he cannot attack the city. Tell him to go home."

Nihl, still kneeling, eyed her without changing expression. Then he rose and said, "We will leave immediately."

When he had gone out, Deirdre stood and smoothed her dress as if trying to gain inner composure. She set her shoulders and reached a hand to the Counselor. "We will hold audience now. Come—I need you to stand beside me."

As they walked the corridor en route to the audience hall, Deirdre slipped into reminiscing about the events she had witnessed in that hall. She thought of the day eleven years ago that her father Karel had gestured, and Roman had stepped out from the crowd in the hall. *I am appointing a guardian for you. His name is Roman. . . .* She remembered him then exactly as she had seen him yesterday morning— strong and brown, his face lined even then.

And she remembered the horror of the day that Karel had dragged Roman bound before everyone in the hall, to pronounce a sentence of death for "indecency with the Chataine Deirdre," when all he was guilty of was lovingly guarding her . . . Her face still burned with indignity at the memory.

But he had escaped. And they had been together as husband and wife for one sweet night before her cousin Jason had taken her away.

195

Still they had been reunited, after the villager's disease had devastated the invading armies at Outpost One. And their son Ariel had been born . . .

Then when she was kidnapped and enslaved at Diamond's Head, Roman's love had driven him to search in vain for her until Galapos, her real father, found her and freed her with his life. So strong had the bond of love between them grown, that he had allowed her to go with him to Corona . . . And in imprisonment, torture, and danger, they had seen a higher Power demonstrated in increasingly vivid displays.

A line began to connect in her reminiscences . . . in all the things that she had experienced, even in all the apparent defeats and hopeless situations, hadn't she seen the Lord resolve every crisis in a manner unforeseen? That line began to glimmer as she saw it move from instance to instance, picking happenings and persons at will, to form them into a pattern of purpose and convergence. Years after the fact, she could see the good that had resulted from those things which before had been incomprehensible.

What it meant was that now the Hand which controlled those events was still holding the reins. When even the worst happened, she could still know that the Lord of heaven and earth was fashioning that glimmering line into something of eternal significance.

That was how Deirdre was able to walk into the audience hall in the midst of a milling, curious crowd, and sit with an air of finality on the throne.

"Surchatain Roman is dead," she announced to the crowd, which stilled to near lifelessness. "As he intended, I am ruling in his stead. I will enforce his decrees and carry out his commands. But I warn you that I am angry and will not show the tolerance he showed. My husband's assassin has gained you a tyrant in his stead. So go away— I will not hear anything from you today."

She rose from the throne and paced through the crowd, not looking to the right or the left. After some confused hesitation, the people went down on their knees as she passed.

In the corridor, she saw Captain Olynn running toward her, his face full of suppressed excitement. "Surchataine! By accident, the men have found—"

"Roman?" she exclaimed, in a spasm of hope. "Roman?"

"No, Surchataine." His face fell. "They have found the chief emissary from Qarqar still in Westford."

Deirdre's brows contracted in puzzlement, but Basil, beside her, practically shouted, "Bring him to the library! And Orenthal the weaver as well!"

196

Olynn raced out and Deirdre spun almost angrily toward the flushed Counselor. "What are you doing?"

"Forgive me, Surchataine," he urged, taking her arm. "I am acting on facts I forget you do not know. Come." He steered her toward the library, saying, "I never finished telling you—Orenthal is the weaver who warned the Surchatain he had overheard an assassin being hired. Orenthal's description of the man who did the hiring seemed to fit the Qarqarian emissary. We wish to make sure of that now."

"I see," Deirdre murmured, coloring at her hasty, imperial manner toward an old friend. "Why would Qarqar wish Roman dead?" she asked humbly.

"For more reasons than I have time to recount. I suspect it may hinge on Troyce's discovery of their horde of gold. They may have decided to ensure that Roman could not demand it at some point in the future."

"Ah," said Deirdre, nodding serenely while receiving all this as new information. She began to wish she had paid more attention in the past to what was going on around her.

They entered the library. Basil did not seat himself, but waited for her to sit first. Deirdre, unaware of this, walked to the great double windows and placed her hands on the diamond panes of greenish glass. *Roman* . . . an intense longing for him passed through her with a shudder.

Before she could sink into self-pity, the library door opened and Olynn entered with the emissary. They both bowed to Deirdre and Basil. "My lady," said the emissary, "may I ask what prompts you to arrest me like a criminal and bring me here?"

"You may ask nothing of me, and it is presumptuous of you to address me," Deirdre said coolly, and turned back to the window.

The emissary's high forehead wrinkled at the rebuke. He did not look chastened, but rather mildly irritated. He began to sit, but Olynn restrained him and Basil narrowed his eyes forbiddingly. They all stood, as Deirdre stood.

They waited in ominous silence, Deirdre still at the window. Then she turned expectantly, and within minutes a guard arrived with a bushy-headed tradesman. He glanced all around, particularly staring at the emissary.

"Are you Orenthal the weaver?" Deirdre asked.

"Yes, my lady—er, Surchataine," he said, bowing awkwardly, a little to the side.

"Do you know this man? Or have you seen him before?" she asked, pointing to the emissary.

"Yes, Surchataine; he's the one," Orenthal answered firmly. "He's the one I heard hiring to get Surchatain Roman killed. I wish he'd 'a' listened to me." The emissary went pale and slack-jawed.

"I wish so also," said Deirdre, sternly preventing her eyes from watering. "But you did your part, and that deserves reward. Guard, take Orenthal to Sevter and see that he is paid one hundred royals for his service to the Surchatain."

"Thank you, my lady!" exclaimed the weaver, and he slapped the guard on the back as he was escorted out.

Like a crouching lioness, Deirdre turned to the emissary. He huffed, "That man is a demented liar—" but the Surchataine interrupted him with a command uttered through gritted teeth: "Go back to Qarqar," she said. "Go back to your Surchatain, and tell him to prepare for an assault such as he has never seen. When we leave Hornbound, there will not be a grain of your precious gold anywhere, nor even will a corner of a building remain upright to hide it in."

She finished but he remained, gaping at her. "Go!" she screamed. Thus impelled, he fled.

Deirdre raised blank, weary eyes to the gentle Counselor, who smiled wryly. "A just retribution," he murmured, "and maddening at that. Roman could not have done better."

"Oh Basil!" She fell on him, too enervated to express the ache within except by weeping.

CHAPTER 23

EFFIE SAT by the cot on which her visitor lay, methodically stroking his hair. She would get up and pace the room, then sit again abruptly to check on him. In an instant, it seemed, his face had gone from pale grey to hot red. He was burning with fever, and she was unable to do anything but bathe him with wet rags. Now and then he would groan for water, though he never seemed to come fully awake when he drank from the ladle she held to his mouth.

After he had settled down somewhat, she pulled back the oiled window covering for air and went outside to work restlessly. She tossed a handful of grain to the geese, then with only half a mind weeded her garden of leeks, carrots, cabbage, and beans. She stopped by the

198

lean-to window to look in on him on her way to the well, and stopped there again on her way back to the garden with a full bucket. She watered the vegetables, then headed back to the well. She kept glancing through the window at him until she grew irritated with herself for being so solicitous.

On her last return trip she saw him stirring again, so she ran with sloshing water through the hut and into the lean-to. He was raising himself up weakly on his right forearm facing the window, eyes closed. He uttered, "—thirsty," before his head dropped down again.

Effie brought the ladle and bucket to him. He started to raise himself up on his left arm to drink for himself, but when he put weight on the arm, it buckled and he recoiled in pain. She steadied his head with one hand and brought the ladle to his mouth, but he was still struggling to do it himself. He managed to knock the ladle enough to soak the cot but not get one drop in his mouth. Finally he seemed to realize he was interfering with his own comfort, so he gave up and let her ladle the water to him as before. As he finished it, he opened his eyes just a crack to see her before laying his head back down with a moan.

The girl sat transfixed, for he had laid his feverish head on her open hand, his cheek resting in her palm. She kept very still, not wishing to remove her hand and disturb him. But, watching him, a warm feeling poured over her, causing her to slide her other arm over his shoulder and lean down on his neck. "You're going to be well," she promised in a whisper. "I will take care of you."

Then she jerked up, hearing hoofbeats outside the hut. Quickly, she drew the tattered parchment covering over the window and threw the blanket over him. Fearfully, she peeked out the door of the hut.

Three soldiers were dismounting and coming toward the doorway, scattering the honking geese. The one in front, a big blond man, saw her and stopped his companions. "Greetings, young lady," he said amicably. She did not answer.

"We are looking for a man perhaps you have seen," he continued. "Tall and dark-haired, dressed as one of us. He may be injured, or dead, yet even so we are offering a large reward to anyone who can lead us to him, in whatever state he may be." He held out a bulging money bag to give weight to his words.

The blood drained from her face as the panic rose. Did they know she had found him? Why were they offering such a large reward for him, dead or alive? He must be a criminal. Only dangerous criminals carried that kind of bounty. But if she asked what he had done, they would become suspicious.

"No," she whispered. "I have seen no one."

He cocked his head to catch her reply, then said, "Remember, we are anxious to find him," hefting the money bag again. She nodded and withdrew into the hut, peeking out as they mounted their horses and rode away.

When they were out of sight of the hut, one soldier asked Captain Olynn, "Don't you think we should search the places we stop at, sir?"

"What for?" asked Olynn. "That would only annoy the people needlessly. There's no one they won't give up for a bag of gold."

"But why don't we at least tell them it's Surchatain Roman we are looking for?" persisted the first.

"On the outside chance that he may actually be alive, though wounded or captured. If such is the case, I fear to think how many people would finish him off if they knew he was the Surchatain, when they would let a stranger live in peace." The first soldier nodded sadly at the truth of this.

Effie, trembling in relief to see them gone, backed into the hut and stood over Roman again. "Who are you?" she whispered. His closed eyes did not so much as flicker. "What have you done that they offer so much money for you?" She put her mind to trying to recall any outlaws she had heard about lately—what they looked like and what had become of them. But she could not recall any in particular that he might be.

"Effie! Effie! Are you home, child?"

She jumped at the voice and ran outside to see a smiling, middle-aged woman in a fashionable linen dress, full and flowing. She had a laughing face that once had been very beautiful, with dark eyes and clear skin. The laughter, now permanently etched around her eyes and mouth, revealed her age but gave her an appeal that younger, more vain women did not have.

"Oweda!" Effie threw her arms around her the way a child would a beloved grown-up, but being just as tall as the woman, almost knocked her down. "Oweda, I didn't know if you would ever come see me again!"

The woman sighed, "I'm sorry, dear; I kept trying to come, always feeling anxious about you, but the most absurd things held me up time and again. I could only pray the good Lord would keep you safe till I got here to see you for myself. Is . . . is your brother here?"

"No! He's gone for a few days. What did you bring me?" Effie asked eagerly, poking at the matron's basket.

"Let's go have a look," Oweda answered smiling, and Effie took her into the hut.

Remembering her secret, Effie exclaimed, "Oweda, you won't believe what happened yesterday!"

"I want to hear all," Oweda declared. "But first look at these."

200

She pulled a handful of brightly colored ribbons from the basket.

"Oweda!" squealed the girl. "Oh—put them on! Put them on me!" She yanked off her dull brown scarf and turned the back of her head to her friend.

"Only two or three at once," Oweda smiled indulgently, taking Effie's hair to braid it.

Effie fingered the embroidered ribbons and murmured, "They must have cost you a lot of money."

"Oh no, not too much," Oweda answered lightly. "A seller we met on the road gave us a good price on them when we told him we had a girl who would look so pretty in them!"

Effie smiled shyly, then looked toward the open door. "Where is Mathias and your cart?"

"He is in Westford, selling the rest of our pottery. I think we might make thirty royals on this trip."

"That's *wonderful!*" Effie gasped, sincerely without envy.

The matron tied ribbons in Effie's hair, studying the effect with satisfaction. But her expression changed to seriousness when she turned the girl around. "Effie, I worry about you, staying here alone. And I worry more when your brother is here!" Effie began to speak but Oweda continued, "There's so much bad happening. We just heard in Westford that Surchatain Roman has been killed. Murdered, and they haven't caught the murderer. This is just not a good place for a child to be alone. Mathias and I have been talking, dear, and since we cannot come by often enough to take care of you, we want you to come live with us, and be our child. You know how Mathias and I love you. Come home with us."

Effie almost shouted her acceptance before remembering the man on the cot. *So what? Leave him here,* she thought. But he might not live without some attention, and then what good would all her effort have been? *Oweda will help me care for him,* she reasoned, then gasped as Oweda's comments suddenly shed light on his identity. Oweda would not tend *him.* Only one person in the whole world would do it. . . .

Effie dropped her head and whispered, "I wish I could come with you."

"Well, why don't you?" exclaimed Oweda.

Effie glanced dismally toward the back room. "I . . . can't. He needs me."

Oweda pursed her lips. "Effie, one of these days he's going to leave and not ever come back. This might be that day. Then what will you do?"

The girl's lip quivered. "I can't leave yet. I want to, but I can't."

Oweda sighed. "I shouldn't fault you for being loyal to your brother,

201

scum though he is." She began pulling other items from the basket—sausage and cheese, a little pair of slippers, a comb, and a crock of jam and bread.

"Thank you, Oweda, thank you," Effie murmured as she gathered the things to her.

Oweda stood reluctantly. "I cannot even stay the day. We must refill our cart and leave for a fair in Calle Valley. But I will come again to see you, dearest, and to see that you are well."

Effie stood to hug her. The matron held her in disappointment, then smiled slightly. "You haven't told me what happened yesterday," Oweda reminded her. But the matron glimpsed something shiny on the dirt floor and wonderingly bent to pick up two gold royals.

"That is what happened," answered Effie. "Pax gave me some money."

Oweda carefully pressed the coins into the girl's hand and observed, "Miracles yet happen, then." She kissed Effie's face. "I love you, child."

Effie held on to her—so very close to leaving with her and not looking back. But then she let go of Oweda and said miserably, "Please come back some day, Oweda. Please."

"You know I will, Effie. Goodbye, little dear."

Effie watched her disappear in the direction of Westford, then listlessly went to the back room to check on her visitor. He was sleeping in the same position as before, skin still burning.

Effie sat beside his cot and put her head in her hands. "So that is who you are," she murmured. "Why did you kill Surchatain Roman?" Her head dropped down. "And I have saved the life of a murderer. I could have gone to live with Oweda and Mathias, but for you, and here you are nothing but a murderer. Why should I stay for you?" she demanded. He did not even twitch.

Sighing, she cooled him with wet cloths once more and went out to fix herself a dinner of sausage and cheese.

He awoke only once more that day, again to ask for water. But once he drank it he lay right back down and did not open his eyes. Effie then saw that the gash in his shoulder was draining a foul pus. She washed it clean, but pus continued to drain from the wound.

"I should bandage that," Effie told herself, looking about for something to use. She retrieved his shirt to make bandages of it, but it was dirty and bloodstained—"No, it won't do like this. It must be clean." She boiled the shirt over the fire and hung it out to dry on a bush. Then she thought of his other clothes—specifically, the leather shortcoat beneath his cot.

Examining it, she shook her head sadly. It was caked and stiff with dried blood—just unsalvageable. "Shame," she murmured. "Once it

202

was a nice coat." Well, if it couldn't be cleaned, she had best get rid of it.

Effie wadded it up to throw it in the fire, but caught herself. "No, no. It's tanned. It will stink horribly." She decided to bury it. So she took it out beside the garden, where she remembered with irritation that her gardening spade was inside. Dropping the coat, she trudged back to fetch the spade, casting an eye on her visitor, as always.

Coming back around the corner of the hut with the spade, she startled at the sudden, agitated honking of her geese. She ran forward and muttered, "Oh no!" A mongrel dog was crouching over the shortcoat, chewing on it happily.

"Go away!" she shouted, brandishing the spade. The dog scurried off, taking the coat with him. "No!" She caught hold of one coat sleeve, but the mongrel held the other, shaking it playfully. "Let go—you—" The dog growled fiercely, much enjoying this game.

Effie went for stronger tactics and raised the spade to beat the mutt. But he stole the coat out of her one-handed grip and raced with it into the trees.

She chased him, but lost him in the brush. "Oh, piff," she muttered. "I hope no one else finds it. Why do things always go wrong for me?" She turned dismally back to the hut, stopping at the bush to check the shirt. It was still a bit damp, but now that it was clean she spread it out to inspect it more closely.

It was a very nice shirt, of some shiny cloth with a tiny, tight weave. A person didn't see that kind of cloth everyday. At least, Effie didn't. Its only flaw was the rip in the back. "I hate to tear this up for bandages," she mused, and then decided that she would not.

Effie left the shirt on the bush and ran to dig around the cot in the large room. Triumphantly, she pulled out one of her brother's shirts, left for her to wash. She threw it with a cunning grin into the kettle over the fire. "I'll wash it," she said agreeably, as if speaking to its owner, "—before I rip it to pieces."

Once the shirt was washed and dried and torn to proper lengths, Effie took it into the lean-to and hesitated over the wounded man. "I have to be careful not to make him bleed again . . ." She gingerly pushed one end of a strip under his chest, then brought it up under his left arm. The other end she passed under his right arm, then she tied the two ends. The bandage just barely covered the wound, which was almost too high, and she saw the need to pass a length over his left shoulder as well.

Effie tied the strips on in layers a little nervously, dogged by a nebulous fear that he would wake up or die during the process. But she finished without disturbing him, and proudly admired her handiwork.

Then she looked distastefully at his belted trousers, spotted with blood and sweat. "I should wash those," she said. But she could not work up the courage to take them off him, so she rationalized that bandaging him was enough for one day.

It was getting on twilight now, so Effie gathered up some brush and small logs to replenish the fire for the night. She sat at the table and spread some of the currant jam on bread while she considered how quiet and comfortable it was here when her brother was gone.

When she finished eating, she remembered the man's shirt was still outside, hanging exposed. So she brought it in quickly, bolting the door against the night, and sat by candlelight to mend it. She found her needle and thread, but the darkness around made her want company, even that of an unconscious stranger.

Effie took her candle to sit beside his bed and work. She looked him over before she sat—to make sure he was still alive, and also to make sure he was still asleep. Finding both to be the case, she sat in some confidence, taking up the shirt. "I don't know why I'm bothering about you," she told him disdainfully. But then the thought crossed her mind, *You thought the shirt worth saving. Is the man less so?*

She glanced at him uncomfortably and stitched the tear in silence.

After the usual sumptuous dinner in the palace of Westford, during which Deirdre was silent, Basil ordered musicians to come play before the table. Privately, he had told them he wished nothing rowdy or gay, as the whole of Westford was in mourning for Surchatain Roman. So with lutes, flutes, and sackbut, a troupe bowed to Deirdre and began to play.

It was apparent they had chosen tonight's selections with care. Their melodies were laments in minor keys: sighing, airy strains on flute and low, resonant bellows on sackbut that were reminiscent of the trumpet blare honoring the dead.

Basil glanced at the Surchataine as they played, sensitive to how the music might affect her. But she stared ahead, focusing on nothing, nor changing expression. She seemed far away at the moment, in secret realms.

A soldier came to the doorway and gestured to Captain Olynn. Murmuring apologies to Deirdre, the Captain rose and went out to speak with him. Deirdre blinked. Olynn turned his back to the hall as he took something from the soldier's hands. Only a word or two passed between them, then they hesitantly eyed the table.

As the musicians finished a piece, Deirdre dismissed them with a wave. She shifted expectantly toward the doorway, her eyes on the floor.

Olynn did not come forward, so Deirdre said matter-of-factly, "You have something to tell me."

He entered the hall carrying something bundled up, and cleared his throat. "One of the men took this from a stray dog, Surchataine. We thought you might recognize it." With greatest reluctance, he held out the bundle.

Deirdre took it from him, not meeting his eyes. There where she sat she unfolded a ripped and soiled leather shortcoat, heavily caked with dried blood. Deirdre turned it over in her hands, touching the collar, caressing the sleeves.

"It is Roman's," she said softly. "I made it for him when I was just a child. It was his favorite coat."

Olynn lowered his head and Basil blinked to contain tears. There could be no doubt now. They had all been stubbornly hoping that Roman had eluded death once again, but in the light of such evidence, all such hopes were seen to be nothing more than mocking wishes. The others at the table were speechless, some with their heads down in sorrow.

The Surchataine stood and walked away from the table. Basil quietly dismissed the guests. Holding the coat to her chest, Deirdre went slowly up the stairs to her chambers. She let herself into the inner room, now dark and somber, and lowered herself to her knees. She spread the coat out on the floor, as to the eyes of someone who could see in the dark, and raised her face to God in the agony of loss.

There were no words that would come at such a time, but as her soul looked upward, it was met by a force that embraced her like a lover—a warm, compassionate flow that held her in consoling arms.

She let her tears out freely, feeling they were accepted, and let herself weep out the full measure of grief, knowing it was understood.

CHAPTER 24

EARLY IN THE MORNING Deirdre rose and opened her chamber window to a lush, sparkling dawn. She sat for some time at that window, groping for a reason to face the day. And then, as on every other morning of her life, she had breakfast in her chambers and dressed.

She summoned Basil to her receiving room, and as he bowed, he appraised her anxiously. He did not know what to make of her quiet, settled air, nor of the new depth in her eyes. "Basil." She gave him the soiled shortcoat. "I wish to honor Roman with a funeral barge, tonight, set off from Hycliff. With this on it. Please begin preparations, and send criers to announce it."

"Of course, Surchataine," he answered with a full heart. "He will receive all the honor he so greatly deserved." She nodded slightly. "Surchataine," he began hesitantly, "I am loath to press you, but an emissary is here from Calle Valley. Surchatain Roman saw him last week and refused his request, but he remained in the city, and now he has asked to see you."

"I assume he asks that because he has heard of Roman's death," she said bitterly.

"That is a fair assumption," Basil acknowledged. "Still, it may be wise to hear him, if only for diplomacy. Our reports are that Calle Valley has made strong gains recently, and is no longer safe to ignore."

"If that is what you advise, then I will hear him this morning," she said.

"I will go summon him to the audience hall to wait for you," the Counselor replied, bowing.

But an errand boy caught him in the corridor and directed him first to the foyer to see Kam, the Second in Command. Kam himself had been directing the search for the Surchatain along the north market road. Always ardently loyal to Lystra's interests, Kam had developed a deep personal loyalty toward Roman since the death of Surchatain Galapos, and that feeling had been heightened by recent events.

Kam, his face tense under the black curly hair and beard, began, "Counselor, I thought to report to you on the progress of the search, now that—now that—"

"What is your progress?" Basil interrupted.

"None, Counselor," the Second replied in disgust. "If anyone saw

206

anything, they aren't saying. We found no blood or articles along the road, though we searched practically into Seleca. Of course, if there were any dropped, someone probably has taken them by now. From the condition of his coat, it looks as if he was killed, then his body removed on a cart. Nothing else would do it so neatly." He stroked his beard in agitation, his barrel chest expanding in a sigh of futility.

"Then we are looking for a body now," Basil said quietly. "Continue your search, offering the same reward. Deirdre wishes to send off a funeral barge tonight, and I think it would comfort her to have found the body."

"Yes, Counselor," Kam acquiesced, inwardly cursing their failure.

From there, the Counselor sent a summons to the inn where the emissary from Calle Valley was staying, then went to the audience hall. But he found the emissary already there waiting—on the chance that he might be given an audience with the Surchataine. The townspeople in the hall were still a little edgy, talking in muffled tones, but Basil gleaned from what little he overheard that they had no doubts concerning the transfer of power to Deirdre. The emissary seemed nervous at having been thrust unknowingly into such a volatile situation, even though he hoped to profit from it, and was about to address a tentative question to the Counselor when Deirdre entered.

The spectators went to their knees as she passed by them and sat on the bronze throne that Karel, Galapos, and Roman had occupied before her. "I wish to announce first," she began, "that a funeral barge for Surchatain Roman will be cast out from Hycliff at sunset today. Those who wish may attend."

This drew a murmured approval from the crowd, for such spectacles were highly appreciated by the public. It would also appease the citizens who were disgruntled that the athletic games had been canceled abruptly upon the Surchatain's disappearance. The setting of a funeral barge was not only a good show, it usually involved a free meal of cakes and ale.

"Before I leave for Hycliff this morning, I will hear from the emissary of Calle Valley," Deirdre said.

The emissary was prepared to make the most of this opening. As he bowed deeply before her, he said, "Surchataine, I am Virl. I cannot express the grief I feel, and all Calle Valley will feel when they learn of the Surchatain's untimely death. Please accept my sorrow as your own." Deirdre merely eyed him skeptically.

Virl continued, "I have brought a small gift of wine from our valley— fifty casks—which I ask you to receive as a token of our good will." Deirdre nodded slightly.

"Surchataine," he went on, "my reason for coming was to invite your gracious participation in the first summer fair in Calle Valley. Our Surchatain has labored long to build up the fortunes of the area to provide the fair, and now it will come to pass—"

"Who is the Surchatain of Calle Valley?" Deirdre asked suspiciously. The last Surchatain she knew of had been Merce, who had allied himself with Lystra's enemies in an attempt to conquer her. Merce had been killed at the battle of Outpost One.

"Caspar, son of Merce, is our ruler, and sends you his warmest greetings, Surchataine."

Caspar . . . Deirdre's eyes hazed over in concentration. Evidently he had not fought beside his father, else he would have been killed also. Caspar had been one of her suitors—that is, before she had run away from Westford to marry Roman. Of all those she had rejected, Caspar had been the one least offensive to her . . .

The emissary was explaining, "The fair, which opens in Crescent Hollow three days from now, promises to be a great success, Surchataine. We have merchants en route from all parts of the Continent. And it will certainly benefit the autumn fair in Hycliff, for many merchants will remain in the South, selling and replenishing their wares, until the time for the Hycliff fair." Deirdre did not reply, but he saw interest creep into her face.

Encouraged, Virl came to the point. "However, our most pressing concern is the safety of the overland trade routes through Lystra. Most merchants coming from the East will of necessity travel through Lystra, as the mountains north of Crescent Hollow prevent a direct northern access. If we could prevail upon you to provide protection to the merchants traveling to the fair through Lystra, I am sure it would prove to be mutually beneficial."

Deirdre studied him without answering. The emissary gauged her also, and the great risk of what he was about to say next. But, relying on his years of experience in reading capricious rulers, he said it: "If my lady deems our plan to be good, then Surchatain Caspar wishes to extend to her his personal invitation to be his guest at the fair."

While Deirdre considered his words, he waited, marveling a little at the hardness of such a young, comely face. Her blue eyes seemed to beckon, even when it was obvious that what she was contemplating was not love. Virl was ruefully reflecting that he was probably too old to be attractive to her when she abruptly answered, "I give permission for my soldiers to patrol trade routes to Calle Valley for your fair. You may meet with Basil and the Second Kam to work out the particulars. As for Caspar's invitation . . . I will think about it. You are dismissed."

208

Before leaving the hall she told a soldier, "When Sevter and his staff have assembled all they need to take to Hycliff, saddle Lady Grey and summon me from my chambers."

"Surchataine," he bowed.

Then she forced herself up the stairs. She had been avoiding Ariel since the day before yesterday, when Roman had disappeared. Now, she must tell her son that his father would not be coming home again. The boy was not yet three, and she did not know if she could make him understand the meaning of death. But he needed some explanation for the fiery show he would see tonight.

Deirdre put her hand unwillingly on the latch of the nursery door, and opened it.

Effie roused sleepily that morning, a little later than usual. Yawning, she stoked the fire and threw a few more pieces of wood on it, then picked up the bucket to go draw water.

Outside, the morning sun had already topped the trees to send light splashing down in golden puddles around the hut. The air was heady with the scent of pine trees in summer. On her way to the well, Effie kicked through the fragrant thatch of pine needles on the forest floor. She dawdled outside a while, playing with the geese and enjoying the coolness of the morning before returning to the hut with her filled bucket.

She drank and washed her face, then lazily spread jam on a thick slice of bread. Munching it, she stepped to the door of the other room to look in on her visitor.

At the door she gasped and dropped the bread splat on the floor, jam side down. The man was lying on his back, awake, watching her.

Her first impulse was to run. But he said in a whispered croak, "I need water. Please."

His appeal didn't sound very dangerous, so she backed out and cautiously brought in the bucket and ladle to him. He lifted up, wincing, to prop himself on his right elbow. But when he reached out with his left hand to take the ladle, a spasm of pain froze his fingers. He could not even extend the arm. Effie bypassed his clenched fingers and held the ladle up to his mouth.

Once his thirst was sated, he lay down again. She watched him as he gingerly worked his swollen shoulder around, trying to find a comfortable resting position. Then he looked up to meet her gaze. As they studied each other, a slight smile appeared on his face. Effie noted that his fever was down. He said, "I am hungry, if you have any more bread you have not trampled."

"Oh—?" She looked down at the bread and jam, which she had

indeed stepped on in bringing his water. She laughed impulsively and he smiled at her. Not understanding his smile, she retreated at once from his bedside.

In a few moments she came in again with cheese and bread on a wooden plate. She helped him raise up and shift around to lean against the wall. Holding the plate in his lap, he ate with his right hand, resting the useless left one on the cot. He swallowed and said, "You are very kind—Effie, isn't it?"

She jumped. "How do you know my name?"

"I heard a woman say it, from the other room," he said, leaning his head back against the wall. He appeared to be tiring from even this little effort.

"But you have been asleep all this while!"

"Most of the time," he said. "But at other times, I was aware of voices around me."

She squirmed at all he might have heard. At this point he sank weakly down to the bed again, and she adjusted the goose-down pillow under his head. "Tell me how I came to be here," he whispered.

"I found you bleeding on the market road," she replied. "I brought you here and bandaged you up."

He closed his eyes, nodding. "I was ambushed. I remember the sound of the arrow." He opened his eyes again. "Who knows that I am here?"

"No one besides me," she assured him. "Soldiers came around offering a reward for you, but I told them nothing."

He cocked a brow. "Not for money? Why not?"

"Because I . . ." She hesitated, unsure she should tell him. "Because I know who you are." He might as well know. He could not hurt her, weak as he was.

He frowned slightly. "Then why didn't you give me over to the soldiers?"

Now she frowned. What did he want her to say? "Because after all the trouble I had saving you, I did not want to see you hanged!"

His languid smile in response made her boil in irritation. "Why would they hang me, Effie?"

She composed herself, thinking to see through his game. He wanted to see just how much she knew. "Surchatain Roman is dead," she told him, "and they have not found the murderer."

He blinked at her. "I am Surchatain Roman."

Her heart bounded up. The Surchatain! She had saved the Surchatain! But then came a snide thought: *Gullible fool, that's impossible. Can't you see he is lying?* She jerked to her feet, angry and hurt. "Liar! How big a fool do you take me for? I should have left you to die in the road!" She yanked the plate away and ran from the lean-to.

210

What a liar, she seethed, illogically taking up the hoe to jab at the garden rows. *A man who lies like that might do anything. He's dangerous. What am I to do with him now? Once he mends, he's likely to turn and kill me for saving him! I can't let him mend . . . I must undo what I have done . . .* She rested her weight on her hoe and began to cry in frustration and despair. It was the pattern of her life to never do anything right.

Resolutely, she sniffled and straightened. Hoeing again, she pondered what to do. Her eye was drawn to a spot of orange a few feet from the edge of the garden, near the trees, and she cursed. Walking over to the spot, she lifted her hoe to destroy once again a tenacious patch of fly agaric. Effie knew these mushrooms were deadly poison, and would never eat them, but someone else who was hungry might not know . . .

She paused, hoe upraised. Then she lowered it and chewed on a fingernail, thinking. In a moment she had decided. She left the hoe and quickly gathered some ripe vegetables, which she took inside and cut up in the kettle, with some water and salt. She rekindled the fire with the flint and stood over the pot to watch the stew boil.

When it was almost done, Effie took a knife outside to the mushroom patch and carefully dug out the largest, orangest one. She cut it up in tiny pieces, all of which she scraped into a wooden soup bowl. Then she filled the bowl with vegetable stew and took it to Roman.

"I have made you some dinner," she said.

He opened his eyes and inhaled to gain strength. He began struggling to sit up, so she helped him lean against the wall and then handed him the bowl and spoon. "Thank you, Effie."

He blew on the stew, which steamed very hot in his hand. Gingerly he balanced it on his lap, waiting for it to cool. He rested his head back on the wall and said, "I *am* Roman, Effie. What can I do to convince you?"

"Oh, I believe you," she said lightly.

"I think you do not, but you are afraid of me. Ask me questions, and I will tell you things only the Surchatain would know."

"I would not know what to ask, nor if what you told me was right," she answered.

He winced. "That's true. What would convince you, then?"

She looked him in the eye. "I am convinced."

"You said they have not found the murderer," he said suddenly. "I know who is responsible. The chief emissary from Qarqar hired someone locally to kill me. Of this I was warned, and I ignored it."

"I believe your stew has cooled," she said. He raised the spoon to his mouth and blew on it, but found it still too hot.

211

He sighed, studying her, and she turned her face away. He began discoursing softly, as if more to himself than her: "I once was guardian of a little girl much like you—smart, and stubborn, and unable to believe anything but the worst. I grew to love her, but for years she could not accept the love I showed to her as real because everyone else lied to her about everything. Then one day she believed me, and God gave her to me to be my wife—"

Effie stood and so abruptly snatched the bowl from him that some of the stew sloshed into his lap, sending him up with a gasp. "Your stew has gotten cold. I must get you another bowl," she said, as he stared at her in astonishment.

After Roman had eaten, Effie brought him water for bathing. She helped him remove his boots, but shyly retreated after that, and he did not ask for further help. She puttered outside, feeding the geese and collecting sticks for the fire, until she felt it safe to go in again. When she finally put her head in the door of the lean-to, she saw him lying on his back with the blanket pulled up to his chest. His trousers were on the chair.

"Would you like me to wash those for you?" she asked timidly.

"Come sit first, a moment," he said, brushing the trousers off the chair. "I want to know more about you."

She sat stiffly as if for an interrogation. "Who lives here with you, Effie?"

"My brother." She could answer that one.

"Where is he?"

"He is away for a while."

"How long?"

"I don't know," she said straightforwardly.

"Where did he go?"

"I don't know." Her tone implied it was none of her business.

"Does he leave you alone like this often?"

"Sometimes. Whenever he comes into money."

"How does he earn money?"

"I don't know."

By this time, Roman had dropped his head back into the pillow as if it hurt. "Effie, how does he provide for you?"

She had to think about this. "Sometimes he gives me money. And sometimes he brings foodstuff. But I have my garden and my geese when he doesn't. And whenever Oweda and Mathias come by, they bring me things."

"Who are they?"

"They're a merchant couple I met in Westford a few years ago.

They travel a lot, and can't pass by here very often, but they try to, because they don't have any children and they want me to be their child."

"Do you want to be?" he asked.

"Oh yes!" she said, her face lifting. "But I did not know they wanted me to come with them until Oweda told me yesterday. She was just here. It was her you heard. She asked me to come with her."

"Why didn't you go?"

"Because I had to stay here to take care of you!" she answered crossly, as if he should have known why.

He looked at her with an expression of respect. "You'll be rewarded for it, Effie. I promise you that."

She shrugged and took his trousers out to wash.

That evening, a visitor in Hycliff would have been drawn to the ports by the crier's call and the curious crowd. There, he would have been given sorghum cakes and cupfuls of ale as he listened to the lament of the trumpeters and the mourning of the weepers. Then he would have seen from a distance a golden-haired Surchataine and a very small child set torches to a barge loaded with kindling. And he would have watched with the crowd as the barge was launched to sea, further ignited by thrown torches and flaming arrows until it was a fireball in the midst of the dark waters.

CHAPTER **25**

SHUFFLING, CLUNKING NOISES awakened Effie in the morning. She blinked around bemusedly to see that Roman had retrieved his trousers from the hearth, dressed, and was now attempting to cross the room to the outside door.

"What are you doing?" she demanded, irritated that he had gotten up without her help.

"I need to get outside, little nurse," he said with a wry smile.

She took his good right arm and unbolted the door. He gratefully breathed in the sweet morning air. "I had forgotten how good it is just to wake up," he murmured. Not ever having experienced that particular feeling, Effie did not reply. Still smiling in that wry manner, he shuffled out through the curious geese.

When he came back in, he found her boiling goose eggs for breakfast. She pulled up the stool and let him lean on her to sit at the table. As she placed two eggs in a bowl before him, he said, "Thank you, Effie."

She went to the hearth and stood over the kettle. The way he spoke to her was strange to hear. Pax certainly never talked like that. Mathias was kind, but always a little distant and preoccupied. This man, however, talked to her as if she were a friend. Someone worth talking to.

She stood over the kettle so much longer than necessary that by the time she had turned back around, he was watching her. "Why are you crying?"

"I just wish . . . my brother treated me the way you do."

"Does he hurt you?"

"No," she answered quickly. "No." But he kept watching her as she nonchalantly set her eggs on the table and brought the chair from the other room to sit with him.

"Besides, you needn't worry about him," she added. He cocked his head. "He had a lot of money with him when he left, so he won't be back for a long time."

"A lot? How much?"

"I don't know. More than I've ever seen. He had it in one of those fancy leather purses that rich people carry."

His face paled somewhat. "A brown leather pouch?" he asked. She nodded. "Did it have an imprint?" She nodded again. "Was the imprint a lion and a cross, Effie?"

"I don't know. I didn't see it that well. Why? Have you lost . . . a . . ."

"Never mind." He straightened so abruptly he winced. "May I have another egg, Effie? They're good."

She rose and took the bowl he held out to her. She dipped two more eggs from the kettle into the bowl, then looked down in surprise to see how they rattled in her hands.

"You don't act like a Surchatain," she observed peremptorily as she gave him the bowl.

He raised his face at this unexpected statement and laughed. "How does a Surchatain act?"

"Well . . . lordly."

"Arrogantly, you mean," he replied. She shrugged. "I have had my fill of pride, Effie. And it is hard to be arrogant to the one who held my life in her little hands."

214

Effie folded her hands in her lap, blushing. They were bony and gawky, but certainly not little. "But there is something more I must ask of you," he added. She gave him her full attention. "I must let my wife know that I am all right. I need to get a message to the palace, but I am too weak to walk there myself."

"I can go for you!" she exclaimed.

"I was hoping you would. Go to the palace and ask to see Surchataine Deirdre. Tell her what happened, and where I am, and that I am mending. If she asks proof that it is I who sent you, tell her . . . tell her that I have been humbled under a mighty hand, and that from now on I will listen to Basil. Can you remember that?"

"Yes, I can do that," she said importantly. She paused to tie her hair back with one of her new ribbons, glancing self-consciously at his smile. Then she hurried out, feeling so responsible on this mission that she could barely restrain herself to a brisk walk.

Relaxed and smiling, Roman waved as she trotted away. But as soon as she was out of sight, his face took on an expression of concern and he began straining to work his unresponsive left arm.

Effie ran down the market road to within sight of the formidable gates of the palace. Here she slowed to a timid walk. Who was she to demand to speak with the Surchataine? But remembering who sent her, she boldly approached one of the guards at the gate and looked him in the eye.

"I need to see the Surchataine," she announced.

The guard turned up a corner of his mouth. "Why, kitten?"

"I have a very important message for her. You must let me speak to her," she said gravely.

He arched a brow. "What's your message?"

"Surchatain Roman is at my house, mending from a wound. He wants her to know he is well, and he has a special message for her."

The guard's smile vanished. "The Surchatain is dead, girl."

"No, he is not," Effie insisted. "He is at my house. He sent me to tell her this."

The guard hesitated, then said, "Come with me." He took her into the palace foyer, where they chanced to see the big blond soldier who had come to Effie's hut.

"Captain!" the guard called, and he turned.

"Sebastian?"

"Captain Olynn, this girl says she has a message for the Surchataine."

"Is that right?" the Captain looked her over lightly. "What's your message?"

Effie said importantly, "Surchatain Roman is not dead. He was wounded, but he is healing. He is at my house. He wants to tell the

215

Surchataine that he is all right, and he had a special message for her so she would know he really sent me."

"What's that?" asked Olynn.

"He said he's been humbled under a mighty hand, and from now on he will listen to . . . listen to . . ." What was that name? ". . . Bannon . . . ?"

The guard and the Captain glanced at each other. "You've given your message. Now go home," said Olynn.

"But he wanted me to tell her in person," Effie argued. "No, not Bannon—it was . . . Bayer?"

"I will tell her whatever she needs to hear," Olynn said gruffly, motioning. The guard began to lead her out.

"Wait!" demanded Effie. "He told me to tell her myself!"

As the guard took her away, Basil passed through the foyer and glimpsed her struggling as the great doors closed. "Who was that?" he asked Olynn.

"A village prankster," answered the Captain. "Do you need me, Counselor?"

"Yes, Captain; please come with me to see Kam."

"Certainly, Counselor."

On the outside, the guard dragged Effie protesting to the gate. "You must let me see her!"

"Your message will be delivered," he said coolly.

"Basil! That was the name! He said from now on he will listen to Basil!"

"Go home, girl!" The guard shoved her away.

Despondently, she returned to the hut. Roman was resting in bed, but raised himself up expectantly as she entered. She pulled up the chair beside his bed and plopped into it, hanging her head.

"I gave them the message," she said dejectedly. "But they did not believe me."

"Who did you speak to?"

"The guard at the gate. He took me to an officer, but they would not let me speak to your wife," she said. He lay back, perturbed. "Are you *really* the Surchatain?" she demanded.

He pursed his lips in exasperation. "How does it feel not to be believed?" he countered. "Effie, it's going to be you and me for a while, until I get strong enough to make myself known. You're going to have to trust me till then."

"I will," she promised. "I do."

At the palace, Basil was in Deirdre's chambers to make a report to her—the kind of report that every counselor dreaded to make, and

216

only the most faithful could be trusted to make at all. Therefore, he unconsciously rubbed his hands nervously as he said, "Surchataine, I have been conferring with the Second Kam and Captain Olynn, and it seems we have worked ourselves into a quandary with the soldiers."

"What do you mean?" Deirdre asked.

"Surchataine, as you will recall, when you sent the emissary from Qarqar home, you promised him an invasion. If we do not make good on that promise quickly, Kam believes they will muster and attack us in their own defense."

"They *will?*"

"It is likely. Also, we have not forgotten Commander Nihl's mission to Corona. If he is unsuccessful in persuading Bruc to leave, and the Polonti attack Corona, we *must* be ready to aid Surchatain Titian as promised. It was a high priority with Roman."

"It *was?*" she asked lamely.

"Yes. And I am afraid that either of these two endeavors alone would require the concentration of our forces. However, now that we have additionally promised our soldiers to protect trade routes to Crescent Hollow for the fair . . . all three demands are likely to coincide. Yet only one can be accomplished, Surchataine."

Deirdre sinkingly perceived the implications of her scattered directives. How could she have made such rash promises, without any foresight or plan? "What shall we do?" she murmured.

"It seems all we can do now is watch to see from which direction comes the greatest threat, and act on that one. And hope the others will wait."

Deirdre nodded feebly. "Thank you, Basil."

After the Counselor had quietly closed the door behind him, Deirdre plopped down in despair at the chamber window. "Oh Lord," she moaned, "look at what I have done! I have made such a midden of matters already. What shall I do now? Oh Roman—how I wish I had listened to what you tried to teach me!" She placed her chin dismally into her palm.

That day Roman seemed tired of resting and impatient to get up, so Effie helped him out to walk around. "Be careful!" she scolded when he pulled from her grasp. "Only a few days ago you almost bled to death!"

"And because of your care, I am better today," he answered agreeably, stretching in the sunlight. He *did* seem better, except for the stiff and swollen shoulder which impeded movement of his arm.

He walked around while Effie hovered at his side. "Not dizzy?" she asked.

"Not any more."

"Nor weak?"

"Yes, weaker than usual, but I am getting stronger," he assured her.

"Good," she said. "Good. Then you'll soon go home and not need me any more."

He did not notice the change in her voice. "I fear to think what is happening at the palace, with Bruc attacking Corona and the emissary from Qarqar gone mad." He paused to shake his head. "I must get back in control as soon as possible—" He went silent, feeling a conviction akin to a thunderbolt that this was *not* what he must do.

Effie slipped an arm under his to help him walk, whether he wanted help or not. "It has been good for me to take care of you," she mused. "I feel like a—a different person. I feel things will not ever be the same . . ."

Roman glanced at her. What she said troubled him, but he did not know why. "I think I should go lie down now," he murmured.

On the cot, he unwound the bandages, which had become uncomfortable. It was then that Effie saw the brand on his chest. "What happened to you?" she exclaimed.

He pressed his chin down to look at the mark of a cross and smiled briefly. "I tangled with a nasty little man who had a fondness for torture."

"How did that happen?" she grimaced.

He made himself comfortable on the goose-down pillow, then began to tell her the story of his trip with the scouting party to Corona. As he talked, she listened in rapt attention, eyes widening now and then, but never interrupting to question him. He tried to concentrate on the story he was telling, but found that inner impressions kept demanding his attention—impressions that focused on her.

Roman saw her clearly as a sensitive and hungry child, yearning for affection and security. He saw her also at a crossroads, trying to decide what manner of person she would be and what kind of life she would live. He saw all this far more distinctly than she probably did herself. What perturbed him, however, and made him pause repeatedly in his narration, was the realization that somehow he had become crucial to this struggle of formation, and that she needed him now as much as he had needed her.

It was not his pride of independence that was threatened here, for he had learned (he thought) the necessity of occasional dependence on others. But he feared the fondness in her eyes might grow beyond safe bounds, and how would he handle a young girl in love?

In considering this dilemma he paused again, and a look of impatience crossed her face. Then a silent voice chided him: *Don't flatter yourself. Leave the dangers to me; you just be kind.*

With a laugh at his exaggerated ideas of his own attractiveness, Roman cleared his mind of self-centered distractions and concentrated on telling Effie the mighty things God had done in Corona.

CHAPTER 26

LATE THAT EVENING, when most in the palace had long been asleep, a group of soldiers arrived at the gates, causing much excitement among those who were on watch. Deirdre was awakened by pounding on her outer door. Leaping up for fear of what might need her attention at this hour, she pulled on an overrobe and opened the door herself, waving the sleepy chambermaid away.

A guard at the door began, "Surchataine—" but was brushed aside as a weary-looking Commander Nihl stepped into the receiving room.

"Nihl!" Deirdre was so relieved to see him that she forgot all propriety and threw her arms around his neck.

He leaned down to allow her to hold him, but did not embrace her in return. The stares of the guard and the chambermaid brought her back to reason and she released him, chagrined at her carelessness. "Thank you, Surchataine," he said with a gravity that smothered any hopes of gossip the witnesses might have been entertaining.

"Nihl . . . what news have you brought from Corona?" she asked dismally. Then suddenly: "But how is it you are back so soon? You left only two days ago!"

"Such a remarkable thing happened, Surchataine, that we rode back to report to you without stopping on the way. We were successful beyond expectation in the task you gave us. And this is how it happened: We left as you commanded, but by the time we had reached Outpost One, we still had daylight to travel. We knew even then Bruc might be at Corona, so we continued to ride, and camped at the foot of the Fastnesses.

"That enabled us to reach Corona before noon of the next day. And how fortunately timed, for at the moment we came to the gates, we saw the Polonti army approaching. I sent a man within the city

219

to warn Titian. The rest of us waited at the gates. When the army met us, I saw leading them none other than Asgard, my brother. Bruc had made him Commander of his army.

"So we two faced each other. And he said, 'Stand aside, little brother.' I told him no, but that I had been ordered to turn him away from Corona. He said that he would have to kill me then, for he had orders to plunder Corona.

"I said, 'Plunder what? Your scouts are miserable liars, if they told you there was any plunder here. This city has already been so ravaged that there is nothing left but poverty. Surchatain Roman has determined that Bruc will not prey on the helpless.'

"Asgard drew his sword and said, 'Stand aside! I cannot return empty-handed.' At which I remembered Qarqar, and their horde of gold. So I told him, 'If it's plunder you're after, another three days' march to the west will bring you to all the gold Bruc could want.' I told him of the treasure hidden in Hornbound—how Troyce had discovered it but Roman had been unwilling to force it from them. But since their chief emissary had betrayed our goodwill, according to Basil," (Deirde nodded confirmation), "then Bruc would be avenging Lystria by attacking Hornbound.

"Asgard listened, then said, 'Swear to me you are not lying.' And I swore on our father's grave that I spoke the truth. He conferred with his officers, and they voted to march to Hornbound. The last words he told me were, 'If I find you have lied, I will come with my army to bury you in the ruins of Westford.' I told him, 'Then I am as safe as a cub in its mother's lair.'

"They did not even rest, but started immediately to Hornbound. We watched them march as far as we could see, then I sent a pair of scouts to follow them. I left a pair also in Corona, to stay on watch, but I am sure the city is no longer in danger. When Asgard decides on a course, he is set in it.

"Then we hastened back. I left most of my outfit at the outpost to rest, but I could not sleep until I had reported this to you. The Lord was with us in a mighty way, Surchataine."

For a moment Deirdre was speechless. "Oh Nihl . . . you have no idea how much so, and how much more you have accomplished than you think. You have saved us, Nihl."

He shook his head in pondered disagreement. "Surchataine, I took the only course open to me. On our return march, I had time to consider that the circumstances were laid out for me to act just as I did. There was a stronger arm at work—of this I am certain."

"I know, and I am grateful. But I am also grateful you had the courage to go as I asked without question."

A mild change of expression crossed his face, which for a Polonti meant astonishment. "That is my duty, Surchataine. To serve you as well as the Surchatain."

At this, Deirdre collapsed into a chair. "Roman is dead, Nihl," she whispered.

His face set into hard lines, and he asked in a low monotone, "How did he die?"

"We don't know. By a knife or arrow in the back, it seems. It was the Qarqarian who ordered him killed, after all."

Nihl paused as if he had missed something. "Where did you find his body?"

"We haven't found him. But a soldier found his coat, ripped in the back and drenched with blood."

"That is all?" Nihl asked. "Where is the coat? I wish to see it."

"We put it on the funeral barge last night," Deirdre said. "But what would it profit you to see it? It was just as I have described." She felt irritated at his reservation.

"Surchataine," Nihl said plainly, "if that is all you have found by now, the chances are much greater that he is alive. He could merely be wounded—"

"No, Nihl! There was too much blood!"

"—or it may not have been his blood at all. You underestimate your husband's ability to survive."

"That isn't so! I know better than anyone his abilities! But if he is alive, then where is he? Why hasn't he come home?"

"There may be many explanations, depending on what happened to him. But now there is more reason to assume he is alive than dead."

Deirdre fell back into the chair, holding her head. "No. Don't make me hope—I can't endure it. I can accept his death better than to hope uselessly." Her words were faint and despairing.

Nihl studied her, then bowed. "I have made the report I came to make. Goodnight, Surchataine." She nodded listlessly.

On leaving her chambers, Nihl quietly ordered the guard, "Summon the Second to my quarters immediately."

Nihl had hardly walked into his chambers and greeted his wife Izana before they heard a knock. He opened the door to Kam and Olynn while Izana hung on his neck, disappointed. "Wait for me in bed," he whispered to her with a gentle pat.

Meanwhile, Kam and Olynn sat at a small round table, Kam whistling, "What luck in Corona, Commander! We just heard it all from Cy."

Nihl pulled up a chair. "Not luck. Providence. But now I wish to know what you have found of the Surchatain besides his coat."

"Not a blessed thing," spat Kam. "No one saw anything. No one heard anything. The earth has just swallowed him up."

Nihl poured them ale from a flagon on the table, and sat back chewing on the rim of his cup. Kam added, "We did find out for certain that it was the emissary from Qarqar who hired his killer." Olynn told Nihl of Deirdre's confrontation with the emissary and her expulsion of him from Lystra.

The Commander smiled. "It is all the more remarkable, then, that I felt impressed to bait Asgard with the gold in Hornbound."

"It saved our necks," muttered Kam. "But it's done Roman no good."

Nihl fixed his hard brown eyes on Kam. "Why are you all so convinced the Surchatain is dead?"

Kam seemed confused. "Wouldn't we have found him by now if he were alive?"

"Not at all. Most likely, you would have found him by now if he were dead. The killer would want his death known and proven. Else how would he collect his pay? And how much would the Qarqarians profit from Roman's mere disappearance?—which we should have minimized. No—the killer would not hide the body. But a living man can hide himself."

Kam looked thunderstruck at the obvious logic of this reasoning. Olynn went suddenly slack-jawed. "Why would Roman hide?" Kam whispered.

"Let us suppose," said Nihl, "that on the road to Corona he made contact with the assassin—or rather, the assassin with him—and yet survived. Let us also assume the assassin escaped. Now, if you knew someone was out to kill you, and that this someone was roaming free, would you allow yourself to remain an open target?"

"Or he could be wounded, recuperating from the assassin's strike," Olynn said dully.

"That is another possibility," agreed Nihl. "I tried to explain this to the Surchataine, but she is too distraught to think of it . . . what is it?" he asked, as Olynn was numbly shaking his head.

"Commander, for what I am about to tell you, you will boot me down to slophand. But it appears the Surchatain is indeed alive, and is staying in a villager's hut, mending from an injury."

Nihl's face sharpened in excitement. "Whose hut? Where?"

"I don't know," gulped Olynn. "Just this morning, a peasant girl came to the palace demanding to speak to the Surchataine, and claiming to have an important message. The girl swore Roman was alive, but injured, resting in her hut. We . . . ah, we sent her away, thinking her full of foolery."

222

"Who else spoke with her?" Nihl asked calmly.

"Sebastian, on guard duty at the gate."

"Summon him."

They waited as Olynn sent a guard after Sebastian. Nihl drained his ale and looked such a philosopher that Olynn sheepishly asked, "You're not angry, Commander?"

"I would not expect you to understand these things as I do. That is why I am Commander." From anyone else this would have sounded intolerably arrogant, but Nihl's flat tone made it just another fact.

Sebastian entered, sleepy and disheveled. "Commander." He barely suppressed a yawn as he saluted.

"Tell me about this peasant girl who came to you with a message from Surchatain Roman," Nihl said.

Sebastian woke up immediately, glancing at Olynn. "She said the Surchatain had sent her to tell Surchataine Deirdre he was wounded, but healing."

"Is that all she said?"

"Well, no; she said he had sent a special message to the Surchataine . . . something like he had been humbled, and from now on would listen to Basil . . ." Sebastian again glanced toward Olynn and exclaimed, "You think it really was from him?"

"That is exactly what I think," responded Nihl. "Do you know her name? Or where she lives?"

"No, Commander," Sebastian answered miserably. "We did not take her seriously."

"She's probably one of those who live around the Village Branch," Kam said eagerly. "What did she look like, Sebastian?"

"A village girl, like any other village girl. Not pretty, nor ugly, just . . . a peasant," he said helplessly.

"We four will begin searching huts in the morning," said Nihl. "Don't ask permission, don't say what you're looking for, just look."

"We should have more men to help, Commander," suggested Kam.

"No. I order you to tell no one of this. The Surchatain may have good reason to stay hidden, in which case the cover of his 'death' will work well for us."

"Shouldn't the Surchataine be told?" Kam asked.

Nihl paused, then uttered, "No. I will inflict no more pain on her until I can present Roman to her, alive and whole."

They understood him. Harboring the intensity of suppressed excitement, the three went back to their rooms for an hour of sleep while Nihl went in to Izana.

The next day Nihl, Olynn, Kam, and Sebastian rushed through perfunctory duties so that by midmorning they were able to meet secretively at the stables. "You three search every hut along the Village Branch," whispered Nihl. "Sebastian, you and Olynn watch for that girl. I have an idea to search elsewhere."

The others saluted, and they all casually rode out the front gates, which stood open. Nihl watched as the other three turned westward toward the branch of the river around which the poorest of Westford lived in clustered huts. He himself then went north along the market road, where Roman had last been seen. Nihl rode a measured distance, scanning the sides of the highway continually, until he selected a place to turn off into the forest, where he began his own search.

That morning, Effie awakened late—again—and roused quickly to make breakfast, aware that her visitor was probably hungry by now. When she had finished boiling goose eggs (quietly, in case he was still asleep), she peeked into the lean-to. "Are you ready for—"

He was gone. She stood mutely staring at the rumpled blanket on his bed. She walked to the cot and mindlessly folded the blanket. He was gone. "I guess he felt good enough to leave," she explained to herself. "That's to be expected."

What was unexpected was the way it rattled her. "What difference does it make?" she demanded. Then she realized that she had counted on it—on him—to *make* a difference in the treadmill of her day-to-day existence.

She shrugged violently. Who needed him? Oweda and Mathias wanted her. They wanted her to come live with them . . . didn't they? Yes, of course. They would be back to get her . . . wouldn't they?

Effie sank down onto the cot, drained of faith in anyone. She put her face into the blanket, hiding from habit as she sobbed out the pain of abandonment. It was an outpouring that she had not allowed herself in a long time.

A movement in the room hushed her sobs, as she thought with dread that Pax had returned. She kept her face down in the blanket. But then whoever it was knelt before her and a hand closed over hers, gently pulling the blanket away. She looked up into Roman's pained face.

"What're you doing back?" she blurted gruffly, rising to illogically spread the blanket back on the cot.

"I was just walking outside, stretching my legs," he said softly, not adding aloud, *and testing whether I am strong enough to leave.* "You thought I had left?"

"Makes no difference," she said carelessly. "You can leave anytime you want." He gauged her tensely, and Effie's fragile façade crumbled.

She began crying afresh, reaching out to him. With his one good arm he gathered her to his chest and held her.

"I will not leave you alone, Effie," he whispered. "I promise." But inside he was in turmoil. *I don't want this. I can't help her.* With the crises facing Lystra, he must return to his first responsibility of rulership as soon as he was healthy enough to do it. But he had promised her, and he would not break his word. What on earth could he do?

She shook her head in his chest as if denying that he owed her anything. But she could not even stop crying to say it. *Lord Jesus,* pleaded Roman, *what am I to do?*

CHAPTER 27

DEIRDRE MET with Basil that day, and as they sat in the library to talk, he noted with relief how bright and refreshed she looked. "Did you hear Nihl's report?" she asked eagerly, the first thing.

"Yes, Surchataine," he smiled. "All our fears seem to have been banished in one sweep."

She sighed, relieved. "And now, is there any reason our soldiers cannot be sent to protect trade routes to Crescent Hollow?"

"None that I know of, Surchataine. And it may precede what could be a valuable alliance with Calle Valley."

"Then go make arrangements with Nihl and Kam to dispatch the soldiers. And tell the emissary," she said lightly, "that I accept Caspar's invitation. He can expect me in a week for the fair."

That day passed in a string of routine events for most folks at Westford. The first installment of copper and iron ore from Qarqar arrived at the smiths'. The Qarqarian merchants knew nothing of the recent turmoil, having set out with their payload when the chief emissary's companions had returned to Hornbound with the trade agreement. So the copper smith, blacksmith, and armorer took their ore gladly, paid them, and sent them cordially on their way. It was a good deal for the smiths, because the ore was very cheap as compared to refined metal, and the smelters around Westford were superior to those in

Qarqar anyway. These particularly profitable transactions generally promoted good feelings among the community as they felt their strong economic pulse.

Other events took place that day, which in comparison were invisible but far more important. Deirdre took Ariel out to the grounds to practice archery with his half-size bow and arrows, as Roman had done so often. But once at the grounds, Ariel refused to begin practice. He stood patiently waiting, watching the army's archers take practice.

"Ariel, don't you want to shoot?" Deirdre pressed him.

He looked up at her with a grown-up expression of mild irritation. "Wait for Fada," he instructed.

Deirdre lowered herself to be eye level with him. "I explained that to you, Ariel," she whispered. "Father is not coming. He is never coming back. He is dead."

Ariel did not answer, but imperially looked over the archers. "Come practice, Ariel," she urged.

"Wait for Fada!" he insisted.

"Baby, he's dead! He's not coming!" Deirdre cried, shaking him.

This time when he turned his face to her, it was a picture of impassiveness in a crisis that was a perfect duplicate of his father's face. Deirdre released him, moaning, and he dropped the little bow to go inside with his nursemaid.

Deirdre maintained her composure until she could get to her chambers and send the maids away. Then she grasped the casing of the magnificent window in the sleeping chamber and screamed, "How could you do this? How could you leave us like this? Stubborn, proud fool, to think you are indestructible! How could you get yourself killed when we need you so?"

She inhaled calming breaths and uttered, "I love you, Roman . . . oh, how I yearn for your touch again . . ." She leaned back against the window, eyes closed, dreaming of the way he used to love her.

A knock at the door interrupted her dreams. She ignored it. It was repeated, insistently. She tore herself from the window and opened the outer door to her receiving room.

Basil stood outside. Before speaking, he took her hand in both of his and simply held it. Then he quietly told her, "Surchataine, the emissary from Calle Valley was delighted that you accepted Caspar's invitation. But he urges you not to delay, but to return with him now to Calle Valley. He says that his Surchatain is most anxious to see you."

"But . . . unannounced . . ." murmured Deirdre.

"If you accept, he will send a fast messenger ahead today to Crescent Hollow. You and your retinue may then leave with the emissary tomor-

226

row morning, and be assured of a welcome waiting."

She stared off blankly. The Counselor added in the gentle way so becoming to him, "Deirdre, I think you should go. You need to leave this palace for a while. And . . ." he continued delicately, "it is prudent for us to—to *not* discourage Caspar at this point."

That jerked her eyes back to meet his pale blue ones. She perceived immediately that Basil was talking about paving the way for a marriage alliance. Her mind filled with a stream of angry, vituperative words to lash him for his callous disloyalty. His face braced for what was coming and Deirdre's eruption evaporated. Again, she was forced to see that he was the best advisor she could possibly have, his main concerns being what was best for her and for the province.

"But Basil," she murmured, "there must be a period of mourning. I must have that."

"You will. But what would Roman think of a mourning period which weakened Lystra before her enemies?"

"I will do as you say," she whispered. *But Roman—know that I will always love you.*

Another conversation took place that afternoon. Nihl, Kam, Olynn, and Sebastian met again at the stables after a fruitless search. "We went inside every hut along the Branch, Commander," said Kam. "Not a sign, not a hint of him anywhere."

"I did not see the girl, either," added Sebastian, shaking his head. Olynn did not comment. They were tired, and their faces carried expressions of doubt about this renewed search.

"I did not expect you to find him at the Village Branch," Nihl replied. "It is too crowded there for a wounded man to hide and no one know of it. But I wanted you to search it anyway just to make certain we have covered all ground."

"Where were you looking, Commander?" asked Olynn.

"In the forest, near the northbound market road. I did not find him either, but I did find that there are isolated huts along that route. I believe he may be in one of those." The others glanced at each other dubiously. Most of the conviction that they had worked up in the predawn hours had now been put to rest.

The Commander said, "You are all dismissed from duty for the day." But he climbed back on his horse and went out to search again while daylight remained.

The Counselor was not able to locate the Commander that day until the dinner hour, after which Basil directed him and Kam to the Counselor's chambers. They exchanged formalities, then Basil asked, "Commander, what do you believe is our position with Polontis?"

"We are secure," Nihl said. "I see no reason they would abandon their quest for Qarqar's gold to return to Corona—or to come here."

Basil nodded. "And Qarqar?"

Nihl almost smiled. "I am eager to hear the scouts' report of what they did when Asgard came."

"Then we have nothing to fear from them, either," said Basil.

"All this you know, Counselor," said Nihl. "What is on your mind?"

"I am thinking that there is no reason to withhold our soldiers from protecting the trade routes as the Surchataine promised."

"What?" exclaimed Nihl. He swiftly regained his impassive demeanor and stated, "No, Counselor. Surchatain Roman denied the emissary's request for protection of their trade routes."

"Roman denied it, but Deirdre has granted it now. I think we should acquiesce and do it," said Basil, a firm edge to his voice. Saying this, he went to a desk and drew out a scroll. "Here is a map of the routes in northern and western Lystra. You shall begin posting men immediately, for the Surchataine leaves in the morning for Crescent Hollow."

"Why is she going to Crescent Hollow?" asked Nihl, eyebrows arching. Kam was uncharacteristically silent throughout this interchange.

"To meet with Surchatain Caspar," answered Basil. "To establish grounds for a future marital alliance."

"No!" exclaimed Nihl, jumping forward in strange passion. "Counselor, she must not go to Crescent Hollow yet!"

"Mind your place, Commander!" threatened the Counselor. "Remember your loyalties and your duties, or I will remove you from your post!" Kam closed his eyes as if he had a sudden pain. Nihl straightened, his face rigid. "Now you will dispatch your men as ordered," Basil demanded, thrusting the map at him. "You are dismissed!"

Nihl took the map and bowed. Outside Basil's door, the Commander handed the map to Kam. "I am charging you with coordinating the men. I will not take an active role in this until I find Roman."

"Commander," Kam saluted, not daring a word of protest or doubt.

Nihl went down to the chapel then, feeling an intense need for help. He looked in the doors and saw Brother Avelon, the old holy man, on his knees at the front of the chapel, head bowed on a bench before him.

Nihl slipped in quietly to kneel at his side. "Brother Avelon, please pray for me," he whispered. "And for Roman. I know he is alive, and I must find him soon . . ." When the holy man did not respond, Nihl took his shoulder. "Brother Avelon?"

The old man fell back on the bench, and Nihl saw that he had died peacefully while in prayer. Nihl sighed and looked up at the rough wooden cross to carry his request himself to the Lord.

One final turning point occurred that day, this one totally invisible. While Effie was cooking dinner over the hearth in the hut, Roman sat on the cot in the lean-to, trying to work his left arm.

The arm appeared uninjured to the eye, but was stiff and numb. Only with intense effort and considerable pain to his shoulder could he move the arm. He could grasp, but not strongly enough to hold a weapon reliably. The arm even pained him when it dangled loosely at his side.

Like a cripple, he thought grimly. He took one of the cloth strips Effie had used as a bandage and made a sling to hold the arm more comfortably. *Better to look wounded than crippled,* he thought.

Then, with a jolt, he realized that he *was* crippled. He—the pugiling champion, the Chataine's personal guardian, the warrior Surchatain—could hardly heft a spoon in his left hand.

Being forced to face the reality of his own sudden limitation was almost intolerable. In all the crises of his life, at least he had had his physical resources to draw on. But this—*Oh God! Let me face anything but this impotence!*

My grace is sufficient for you, for my power is made perfect in weakness. Roman closed his eyes. If anyone had dared to recite that scripture to him at this time, he would have exploded in a rage. But from the mouth of the Creator, the One who had formed him in the womb, and then saved him from destruction many times over, it carried an indisputable weight of righteousness. *He* was right, and there was no ground in heaven or on earth for arguing.

Roman looked down at his limp arm. "Are my days of strength ended?" he whispered. "Then here am I, God: a useless warrior."

When Effie called him to dinner from the other room, he shuffled in and sat at the table like an old man. She bustled happily about, putting out cracked pottery and pouring well water to drink, as the ale had run out.

Her effervescence certainly did not lighten his load any, for it merely reminded him that she was expecting him to do something for her which he did not know if he could do. Indeed, he did not know what to do for her at all. Take her to the palace? As what? What would she do there? What would Deirdre think of it? And what was to be done about brother Pax?

Effie cheerfully put a spicy cabbage salad on the table, and then a roast goose. Roman stared. "Effie—you killed one of your geese!"

"Of course I did. I can't have goose every night, but I will when the Surchatain comes to visit!" She said it laughing, but with utter faith that he was who he said he was.

A smile cracked his dour face. She hugged his neck, urging, "Let's celebrate! You and I!" She insistently pulled him from his chair to make him dance with her.

"All right, Effie; you win, you win." He tried to maintain some dignity and balance as they stepped around in a jumble of a dance, but finally succumbed to a grudging laugh. Then it struck him—"You're right, Effie, it's a time to celebrate. You finally believe me . . . and I believe Him." She laughed, too caught up in her homemade fun to ask what he meant.

CHAPTER 28

WHEN THE EMBERS on the fire had burned down to a soft orange glow and Roman had retired to his cot in the lean-to for the night, Effie, still smiling, cleaned up the remains of their celebration. She took extra care to sweep the floor and rinse out the kettle; for some reason, she felt the need to set the hut in order.

She was just going to the door to bolt it when she heard hoofbeats. Apprehensively, she peeked out and saw a rider approach and dismount. Paling, Effie backed into the hut. The rider swaggered in, pushing her aside to flop down at the table and demand, "Here I've come home and you don't even have a pot on the fire! Where's my dinner, snip?"

"Pax," she murmured, her face tightening at his entrance. "I didn't know you were . . ." she faltered as he slapped the leather pouch, now flat, onto the table by the candle. "Where did you get the horse?" she mumbled, eyes on the pouch. The side with the imprint was down.

"Oh, that nag?" he said smugly, glancing outside. "I just made a smart deal with a stupid old horse trader up near Dansington." He went on to describe how he had outwitted the trader into selling it for a pittance. Pax was so pleased with himself that he temporarily forgot about dinner and neglected to notice Effie surreptitiously turning the pouch over.

"And then this old fool told me he had to have forty royals for

230

this 'mule'—forty royals! And I told him—I told him . . . what are you staring at?" he demanded uneasily. There was anger building to fury in her eyes, and it unsettled him because he had never seen it in her before.

"Where did you get this pouch?" she asked in a low voice, showing him the lion and the cross on it. His brows knitted and he shrugged nervously.

"Where did you get this pouch?" she screamed, shaking it in his face.

"Settle down, girl!" he shouted, grabbing the pouch away.

"You did it!" she cried. "You were the one! You monster!" She landed a fist so solidly on his chest that it knocked the wind from him.

"I am leaving," she declared, backing away to disjointedly gather some things. "I am going to go live with Oweda and Mathias. You take care of yourself. I am leaving."

This snapped him instantly out of his daze. "No, you're not," he snarled. "You're not going anywhere."

"I am!" she countered, dropping her armload of shabby belongings. "Murderer!"

He froze. Then he slowly drew a knife from his belt. "Come here, Effie."

Her voice dripping with sarcasm, she replied, "Are you going to kill your own sister now? Well, I don't think you can. You tried to kill the Surchatain, but you couldn't!" She looked away from him to a point beyond his right shoulder.

"What . . . ?" His expression went from malice to confusion to clouded fear. Hesitantly, he turned to look over his shoulder. Roman stood in the doorway of the lean-to, watching Pax with stony eyes.

Pax wobbled like a drunkard, then clenched his knife. "I got you a good hit. You got to be hurt," he breathed hoarsely.

"Try me," Roman said.

Unwilling to risk a hand-to-hand encounter, Pax lifted the blade to throw it, but Roman pulled his own dagger from his belt. "You had better not miss."

"I have friends!" Pax shouted irrationally. "You hurt me and they'll come after you."

"Finish what you started," Roman baited, taking a step.

Pax wheeled and made a grab for Effie, but she darted away to hide behind Roman.

"Fight *me,* man, not the child!" spat Roman. Pax, sweating, clutched his knife. Roman continued, "Have you ever heard what the Qarqarians

231

do to someone who collects pay when a job's left undone? Or are you too cowardly to fight a man whose face is to you?"

Pax suddenly sprang forward and Roman braced to meet him. Effie screamed as they made contact. There was a quick grappling, movements too rapid to follow, and the glint of a blade between them. They both stopped as if struck, but it was Pax who slumped to the floor.

Gasping, Effie stood over her brother's body. Roman whispered, "Effie, I'm sorry."

"What shall we do? What shall we do?" she moaned, wringing her hands. Roman tried to gather her in to comfort her, but she was not grieving, she was worried. "He *does* have friends, and they're meaner than fighting dogs!"

"It seems I am responsible for you now," Roman muttered. "I had better get you away from here."

"But where can we go?" she asked anxiously.

"That's easy. I am going to take you to Oweda and Mathias."

"But they're not home!" she wailed. "They've gone to Calle Valley for a fair."

"Then we'll go to Calle Valley and find them there," he replied, stooping to pick up the leather pouch. He took the few coins that remained in it and dropped the pouch. "Have you any more money?"

"Yes." She scurried to find her little cloth bag and show him the two royals.

He bounced them in his palm. "That's still not enough. Have you anything else of value?"

"What about the horse?"

"We'll need him to ride." He seemed to be thinking only of getting away as quickly as possible.

"Well," she offered, "I have my geese."

"Round them up, and we'll take them to the poulterer tonight," he instructed. "Perhaps he'll give us a bed for the night, too." Effie darted outside as Roman ransacked the hut for supplies. When he came out, he helped her herd the eight geese together. Effie led them away from the hut with a leash on the neck of the biggest gander while Roman and the horse comprised the rear guard.

"Which way to the road?" he called quietly.

"We had better stay off the road tonight," Effie returned. "That is the surest place to meet Pax's friends."

"Robbers? On my road?" Roman asked indignantly.

Effie smiled sardonically at his naiveté. "They forgot to ask your permission." She took him instead on an obscure path parallel to the road and within a half hour they detected the livestock section of Westford close ahead.

232

They coaxed the geese into the dark, smelly streets, past the butcher's and tanner's, then stopped at a house flanked by pens of chickens. Roman beat twice on the door, and a dog inside began barking. A voice called, "What? Who's there?"

"Surchatain Roman," he replied, his mouth close to the door.

"Should you tell him that?" Effie whispered.

"Sure, and I'm the Almighty," the voice answered irately. "Go away!"

"I am the Surchatain!" Roman put more depth in his tone. "Stop your profaning and open the door!"

There was a sudden quiet within, then the door barely opened a crack. A hand stuck out to lift a candle to Roman's bearded face. "By my mercurial stars, it is the Surchatain! Hey, Elyria, we got the Surchatain out here!" A voice in the background replied something in the vein of that being impossible and his needing to soak his head to clean his ears.

The poulterer left Roman standing at the door while he argued with the unseen Elyria that he had seen the Surchatain often at open audience in the mornings and he knew that it was in fact Surchatain Roman standing on his doorstep at this very moment. So Elyria came to the door herself to scrutinize Roman, Effie, the geese, and the horse. "What do you want?" she asked suspiciously.

"Forgive the intrusion, my lady, but I have been put out of pocket by an assassin's attempt on my life. I have some work to do, and we want to know if you will buy this girl's geese and put us up for the night," Roman said politely.

"We'll buy the geese," the woman said, "but if you're really the Surchatain, why don't you go home and sleep in your palace?"

"I will. But first I promised to deliver this girl safely to her guardians, and then I must find the man who paid for my murder. Until then I need to stay out of sight, so please do not tell anyone you have seen me."

"Of course," she said sarcastically. "There's the pens. Go put up your animals and make yourself a bed there," she pointed.

"In the pens?" Roman asked, embarrassed.

"Yes, in the pens," she said firmly. "I'll send my husband out to pay you for your geese in the morning." And she closed the door.

Roman and Effie glumly fenced the geese, tied the horse, and gathered dry hay to make a bed. She kept glancing sideways at him until he pointed a fistful of hay at her and threatened, "If you ask me whether I'm really the Surchatain, I will turn you over my knee!" She hastily mumbled that the doubt had never crossed her mind.

The poulterer sheepishly came out to them with leftovers from dinner.

"Beg pardon, Surchatain, it's all she'll let me bring you. She doesn't believe you."

"I can understand that. But why doesn't she believe you?" Roman asked testily.

"Women. You know how they are," the poulterer replied vaguely.

"No, but I'm learning. Tell me, have you seen any Qarqarians in town? They like to wear those long red robes, even in summer."

"Yes, they've had merchants here, with a good load of ore."

"You mean Lystra is honoring the trade agreement with them?" Roman demanded.

"And why not? It's a profitable deal, Surchatain."

"I was hoping Nihl would raze Hornbound," Roman muttered honestly.

"What's that?" asked the poulterer, turning his ear.

"Can you deliver a message for me?" Roman asked suddenly.

"Readily, Surchatain. Tell me what you want said, and to who."

"No," Roman said, dropping his shoulders. "That won't work—I tried that once. Do you have paper?"

"Of course," the poulterer said huffily.

"Then bring me some, and a quill."

The poulterer brought the items, and Roman sat down to write out a few lines. Then he rolled it up and tied it with a leather thong. "Please give this message to Commander Nihl. You can find him any morning on the palace grounds, watching the soldiers drill. Tell him it is for the Surchataine Deirdre. When she sees it, she'll know it's from me because she'll recognize the hand."

"Right, Surchatain."

"If Nihl is not there, give it to the Second Kam—but no one else. Will you do that?"

"Yes." The poulterer took the scroll. "Oh—Surchatain—one more thing . . ."

"Yes?"

"I'm going to pay you for the geese tonight. Regardless of what the missus says, I trust you." He handed Roman a few silver pieces.

"Thank you," Roman replied in a slightly imperial tone.

"But—could you be out of the pens before sunrise? Our customers come early and the missus doesn't want anyone to see you here."

"Yes," Roman said, shrinking at the remark.

"Fine. Good night." Leaving the Surchatain in the hay, the poulterer returned to his house. He tucked the little scroll beside his clothes and climbed into bed.

The following morning, his wife Elyria shook out their clothes as she customarily did, and discovered the scroll. Curious, she unrolled it and read, "My love. I am well, but I cannot come home yet. Wait for me. Tell Ariel to wait for me. I long for you, my love, and I will be home soon."

"Rubbish!" she snorted, and tossed the paper into the fire.

At that moment Deirdre's retinue was preparing to depart and Kam had already begun dispatching soldiers to cover the trade routes. As for Commander Nihl, he had ridden out to search along the north market road again. Today when he entered the surrounding forest, he happened to ride in just the right direction to come across a little footpath. He followed it one way until he spotted a hut sitting off from it. He climbed down from his horse and poked his head into the hut. A man and a woman lay sleeping on a straw bed on the floor. A dog near them raised its head and growled.

Nihl withdrew quietly and continued down the footpath until it took him up to the city. Then he backtracked the other way. He came across another hut which had been partially destroyed by fire. Nihl dismounted uneasily to inspect this one; it had a wild and desolate air about it. He looked down through a burned-out hole in the side of the hut, and paused gazing at a skeleton.

Almost without blinking, Nihl left that hut and continued up the path. But the dead man's bones had rattled him. Could everyone else be right, and he be wrong? Were those bones an omen of what he would find if he did find Roman?

He came across another hut, this one boasting a small garden. Nihl listened at the door, then pushed it ajar. Stepping in, he paused at the sight of a body on the floor. Noting a door opposite him, he warily drew his sword and silently crossed the room to look there. But all that was beyond the door was a small, rumpled cot, stained with dark spots that looked like blood.

On his way out, Nihl stopped over the body. Then his eyes popped wide open and he quickly bent to pick up the leather pouch with the Surchatain's insignia.

"He was here," he breathed. "He was here and left—then he must be back at the palace by now!" Still gripping the pouch, Nihl leapt on his horse and raced down the path.

When he arrived at the palace, he saw Kam, Olynn, and the Counselor, Basil, standing together in the front courtyard. "Is he here?" Nihl shouted. Olynn blinked and Kam looked at the ground.

"Where have you been, Commander?" Basil asked.

In his excitement, Nihl did not notice Basil's strange tone. "Counselor, I have found Roman's pouch in the hut where he was staying— he was there, but has left."

The Counselor hardly glanced at the pouch. "If that is indeed his, then what you have found is what the assassin discarded." Nihl was beginning an argument but the Counselor continued, "Then you were not dispatching soldiers as I ordered you?"

Nihl grew still. "I delegated that to my Second, Counselor."

"But I ordered *you* to do it!" said Basil. "Because you have disobeyed my order, you are relieved of your post as Commander and dismissed from the palace. Gather your things and be gone within an hour!"

Basil turned his back but Nihl took a step toward him. "With all respect, Counselor, is this an order from the Surchataine?"

Basil's head jerked back over his shoulder, his pale blue eyes sparking. "That is *my* order, and if you attempt to approach the Surchataine, I will have you put in prison. Take your leave, before I have you thrown out!" Basil stalked from the courtyard.

Kam and Olynn stood with Nihl while he absorbed the shock of his dismissal. "Commander—" Kam began hesitantly.

"I am no longer Commander," Nihl said calmly. "Who is?"

"Ah, the Counselor appointed me," Kam answered uneasily. Nihl did not comment. "If you remember what happened when Troyce tried to usurp the throne and all, I think you'll understand why the Counselor is so touchy about insubordination," Kam went on rapidly. "But once you find the Surchatain, I'm sure—"

"Surchatain Roman is no longer in the peasant's hut," interrupted Nihl. "He is beyond my finding."

Olynn and Kam glanced at each other, then Kam added, "I have lodged Izana at my sister's house, until you decide what to do."

Nihl dug his heel into the ground as he thought. "May she stay there a while?"

"As long as you wish, Com—sir. But where will you be?"

"I am going to Calle Valley," Nihl said coolly. "Roman is alive, and Deirdre must not marry another while he lives. I am going to prevent it."

That morning a number of travelers crowded the rocky, westbound thoroughfare leading to Crescent Hollow and the fair: soldiers patroling in pairs; merchants loaded down with wares; wealthy citizens boasting their own bodyguards; money lenders, curiosity seekers, and general rabble.

It had been misting and grey in the early dawn when Roman and Effie had passed through the stone pillars marking the outskirts of Westford. Riding a swaybacked horse, the two of them presented an enigmatic picture—the man unshaven, wearing a tattered sling and a

236

costly white silk shirt; behind him, clutching his waist, the peasant girl bouncing on the horse's rump.

Several hours later the Surchataine's royal entourage passed the pillars, drawing admiring stares and whispered comments from the other travelers. Deirdre, riding the sturdy black gelding, was followed by maids and soldiers, both Lystran and Calle. The emissary Virl rode at her side, talking with grand, sweeping gestures.

Several minutes after they had passed, a Polonti on horseback paused at the pillars. He glanced back at Westford, then gazed up the road at the dimishing party. When they were far enough ahead so that he would not be spotted, Nihl too left the pillars for Crescent Hollow.

CHAPTER 29

As ROMAN AND EFFIE plodded on the westbound road toward Calle Valley, Effie kept shifting uncomfortably in her seat. "It's getting hot, and this nag has the gait of a duck," she complained.

Roman chuckled, "And Pax thought he had hoodwinked the trader—" he caught himself, realizing that he need not speak evil of her dead brother.

"Surchatain," Effie murmured, and he bit his lip for even mentioning Pax's name. "Are you sure you should take me to Calle Valley? It's a long trip, and you must be needed at the palace. They think you are dead."

Roman exhaled. He knew the most logical course of action was to return to the palace and delegate the task of finding Oweda and Mathias. But for some reason he felt pressed to do this *personally*—to give her welfare the priority she had given his. He feared that once he became Surchatain again, other matters of state would squeeze her out.

"I promised to see you safely to your friends," he told her. "I must keep that promise, for my sake as well as yours. Besides, whatever they tell the people at large, I am sure Basil and Nihl and especially Deirdre do not believe I am dead. And that should be confirmed by the poulterer's message."

237

She frowned, "*I* tried to deliver a message, too. It's not as easy as you make it out to be. It seemed to me they all really think you are dead."

He condescendingly patted her hands on his midriff. "Don't worry over it, Effie." Their nag started into a sudden lope as they were passed closely on either side by a pair of Lystran soldiers. The pair glanced, smirking, at the broken-down horse with its mismatched riders. As Roman watched them gallop down the road, his face darkened and he muttered, "I would like to know what urgent mission those two are on."

"The soldiers are always like that," Effie remarked. "Didn't you know?" Roman glanced over his shoulder at her. She added, "They treat anyone on the outside like garbage."

Shades of the Cohort! Roman stiffened. Were they really like that? *She is a sensitive girl,* he rationalized, but even he had seen their disparaging look. He shrugged, and she answered, "No—you didn't know. Do you know anything that goes on outside of your beautiful palace?"

He delayed answering for a long time, until a bellmaker had driven his cart up beside them and the ringing, clanging, and tinkling of his wares prevented Roman from attending any more disconcerting questions.

Effie was entranced by the music of little silver bells mingled with the peals of big solemn brass ones. The road was barely wide enough for the cart and the horse, so she was able to reach out and rattle several clappers. The bellmaker, fortunately a good-natured man, leaned over smiling to give her a tiny copper bell.

Effie shyly accepted the present. But almost at once there were hoofbeats pounding behind them and angry cursing. Effie, the merchant, and Roman craned around as a Lystran soldier shouted, "Move this cart off the road and let us pass, fool!" His fellow beside him was using his horse to try to bump Roman and Effie onto the rocky shoulder.

The merchant jerked his cart to a stop to let the horses pass him one by one, Roman's first. But as the first soldier passed the bellmaker's cart, he kicked it hard enough to dislodge some of the merchandise onto the side of the road.

Roman whipped the nag around, forgetting Effie on the back, and she had to hold on tightly to keep from falling off. "What reason is there for such violence?" he demanded.

The soldiers gaped at him scornfully. "Keep your mouth shut or get it filled with dirt, peasant!" retorted the first soldier.

"What is your name?" growled Roman.

238

The two soldiers stared at each other and the first hooted, "Why? Are you going to go cry to the Surchataine?"

"I am the Surchatain, and I promise you will be expelled from the army, at best."

The soldiers roared. "You are a dribbling idiot!" They spurred on, spitefully kicking up dust.

Roman angrily wheeled the horse toward Westford. "I'm going back to the palace. Things are already out of control!"

But he felt Effie's arms grip him from behind. "Don't you understand they've always been like this? What are you going to do differently now?"

He paused, thunderstruck. "I don't really know," he stammered. "But here I almost forgot already what I had promised first to do." Dismayed, he turned the nag up the thoroughfare again. "The palace will have to wait. The Lord will have to keep it until I deliver you home where you belong. You saved my life and I owe it to you now."

Effie gratefully squeezed his chest, and they caught up with the bellmaker as he finished reloading his cart. "Please, fellow, accept my apologies for these ruffians," Roman contritely offered. "If you wish, I will ride with you for protection."

The merchant laughed, glancing at Roman's incapacitated arm. "Protect me from the Surchataine's protection?"

"What?"

"Those soldiers are sent out along the roads to protect merchants traveling to the fair."

Roman shook his head, confused. "No, they can't be. By whose order?"

"By order of the Surchataine. Where have you been to not know this?"

"I did not order it, because Bruc's army is marching on Corona!" Roman exclaimed.

The merchant nodded carefully, as if suspicious of Roman's mental state. "As you say. . . . Good day." He slapped the reins briskly on his horse's back.

Roman stared down at the tracks in the dirt road as the merchant drove off. "Do you want to go back now?" Effie asked quietly.

"No," he said with forced decisiveness. "Whatever has happened in Corona, I am too late to alter it. I will just have to do the best I can by you now." He clucked the horse to a walk, then sadly laughed. "Not very long ago, I disguised myself and my wife to look like peasants, just to get away from being Surchatain. Now I find it taken away from me, and I am certainly no happier."

"What does it take to make you happy?" she asked, wondering how anyone who lived in a palace could be unhappy.

"A few less questions from saucy little girls," he retorted, turning the conversation away from too uncomfortable truthfulness. . . .

> Hickory dickory dock,
> The cook forgot the crock;
> The ale went stale
> And killed a whale;
> Hickory dickory dock!

Ahead of them, the loud, joyful song came from a young fellow who was draped across possibly the only horse in Lystra in worse shape than their own nag. Effie giggled and Roman winced, smiling. The fellow's trade was not clearly apparent: his pack showed some barbering tools, but they were old and rusty; there were tin plates and pans, but not enough to sell—he might have been one of the many drifters who just bought (or stole) and sold enough to keep ale in the jug.

As they passed him, he burped and waved merrily. Roman saluted in return, noticing uneasily the embroidered collar set with gems that the fellow conspicuously wore. How a fellow like that came by such a treasure, Roman did not want to know. But drunk as he was, he'd never keep it.

Roman and Effie were mingling with traffic up the road when a sudden clamor behind drew their attention. Travelers were hurrying forward to clear away from the drunk, who was being attacked by two soldiers. Roman watched in incredulous fury as the soldiers yanked the fellow from his seat and began beating him.

Half falling from his horse, Roman ran back down the road, grabbing from behind one soldier who already had a hand on the collar. The soldier was so surprised that he delayed swinging for an instant, during which time Roman flung him face down into the road. Then Roman wheeled in time to see the drunken traveler expertly knifing the other soldier. As that one fell, his companion picked himself up and fled on his horse, mistakenly riding westward at first.

Roman gaped at the drunk, who still had the collar but not his inebriated air. He eyed Roman sharply, stuffing the knife out of sight in his belt. "We had better ride quickly, fellow, before a whole unit comes down our necks." He bent to remove the money pouch from the body of the soldier while Roman stared.

"You baited them!" exclaimed Roman, and the other raised a cynical brow. "But—why?" Roman stuttered.

"Was it unfair of me to make myself an easy target?" he asked, a mock whine in his voice. "But if you want to hear more you had better come quickly. You're an outlaw now as well."

Roman jumped up behind Effie on the nag, then looked down in surprise to see that he had unconsciously reached for the reins with his left hand. His shoulder was still sore, but the arm was beginning to respond. Roman closed his eyes in silent gratitude, but the outlaw was shouting, "Come on!"

The three cut off the road past curious onlookers and delved into a heavily shaded area of forest. The cool green dimness was a welcome respite from the hot dusty glare of the road. They slowed to a walk, while the outlaw scanned the trees around them. Finding what he wanted, he began to follow markings and Roman rode with him till they came to a concealed camp.

As the outlaw hopped down from his horse, several men resting around a campfire stood up. "How'd you do, Thane?" one asked, studying Roman.

Thane threw the money pouch down beside the fire in reply, and one of the men began dividing up the contents. "I've brought new members," Thane remarked, jerking his head toward Roman and Effie.

"I will not rob," Roman said darkly, which elicited humorous glances from some of the group.

"No?" smiled Thane, who as he sat tossed a wineskin to Roman. "Not even a murdering soldier who tries to rob you?"

The blood rushed to Roman's head. From the corner of his eye he could see Effie giving him a look that said, "I told you," but he could not face her and them at the same time. "Those two were rotten apples," he insisted. "The soldiers are for the most part disciplined and honest."

There was some sarcastic laughter from the group in response. Thane smiled almost sympathetically. "What province are you from? Polontis?" No doubt he noticed Roman's characteristically Polonti features—the straight black hair, brown skin, and broad frame.

"I have lived all my life in Westford," Roman replied heatedly.

"Then you are blind and deaf to think so highly of the uniforms," Thane said, not smiling.

"Why should they rob? They are well paid," Roman muttered desperately, squeezing the wineskin in his hand. "And Nihl would never allow it!"

One man on the edge of the group spoke up in a reserved voice. "The Commander expels men caught thieving, but he can't be everywhere at once. And he can't control the factions among the men themselves."

"What factions?" Roman asked tensely. This fellow seemed to know what he was talking about.

"The Lystrans and the Polonti. The Lystrans see the Polonti as foreigners and won't work with them. I'd go so far as to say that a revolt is brewing within the army. The Polonti are the ones holding the army together, and that's only because the Commander is one of them."

"Who are you to know all this?" Roman asked, afraid of the answer.

"I am a soldier—my name is Quint. And I have found out who is responsible for most of the robberies on the road: the Blue Division of the Lystran army. But I can't get back in to report this to the Commander, for they'll kill me on sight."

Roman sat on the ground, sick to his stomach. Effie put a supportive hand on his shoulder. Quint continued, "You could pass for the Surchatain's brother, were you cleanshaven."

"I am he," Roman answered despondently.

"He who?" asked Thane.

"I am the Surchatain," Roman said as if expecting no one to believe him.

"The Surchatain carries a brand on his chest," Quint observed. Roman opened his shirt and showed them the cross.

Thane smiled ironically. "I suspected you might be alive, as no one was allowed to see the body. Why are you running?"

"I never intended to run," Roman said dully. "But now I see why the Lord kicked me off the throne. I had some things to learn."

"You think you'll bring us to justice, Surchatain?" asked Thane. Again the ironic smile, as there were five men around the campfire.

"Bring you to justice?" Roman repeated. "The world has gone mad, with soldiers robbing and renegades patroling the roads." He stood. "No. Rob with my blessing. Then come see me when I return to the throne, and I will give you legitimate authority to ride the roads."

"A man would be a fool to believe that," Thane remarked.

"I swear it," said Roman. "I will appoint a special position for you—to catch uniformed thieves."

"Then ride with us now," Thane offered.

"No. I have a particular duty to perform now. I must take this child to Calle Valley."

"To the fair?" Thane asked, and Roman nodded. "Then let us ride with you. You've been spotted as an outlaw, and you'd best take what help you can get."

Roman studied his angular, youthful face with the habitual smirk and dashing eyes. "Very well," he said cautiously. Eagerly, the renegades packed up their camp and rode with Roman to the edge of the trees, where they peered out to the roadway a hundred feet away.

A retinue of soldiers was just coming into view. The outlaws backed into the trees, watching warily. "That's the one who got away," muttered Thane, nodding toward a soldier riding up to meet the vanguard.

But Roman was watching elsewhere. "Who could be leaving Westford with such a large train . . . ?" Then he moaned, "Deirdre!" as he glimpsed her in the midst of the soldiers. "I told her to wait for me," he growled.

"She did not get your message," Effie whispered, vindicated once again.

Roman nodded. "So she goes to the fair. Oh, my precious Deirdre, who spends money when in distress." He squinted, thinking aloud, "If she ordered soldiers to cover the trade routes, it must have been at Caspar's request. And if she is going to the fair, it must be at his invitation . . ." He froze for an instant, then nodded grimly to himself. "She does think I am dead. She is going to see Caspar. I had better get there myself, and soon—after I have delivered you," he said to Effie.

Thane pointed out, "Our safest course is to ride well ahead of them into Crescent Hollow, since we can travel faster than they. Once you've delivered your package, then we'll see to the Surchataine."

Roman glanced up, not particularly glad that this brash young man wanted to share this critical and highly personal mission. But as Roman didn't see much chance of being able to lose him, he grudgingly nodded. They turned their horses into the woods to take a shortcut that would meet the road further ahead.

To the soldier riding beside her who had just reported the encounter with robbers, Deirdre murmured, "How terrible that they are so close! Please send my personal condolences to the family of the man killed."

"Yes, Surchataine. As the renegades have taken to murder now, do we have your permission to execute on sight? You remember, Surchatain Galapos ordered them under the death penalty when they got so bad after Tremaine's invasion."

"Yes, I remember," she said, though it was just a vague recollection. "I don't really know . . . ask the Commander what is best to do. Nihl will know."

The soldier hesitated, a smile playing across his face. "Yes, Surchataine." He wheeled his horse toward Westford. All the Lystran soldiers with her had heard about Nihl's dismissal. It was obvious that she did not know. Had there been one honest man with her, he would have told her. But they just smirked at each other.

Several miles behind them, Nihl saw the soldier coming and hastily dropped behind the large, lumbering wagon of an armorer. The soldier passed him in a flash. Nihl, knowing the road ahead would be crowded with soldiers due to the Surchataine's edict, realized he would need some way to travel without drawing their attention. Almost any one of them would recognize him, even out of uniform.

He considered traveling at night. But then he would lose sight of the Surchataine's retinue, and besides would lure thieves. He glanced at the armorer. Perhaps he could attach himself to one of the merchants for the trip—the armorer glanced at him and Nihl nodded cordially. But the merchant spat, "Be off, drud," and sped his wagon.

Nihl slowed his mount, burning. The last man who had called him that was dead. Then a clicking sound penetrated his rising anger. Nihl looked over his shoulder to see a leper on a donkey coming up the road. He wore the leper's costume as required by law: a white shroud with hood, gloves, and castanets to warn of his approach. There was little of his offensive appearance that could be seen under his attire, which only fostered the mystery and fear surrounding the disease. Travelers parted like the mountains at Falcon Pass to give him wide berth on the road.

Watching him, Nihl perceived that sometimes the best way to stay hidden was to be as conspicuous as possible. He dropped back to ride beside the leper, who raised his shrouded head. "I have need of your help, friend," Nihl said. "I will give you my cloak and ten royals for your costume."

"Are you mad?" a quiet voice asked.

"No, but desperate," Nihl replied.

"Show me your purse," the leper said skeptically. Whereupon Nihl counted out ten gold royals into the gloved palm. "You don't fear becoming as I am?" the shroud asked.

"I fear failure more," answered Nihl. "If I am unsuccessful in my mission, then I may as well be a—as you."

"Come off the road," said the leper, and they entered the forest alongside the highway. A few moments later a white-shrouded figure on horseback emerged from the trees and took to the road, castanets rattling from his saddle.

244

CHAPTER 30

"EXCUSE ME. Counselor?" Kam poked his head into the library and Basil looked up from amid piles of correspondence and record books on the massive desk.

"What is it, Commander?"

Kam shifted as if uncomfortable with the title. "We've just learned of robbers only minutes up the road from the Surchataine's party— one of our scouts was killed. The men are asking permission to kill the renegades on sight rather than bring them back to Westford for sentencing."

Basil hesitated. "Is the problem that grave?"

"The men think so, sir. And you have to admit, if the soldiers are being attacked, no one's safe."

"Yes, I see," Basil agreed. "Very well, give them permission. But I want the outlaws identified, and if that is not possible, they must be brought back here, dead or alive. We must find out where this problem is coming from."

"Counselor." Kam bowed and withdrew.

Basil shifted back in his chair, pondering how reserved the normally loquacious Kam had become. *The responsibilities of power,* Basil thought, rising from the desk to lean in fatigue against the window casing. *It is such a burden to rule.*

"What am I thinking?" he blinked. "I am not ruling; the Surchataine is." He returned to the desk and selected a letter from the large stack in front of him to answer. "It is still a burden," he muttered.

That evening, Roman and Effie sat at a campfire with the six renegades. The men were relaxed and jovial, but the Surchatain seemed shaken by the events of the day. He chewed slowly on a crudely roasted rabbit shank, which was nearly raw on one side and mostly burnt on the other. Effie, uneasy in this group, scooted closer to Roman. He put his arm around her shoulder in response.

"What are you thinking?" she whispered.

"I am thinking of Deirdre," he replied.

She toyed with the hem of her linsey-woolsey dress. "You're anxious to get her back, aren't you?"

"Yes." He gave up on the rabbit shank, laying it down. "I have a

245

son, too. His name is Ariel." She nodded attentively. "I wonder if he remembers me," he murmured.

"You haven't been gone that long!" Effie insisted, but Roman turned his head to the side, listening to something else. For a few moments his eyes darted around the dark, misshapen trees, then he surreptitiously drew his knife and stared at Thane, trying to catch his eye. Thane saw him, but by the time he had put his hand on his own knife, a horde of soldiers leapt from the trees onto the camp.

Roman shoved Effie to the ground and stood over her as a soldier jumped him. Roman stiff-armed him, then wounded him with a swipe of his knife. Noting the number of soldiers, he yanked Effie up and threw her on the nearest horse, bareback. As he struggled up behind her, kicking a soldier back, one of the renegades yelled, "This way!" and plunged into the woods.

Roman kicked the horse's ribs, but rather than follow the renegade, he dashed off in another direction. Not wasting even a second to look behind, he landed in the road and made the poor creature run like an antelope.

They ran until Effie gasped, "Stop—I'm going to be sick!" Roman pulled the horse, sides heaving, to a halt. The road behind them was a silver ribbon in the moonlight, the dust glittering. It was empty as far back as he could see, so he was satisfied to let the horse walk.

They journeyed several hours, clinging to the side of the road and glancing behind them often. At last, when Roman grew so tired that he could not keep himself upright on the horse, he muttered, "Enough. We must rest."

"Where?" Effie whispered nervously.

"Anywhere," he groaned. They went twenty paces into the trees, where Roman tied the horse and sat.

"Here?" whispered Effie, crouching close to him.

"Yes." He lay on the bare ground, using his arm as a pillow.

"What if it rains?"

"Then we'll get wet," he yawned.

She clutched his shirt as she peered into the darkness around and above. There was just enough light to see shadows—shadows that drifted and changed as if they had a will of their own. "Roman." She felt for his arm. "I'm afraid of the dark."

"Most children are," he said sleepily.

"No—I mean, I'm *really* afraid. I feel sometimes that—things are in the dark around me. That they're going to come out of the dark and get me . . . Roman?" She leaned anxiously toward him, as he had said nothing.

246

He was silent because as she was telling him about her fears, he had felt something manifest itself around them. Not that he could see it, but the weight of its presence bore down on him. It came up and positioned itself at his face like a challenge, and he intuitively recognized it as the same thing he had encountered in a dark, airless room in Corona. Effie was gripping his chest, too terrified to speak.

"Even though I walk through the valley of the shadow of death," he said softly, "I will fear no evil, for *you are with me.*" He felt the thing pause.

"You have no cross, nor charm," Effie whispered.

"We don't need one. We have the name of the Lord. He comes without incantations because it's His desire to protect the simple and the weak." He gained assurance as he spoke, and the air stirred with a nighttime breeze. It seemed to blow the oppression away, leaving in its place the rich smell of humus and strains of a lark's song.

Effie relaxed. "It's gone."

Roman glanced around as moonlight broke through the treetops. "For now."

"I have felt that before," she said.

"You have? When?"

"Whenever Pax came home. It was like—a bad feeling would always come in with him. I could feel it even when he was gone. But I never knew what it was or how to make it go away. Sometimes I thought that if I—if I killed Pax, it would leave." She paused. "But then it did go away."

"When?" Roman asked uneasily.

"The day I brought you home."

Roman pondered this as Effie, unafraid, curled up and laid her head on his chest to sleep.

When the morning sun began making grey inroads into the forest, Roman woke. He lay perfectly still, hearing the crackling of someone's approach, then appraised the distance to where their horse was tied nearby. Through the bracken Thane appeared on horseback, accompanied by another renegade. "There you are," said Thane, smiling cockily.

Roman sat up. "Did you follow us?"

"Yup. We didn't want to lose the Surchatain." His voice was tinged with enough irony to irritate Roman.

"Where are the others?" Roman asked. Effie began to stir and yawn.

"They weren't as quick getting away," Thane answered, dropping from his horse. He seemed to lose a bit of his bravado on the way down, and the other fellow was plainly flagging.

"I thought you knew you were hunted men," Roman said. "It's no game you're playing. The soldiers are not to be toyed with."

"I know," responded Thane testily, "but we've never been ambushed like that before. They must have tracked us all day, then called together a whole unit. That's never happened before."

"It's happened now, so now we have to be smarter than they." Roman stood and stretched his creaking bones. He winced at his sore shoulder, noting how suddenly difficult it had become to sleep on the ground. "Old age," he groused. He reached down to help a sleepy Effie gently to her feet. "Come now," he murmured, still thinking. "They'll begin tracking again with daylight." He suddenly peered at Thane. "Or could they have followed *you?*"

"No!" Thane said scornfully, then glanced at the other renegade for support. "Did they, Braxton?"

"How would I know?" Braxton muttered. So they lost no time getting on the road. There, they mixed warily with the early risers who occupied the thoroughfare. They shared bread from Thane's pouch, darting out of sight whenever they spotted the rich brown uniforms of the soldiers far down the road.

Roman felt befuddled and weary. How had this ridiculous situation come about?—running from his own soldiers, unable even to contact his grieving wife. He felt immersed in a nightmare which had to run its course before he could awaken.

He thought of the evil presence he had encountered last night. Was it only his imagination? But Effie had felt it, too. It was the reason she was afraid of the dark. How was *that* affecting what was happening to him?

He tossed his head in mounting apprehension, but as he did a glint of pink from the new morning sky caught his eye. Roman looked upward in amazement. It was *the* sky—the exact same sky that he had seen when he had been lifted from the pit of hell, only now the Man was not stretched across it.

Or was he? If there were invisible presences in the dark which could oppress and terrify, then wasn't His presence also in the light, to protect and encourage? Abruptly he recalled pieces of a psalm: "Even the darkness will not be dark to you; the night will shine like the day, for darkness is as light to you."

Roman exhaled. How many times did he have to be reminded that God reigned in every realm? These terrible powers could stretch only so far as God allowed, then they were checked. And they were reduced to puffs of wind when confronted by the Name of the beloved Son. So he was not riding along powerless in this nightmare, rough though the ride was.

248

Thane spoke up: "Eyes ahead!" A hundred yards up the road was the border to Calle Valley. At this crossing stood four Calle soldiers inspecting travelers who desired passage. The forest had been cut back extensively from the crossing as a guard against secret entry.

The travelers paused and let traffic flow around them. "There are only four," Thane muttered. "We can take them."

"And have the Calle army chasing us as well?" responded Roman. "Think a moment." Travelers who had to go around them cast irritated glances their way. Effie, sitting behind Roman, returned their looks curiously.

"Then let's just leave the road and go around them," Thane suggested impatiently.

"Not possible. They've already spotted us," replied Roman, peering ahead.

"So we'll backtrack and take another route!" Thane was already turning his horse.

"And have you forgotten who is back there chasing you?" Roman asked sharply.

"We're stuck," muttered Braxton. Roman chewed his lip as he silently prayed to the Power that moves mountains.

They sat on their horses, Thane eyeing Roman as Roman watched the road. The heavy traffic forced them off to the side. The Calle guards looked up at them occasionally, but did not leave their post.

"Well?" Thane prodded.

"Wait," Roman said, eyebrows gathering slightly in anxiety.

They waited a few moments, Thane nudging his horse so that it danced restlessly. Finally he taunted, "Can't you decide? Do we go forward or back?"

"If you are that bold, you go forward," Roman answered.

Thane muttered a reply which Roman was glad not to hear, then the renegade spurred forward to the crossing. The other three watched as he was stopped by the guards, and spoke to them. One of the guards gestured to Thane's companions, and he shook his head. Another guard pointed to Thane's horse, then waited for a reply. Thane's answer apparently did not satisfy him, for he waved Thane back with his sword.

The renegade returned to the three while the guards watched intently. "They won't let anyone pass who doesn't have a clear and identifiable occupation," he muttered. "I told them we were bodyguards for merchants at the fair, and they wanted to know who. So I said we were for hire, but they said we had to be hired before passing. That decides it. We'll have to go off the road."

"It won't work," Roman insisted irately.

"Then what do we do?" Thane countered.

"Wait," Roman said, and Thane groaned in frustration.

Suddenly Effie squeezed Roman's waist. "Oweda!" A woman on a passing cart jerked around.

"Effie! What are you doing here?"

"Looking for you, Oweda!" Effie scrambled down from Roman's horse to clamber up in the cart. The renegades looked at each other and the merchant couple bemusedly. Mathias scrutinized the three men while Oweda hugged Effie. "Oweda—and Mathias—this is—" Effie began excitedly, but Roman gestured, glancing at the passing crowd.

"Tell her later, Effie. Let's say now that since you saved my life, I promised to deliver you to them. I seem to have done that, although I'm not sure how . . . But they can help us now, if they will."

"They're all right, Mathias," Effie reassured the dark-faced man. Oweda exchanged glances with him and shrugged her shoulders. "He killed Pax," added Effie, and Mathias immediately asked, "What can we do for you?"

"Tell the guards ahead that we are your bodyguards," said Roman. "But once we get to Crescent Hollow, we need to go our own way."

"That we can do," replied Mathias, and the group started toward the border crossing.

A unit of Lystran soldiers marched triumphantly into Westford, then down the streets and across the bridge to the palace. In the front courtyard, they threw down four bodies and summoned the Counselor. A lead soldier bowed at Basil's appearing and said, "Counselor, Iven here. As you ordered, here are the renegades we caught. We don't know a one of them. Some others got away, but we'll have no trouble catching up with them. We know where they're heading—the fair at Crescent Hollow."

The Counselor looked up sharply, as did Kam, who had joined him. "You think they are following the Surchataine's party?" the Counselor asked.

"Could very well be."

"Then why are you standing here? Go stop them at once, by any means!" shouted Basil. Iven saluted, leading the unit out at a heroic run. Basil pulled his grey hair in distress, turning to Kam. The new Commander was staring down at the bodies. "Commander, gather all the men at your disposal and join the Surchataine's escort!"

Kam's black beard began to twitch. "I don't think that would be wise, Counselor," he mumbled.

250

"What are you saying?" exclaimed Basil, astonished that Kam would refuse a command.

"Something is not right, Counselor," whispered Kam, then looked around as if afraid of being overheard.

"Whatever are you talking about?"

Kam whispered, "I know one of these fellows they caught. His name is Quint. He's one of us."

"You mean he *was;* he turned renegade," Basil corrected him.

"No, Counselor. Not Quint. He was as sure as the seasons. The Commander had sent him on a special mission to search out the source of these renegade attacks."

"Apparently he found it," the Counselor remarked sarcastically.

"Apparently, he did. But before you judge, let me tell you something else: Iven was lying. He knew Quint. They all did. He was in the same unit—check the rolls to see for yourself. And what is more, if these were really renegades, they would not be traveling to the fair, nor would they accost the Surchataine's party—that would be suicidal. Real renegades stake out a territory where they know every rock and hole for hiding, and then they stick with it. Whoever this is the soldiers are chasing, I'm afraid to guess." A possibility crossed Kam's mind, but he dismissed it at once as too wild.

"So what do you suggest, Kam?" Basil asked, eyes on the four bodies.

"I recommend that we get Commander Nihl back at his position right away."

"Then find him," Basil growled, and called a soldier to remove the corpses.

Out of the corner of his eye Kam watched the soldier, a Polonti, walk over to the bodies and pause. Kam guessed that he, too, recognized Quint. But the soldier turned on his heel, signaling to another soldier, who disappeared toward the stables. Kam grabbed Basil's arm as Polonti began gathering on horseback like thunderclouds.

"What are they doing?" gasped the Counselor. The Polonti were discarding their Lystran shortcoats as they rode toward the front gates.

"Counselor, if you've ever taken charge, do it now!" Kam exclaimed.

Basil hesitated, staring, then jumped into the midst of the mounted Polonti. He seized the reins of the leader's horse, demanding, "What are you doing?"

"We will not serve under you any longer. The Surchatain is dead, and you have dismissed his Commander. We will not serve in an army of robbers."

Basil gaped, speechless, but Kam interposed, "You know where these attacks are coming from, don't you?"

"Yes," said the Polonti.

"They are not renegades, are they?"

"They have never found it necessary to quit the army," replied the Polonti.

Pale with anger, Basil flung his hands up. "Then I charge you to go stop them!" The Polonti cocked a brow at him. Basil added, "And if you find Commander Nihl, send him back to me. He is reinstated to his post."

The Polonti half turned in his seat to the others behind him, and one nodded. "It will be done," he said.

The Polonti rode out, and Basil murmured, "The Surchataine . . . she is not in danger, is she?"

"Surely not," said Kam.

"Then who is it Iven is pursuing into Calle Valley?"

The stubborn possibility resurrected itself again to Kam, and he reluctantly mentioned, "Commander Nihl was convinced the Surchatain is not dead."

Like a man sinking in turbulent waters, Basil took Kam's arm for support. "The Chatain and his nursemaid will share my quarters. They will not leave my sight until . . . the Surchatain comes home."

CHAPTER 31

THE BORDER GUARDS stood at rigid attention as the Surchataine's party passed. The Calle emissary Virl smugly told Deirdre, "You will find a highly trained, loyal army in the Valley. Surchatain Caspar has exerted much effort and expense to train them properly."

"That is good," Deirdre agreed, nodding benignly at a passing merchant who saluted. "A country is only as sturdy as its army."

"My lady need have no fears on that matter. And in Calle Valley, the Surchataine has as much power as her husband—unlike in other provinces."

"Oh, I had as much authority as Roman," Deirdre answered briskly. "Except, of course, where our opinions differed . . ." She trailed off,

252

remembering in a surge of love and grief how often he had acquiesced even then.

"In which case his prevailed," Virl observed. "It is not so in the Valley."

"Then how are decisions made?" Deirdre asked vaguely.

"Either party may submit to the other's wishes. Often the Surchatain may do so, to please his lady. It is very important to him to please her."

Deirdre thought that was fine, although not really much different from Lystra. She would have to study the laws of the Valley to see how much power the Surchataine actually had.

On this leg of their journey the mountains were clearly visible now, rising up in mottled green along the horizon. The road dipped slightly as the landscape rolled around them, thick with lush vegetation. In the growing season, everything seemed bursting with fruitfulness, even in the wildlands. This was superior country to the land around Westford, she considered.

She was beginning to ask a question about Caspar when shouts behind them turned their heads. The border guards were vehemently denying a white-robed person on horseback permission to enter. They were cursing and threatening with drawn swords, demanding that the leper turn back. A traveler threw a rock which grazed the leper's shoulder. Their hostility toward someone who had suffering aplenty kindled a burning anger in Deirdre. She suddenly commanded, "Let him pass!"

The white-hooded head looked up toward her and the guards froze in dismay. "My lady, that is a leper!" Virl cried.

Deirdre insisted, "I said to let him pass. In Lystra, Roman always showed mercy to the unfortunate. Would Caspar do less?"

"Ah—of course not," sputtered Virl.

"Then let him pass." The guards stood far apart as the white figure rode through. The other travelers scurried aside. "Furthermore," Deirdre said in rising defiance, "he may travel with me."

The soldiers escorting her almost broke formation. Virl panicked. "Surchataine, I must protest!"

"To whom?" Deirdre asked, amused. "Or were you lying about the lady having as much authority as the lord in Calle Valley?"

Virl was close to blubbering. "I beg you to be reasonable, Surchataine!"

"I believe I am." She nodded to the leper, who was now within six feet of her, and he bowed his head. As the party progressed again, disjointed and somewhat spread across the road, not even Deirdre had the courage to draw the leper nearer for conversation. So not much was said for the next several hours.

"So that is what happened with Pax, Oweda," Effie finished explaining all the recent events. She talked quietly, so that Thane and Braxton had to ride close by the cart to hear. Roman rode further apart, keeping a watch out for soldiers. Everyone else seemed to lose awareness of being pursued while Effie was telling her tale. Even Thane had been listening without his usual sarcastic comments.

Oweda tentatively asked Roman, "Is there anything more we can do to help you now, Surchatain?"

"Nothing, lady," Roman replied without seriously considering her offer. "I am quite on my own now."

Mathias said, "We should reach Crescent Hollow by eventide. Can we pay for your lodging there?"

"Perhaps," Roman mused. "Only when I reach Crescent Hollow, the first thing I must do is get into the palace. I may not have time to be lodged."

"*We'll* take the money, instead," Thane offered, but Roman turned on him so irately he backtracked: "Do you have anything to eat?" The merchants opened their packs to the renegades.

At this point the traffic, which had been steady throughout the journey, increased to the point of packing the road. "This is mad," muttered Thane. "I've never seen crowds like this outside the cities."

"This is the only route from the east to Crescent Hollow," Roman informed him. "The mountains north of here are impassable, so anyone coming to the fair must come this way."

"Is that so?" muttered Thane, scanning the mountains rising up in gentle green slopes. "They look tame to me."

"Have you ever tried to traverse them, hothead?" Roman asked testily. "The slopes are the least of the problem—it's what lives on them. There are snakes and scorpions in every crack, and in the higher regions, bears. You can't cross them running, and you certainly can't stop and rest."

"How do you know?" Thane questioned almost sarcastically.

"I had to skirt them every time I made a messenger run between outposts," Roman replied, looking over the deceptively peaceful hills. "From a distance, they look easy to cross—even pleasant. But anyone who is lured into them finds a deathtrap waiting for him."

Thane shrugged, but Oweda and Mathias were silently nodding. They knew the travelers' name for these mountains: the Poison Greens.

As they descended further into the valley, the air became sultry and still. The sun was not overbearing, but still uncomfortable. "Ugh, it's getting hot," muttered Braxton, wiping his face with his sleeve. Roman looked over at the hills, wishing for a breeze. "It doesn't ever

254

get this humid in Westford," he remarked, as if that should make them feel better. Anonymous travelers near them didn't seem as troubled by the stifling humidity; perhaps in their concentration on getting to the fair, they noticed it less.

But one of these travelers did notice the party. He was a scruffy, unkempt fellow whose age was disguised under layers of dirt and wild hair. He rode along on a donkey beside Thane and kept eyeing him and Braxton until Thane uttered an obscenity in his direction. Roman, riding abreast of Mathias's cart in front of them, turned around.

But the wild man let out a rolling laugh and said, "You need what I got!"

"What are you talking about, fool?" growled Thane.

Roman muttered, "Best watch your tongue with strangers, or you'll find yourself courting a knife in the belly." Thane bit back his next remark and determined to ignore the fellow.

But he would not be ignored. He swerved his donkey up against Thane's horse and insisted, "You need what I'm selling."

"What are you selling?" Thane asked skeptically.

"You get bested in a fight. Or you get in a crowd that you don't want to be in, see? I bet you get in scrapes sometimes."

"So?" muttered Thane.

"You need something when a knife won't work. You need one of these. Just drop it into a boot, or a sleeve, and it'll do your work." From his coat he took a little metal box punched with holes and opened it.

Thane leaned sideways to look. "What have you got—whoa!" He jumped back at the sight of several small, huddled scorpions. "You're mad! Where'd you get those?"

"The Greens," chuckled the wild man. "Only five pieces for the box, and they may do you a good turn."

Thane sat back and studied the fellow. Roman cast a tense look back, but did not intervene. "Would *you* want a fight with a man who had these?" pressed the fellow, winking.

"Curse you, you're right!" said Thane, and he dug into his shoulder bag for the silver pieces. When the fellow had the money, he surrendered the box to Thane and saluted with two fingers. Then he dropped back on the road, and they did not see him again.

Thane gingerly tucked the box into a pocket in his loose shirt, then changed his mind and put it in his saddlebag. Braxton swerved away from him. "Stay away from me."

"They work already," smiled Thane.

Roman shook his head as if disavowing responsibility for this young daredevil, then glanced into Mathias' cart. There was a variety of wares—trinkets, pottery, soaps, and a locked cabinet of spices. "What do you sell?" he asked Mathias.

"Whatever seems to be in demand," the merchant answered. "We buy from sellers who can't travel and take their wares on the road. That way we can pick the best to sell, and don't get stuck with any one commodity. Makes for a nice profit. It has become easier too, with the fairs. We can sell our whole stock at one fair." Mathias continued to outline their buying and selling strategy in detail. Roman nodded politely, listening with half an ear. When Mathias gleaned that his audience had become uninterested he stopped talking, and Roman failed to notice. The party lapsed into the routine of travel, speaking little as their horses plodded on.

It was about midday when the now-familiar sounds of running hoofbeats and shouts behind them snapped them out of their boredom. As the Lystran soldiers came closer, Roman whispered, "Hold your own—don't run. We're bodyguards. There's a chance they won't recognize us if we act as if we belong here—" He hushed as two soldiers came abreast of him. They were scanning everyone on the road, and the outlaws by no means escaped their attention. One soldier glared at Thane and demanded, "Who are you and what is your business?"

"I'm just an arm, hired by this merchant family to protect them," he said respectfully. Then he cast a long glance at his saddlebag.

The soldier caught the glance. "What are you carrying?"

"Nothing! Nothing you would want!" Thane exclaimed nervously.

This denial strongly piqued the soldier's interest. "Open your bag," he ordered. The first soldier, who had been rifling through the merchants' cart, took a string of glass beads and fell back to watch. Oweda breathed out in gratitude that he had overlooked the expensive spice cabinet.

With intense reluctance, Thane unstrapped the bag, but declined to open it. The soldier reached in himself and pulled out the little tin with punched-hole designs. He grinned up at Thane, whose face conveyed crushed disappointment. The soldier began to open it, but when they saw a third soldier riding in haste toward them, he stuffed it in his breeches unopened.

The soldier gained them and gasped, "One of you return with me and one of you ride ahead to alert the others—There's been a revolt by the Polonti and we have to gather quickly to stop them." At this point he stopped and eyed Roman, whose distinctly Polonti features

256

must have made him pause. "Do I know you, fellow?" he asked menacingly.

"No," responded Roman. "I am not one of you."

He narrowed his eyes but reined around, and the three split up and rode off—one with a tin of scorpions in his breeches pocket. There was a quick burst of ironic laughter from the traveling party, and Braxton slapped Thane's shoulder. Then Thane's sly eyes settled on Roman and he asked, "Why didn't you tell him the truth?"

"I did. I'm not one of them, and whatever they are, they're not my soldiers. That will become apparent very soon," Roman said.

"What are you going to do?" Thane asked eagerly.

"I'll know that when the time comes to do it," Roman said, with the assurance of experience.

They slowed cautiously as another Lystran soldier approached from the west, galloping in and out around carts and horses. But he passed the party without a glance, apparently returning in response to the alarm. Roman murmured, "I wonder what the Polonti are doing. That doesn't sound like Nihl, to revolt. He always controls his men better than that . . ."

"Then he's probably not in control," Thane remarked. It was a casual observation, but Roman's hands became clammy.

"Now," Roman muttered with finality. "Now that Effie is where she belongs, it's time to straighten matters out."

They arrived in Crescent Hollow at twilight in the midst of a jostling, jangling crowd. Signposts pointed out the way to the fair and directions to lodging places. Even from the main thoroughfare they could see the merchants' booths—tents crowding each other along the street, decorated with gaudy banners and signs. They heard criers hawking wares for the merchants who were too proud to shout, and minstrels singing loudly in competition for a few coins. Effie began to bounce in excitement.

Oweda put an arm around her. "Effie, a friend is letting lodgings to us on Short Street." She glanced at the men. "You need to say goodbye to your friend."

Roman dismounted, and without hesitation Effie embraced him. "I love you," she whispered.

"I will never forget you, Effie," he promised.

As Oweda drew her gently away, the last words Effie told him were, "I hope you find her." He smiled and nodded.

"Well, Surchatain," Thane said cheerily, "it'll be hours before the lady's party arrives. What do you say we find an inn with good ale and get comfortable?"

"Good thought!" said Roman, a shade too agreeably. "Only I need to do some scouting first, on foot. Take my horse with you, and when I'm done I'll come find you."

"Right," Thane said, taking the reins. "Wait . . . you don't have a royal, do you?"

"My last one." Roman dug in his pocket and tossed it to him. "Save some of the bottle for me."

"Right," Thane grinned, winking at Braxton. Roman let them go with relief, then began striding down a narrow, dirty street with tall houses almost touching high above his head. He did not wish to tell Thane he was going to do more than scout. He was going to finally meet the Surchatain of the Valley.

Roman traversed the city and found the palace in the center of the banker's district. It was not as large as the palace at Westford, but it was protected by high, formidable walls—and a moat. He paused at the water's edge, observing that the drawbridge was drawn up tight. He knew Deirdre had not arrived yet. He also knew that Caspar was not expecting him. So if he walked up to the drawbridge and demanded entry as the Surchatain of Lystra, what would Caspar do? Throw him in the moat, probably. If he waited until Deirdre arrived and demanded entry as her husband, *then* what would Caspar do?

"Throw me in the moat," Roman muttered. He sighed and glanced around—no guards had come into sight yet. He knelt by the moat and splashed lightly with his fingers. Answering ripples which progressed toward the splash confirmed that there were creatures of some sort in the water to discourage attempts to swim it.

Standing, he gauged the width of the moat to be merely twenty feet. To be thorough, he looked around for a possible medium of passage—a pole or a plank—but of course the ground was kept free of litter. He studied the drawbridge for a way to cross unnoticed on it, perhaps underneath, when it was lowered. But he could see the hinges were dead level with the water.

A guard appeared, making perfunctory rounds, and Roman ducked out of view. The guard carelessly passed within ten feet of him as Roman lay flat on the ground, hidden only by an irregularity in the mound around the moat.

He raised up again as the guard passed and tested his injured shoulder. It was sore, but mobile. Looking at the murky water, he drew in a long, fortifying breath. "Lord . . ." he murmured as he backed up. Then he ran at top speed and flung himself in a headlong dive into the moat.

Two strong strokes brought him immediately to the other side, but

258

he already felt a nip on his thigh. Struggling up the muddy side of the moat, he felt powerful teeth puncture his boot leather and prick his heel. His other foot stepped on something black and slippery and he fell under the shadow of the wall just as the guard came running back around to investigate the splash.

Roman pressed against the wall while the guard watched the water. If he had raised his eyes only degrees, he would have seen the black thing thrashing from Roman's heel. However, he was watching the ripples fade and the water grow quiet again. Satisfied that the moat had done its job, the guard continued his rounds.

Roman slumped down, watching the creature twitch on his foot. Cautiously, he grasped its head and squeezed, dislodging the teeth. Then he tossed it, injured, back into the moat. The water instantly churned again, then subsided.

Dripping, Roman crouched next to the stone wall and waited for the drawbridge to open to Deirdre.

Effie, Oweda, and Mathias rode in the clattering cart toward Short Street, passing sections of the fair, all lit and lively. Effie was almost incoherent in the excitement of retelling Oweda in greater detail all that had happened with Roman while observing the fair all at once. She had never imagined, much less seen, so many handsome treasures displayed together, and her narrative was going something like this: ". . . and then I finally got the bleeding to stop, but oh, he looked like a dead man—actually, it was still trickling when Pax came home and—Oh! look at the beautiful cloth! Anyway, Pax came home and I had to leave him—Roman—all night without knowing whether he was dead or alive, then in the morning I went in and—Look at the *dolls!*"

Effie was brought to a speechless gaze by the sight of the dollmaker's booth, crowded with lovely little things in genteel little clothes. Oweda cocked her head, smiling, and Mathias stopped the cart. "Look at that," he pointed. A train of soldiers and officials stood in the street outside the booth as if waiting. Effie was so entranced she did not see them; in an instant she had slipped into the booth for a closer look at the dolls. There was only one person inside with the dollmaker—a beautiful woman in rich attire who was lovingly caressing a doll.

Then Effie glimpsed a white figure hiding in the doorflap of the booth, and heard it whisper clearly, "Surchataine . . . Deirdre."

The woman turned to look at Effie. "Did you speak to me?"

Effie gaped in dumb terror. It was her! This was the Surchataine, standing right here, thinking this dirty peasant girl had the audacity to address her—!

Deirdre was frowning. "Did you have something you wanted to tell me?" She did not see the silent white figure on the edge of the tent.

Yes! Effie opened her mouth, but nothing would come out, and she wanted to run for embarrassment. Deirdre turned her back on the girl in momentary impatience, then smiled over her shoulder. "Do you like dolls, too?"

"Surchatain Roman is alive," Effie blurted out her carefully rehearsed message. "He wanted me to tell you he was wounded but healing. He said he has been humbled under a mighty hand, but from now on he will listen to Basil!"

Deirdre dropped the doll. The dollmaker hastily picked it up, brushing it off. Before the stunned Surchataine could say anything, the white figure stepped into clear view, lowering his hood. "It is the truth, Surchataine. He is alive."

"Nihl—!" Deirdre gasped. She threw her arms around him and clasped him, leper's clothes and all.

"Are you the girl who tended him?" Nihl asked Effie.

"Yes!" she answered, a thrill rising up from her toes. "Yes, it was me! I saved his life. And because he was grateful, he brought me here to Oweda—"

"Roman—is—here?" Deirdre croaked, choking on her heart in her throat.

"Yes," Effie said importantly, gratified by their expressions. "He is looking for you."

Deirdre turned to Nihl, whom she still grasped. "Nihl, what shall I do? I am to meet with Caspar!"

"Go meet with him," Nihl answered calmly. "Roman will certainly come to the palace."

"But I do not know that Caspar will receive him!" she said, panic tinging her voice.

"I'll wager Roman would guess that," Nihl replied with a half-smile.

"Nihl—come with me!" Deirdre urged.

He paused. "I should find the Surchatain first."

"Please, Nihl!" she begged. "You said he would come to the palace, and I need you until he does. I need someone near me I can trust!"

"Very well. I can hardly refuse you on that ground."

Deirdre turned to Effie. "And how can I repay you?"

Effie took in at one glance her rich clothes, her jewels, the dolls surrounding them. But suddenly she remembered at what great cost to himself Roman had foregone the throne to bring her here, as he had promised.

She looked the great Surchataine in the eye with a dignity and maturity matching her own and said, "I have been repaid." Deirdre nodded wonderingly and Effie left, filled with the thrill of having done right and done it well.

Meanwhile, Deirdre and Nihl rejoined the royal train, with Nihl casually removing the leper's shroud amid startled exclamations. "What is he doing? Who is that?" demanded Virl.

"This is Commander Nihl. He is accompanying me into the palace," Deirdre explained sweetly. The Lystran soldiers behind her looked suddenly confused.

"My lady, this ruse was unnecessary; you are well protected," Virl argued faintly.

"Are you countering my order *again?*" Deirdre asked in mock exasperation. "I wonder how your Surchatain could really consider the wishes of his lady when even his emissaries do not."

"Graciousness forbid! You may take anyone you wish into the palace," Virl corrected himself hastily. Deirdre smiled brilliantly on him. *I certainly will, and more than you realize.*

CHAPTER 32

ROMAN WATCHED from the cover of a protruding corner tower as the great drawbridge was lowered groaning to the ground and Deirdre's party crossed it. Torches carried by palace servants enabled him to pick her out at once, and, to his shock, Nihl beside her. "What . . . ?" His thoughts leaped ahead in angry confusion. *What is he doing here with her, when his own men are rebelling?* An insidious suspicion crept in as he recalled Nihl's confession of his feelings toward Deirdre. But before his suspicions could rise out of control, Roman checked them with a conscious, willful decision to trust his Commander. He had to. He needed Nihl.

The last man crossed the bridge, and it began to rise on screeching chains. Roman darted to the closing crevice and jumped up on the bridge. He rolled down it, falling to the side. One of the drawmen caught the movement in the sparsely lit bay and came closer to the door to look, but Roman had slid out of sight behind the lower pulley.

The drawman watched the door close securely, then he locked the chains and left.

Deirdre and Nihl, along with the emissary Virl, were ushered into a foyer glowing with colored fabrics and warm wood. Deirdre paused before a likeness of Caspar painted on the wall, and she wondered how closely the attractive image mirrored its model—it did not look like she remembered him to look.

"Deirdre." She turned, and saw that it was a good likeness. Surchatain Caspar crossed the room wearing a short military cape that swirled with each stride. "Thank you for coming." He took her hands in his and kissed them warmly.

All at once she was confused and jittery. He *was* the same Caspar—sincere, intelligent, but now older and more seasoned.

"I am sorry to hear of your husband's death," he said softly. "Roman's victories were known even here. But . . . I have been waiting a long time for this meeting, Deirdre."

She opened her mouth slowly, trying to think of a rational response. How could he be so honest and appealing? It would be so much easier if he were an ogre! Nihl was watching her. "I am glad to see you also, Caspar," she said evenly. "And I have something to tell you . . ."

"Tell me in the banquet hall, over wine and pomegranates," he said. Placing an arm around her shoulder, he steered her to a private room, leaving Nihl and Virl behind. The Commander started to follow, but as Deirdre did not indicate he was to come, he was prevented by a Calle guard. All he could do was watch the two disappear down a corridor while Virl stood smiling. Then the emissary nodded toward Nihl and growled, "Get him out of here," and two guards took his arms to forcefully lead him away.

Deirdre reclined on satin cushions beside a low table set with fruit, cheeses, and wine. Caspar leaned likewise on a pillow near her and reached out to fill her goblet, then his. There was no one else in the room, not even servants. "Deirdre, I have so much to tell you, and so much to offer you," he began earnestly.

Deirdre felt suddenly anxious to slow down his rapid advance. "Caspar, how is Laska?" she asked, recalling his sister, her girlhood friend.

A corner of his mouth turned up in a bitter smile. "Laska is the Surchataine of a little, inconsequential province in the northern regions. She has been sending us spies disguised as emissaries for years now, and recently she sent a raiding party to try to disrupt the fair. We chased them into the Poison Greens, and I do not believe they came out again."

262

Deirdre began to offer hasty excuses for her friend, but Caspar interrupted. "Forget her. I want to talk about you and me, Deirdre. I've already lost four years with you. I'll not lose any more."

"Caspar, I—"

He shifted closer, his voice lower: "Don't you realize I have loved you all this time? Even after I heard of your marriage, I still took no one. I chose to wait, to see if some day you would be free again. I have been waiting for you to come back to me, Deirdre. I am the one who was meant for you from the beginning."

Utterly confounded, she gazed at his earnest, handsome face. He chose that moment to cross the vast inches to her lips and kiss her. Against all reason, she found herself responding, to the point of sinking back on the downy pillows.

A nagging began at the back of her brain. Roman was not dead. Caspar was not for her. The one meant for her was the one she had sworn vows to . . .

"Quiet down," she murmured, and Caspar rose up laughing, "What?" Confused, she blushed and fanned her face. Then, they heard a commotion outside the door. There were muffled shouts, a kick on the door, and scuffling sounds.

Caspar leapt up and opened the door, with Deirdre standing fearfully behind him. Outside they saw Nihl, wrestling with two guards. "Stop!" ordered Caspar, and the three paused, winded. "What is the meaning of this?"

"Tell him, Surchataine," panted Nihl. Deirdre stared in mute distress. Nihl's eyes grew wide. "Tell him, Deirdre!"

"Look you, whoever you are, you certainly will not address the Surchataine in that manner!" Caspar declared angrily. "Escort him out of the palace!"

"No, please, Caspar," Deirdre said hastily. "He's a good friend—he means well." She did not dare look into Nihl's angry face.

"Very well, then, if you say so. Guards, take our—our guest to a room for the night," Caspar instructed coolly. Nihl did not resist as they took his arms, but Deirdre would not meet his eyes. As they led him away, Caspar whispered to a guard, "And lock him in." He did not know who this "good friend" was, only that he was a nuisance to be kept away while Deirdre was being wooed.

"Now then." Caspar turned back to her, taking her hand. "We will not be interrupted again."

Deirdre's guilty conscience spurred in her a desire to talk, and she deliberately stalled returning to the private dining room. "Caspar . . . tell me . . . tell me what happened after your father was killed."

263

"What happened? What could happen? I became ruler of a wasteland. We had nothing but half a summer harvest to start over with. There were times when I was out in the fields working with my own hands. We filled up the granaries and leased out farmland to anyone willing to work it. The craftsmen returned, then the merchants and money-lenders . . ." As he talked, he reached up to stroke her hair, and became so caught up in what he saw that he quite forgot what he was saying.

"Deirdre . . . you need never go back to Westford, if you wish. I would give everything I have to make you my lady."

"Caspar—I have to—" she gulped. "I have to go to bed now," she mumbled.

He smiled faintly. "We have all the time there is. I will persuade you yet." He motioned to a guard to escort her upstairs to her sumptuous quarters. Once within the colorful, candlelit walls of her sleeping chamber, she dismissed the housemaids and nervously paced up and down the room.

"What am I *doing?*" she moaned, beating her forehead. "Why didn't I tell him right away that I can't marry him?" Even as she posed the question to herself, she knew the answer. She enjoyed being courted by him again. She was awed that he had waited so long for her, and she wanted to milk his anticipation of having her at last for as long as she could.

Facing the ugly truth squarely made her flinch. Not only that, but every moment that she delayed the truth made it harder to ever say it—until she was forced to. Roman would no doubt appear soon, and she trembled to think what would happen if he did come before she was able to set matters straight.

She took a deep breath. "Time to come out of your fantasy, my dear," she told herself. Opening the door into the corridor, she told a nearby guard, "Take me to Caspar."

His sideways smile in response did not register immediately, but then she began to grow uncomfortable as they walked to the Surcha-tain's suite. All of them here needed to know she was still a married woman.

She glanced behind her as a movement caught her eye. There was nothing in the corridor behind them. But a moment later she saw something again, and turned full around. The guard, seeing her stop, glanced back, but no one was there.

They came to Caspar's door, where the guard tapped on it and swung it open into the corridor. Deirdre entered hesitantly, not having heard permission granted. The door was shut behind her. Caspar, naked

264

from the waist up, turned from a marble washbasin and Deirdre blushed, feebly covering her eyes.

He came up so close that her back was against the door. "Something you wanted?" he asked softly.

"Caspar, I have something I must tell you." She inhaled as he attended. "Caspar, I—"

The rest of her confession was lost as the door flew open and she fell backward into Roman's arms. He was armed with a long skinning knife, which came flashing toward Caspar's throat.

Caspar fell back, wrapping a shirt around his forearm and seizing an ornamental sword from the wall. "No!" Deirdre cried, attempting to run between them, but Roman flung her down behind him. The bloodless determination in his face frightened her.

"Who are you?" Caspar breathed, maneuvering to defend himself.

"I am Roman, and I am going to kill you for taking my wife," he said.

Caspar's astonishment was so immediate and real that Roman paused. "That is impossible!" exclaimed Caspar. "My own scouts watched your funeral barge put to sea!"

"Someone was mistaken," Roman replied grimly.

Caspar looked in bewilderment to Deirdre. "Is this your husband?"

"Yes, Caspar; it is," she whispered.

"Deirdre did not know I was alive," Roman said, drawing her to his side. She lowered her eyes as Caspar glanced from Roman to Deirdre and back to Roman.

"Nor did I know," he said cautiously, although something in his manner told Deirdre he now knew what she had wanted to say. "I would never take a living man's wife."

Roman lowered his weapon, reconsidering. "Then—may we leave in peace?"

"If you wish. But I would urge you to accept lodging here overnight and attend the fair tomorrow. My original invitation was to both of you," Caspar replied. In spite of his calm exterior he kept glancing at Roman's knife.

Roman fidgeted with it, looking rather sheepish. "I suppose, then, it would not be very smart to kill you."

"It is quite unnecessary," Caspar assured him hastily. "Though I would be interested to know how you got in." Deirdre was still staring at the stone floor.

Roman replied, "That is a rather long story, best left for tomorrow. Perhaps we could take your offer of lodging . . . ?" He was unconsciously stroking Deirdre's back.

"Certainly." Expressionless, Caspar moved past them into the corridor to summon a guard.

Roman asked Deirdre, "Where is Nihl?"

"In guest chambers—I hope," Deirdre murmured.

As Caspar reentered with their escort, Roman added, "I would like to speak with my Commander, also."

"Your Commander?" Caspar startled. Deirdre flinched.

"My—good friend whom you escorted to chambers," Deirdre explained in a whisper.

Caspar and Roman both stared at her momentarily before Caspar said, "I myself will take you to him."

Roman and Caspar strode down the corridor with Deirdre between them. Her breathing grew deeper and more erratic until finally she stopped and pleaded, "Caspar, please excuse us—I need to speak with Roman."

"I suppose you do," he nodded, walking on ahead.

Roman's expression was tensely restrained as he faced her. "You look neither surprised nor glad to see me."

"Roman—my love—I *am* glad. So glad! You don't know how I grieved when I thought you were dead," she pleaded, placing her hands on his chest. "But I was not surprised because I found out earlier tonight that you were alive. The little girl who took care of you told me." She paused, and he watched her for more explanation. "I did not tell Caspar at first because I feared what he would do. But then I saw I had to tell him, and went to his chambers to do that—"

His jaw dropped in shock. "You *went* to his room? Unsummoned?"

"Y-yes," she stammered.

"Deirdre, how could you?" he sputtered. "Didn't you realize what he would think? I almost killed an innocent man," he moaned, "when *you* were the one trying to cuckold me!"

"No! That's not true!" she cried.

He stared at her as she wrung her hands, floundering to explain herself, and, whether it was an accurate picture or not, what he saw was the little girl who had gotten herself into a scrape again and couldn't get out of it by herself. He tried to maintain a stern expression as she swore repeatedly that she went only to tell Caspar she could not marry him, but when in her anguish the tears came, Roman gathered her in his arms so she couldn't see his smile. "*Believe* me, Roman," she sobbed.

He held her tightly, relishing her warm, fervent embrace and passionate kisses. "On one condition," he murmured. "That you convince me you are glad to see me."

When an instant later a guard came around the corner with Nihl

266

at his side, the Commander grinned at what he saw and said, "Welcome back to the living, Surchatain."

Roman unwrapped one arm from around Deirdre to grasp his hand. "Thank you, Nihl. It's good to be alive." Deirdre pressed her face into Roman's shoulder. "But there is much I need to know," Roman said, growing serious. "Why have the Polonti under you revolted?"

Nihl's eyes widened. "Have the Polonti revolted?" he asked mildly. "I know nothing of this. I was removed from my post because I objected to the Surchataine's coming here."

"Who removed you?" Roman asked.

"The Counselor. The Surchataine was never informed of it."

"But what about Bruc's march on Corona? And what's become of that crazy Qarqarian emissary?"

"All that has been taken care of," Nihl replied calmly. "The Surchataine sent the emissary home, promising him we would attack Hornbound. Meanwhile, I met my brother Asgard at the gates of Corona, and told him to plunder the gold of Qarqar instead. He agreed, and we last saw them marching westward toward Hornbound," Nihl ended, on a note of satisfaction.

Roman studied him. "There is no gold in Hornbound."

"Yes, there is," contradicted Nihl, and he began telling Roman about the graves of the Abode, but Roman was shaking his head with conviction.

"There is no gold in Hornbound. All of that is just legend that the Qarqarians invented to give themselves stature among the provinces. They are a poor mining people, which is why I approved a treaty with them for iron and copper, to help build them up."

Nihl began to lose some of the color in his brown face. "But . . . Troyce said . . ."

"Troyce was *wrong,* Nihl. There *is no gold.*"

Baffled, Nihl exclaimed, "Then why would the Qarqarian emissary kill you over fictitious gold?"

Roman raised his shoulders haplessly. "I don't know! That's why I took the warning so lightly—I could make no sense of it. I suppose he was that determined to protect the legend."

Grimly shaking his head, Nihl said, "Their legend is destroyed by now, along with the rest of Hornbound. And we can expect a visit soon from Asgard. He promised that if he didn't find plunder in Hornbound, he would come to Westford for it."

"He can't! Polontis hasn't the army to attack Westford!" Roman insisted.

"That doesn't matter. He promised it, and he will do it if he has to sacrifice every last man," Nihl said firmly.

"How long ago was that?"

Nihl stopped to think. "Four days ago."

"Then by now they have reached Hornbound, found it empty, and—"

"—are marching to Westford," Nihl concluded.

Roman passed a hand over his pulsing brow. "No time to gather an army. We may have no army at all if the Polonti have revolted, for it is the Lystran soldiers who have been lining their pockets by robbing. We cannot count on them to fight."

Caspar's voice behind them said, "Perhaps I can help you there." They spun toward him. "I wanted you to come so that we might establish an alliance. Well, here is the opportunity. I will lend you my entire army to fight Bruc's soldiers—and I have no small force."

Roman and Nihl studied him. "Why would you do that? No alliance is without cost to both sides," Roman observed.

"There is a price," Caspar acceded. Deirdre grew suddenly nervous.

"Which is?" asked Roman.

Caspar answered, "Deirdre." Her stomach turned upside down. "Give me Deirdre, and I will lend you a fully equipped army, now and whenever else you might need it."

Roman took no time to decide. "That alternative was given me once before, and I made the wrong choice. No thank you, Caspar. That's too high a price, even if it means losing Westford. The Lord will have to show us some other way."

Deirdre leaned gratefully on his chest and Nihl grinned, "I like a challenge, Surchatain."

CHAPTER **33**

WHEN CASPAR seemed finally resigned that Deirdre would not be his, Roman readily accepted his hospitality for the night. Caspar, in turn, simply conducted himself with dignity and surprising grace. In the morning he set them a fabulous breakfast of wine and valley-bred lamb in the private banquet room where he and Deirdre had been alone the previous night. She seemed uncomfortable to be there a second time.

Roman reclined on a plush cushion as a servant filled a massive goblet before him, and he asked, "Do all you Calle eat lying down, Caspar?"

Deirdre flinched at what sounded like a taunt, but Caspar smiled. "It is a custom I observed during my travels, and it appealed to me." He could smile because he was watching Nihl tangle with the pillows— he did not like reclining on them because he kept rolling off, but he could not sit up because that placed him too far above the table. Finally he shoved them aside and sat on the floor.

A serving girl offered him a selection of fruits, which he rejected, not recognizing any of them. When he caught the smirks over his ignorance, however, he sullenly selected a hairy brown kiwi fruit and studied it suspiciously.

"So, Roman," Caspar took his attention from the Commander, "What will you do about these Polonti? Return to Westford and muster what army you have?" Roman nodded grudgingly. Caspar sighed, "You cannot win that way, you know. You should reconsider my offer. Is it worth sacrificing your country to save your pride?"

"It's not my pride that's at stake; it's my wife," Roman returned without smiling.

"Perhaps I was too demanding. I will ask you only to leave Deirdre here, for her safety. You may reclaim her afterward."

"No," said Roman.

Caspar shrugged in resignation. "Then at least I will furnish you and your entourage with fresh horses and provisions for your return journey to Westford."

Roman agreed, "I will take horses for myself, Deirdre, and Nihl. You may keep the servants as compensation for your trouble. The rest of the entourage is dismissed."

Caspar looked surprised. "Am I to host your soldiers while you go fight?"

"You may turn them out, or do with them what you will. They are not mine," Roman said coldly. Caspar lifted a finger to a guard, who left smiling.

After they had eaten, Caspar took them out to the drawbridge bay where horses and bags waited. He ordered the drawbridge lowered, then asked Roman, "May I have your permission to speak with Deirdre alone?"

"Within my sight," he replied.

Caspar took her several feet away and whispered, "This does not change anything. I will still wait for you."

"Please, Caspar, don't," she begged. "You are a good man. You deserve to have someone by your side."

"If it can't be you, I don't want anyone."

269

"Oh, Caspar—don't waste your life waiting for something that will never happen! I am not worth it. No one is."

"Someday," he said. "Someday you may yet be free . . ."

She tossed her head sadly—not for herself, but for him. This romantic stubbornness was not love, it was foolish make-believe. But he might have to reach the end of a long, lonely life before realizing that. Roman said, "Deirdre."

As Caspar escorted her back, he said, "One thing I would like to know, Roman. How did you get in?"

"I flew in an open window," Roman replied with a hint of a smile. He saluted and the three clattered across the wooden drawbridge on the borrowed animals.

Once across, Deirdre gently chastised him, "You did not even thank him for his hospitality or his horses."

Roman glanced at her. "I know why he did it, and it was not for me. I don't feel obligated to thank him for lusting after you."

Embarrassed, she kept quiet for a while after that.

Passing the outskirts of the fair, Roman felt a sinking sensation at the sound of a familiar voice: "Whoa, Surchatain! You never came back for your ale!"

He turned in the saddle to greet Thane and Braxton. "What must I do to lose you?"

"You can't. But you found the Surchataine!" Thane studied her with approval, nodding, and she lifted an eyebrow.

"Deirdre, meet renegades Thane and Braxton. And this is Commander Nihl," Roman told Thane.

"Say, do you know your men have revolted?" Thane amiably asked Nihl, who merely eyed him in return. "I'm glad we found you, Surchatain. You're really going to need us now." Uninvited, the renegades joined the three. Roman tried to ignore them, as well as the fact that he was beginning to like the young rogue.

As they embarked on the eastbound road out of Crescent Hollow, Nihl pulled up close to Roman to murmur, "Surchatain, I don't see how we can make it back to Westford and prepare an army before Asgard comes." Thane leaned forward to hear.

"What choice do we have?" Roman asked dismally. "It's almost hopeless . . . but . . ."

"Whoa!" muttered Thane, and they stared ahead at a troop of Polonti descending the road toward them. "Is it Asgard already? Here?" Roman exclaimed.

Nihl held his breath. "No," he said, exhaling. "No, it's not Asgard. It's Cy, Captain of the Green. He went with me to Corona."

270

"They are not in uniform," Roman observed. "If they have revolted, then . . . we are the first they'd come looking for." His group stopped in the middle of the thoroughfare while travelers scattered out of the way of the approaching Polonti.

They drew closer and closer, coming at a run. The five held their ground as the troop came up to them and halted. Cy, in front, saluted. "Greetings, Surchatain. You are not dead."

"Not yet." Roman returned the salute. "Where are you going, and on what orders?"

"The Counselor ordered us out on the road to stop the soldiers' robbing. And also to find the Commander and inform him that he is reinstated to his post," answered Cy.

"Nihl has always been my Commander," said Roman. "And what have you done about the soldiers?"

Cy shrugged, "We caught only a few. When word got out about us, they returned to the palace to regroup and come after us as one army."

Deirdre gasped, "Ariel! What of Ariel?"

"Your son is well, Surchataine. The soldiers hold no ill will for you. Actually, they think they are protecting your interests."

"You think they will be coming after you on this road?" Roman asked Cy.

"Yes, Surchatain."

"How many are you?" Roman inquired, looking over the horses.

"Two hundred and ten."

"If they muster all that are in Westford, they will have over five thousand," Roman murmured.

Nihl added, "Further, if they are traveling westward now, we can never get them back to Westford in time to fight Asgard, even assuming they obey you at once and without question."

Roman stared in intense concentration at the waiting riders. "How many does Asgard have, Nihl?"

"About two thousand."

Roman deliberately turned his horse to face north. "We can intercept Asgard and bypass the Lystran soldiers if we cross the Poison Greens."

There was not a word to answer him. No refusal, speculation, or question, not even from Thane. But Roman asked Deirdre, "Have you ever heard of the Greens?"

"Virl told me they were impassable," she said, casting a long glance toward the slopes.

Roman offered, "I will allow you to return to Caspar, Deirdre, if you—"

"No! If you are crossing them, I am going with you."

With merely a gesture to signal them forward, Roman led the troop off the road toward the sleepy mountains.

In a very short time they were approaching the foothills, and already their progress was slowed. Before they could climb the hills, they had to cross vast stretches of mire covered with thick, thorny bracken. When the horses became bogged down and tried to jerk their hoofs free, they were scratched and pricked to a panic.

Nihl ordered several of the Polonti off their horses and to the front. Using their long swords, they cut down the bracken in front of Roman so the troop could inch up to the mountains.

It was slow going, and tiring. The men on foot sank in mud up to their ankles as they hacked at the stubborn bracken. When they tired, fresh volunteers took their places, but still it was two hours before they had cleared five hundred feet of briar.

Suddenly the mire gave way to rock, which was covered with a slimy green moss that made it treacherously slick. The twenty-degree incline at which the troop ascended further hindered their progress. All through the company, horses and heads bobbed down erratically as they slipped around. Roman could not resist glancing at Thane, falling back in the midst of the Polonti. "Easy, isn't it?" Thane heard him and grinned sheepishly.

"Should we dis—mount?" Deirdre asked, jolted as her horse took a dip.

"No. The extra weight helps give the horses traction," Roman replied. "Besides—" he pointed down, and Deirdre recoiled. The clattering hoofs had disturbed a nest of scorpions, which came crawling en masse from a crack. One or two tried to climb up on some of the horses' legs, but the riders were very alert to knock them off.

After conversing momentarily with Cy, Nihl gingerly guided his horse to Roman's side. "Surchatain, the men are discussing how best to camp on these mountains—"

"Camping is impossible," Roman said briskly. "We must cross them today."

Nihl paused as his horse staggered. "I do not believe we can get over them by nightfall."

"Then we will have to cross at night."

Nihl nodded, plans and contingencies sweeping through his mind. He edged over to Cy, and Roman could see the Captain become animated with gestures. He knew what Cy was saying, but it did not deter him. There was no other way.

Nihl spoke to Cy uninterrupted for several minutes, then two other Polonti joined their conversation. Roman noticed all this because he respected his native brothers as hunters, trackers, and fighters. He could not safely ignore their opinions.

By the time Nihl skidded toward Roman again, he and Deirdre had reached a plateau of lush green weeds. "Watch your skirts," Roman warned Deirdre. "Stinging nettles." She quickly gathered up the folds of her skirts and tucked them tightly beneath her.

"Surchatain, the men are agreed on several points," Nihl began cautiously, and Roman's jaw tightened. "One, we cannot cross the Greens before sundown, and no one with us has flint or torch. Again, if we somehow managed to cross in time to meet Asgard's army, we are not enough to stop two thousand Polonti, nor even slow them much."

"You are right, Nihl," Roman murmured, feeling his confidence crumble before these facts. Inwardly he prayed, *Lord, what do I do? I am responsible for these men—and Deirdre—but how do I stop the Polonti?* He waited, listening, but received no answer.

Just as the last riders were clearing the slippery rocks, they were suddenly met by a bedraggled man riding a donkey. He cut across their path and Roman reined up. When the lone rider turned a gap-toothed grin his way, Roman recognized him as the seller of scorpions.

"Where are you *going?*" the scorpion man laughed, as if at a joke.

"We must cross the Greens. I will pay you well to lead us," Roman answered, feeling a great relief.

"I?" the other laughed. "No, no, ha, ha, ha!"

"I will pay whatever you demand," Roman offered urgently.

"No, no. You're a stranger to the Greens. There's more to fear here than scorpions," the fellow insisted.

"Yes, I see, but—"

"No, no. You *don't* see. You can't see them all. But they're here—all around. And they come out at night. Lead you through? No!"

"What? Who is here?" called Roman. The wild man was kicking his donkey to run out of sight.

They could no longer see him, but his shouted answer came echoing back off the mountain: "The dead!"

Roman stopped, and the Polonti were quiet behind him. Was this a warning to stop or a challenge to go on? Back, or forward? What did the Lord say? Roman sought desperately for an answer, but the Lord was silent.

Roman kicked his horse to go on. The Polonti followed without a murmur. But Nihl rode up close to Roman's side and asked so that no one else could hear, "Is this wise, Surchatain?"

"I see no other way," Roman mumbled. "I have to trust that the Lord will guide us safely through."

"Yes," Nihl agreed. "But . . . every mortal man must die some

273

time. When his time comes, the Lord will not let him pass untouched."

There was no disputing this. Roman fought off a rising dread in his belly, then reached for Deirdre's hand. "Go back to Caspar," he pleaded.

"No. I am with you." Her stubbornness would remain intact to the end.

They reached an area of thick scrub trees, dense with a strange grey moss which hung down from the branches. The riders fell into a line formation of two abreast as they entered the murky, shrouded world. Their hoofbeats were muffled by damp forest debris, so the men could clearly hear the hissing of snakes and the clicking of unseen insects all about. Deirdre glanced up uneasily and startled at a snake dangling down from a tree branch above her. She quickly passed it. As long as they kept moving, they were all right . . . she hoped.

One of the Polonti behind her reached up and cut the snake down from the tree with a stroke of his sword. Here and there a large winged insect would fly into someone's face, who would duck or bat it away. A stale, stagnant smell rose up from a pond near them. When Deirdre looked across it, the green scum on its surface rippled as something beneath it swam from the center to the edge.

They kept moving. Soon, the sun began its afternoon decline, and they had not seen the end of the trees yet. Roman urged his horse to a faster trot. They needed at least to clear the timberline by nightfall.

The hoofs quickened to a gallop, plopping in damp, sticky ground. "Please, Lord," murmured Roman, "Please let the light last until we get through the trees."

Almost immediately there was a perceptible darkening. The men looked up through the treetops in startled apprehension. Grey thunderclouds were slowly rolling together from the north. A few horses began snorting and shaking their reins, smelling a change in the air.

Nihl's face became taut with tension. "We must have the sun to guide us," he muttered. A deep growl rumbled across the mountain. "Is that thunder?" Nihl startled.

"No, I don't think so," Roman replied. Deirdre's horse whinnied in fear, and she reached down to stroke it comfortingly.

Minutes later, in midafternoon, the sun disappeared behind clouds and the troop was enveloped in shadowy darkness. "Set your eyes ahead!" Roman ordered. "Don't slow and don't look aside!"

They galloped ahead in the dim woods, skimming trees and breaking branches. The air grew very still, then was shaken by the crackling of thunder. Roman wove through the trees as he led the troop on an essentially straight course—correcting a left swerve with a right, alternating turnings.

274

Suddenly their path ahead was blocked by a thick tangle of underbrush. The vegetation had changed, and the forest ahead was impenetrable. Several riders crashed together as they came to an abrupt stop. "To the left—this way. Count your paces!" Roman ordered. They began that direction, but promptly ran into a den of hissing adders. Roman's horse reared in fright. "Back up! Back!" he shouted. They jumbled back and rode to the right, but the brush persisted at an irregular angle. Roman started to turn in at a gap, but Nihl said, "No—we can't get through there."

Roman nodded and corrected his course, then paused. "How many paces have we gone since we turned? Thirty?"

Nihl slowly responded, "Ah . . . I was thinking . . . forty." A fog began to thicken about them.

"Forty," Roman agreed. But the farther they followed the edge of the tangled growth, the farther to their right they had to turn. At last, the mass of vegetation ended—at an impassable rock chasm. The bottom could not be seen.

Roman gazed down at the chasm. *Lord, help us get through!*

Thunder crackled again through the sky, very close, as lightning brightened the forest for an instant. Roman used the flash of light to take in their surroundings. "Back to the left again. We must find a way through these trees." They turned and rode the way they had come.

Raindrops began pelting the trees overhead, some finding a clear path to beat on the riders. Obstinately, they pushed through the rain. It was not so heavy as to obscure their sight, but with the mist and the dark, they could not discern details in their path. All of a sudden Roman heard several behind him shouting. He jerked back on the reins, but could not understand what they were saying. "What? Nihl?"

"They say these are not the same trees!" Nihl gasped. "They're not!"

Roman wheeled to look at the trees. What kind of trees were these? What kind had the other been? "Lord God, we're *lost,*" he pleaded.

The rainy fog around them thickened, as if to hem them in. The forest became eerily quiet. The only sound was the patter of the raindrops.

A sigh came through the trees. "Roman . . ." it breathed. "Roman . . ." He sat still while ice engulfed his heart. "It's time, Roman. It's time . . . it's time . . . it's time."

"No," he choked. "Not like this."

Lightning crashed through the sky, and on the tail of its dying growls came other voices: "Yes, it's time . . . you cannot fight it. Your destiny waits here . . ."

"No!" shouted Roman, spurring his horse to a prancing frenzy, as it had nowhere to go. Nihl restrained him, and the other Polonti looked at each other. They had heard no voices but Roman's. Deirdre's face glistened with rain and tears as she watched her husband thrash around. Thane and Braxton looked white and confused.

"That oppression—it's here . . . I feel it—"

"Roman—" Nihl began. Lightning struck in the trees near them, sending them reeling back. A blaze erupted in its wake.

"Look! A gap! We can go through there!"

"No, Roman! It's a fire!"

"But there's a path through it! Don't you see it?"

"No! We can't ride through the fire!"

"Come on!"

"Roman—*stop!*"

The Counselor met Kam in the palace foyer. "What is happening? What are the men doing?"

Kam caught him by the sleeve. "Scouts have returned from Qarqar saying there's an army coming—"

"The Qarqarians?" Basil startled.

"No, Counselor: Polonti! Marching toward Westford!"

Basil paused with furrowed brow. "Then—Nihl's brother must not have found what he was looking for."

Kam almost stopped breathing. "You think so? The soldiers thought it was the renegade Polonti returning to fight."

"Where are the scouts who spotted them?" asked Basil.

Kam lifted his arms helplessly. "I don't know. They vanished."

"Well, it couldn't be the 'renegade' Polonti," Basil argued. They headed out toward Calle Valley, not Qarqar. And you saw how few of them rode out of here. Certainly not enough to make up an army."

"Their number seems to have grown as word was passed along about them," Kam remarked ironically. "If it is Bruc's army, they will be several thousand frustrated Polonti looking for a fight . . ."

At that moment Iven burst into the foyer. "Counselor Basil, I have assembled the men to ride out and meet the renegade army. We are ready to crush them at your command!"

Basil seemed to grow with power. "Well done, Iven. I give you the command to lead the men in this countercharge. But sift them carefully first—only stalwart volunteers may ride with you. Only those who hate the Polonti and wish to fight them may go. And inform Captains Colin and Olynn that they are dismissed from their posts for cowardice and may not go at all!"

Iven swelled. "Yes, Counselor!"

When he had charged out, Kam and Basil nodded to each other.

276

"We are done with the *real* renegades," Basil noted.

"A fitting end for them," said Kam. Then he laughed, "I can hardly wait to see Colin and Olynn when they find out you saved their necks by charging them with cowardice!"

Basil smiled faintly. "Have them and Captain Reuel assemble the remainder of the men to defend Westford, in case Iven is run over too quickly."

Shortly thereafter, an army of two thousand Lystran soldiers poured out of the gates, taking a northwest tack along the Passage toward Qarqar.

As dawn spread out over the Continent, stretching from east to west, It revealed two armies meeting on the plain north of the Poison Greens. With proud banners whipping in the wind and polished armor gleaming, they assembled in ranks facing each other. Then, at the trumpet blast, they clashed with shouts, and the pounding of hoofs. Swords clanged together and horses fell. Screams and groans, cries and curses drifted up like souls fleeing the terror of the battlefield.

High above, on the jagged northern crest of the Greens, forms lined the cliff and looked down on the battle below. They watched silently, the only sound from among them being the snorts of horses and the rattling of bits.

"We are too late," observed one rider.

"We are just in time, Nihl," corrected another. "We have already fought our battle. This one we were meant only to stand and watch."

Nihl turned to the speaker. "How did you see the path through the flames? None of us saw it—not even Deirdre."

Roman smiled wearily. "I was the one who prayed for it."

Nihl returned his gaze to the fighting, and his hand trembled slightly on the reins. "But . . . it burned all night through the trees, on our right and our left as we passed . . ." He paused in bewilderment, then looked at Deirdre. "Do you believe it really happened?"

"After what I have seen the Lord do, I would believe anything," she murmured. "It is no greater a miracle than His transforming me from what I was . . ." *And saving me from what I might have become.* She shuddered at the thought of a selfish, bitter little girl growing up only to become a selfish bitter woman. Even at her best, without Him, she would have chosen the luxury of Caspar's palace over the treacherous Greens—and never would have experienced such marvelous things.

They watched the battle scene a moment more but it was clear that there was nothing more they should do. Then Roman sighed as if the weight of armor had been taken off him.

"Let's go home," he said.

GLOSSARY

Abode—the cemetery in Hornbound where, according to legend, the Qarqarians hid their gold.

anakim (a NAHK im)—spirits which controlled a village though confined to figures of wood or clay.

Ariel (AIR e uhl)—Deirdre and Roman's son.

Asgard (AZ gard)—the Commander of Polontis' army under Lord Bruc; Nihl's older brother.

Avelon (AV e lawn)—the holy man who had won Roman's mother to Christianity.

Azrael (az RE el)—the name engraved on the sword Roman took from the palace of Corona; according to legend, the angel who separates the soul from the body at death.

Basil (BAY zil)—Counselor to Surchatains Galapos and Roman.

Berk—the Captain of the Bloodclad who served Tremelaine and Graydon.

Bloods (the Order of the Bloodclad)—in Tremaine's day, a special unit of highly trained, savage soldiers; the order was revived by Tremelaine with less success.

Braxton—a renegade, friend of Thane.

Brock—a cook in the palace of Westford.

Bruc (bruhk)—the Surchatain of Polontis.

Calle (kail) **Valley**—the province west of Lystra ruled by Merce, then his son Caspar.

Caspar—Surchatain of Calle Valley and former suitor of Deirdre; Merce's son.

Cass—a soldier of the Bloodclad.

Chatain (sha TAN)—title given the son of the Surchatain; the heir to the rulership; feminine—Chataine (sha TANE).

Clatus (CLAY tus)—the Captain in command at Outpost One.

Cohort—a special unit of soldiers created during Karel's rule after the pattern of Tremaine's Order of the Bloodclad; however, Karel's unit quickly disintegrated into a snobbish, self-serving order which lacked any outstanding characteristics.

Colin (CAWL in)—Deirdre's cousin, who brought the wealth of his father Corneus' province to serve Roman after Corneus was killed at Outpost One.

Coran (KOR an)—an emissary from Polontis.

Corneus (cor NEE us)—the wealthy Surchatain of Seir who betrayed an alliance with Galapos to fight instead with Tremaine. After Corneus was killed by Tremaine, Corneus's son Colin offered his service and wealth to Roman.

Corona (cor OH na)—capital of Seleca, which Tremaine formerly ruled; later Graydon and Tremelaine ruled it in emulation of him.

crenelation—the squared notches edging the top of a wall.

Crescent Hollow—capital of Calle Valley, ruled by Caspar, and site of the summer fair.

Cy (sigh)—Captain of the Green Unit of the Lystran army; a Polonti who went with Nihl to Corona.

Deirdre (DEE dra)—the Surchataine of Lystra, wife of Roman.

Diamond's Head—the capital of Goerge ruled by Sheva before the province was annexed to Lystra by Roman.

drud—epithet attached to all Polonti who were in slavery at Diamond's Head.

DuCange (du KANJ)—the trouble-making silversmith of Westford.

Effie—a peasant girl who saved Roman's life.

Eledith (EL e dith)—capital of Polontis, situated in a mountainous area of the province.

Elyria (il LEER ee ah)—the wife of Westford's poulterer.

Fastnesses—the mountain range running through Seleca and Polontis.

Fidelis (fi DEL is)—Roman's horse, a spirited white Andalusian.

flagon (FLAG en)—a flask with a handle.

Galapos (GAL a pos)—the Commander Roman served under as a young man; became Surchatain of Lystra after Karel's death; Deirdre's natural father who gave his life to free her from slavery at Diamond's Head.

Galen (GAY len)—Tremelaine's name before he began to rule in Corona.

gimlet (GIM let)—a hand-held boring tool.

gimmal (GIM ul)—a ring of interlocking circles.

280

Goerge—the province east of Lystra, formerly ruled by Sheva.

Goldie—Deirdre's alias during her enslavement at Diamond's Head.

Graydon—Tremelaine's brother, a sorcerer.

Gusta—Ariel's nursemaid.

hauberk—chain-mail armor.

High Lord—a title used by many Surchatains, but rejected by Galapos and Roman as blasphemous.

Hornbound—the capital of Qarqar.

Hycliff (HIGH cliff)—port city in Lystra which hosted a fair every spring and autumn.

Iven—a robber-soldier of Lystra.

Izana (eye ZAN a)—a maid in the palace of Corona whom Nihl married.

Jason—Colin's older brother, who had "married" an unwilling Deirdre after she had just married Roman. Jason killed himself after hearing the outcome of the siege at Outpost One.

jess—the strap fastened to a falcon's leg.

Josef—a slave at Diamond's Head who taught Deirdre about God.

Jud—one of two scouts sent to Corona to gather information before Roman went to face Tremelaine.

Kam—Nihl's Second in Command, who was over the captains in the Lystran army.

Karel—former Surchatain of Lystra, whom Deirdre supposed for years to be her father; he was killed before Tremaine invaded Westford.

Lady Grey—Deirdre's favorite horse, a grey mare selected for her by Roman when she first learned to ride.

Laska—Caspar's sister, who had been a good friend of Deirdre's when they were young girls.

Lew—a citizen of Corona with a keen mechanical aptitude.

Lystra (LIS tra)—province ruled by Roman and Deirdre.

Magdel—Graydon's daughter.

Mara—Graydon's wife.

Mathias (math I as)—Oweda's husband, a traveling merchant.

Merce (mers)—the former ruler of Calle Valley who joined with Tremaine and was killed by him at Outpost One; Caspar's father.

Merry—the head cook at the palace in Diamond's Head who came back with Deirdre to Westford.

Milcom—the name of the gold idol which Tremelaine erected.

Nanna—Deirdre's nursemaid from infancy who fell under the witch Varela's power and was killed by her.

Nihl (neel)—Commander of the Lystran army under Roman; a Polonti who had been enslaved at Diamond's Head. When freed by Deirdre, he returned to Westford with her.

Olynn (AWL in)—a captain in the Lystran army, whom Roman made acting Commander while he and Nihl were gone from Westford.

Ooster—capital of the province that was formerly Seir, ruled by Corneus; Deirdre had been held captive there while Roman and Galapos fought against Tremaine at Outpost One.

Orenthal (OR en thal)—the weaver of Westford who overheard an assassin being hired to kill Roman.

Orvis—a tailor of Corona who aided Roman and Deirdre.

Oweda (oh WEE da)—Mathias' wife, a traveling merchant who wished to adopt Effie.

Passage—the only navigable river which emptied into the Sea on the southern coast of the Continent.

Pax—Effie's brother.

pentices—covered external passageways joining wall to wall of a castle.

piece(s)—a coin used throughout the Continent, which contained 15–20 percent silver; fifty pieces equaled the value of a gold royal.

Pindar—a soldier of the Bloodclad.

Poison Greens—the mountains north of Calle Valley, considered impassable.

Polontis (po LAWN tis)—province northeast of Lystra, home of the Polonti (po LAWN tee).

Qarqar (KAR kar)—the province northwest of Lystra, which exported mostly ore.

Quint—a Lystran soldier who posed as a renegade to track down the source of frequent attacks on travelers.

Reuel—a Captain in the Lystran army.

Rollet (rawl LET)—Tremaine's son, a former suitor of Deirdre who was killed by Roman's men in Corona.

Roman—the Surchatain of Lystra upon the death of Galapos; a half-blooded Polonti who was the Chataine Deirdre's personal guardian until their marriage.

royal(s)—a coin used throughout the Continent which was supposed to contain 10 percent gold, but seldom did (with the exception of coins minted during Roman's reign); one royal equaled 50 silver pieces.

Sebastian—a Lystran soldier who rescued Basil from the hanging rope.

Seir (SEE ir)—the province northwest of Lystra, ruled by Corneus before it was annexed by Roman.

Seleca (SEL e ka)—the province north of Lystra, once ruled by the mighty Tremaine.

Sevter—palace overseer at Westford, formerly the overseer of domestic slaves at Diamond's Head.

Sheva—widow of Savin who ruled Goerge until she was killed in an attempted overthrow by her soldiers.

282

sigil (SIJ il)—a design having occultic significance.

Surchatain (SUR cha tan)—title for the ruler of a province; feminine— Surchataine (SUR cha tan).

Tarl—Captain of the Ninth Unit of the Selecan army (the Bloodclad).

Teaching Room—Tremelaine's torture room in the palace of Corona.

Thane—a renegade who attached himself to Roman.

Titian (TISH en)—the head cook at Corona whom Roman made Surchatain of Seleca.

Tremaine (tre MAIN)—powerful ruler of Seleca who died of disease while sieging Outpost One.

Tremelaine (TREM el ain)—the name Galen used after becoming entranced with Tremaine and assuming power in Corona; a sorcerer like his brother Graydon.

Troyce—palace administrator at Westford, who had formerly been administrator at Diamond's Head.

Tuss—a kitchen servant in the palace of Corona.

Varela (va REL a)—a witch who had attempted to destroy Roman and Lystra; she vanished mysteriously after Roman determined to confront her.

Vernard—one of two scouts sent to Corona to gather information before Roman went there to face Tremelaine.

Vida (VEE da)—Orvis the tailor's wife; a woman of courage who aided Roman and Deirdre.

Village Branch—a branch of the Passage where the slums of Westford were located.

Virl—an emissary of Calle Valley.

wainwright—a wagon maker.

Wence—a Polonti noted for his size and strength who served in the Lystran army.

Westford—capital of Lystra, where Roman and Deirdre ruled.

About the author:

Robin Hardy writes about *High Lord of Lystra:* "This book involves an encounter with supernatural evil, in which the 'hero,' Roman, discovers his own limitations and the sufficiency of Christ. It has always disturbed me to see the fascination of our entertainment media with the occult and how this 'entertainment' focuses on all the ways innocent persons can be tortured by these forces. The endings are never wholly satisfactory, because no one can imagine a supernatural good to match the evil. But we have the perfect picture of that good in Jesus Christ. In this book, I wanted to explore what could happen when a Christian is confronted by this kind of evil. And what I have found is that God is Lord of every realm.

"I have put in this book a few of my experiences, such as Deirdre's encounter with joy (p. 165). This happened to me over a year after my mother, Ruth's, death from cancer, but whenever I think of it, I think of her. It was somehow a validation to me of her faith in the Lord, and a promise of the confirmation of my own faith if I hold on to all He has been teaching me in His Word.

"I have tried to balance all this heady supernatural stuff with the less spectacular, more ingenious ways the Lord works in a life—how He changes a person's character by the slow grinding of little, daily trials, moments of joy, invisible insights, all spelled out plainly in Scripture for us to understand. All these little things seem unremarkable by themselves, but collectively are so astounding that I find I cannot relate the process fully in fiction—no one would believe it!

Robin and her husband, Steve, have a daughter, Stephanie, and a son, Glenn, whose arrival coincided closely with the completion of *High Lord of Lystra.*